Vampires of the Scarlet

"David Lee Summers offers vampire lovers an inventive and elaborate conspiracy laden story about a band of vampiric mercenaries known as the Scarlet Order ... From the dungeon strongholds of medieval Europe to the untamed desert plains of the early American Southwest, the storyline follows several members of the order and their 'fall from grace' ... he does an excellent job of bringing it all together with a thrilling endgame." Christine Filipak, *Dark Realms Magazine*

"We now have our very own Southwestern vampire lore and tradition thanks to the imagination and painstaking research of Summers." S. Derrickson Moore, *The Las Cruces Sun-News*.

"Worthy... the vampires form the Scooby-Doo gang to fight evil. They must infiltrate Los Alamos and rescue fellow vampires being used for government weapon's reasearch." Fred Cleaver, *The Denver Post*.

"Summers writes richly, making us care about and identify with the ultimate group of outsiders who band together to protect the human race from its destructiveness and ultimate lack of humanity... This is a fun book to sink your teeth into and a good addition to the libraries of those readers with a taste for inventive vampire fiction." Roy Van der Aa, *The Ink*.

Books by David Lee Summers

The Solar Sea
The Astronomer's Crypt

The Space Pirates' Legacy Series
Firebrandt's Legacy
The Pirates of Sufiro
Children of the Old Stars
Heirs of the New Earth

The Clockwork Legion Series
Owl Dance
Lightning Wolves
The Brazen Shark
Owl Riders

The Scarlet Order Vampires Series
Dragon's Fall: Rise of the Scarlet Order Vampires
Vampires of the Scarlet Order

Vampires of the
Scarlet Order

David Lee Summers

THE VAMPYRE LIBRARY BOOK CLUB
feelthebite.com

Embrace the night!

David Lee Summers

Hadrosaur Productions, Mesilla Park, NM

Vampires of the Scarlet Order
Hadrosaur Productions
Second Edition: August 2020
First date of publication: May 2005

ISBN-10: 1-885093-94-2
ISBN-13: 978-1-885093-94-3

To Kumie, enchantress of my heart forevermore.

Acknowledgements

First off, I would like to say a very special thanks to those independent press editors who believed in these characters and situations and encouraged me as I developed the Scarlet Order Vampires. In particular, I'd like to thank Kate Hill and Portland Elizebeth of Anxiety Publications, Dawn M. Callahan of *Night to Dawn*, Margaret L. Carter of *The Vampire's Crypt*, Terrie Leigh Relf of *Hungur*, and David B. Riley of *Trails: Intriguing Stories of the Old West*. Last but far from least, I'd like to thank Leslie X. Council of *Rigor Mortis* and *Message of the Muse* who edited and polished the earlier edition of this novel.

Thanks also to: Janni Lee Simner who jump-started this novel with a question about vampires living in Las Cruces – the city of crosses; Nick Perry whose knowledge of history and government proved invaluable; Dr. Mildred H. Rowley and her staff for answering what must have seemed the most bizarre medical questions; Kumie Wise who demanded to see every chapter as it was written; Autumn and Verity Summers who motivated me daily with smiles and laughter and helped by not interrupting me while writing; Chaz Kemp who visualized the Scarlet Order vampires for the cover; and Jacqueline Druga who oversaw the team that brought the first edition of this novel to print.

I appreciate all the readers who took the time to join the Scarlet Order Vampires for the fifteen-year run of the first edition. Michael R. Donohoe and Eric Schumacher both suggested this novel might be stronger if I started the story in the present day and revealed the history as we went along. This new edition has all the chapters of the original, but rearranged to do just that.

Finally, thanks to all my Patreon subscribers and particularly Robert E. Vardeman and Gary W. Davis who provided support and feedback as I developed this new edition.

Vampires of the
Scarlet Order

Prologue

Desmond, Lord Draco's Estate, Near Cardiff – 1821:

Desmond, Lord Draco sat at one end of a long table writing on a parchment spread out before him. Recently summoned from Paris, Roquelaure drifted into the room and sat down near his master and evaluated the words Draco had already set down. "Not another letter to Rome, my lord," he mused. "The Catholic Church won't continue to pay for your personal war with the Ottoman Empire indefinitely."

Draco lifted his quill and looked into the handsome vampire's eyes. "I have just received word that the Greeks are fomenting a rebellion. They may just succeed in driving the Ottomans from their territory, especially if they have the Scarlet Order's help." He referred to the band of mercenary vampires he commanded.

"Of course, extra funding from the Church for more supplies would help," came a voice from the shadows. Roquelaure turned his head and faced the two-thousand-year-old vampire at the table's far end. Alexandra the Greek sat so still and her features were so smooth, she reminded Draco of a doll crafted in china by a master toymaker. "No doubt, the Church would like to see more distance between themselves and the Ottoman Turks."

"So, what can you tell me of this rebellion?" Roquelaure rested his head on his fist.

"Alexander Ypsilantis is a nobleman who has been making friends in surrounding countries," said Alexandra. "He served in the Russian army during the Russo-Turkish war and he may be able to get their help. Besides, I rather like his given name."

"You would." Roquelaure laughed.

"There's more," interjected Draco. "Ypsilantis has friends among the Serbs…"

Roquelaure sighed. "This isn't about your lands in Transylvania again? I thought you wrote those off after that business with Prince Vlad."

"It was a lovely castle and I grew rather attached to those mountains." Draco set his quill down. "I still haven't come close to restoring my library to its former grandeur."

Alexandra's eyes moved from Roquelaure to Draco while she continued to sit statue-still. "While I favor helping the Greek rebellion, presuming we can obtain funding, I do agree with Roquelaure. You dwell on the past. If we succeed and beat back the Ottoman Turks one more time, why not go to America? I hear there are rugged, beautiful lands there."

Draco snorted. "Would the Americans welcome mercenaries? I wonder…"

Roquelaure leaned forward. "Have you ever heard from Rudolfo since he sailed over the ocean?" He referred to the only vampire Draco ever made. His departure seemed to hurt the vampire lord even more than the loss of his castle in Transylvania.

"No." Draco sniffed and he wiped away a tear. "It's as though he went to America and vanished soon after. I fear he may have been a victim of the Pueblo Revolt which occurred only a few years after he would have arrived."

Alexandra rose to her feet and glided next to Roquelaure, though her eyes remained fixed on the British lord. "Don't you have land in America?"

Draco ignored the question for a time. Instead, he picked up his quill, finished the letter, then read it over. He signed his name with a flourish. Satisfied, he looked up at Alexandra and Roquelaure. "My land is in Spanish-controlled Nuevo México, far from civilization – far from blood to sustain me and farther still from the riddles of the vampire's origin. Perhaps I'll go someday … but that day will be far in the future."

✝✝✝

The Vatican – 1821:

Pope Pius VII found himself concerned with the ebb and flow of empires. Years before, the pope had struggled with Napoleon Bonaparte and his own dreams of empire. Though the Holy Roman Empire had been effectively dead for centuries, Napoleon did away with the last vestiges of the empire when he ordered Frances II to give up his title as Holy Roman Emperor. At the same time, it seemed as though Englishmen were spreading all across the globe. Even the young United States of America demonstrated imperial ambitions.

Upon this backdrop, Pius VII received news of a rebellion against the Ottoman Empire in Patras, Greece. Shortly after, the pope received a letter postmarked from Cardiff in Wales. The pope dreaded receiving such letters. As he feared, the letter was from Desmond, Lord Draco, Knight Commander of the Scarlet Order. For nearly three centuries, popes had been receiving letters from Lord Draco stating that the Ottoman Empire was falling due to actions initiated by the Scarlet Order as decreed by the Council of Trent in 1545. The letter contained the usual requests for funds and volumes from the Vatican Library.

Pope Pius VII crumpled the letter from Lord Draco into a ball and threw it into the fireplace. The pope closed his eyes and bowed his head. Though his attitude was one of prayer, he couldn't have honestly said whether he was speaking to God or to himself: "The time has come for the Church to break its alliance with these demons. They have extorted money from the Church for too long. Empires are the provinces of man. They come and go. The Church's mission is to fight evil – and we will start by abandoning this Scarlet Order to the Lord's judgment."

A knock at the door interrupted the pope's thoughts. "Enter," called the pontiff.

The door opened and a handsome man in flowing robes

entered. He knelt down and kissed the pope's ring. Pius smiled wanly at his old friend Della Genga, Vicar of Rome, and indicated a nearby chair.

Della Genga rose from his knees and sat, looking at the pope with concern. "You are troubled, Your Holiness."

Pius sighed and looked into the fire, where the letter from Draco had already been consumed. "I was just thinking how much a life force money has become in the world."

"It drives empires," said Della Genga sagely. "It allows us to do the Lord's work. We need it to survive."

The pope looked his friend in the eye. "Yet, all of us take money from others. If we take too much from one source, people die."

"You make it sound as though we are vampires," said Della Genga, his brow wrinkled with concern.

"Perhaps," mused the pope, looking back toward the fire. "Perhaps we should aspire to be something better."

Part I

The Physicist and the Conquistador

"Vampire folklorists, such as Montague Summers, suggest that vampires are humans who have lost their souls. Further, the folklorists state that the vampire is possessed by a demon. I regard the soul as a matter for theological discussion and beyond the scope of these observations."

– Dr. Jane Heckman

Chapter One

The New Mexico Institute of Mining and Technology.
Present Day.

Physicist Jane Heckman watched a National Guardsman steer a battle-scarred tank into a cave at the base of Socorro Peak. Heckman's gaze drifted to the mountain's summit where a giant letter "M" was whitewashed on the rocks. The "M" stood for "Mines", as in New Mexico School of Mines. The school had changed its name in the 1950s to New Mexico Tech. Dr. Heckman worked for a division of the school called the Energetic Materials Research and Testing Center which tested ballistics and explosives.

The sun descended behind the mountain. Jane sighed, unhappy that she missed her afternoon target practice session with her crossbow.

The National Guardsman clambered out of the tank and made for a nearby bunker. Jane retrieved a small marble-like plastic nodule from a box in her jacket pocket and carried it over to the tank. She placed it into a depression in the tank's armor, then ran for the bunker as an alarm klaxon sounded.

Two graduate students, Sheila Renault and Lonnie Becket, huddled by a computer in the bunker. On the screen, a window showed the tank in the cave while another window showed a countdown. The countdown reached zero and nothing seemed to happen. Jane, Sheila, and Lonnie leaned in close to the computer monitor. Five seconds later, a flash of light washed over the tank and an explosion rocked the bunker. Sheila and Lonnie fell against the backs of their chairs, whooped and did high fives.

"The nanites worked," whispered Jane in triumph.

✝✝✝

The explosion rocked the cave. Deep in the mountain, in a passageway almost too small for a human to crawl through, a vampire stirred. The vampire blinked dust-covered eyes then coughed as he inhaled swirling grit and dirt. Crawling from his resting place, the vampire spared a moment to wonder how long he had been waiting for humans, for prey, to return to El Pueblo de Nuestra Señora del Socorro. The vampire did not know what had stirred him awake. He only knew he needed blood and he sensed life near the cave's entrance.

✝✝✝

The all-clear signal sounded at the bunker. Jane sent her students out to photograph and examine the tank's remains and surrounding cave while she studied remote sensor data in the bunker. "Be careful," she called on her walkie-talkie. "The entrance didn't cave in, but there may be loose rock around there. If it looks too dangerous, come back and get me. Also, don't get too close to the tank. The nanites should be deactivated, but I don't want anything we missed to crawl on you."

"Will do, chief. We know the protocol," said Sheila's cheerful voice.

Jane sighed and clucked her tongue. She wanted to be with the students. "You're their teacher, not their mother. They won't learn anything if they don't explore on their own," she said to herself.

"Chief." Sheila's call interrupted Jane's thoughts.

Jane fingered the walkie-talkie a little too quickly. "Go ahead."

"We're at the cave entrance. Looks like the tank's pretty well totaled. The cave looks solid."

"Good. Nice contained explosion just like we wanted." Jane continued to stare at a data display, not realizing she still held the transmit button. Sudden movement in the video screen drew her attention. She didn't see anything. Maybe one of the students scrambled over a rock. At last, she realized she still held the transmit button and released it. After watching the video monitor for a couple of minutes, neither Sheila nor Lonnie appeared again. She wondered if they had entered the cave and the rock obstructed the radio signal.

Jane thumbed the transmit button. "Sheila, come in."

She waited a moment. "Lonnie, are you there?"

When she didn't get a response, Jane left the bunker and trudged through reddish sand to the cave entrance.

There was a gaping hole in the front of the tank and the cannon had dissolved. Jane nodded, satisfied, then turned on the flashlight. Something bright red glinted in the flashlight's beam. Jane took two steps forward and stopped cold. Sheila Renault's body lay on the ground at an impossible angle, her blouse torn, and blood oozing from two puncture wounds on her neck. Aiming the light further down the cave, she spotted Lonnie Becket lying on the tank tread, a gaping hole in his throat.

Jane Heckman backed out of the cave. Once she cleared the entrance, she fell to her knees and vomited.

Hands trembling, she reached for the walkie-talkie and called security. Within minutes, a jeep pulled up and two burly men in tan uniforms jumped out. They turned on their flashlights and the physicist led them to the bodies. One of the guards gasped. "Vampiro?" he asked.

"No. It's an animal attack." The second, older guard shook his head. "Let's get the doc back to the bunker and call 911."

The younger guard tried to protest, but the older one shushed him. They led Jane back to the bunker and the older guard made a phone call. Jane's skin tingled and her heartbeat raced. She barely heard what the guard said on the phone call. She forced herself to steady her breathing, then looked at the younger guard's name tag. "Torres."

"Mr. Torres, what did you mean 'vampiro?' Did you mean the bats? We don't have vampire bats in North America…"

Torres shook his head. "There are stories about a creature buried under the mountain called Pedro de Diablo." The guard crossed himself. "Back when the Tech first opened, they say it attacked some mining students out here under M-Mountain, but it hasn't ever been seen again."

The older guard, whose name tag read "Apodaca" hung up. "EMS and the cops will be here shortly."

Jane closed her eyes and tried to compose herself. At last, she looked up at Apodaca. His craggy face and graying hair gave her the impression of a man who had seen almost everything. "What do you think attacked the kids … Sheila and Lonnie?"

The older guard pursed his lips and shook his head. "I'm guessing there must be a mountain lion around."

Jane narrowed her gaze. "But those puncture marks on Sheila's neck…"

Torres opened his mouth to say something, but Apodaca held up his hand to silence him, then tucked his thumbs in his belt. "Some people see chupacabra, La Llorona, or other phantoms whenever they see something strange. I'm guessing the cat, or whatever it was, got startled by the two kids. It disabled one, made a more thorough job of the other, then fled."

"Wouldn't a big cat stay … to feed…" Jane's hands began to tremble despite her attempts at control.

"Not if it were startled." Apodaca shook his head. "It may come back later, to look and see if they're still there. Of course, EMS will take them away."

Jane fell silent. She began to replay her actions. She regretted sending Sheila and Lonnie out on their own. Then again, they were trained and Sheila had assisted on dozens of previous tests. They both knew what to do. If Jane had gone with them, she likely would have ended up just as dead as them. She remembered holding the button on the walkie-talkie mike. Had she missed a call for help? Her chest tightened.

Soon, the police and emergency medical services arrived. The police examined the scene and spoke with Jane. The interview took much less time than she had expected. To them, the events seemed clear. She watched as the EMS crew loaded Sheila and Lonnie's bodies into the back of an ambulance. "I'm sorry you didn't live to see your doctorates," she whispered, then turned away.

When she returned to the bunker to retrieve her things, she found the younger guard, Torres. She knew Apodaca must be right. Lonnie and Sheila had been killed by a mountain lion or something like it, but something about Torres's first impression nagged at her. "Mr. Torres ... these vampire legends. Who could tell me more?"

"Talk to father Juan at San Miguel. He's the parish historian. He knows all the old stories." Torres licked his lips and looked around, then leaned in. "He knows the truth behind all the old stories."

✞✞✞

The next day, Jane Heckman unlocked her office door in the physics building at New Mexico Tech. She checked her e-mail, then rifled through some papers without actually looking at them. A light tapping at the door startled her. Her boss, a stout man who seemed to live in the same brown sweater day-in and day-out, named Richard Condon, stood framed in the doorway holding two Styrofoam cups of coffee.

"How ya' doin'?" asked Condon.

Jane shook her head. "Not well. You heard about Lonnie and Sheila?"

Condon nodded as he handed Jane one of the cups.

She avoided her boss's gaze and concentrated on sipping the coffee. After a moment, she set the coffee on the table, but continued holding the cup to keep her hand from trembling. "Have you heard any news this morning? Are the police any closer to finding the animal that killed the kids?"

"The police have shut down the labs and animal control is scouring the area, but they don't expect to find anything." Condon sipped his coffee. "I imagine they'll let us reopen the site later today or tomorrow. We're doing our best to keep them away from the tank. I know when you're feeling better, you'll still want to study the effects of the nanites. Homeland Security will want to know whether or not those little bugs can be an effective deterrent against terrorists."

Jane released a shuddering breath and a tear fell. "I don't know when I can go back up there…"

Condon cleared his throat and looked as though he wanted to be somewhere else. Jane guessed her grief made him uncomfortable. "Listen, why don't you take a few days off and clear your head. The site will be there when you're ready to go back."

She nodded and closed her eyes.

"If there's nothing else…" Condon looked into his coffee cup, and started to stand.

"There is one thing," said Jane. She took a deep breath. "One of the security guards said something about an old legend. He told me there was some old vampire who lived in the mountain called Pedro de Diablo and it once attacked some mining students."

Condon snorted a derisive laugh. "If you look back at the college's history, it was open for a year or so, then closed suddenly. It didn't reopen again for another couple of years. It was all frontier politics, but you know how stories get started."

"So there really is a story?" Jane blew her nose and wiped away the tears, now more interested.

Condon shrugged. "Sure, there are stories, but what do you believe more? A vampire attack closed down the school or the school had serious budget problems?"

She laughed with Condon. "All right. Let me finish up some emails and then I'll take you up on your offer and take some days off."

"Sounds like a plan." Condon stood. "Don't go far, though. It's always possible the police may have more questions."

Jane nodded and watched him retreat. She glanced through her email and considered what Condon said. A mining school closed down for budget problems in a territory where mining was a major industry. Something about that didn't sit right. She began to think there must be more to the story.

After she finished in the office, Jane Heckman drove to the old San Miguel Mission at the heart of Socorro. Founded in 1615, it was one of the oldest churches in the United States. Franciscan missionaries had come to bring Christianity to the people of Pilabó Pueblo. Jane Heckman's rational brain knew an animal had attacked her students, but the old legend of a vampire captivated her. It distracted her from the guilt and feelings of helplessness she couldn't shake.

What's more, the fang marks in Sheila's neck haunted the physicist. She'd never seen the aftermath of a mountain lion attack, but somehow didn't expect something so neat. Where were the claw marks on Sheila's body? Shouldn't there have been more signs of a struggle?

Father Juan had an office at the San Miguel school, next to the mission. Jane knocked on the door.

"Please come in," beckoned a raspy voice.

She entered the small, simple office. An elderly man in black vestments stood and held out a hand, gesturing for Jane to take a seat. In spite of his age, Father Juan had a commanding presence.

"What may I do for you?" asked Father Juan.

"I've come to ask what you know about the early history of Socorro." She released a self-conscious laugh. "This may sound silly, but I was wondering if there were any vampire legends."

The old priest crossed himself. "Vampires in the early history." The grim-faced priest stood and retrieved a book with yellowed pages. He opened it to a drawing of a man in Spanish colonial armor, holding the characteristic helmet of a conquistador at his side. "The early fathers of San Miguel called him 'Pedro de Diablo.' The Devil's Peter."

Jane blinked back surprise. She expected the priest to share a few old folk tales and then send her on her way. She didn't expect an actual history lesson. "Why did they call him that?"

"Peter was the foundation of the church. The early fathers had come to bring the word of God to the Piro Indians who lived at Pilabó. Pedro de Diablo brought the word of Satan."

Jane reached out and took the book. "Did this Pedro de Diablo come with the missionaries?"

"No. The missionaries found him here. They thought he came with the Juan de Oñate Expedition in 1598."

"I thought La Llorona was the local bogeyman ... er ... woman," mused Jane.

Father Juan arched an eyebrow. "La Llorona is a folk tale. By all accounts, Pedro de Diablo really existed."

Jane narrowed her gaze. "What happened to this Pedro de Diablo?"

Father Juan gently retrieved the book from Jane and shook his head. "No one knows. The missionaries left during the Pueblo Revolt in 1680. They didn't return to Socorro until 1815. There's been no word of Pedro de Diablo since the 17th century."

"I've heard about an attack in the 1880s, soon after the New Mexico School of Mines opened..."

The priest nodded. "I've heard those stories as well, but Pedro was a well spoken, articulate man. I think he was a real man and no vampire. The stories from the 1880s speak of a mindless horror. I give them little credence."

Jane considered that. "Yet, if this Pedro came in 1598 and still lived in 1680, he would have been over a century old."

The old priest shook his head. "Perhaps his life span was exaggerated. He stood. Even hunched over, he looked intimidating. "Why do you have such an interest in this old story?"

"I'm a physicist up at the Explosives Center at Tech. Two of my students were killed last night by something. The police think it was an animal..."

"And part of you wonders whether it could have been a man or even Pedro." He shelved the book, then returned to his chair. "Do you feel responsible for the loss of your students?"

Jane's throat constricted and she fought to hold back tears. "I know I shouldn't, but I do."

"It's only natural." The priest's stern features softened. "If you would like to talk about it, I'm happy to listen."

Jane sighed. She'd grown up in a protestant household, but

drifted away from church in her college years. Still it might be nice to have someone to talk to once she gave herself some space. "Right now, I just need a little time."

"I'm here if you need anything," said Father Juan. "May God keep you safe."

Jane returned home, made dinner, then retrieved her crossbow from its cabinet. Outside, she pulled back the bolt, leveled the weapon, and took aim at a target. The bolt flew through the air and struck the bull's eye. She armed the crossbow again, and squeezed the trigger. Tension began to ease from her shoulders and neck. Guilt seemed a million miles away. She longed for strong fingers to massage her neck, but crossbow practice was almost as good.

Ever since she was a child, Jane had loved archery and guns. Her father used to take her skeet shooting. While a teenager, this interest in weapons grew into an interest in the science of ballistics and explosives. She began to study physics so she could learn how guns, bows, and crossbows operated.

Sheila Renault's interest in physics had come from an interest in space. Sheila wanted to learn about explosives so she could understand exploding stars. Lonnie Becket had been a new student and Jane regretted not getting to know him better before he died. They weren't her biological children, but that didn't matter. They had been her responsibility.

Jane loaded another bolt into the crossbow. Her rational mind told her the students must have been killed by an animal, but she began to wonder if a vampire could exist. The priest's story and the guard's belief played on her subconscious. If such a thing did exist, perhaps she could not only destroy it, but record its existence. She doubted a real vampire would fall to ash like they did on some of those TV shows. She leveled the crossbow again and fired.

Chapter Two

The New Mexico Institute of Mining and Technology.
Present Day.

About 9 o'clock that night, Jane returned to the Energetic Materials Research and Testing Center. She flashed her ID badge to the security guard at the gate, then followed dirt roads until she came to a barricade. She donned a headlamp, then retrieved her crossbow from the car's seat. She walked the last half mile to the cave.

Heart pounding furiously, Jane approached the cave's mouth. She craned her neck, trying to see farther than the headlamp beam penetrated. The physicist heard a sound from behind, like a gentle fluttering of wings and tried to turn, but froze in place.

"A beautiful woman." The voice was deeply accented Spanish, but not the typical Spanish spoken around Socorro. "European stock, I gather. Not Piro." He shook his head and sighed. "It would seem my beloved Piro have vanished entirely."

By sheer force of will, Jane turned and faced a man with short, black hair and a goatee. He looked too much like the drawing in Father Juan's book for the physicist's comfort. The man wore a simple white shirt with black trousers – very modern. She struggled to lift the crossbow.

The man backed up a step, but showed no fear.

"Are you the one called Pedro de Diablo?"

"You have been talking to the clergy." The man chuckled. "I

have not been called Pedro de Diablo for a very long time. My name is Rudolfo."

"How can you speak English? I'd heard you came to New Mexico with Juan de Oñate."

"Indeed, I came to this land with Don Juan. I learned to speak English in around…" Rudolfo paused, trying to remember, "the year Fifteen Hundred and Twelve. The exact manner of speaking has changed some in that time. However, it is easy for one such as me to learn new manners of speaking."

"One such as you? What do you claim to be?"

"Over the years, I have been called many things." Rudolfo put his hands behind his back, and walked around the physicist evaluating her. She tracked him with her crossbow. "I think you have already guessed that I am a vampire." Rudolfo completed his circle and looked into Heckman's gray eyes. "What are you?"

She blinked at the question. "I'm a physicist."

"A physicist?"

"What you might call a natural philosopher."

"Ah! Like da Vinci or that man who was just coming to be known when I left Europe … what was his name?" Rudolfo snapped his fingers. "Galileo."

"That's right."

"What is your name?" Rudolfo sighed as the physicist hesitated a little too long. "I told you my name. Surely you can tell me yours?"

Jane Heckman bit her lower lip, but finally acquiesced.

"Now, Señorita Heckman, wouldn't we be more comfortable sitting down somewhere." Rudolfo indicated the bunker just a short way off. "I found some rather comfortable chairs down there."

"Señorita?" At forty-three, Jane was not used to being called 'señorita.' "You are either flattering me by assuming I'm younger than I am, or you're assuming I'm not married?"

"One so lovely as yourself would have her husband with her if she were married."

"Times have changed," said the physicist, coldly.

"Indeed." Rudolfo's lips curled upward.

She followed Rudolfo to the bunker, but maintained some

distance. Given the facility's guards and the police barricade, no one bothered to lock the bunker. Rudolfo let himself in and sat. Jane also took a chair. She relaxed her aim, but continued to hold the crossbow.

"A woman who is a natural philosopher," pondered Rudolfo. "You must be truly remarkable."

"I like to think so."

Rudolfo grinned at her self-assuredness. "Why did you come to seek me out?"

"I was curious. I wanted to know if there really were such things as vampires."

"I am a lonely creature, just now learning about your world. I have been asleep a very long time." Rudolfo leaned forward and gazed into the woman's eyes. His voice turned velvety, seductive. "As a natural philosopher, a physicist, what is your passion?"

"My passion?" She blinked at the sudden change of subject, then pursed her lips. "My passion is the natural world. As a physicist, I can imagine how the world works at the deepest levels."

"Indeed." The vampire looked at the crossbow. "Would you please put that thing away? I have no need to kill you."

"Have you already killed tonight?" Jane forced an even tone, though the bile rose in her throat as she questioned why she'd come out to the facility all alone. She did not release the weapon.

"Would it be so horrible if I had?" Rudolfo sat back, folding his arms. "I am a vampire. I know how the world works at the deepest levels. I have no need to imagine. I can move faster than any human, I can hear more, see farther." He reached over and touched a computer monitor. "There's more. I have seen history itself unfold."

"If you're a vampire, why did you disappear into the cave?"

"When the pueblos in the north revolted, the Piro people and the Spanish fled south. I thought the wait would be a short one. After a hundred years, I was so far dead that it took a violent shaking to awaken me."

"Couldn't you have lived off the land? Couldn't you have killed animals for food?"

Rudolfo's face wrinkled in distaste. "On the trip to this continent, some of the lonely conquistadors made use of the livestock." Seeing the physicist's confusion, Rudolfo explained further. "The soldiers mated with the sheep." Seeing the look of disgust on her face, the vampire nodded. "For a vampire to feed on wolves and rabbits is like a human mating with sheep."

Jane shuddered as she actually considered what it would be like to drink a human's blood, much less an animal's. She shook her head, realizing this person, this probable murderer had pulled her into believing he actually was a vampire. She decided to press for more details. "There are also stories you arose during the 1880s."

Rudolfo's brow furrowed and he leaned forward. "I don't know. There are flashes of memory. Perhaps I did awake briefly once or twice. If people did visit, they left me alone in the dark." He sighed. "I am lonely, Señorita Heckman. You could join me and I could make you a vampire. You would know the natural world more intimately than you could ever imagine."

"Is that why they call you Pedro de Diablo? You're trying to find disciples?" She released a nervous laugh.

The vampire shrugged and his eyes narrowed. A chill crept down Jane's back as she looked into Rudolfo's eyes and recognized his hunger. She lifted the crossbow again and aimed at Rudolfo. She stood and kept the weapon pointed at him as she moved toward the door. Once outside, she ran for the car.

Rudolfo already stood beside the vehicle. He no longer looked charming. "Why do you run?"

"I don't want what you have to offer," she said.

"What I offer is immortality ... and love. You know I am a vampire, but do you know what else? Before I was a vampire, I was a conquistador."

Jane Heckman bit her lower lip, her eyes darting from side to side, evaluating options. If the creature before her told the truth, he could teach the world about the early history of the Spanish in America. A creature such as Rudolfo would also be fascinating to study. However, the creature before her threatened her and most likely killed her students. Now that she had him in her sights, could she kill this man in cold blood. Was he really a vampire, or just some maniac? Either way, she needed to get help. She decided to play along with him. "From what you say, you must have braved Jornada del Muerto. You must be very strong." She referred to the barren, rocky desert south of Socorro. The name meant the Journey of Death.

Rudolfo sneered, revealing fangs. "I *was* Jornada del Muerto, my lovely, natural philosopher. Conquistadors died, but I survived."

Jane's arm grew tired from holding the crossbow. The vampire struck out and knocked the weapon from her hand before she could squeeze the trigger. She turned to run, but a hand hammered the back of her skull and she fell face-first into the ground. She sputtered and tried to get up but was rolled onto her back.

Rudolfo's eyes were afire. He licked a tongue across a fang. "I am a conquistador, Señorita. I take what I want by force." A claw-like fingernail slashed and tore through her blouse. The vampire seemed perplexed by the bra underneath. Heckman took advantage of the pause and swung at the vampire's face. He blocked the blow. It was like hitting a metal post and she cried out. His attention returned to the bra and he sliced the lacy fabric with his fingernail. A trickle of blood oozed from the scratch on Heckman's naked breast. Rudolfo smiled and sank fangs into the scratch, just above the physicist's nipple.

Jane swallowed a deep breath, then another. She fought to hold back sobs. She wanted to fight the vampire, but had nothing to fight with. The crossbow was gone. Images began to impact her mind. While the vampire fed, she experienced the world as he saw it. The stars seemed closer than ever before. Somehow, without instruments, she knew the exact velocity of the wind and where it would carry her if she transformed into a bat. The ability to know the world this way was seductive in itself.

Rudolfo sat up and pulled the physicist close to him. He spoke to her softly and caressed her shoulder. "So much time as a scientist, learning about the world, being a mother to your students. There's never been time for another that's your equal. How sad," he lamented.

Coming out of her stupor, she bit the vampire on the shoulder. He cried out but held her as she bit harder. Blood rushed into her mouth and she had to let go to keep from gagging. She tried not to, but she swallowed some of the blood.

"That should do," he said as he lay her on the ground to begin her own journey of death. "Until tomorrow."

The vampire vanished. Tears streamed down Jane's face as she watched the stars circle above. She grew cold and eventually willed herself to stand. She climbed into the car and drove home. She peeled off her filthy clothes, lay in bed and fell asleep for the last time as a human.

✝✝✝

The next day, Jane Heckman awoke, feeling like her shoulder was on fire. A streamer of sunlight came through the bedroom window, touching her bare skin. Jumping out of bed, she dropped into the shadows against the wall. Without looking at her bedside clock, she somehow realized sunset already approached.

Coming alert, a bone-deep craving made her stomach churn. At first, the craving felt like thirst, then hunger. Then instinct kicked in and told her she needed blood. "I don't want to kill a person," she said in near panic. "What's happened to me?"

The sunbeam striking the bed faded and Jane made her way to the bathroom and looked into the mirror. She opened her mouth and touched her new fangs with her tongue, not quite sure they were real. The doorbell chimed and she became aware of a heart beating outside her front door.

The all-consuming sound distracted her from all of the other things she began to notice – the footfalls of cockroaches, the gentle breath of air from alongside windowsills, and the vivid colors of her room even in semi-darkness.

The doorbell rang again. Turning away from the mirror, she prowled through the hallway, lithe as a cat. Reaching the door, she sprang.

Dr. Richard Condon stood, open-mouthed in the doorway.

His eyes just had time to travel the length of Jane's pale, nude form before she lashed out and pulled him into the house then slammed the door. Without thought, Jane plunged fangs into Richard Condon's neck. He screeched in pain and she greedily drank the blood that issued from his jugular. As the life left him, Condon babbled, "What are you doing? I just came by to see how you were. You're a vampire? Let me go, please…" The department head lost strength with each word until he fell silent. Jane Heckman drank until Condon's heart was no longer strong enough to deliver fresh blood. Her eyes widened and she dropped her former boss to the living room carpet.

"What have I done?" she whispered hoarsely. The hunger dissipated, replaced by another hollowness, one of fear and desperation.

With a surreal calm, the physicist straightened, took a deep breath and formed a plan. It started with brushing her teeth to get rid of the taste of blood, followed by a shower. After that, she went to her gun cabinet. No more crossbows for this monster.

✝✝✝

Jane Heckman found Rudolfo near the cave at the explosives range. She aimed her Sig Sauer P320 at the center of the vampire's chest. "What was I thinking when I came out here last night?"

Rudolfo shrugged nonchalantly. "You felt a mother's responsibility to your students. You were curious about old stories and legends. Once you met me, you realized you could sense the natural world in a way that you could only guess at as a human."

Jane fought to keep the pistol level, trying to look at Rudolfo's chest, not his eyes then she fired. Rudolfo was thrown into the rock with a bloody, mangled hole just below his sternum, missing his heart, but hitting the stomach or intestines. She cursed. Somehow the vampire must have affected her aim.

Rudolfo sighed, and put his hand to his abdomen, wincing as he touched it. "You thought you would kill the vampire, then you would kill yourself, ridding the world of evil." The flow of blood slowed then stopped. The wound already seemed to be closing. "There is a certain magic in vampires. A healing magic, not unlike love."

"I don't believe in magic."

Rudolfo eased himself to his feet. "Then the world is a sad place for you, indeed." He reached around to his back and grimaced. After a moment, he held out his hand and stepped forward. "Let me show you the world as I know it. Last night, you were skeptical of the existence of vampires. Now you are one."

Jane leveled the pistol again. "I won't be your lover. I'm not someone you can conquer."

"Love takes many different forms, as does conquest." Rudolfo narrowed his gaze. "Have you fed tonight?"

Some new part of Jane Heckman's consciousness understood the concern in the question. She nodded.

"Now you know the awful hunger," he said. "You understand that I am sorry I hurt you by hurting your students, but now you know why I couldn't resist."

"You fucking bastard."

Rudolfo lashed out and grabbed her wrist, forcing her to drop the pistol. Growling, she twisted her arm, trying to break free. Rudolfo pulled her closer. Gingerly, he reached out and curled his fingers under her long, graying hair. He let it flow through his fingers. Jane stopped struggling, and watched him, wary. "Will you come with me? You can introduce me to your modern world and I can introduce you to the world of the vampire."

She nodded, her teeth gritted, her knees shaking, tears flowing. She hated this feeling of being conquered, but she was now a vampire and had no choice but to learn to live with it. Rudolfo helped her to sit on the cold ground. He began to rub the tension from her neck and shoulders.

A coyote howled in the distance. Jane Heckman wiped away her tears, resigned to be a child of the night but determined not to be conquered. She stood and retrieved the Sig, knowing there would be other chances to avenge her students. Then she helped Rudolfo to his feet. "The first rule of survival in the modern world," she began, "is not to live on an explosives range." With that, she led Rudolfo back to her house.

Once there, he showed her how to dispose of Dr. Condon's body and he helped her clean the house. As they worked, he told her the story of how he became a vampire.

Chapter Three

Rudolfo de Córdoba describes his first encounter with a vampire. The Year 1491.

"Rudolfo, come quickly, your father has been killed!" Don Diego cried out as my hand explored a nun's supple breast and my mouth caressed the exquisite curve of her neck. Sister Inez gasped and I sat up in a whirlwind of disbelief and distress over the news of my father's demise. Admittedly, I was also peeved by the interruption of my afternoon's recreation.

"Rudolfo, where are you?" called Don Diego.

I was behind a hedgerow, against the cathedral of Córdoba's whitewashed wall in Spain. The year was 1491, and I hurriedly laced up my shirt while Sister Inez adjusted her dress and hair. Before I continue, I should explain that Sister Inez was by no means a corrupt nun. Rather, like many of the Castilian clergy in those days, she was well aware that she was a creature of both the spirit and the flesh. Her spirit was firmly committed to Jesus Christ. It just so happens that a few moments before, her body had been committed to me. That day, I had been repairing plasterwork around the cathedral when Sister Inez brought me lunch and an offer of an hour's distraction.

In many parts of Spain, the Inquisition insisted that nuns wear black robes to distinguish themselves from the laity. However, we in Córdoba had run our Grand Inquisitor out of town over a year before. Little did we know then how strong the Inquisition would ultimately become.

"Rudolfo!" Don Diego's voice took on a frantic edge.

"I'm sorry about your father," whispered Sister Inez as she brushed my cheek gently with her soft lips. "You'd better go to Don Diego now."

Taking a deep breath, I stood, then stepped through a break in the hedge. Agitated, my father's friend, Don Diego, scanned the length of the cathedral. I clapped my hands on his shoulders, turned him away from the opening in the hedgerow, and looked him in the eyes. "My father's dead?" I asked, not quite grasping the reality of those words.

Don Diego nodded rapidly. Behind him, Sister Inez crept around the corner of the hedgerow, making her way back to the cathedral.

"Don Ricardo was shot by none other than Ibrahim Yousef, Vizier to the Granadan Emir," explained Diego.

My hands fell to my sides and my knees threatened to give way. My father was a captain in the Córdoban militia. The queen had sent him and his caballeros to render aid to the garrison that surrounded Granada: the last stronghold of the Moors in Spain. Don Diego led me to a stone bench and we sat. Covering my face, I hid my lack of tears. Though I mourned my father's passing, few tears remained. A few years before, the black plague had taken many of my family: my beloved wife, my lovely children and my faithful brother. My father and a handful of cousins were all I had left. The church – and Sister Inez – offered some comfort, but I still felt isolated and lonely. "How did it happen?" I whispered.

"It was yesterday evening, shortly after sunset," said Don Diego. "Your father's men heard a pistol's report and ran to investigate. They found your father atop a knoll, shot in the back of the head. They saw the vizier – Yousef – fleeing to the safety of Granada. Several of the caballeros tried to stop Yousef, but he reached the city walls before they could bring him to justice."

Many in the church said the Black Plague was a punishment sent by God. I wondered how a benevolent God could punish innocents such as my children; surely they had not lived lives of excess and corruption. I found myself wishing for a way to avenge my wife and children, but how can one achieve vengeance when the punishment comes directly from God? "Like any father's punishments, God's punishments do not always seem just, but one must trust that they are," said Father Jimenez when I'd confessed my thoughts to him. Father Jimenez was lucky that there had been a wall between us or I would have struck him. Instead, I went home, did my penance, and resigned myself to the fact that there was nothing I could do about the plague, no matter how heavy my heart.

A man, not the plague, had murdered my father. Murder was a crime that could be avenged. "I must join the garrison at Santa Fé," I told Don Diego. "Only by helping take Granada, can I do justice to the memory of my father."

"Your father wanted you here," protested the old man, twisting the ends of his bushy gray mustache. "You're his only surviving heir."

"That may be, but who will inherit the hacienda from me?" I growled. "What will my father's house mean to me if I allow his murder to go unchallenged?"

"Your father's murderer will likely be executed when Granada falls," said Don Diego, trying to talk sense into me. "The city is surrounded, cut off from supplies. It's only a matter of time before the Moors will be forced to surrender."

I stood and stalked off. "I'm going to Santa Fé!"

Don Diego leapt from the bench, following as closely as his short, arthritic legs would allow. "When?"

"This afternoon. There's still plenty of light. I can be there before sunset," I declared.

"You won't get there until nightfall, Rudolfo! You're more likely to be shot by one of the guards than welcomed as a soldier."

"My father's horses are fast, I'll get there before sunset!" I shouted. I strode away, leaving a breathless Don Diego in my wake. A short distance from the church's hallowed ground, I found my horse, pulled myself on and rode out to my father's small hacienda on Córdoba's outskirts. It was almost a joke to call the property a "hacienda." We only had a few olive trees and a press for making oil to sell at market. Still, the land did have plenty of grass and we were able to raise a few horses. We sold some of the horses to caballeros and would-be caballeros to supplement our meager income. Even with that, I still needed to sell my masonry skills. One man could not support our land by himself.

Within half an hour, I arrived at the hacienda. Without pausing, I led my horse to her stall. A little farther into the stables, I found one of the fleet Arabian stallions that were my father's pride and joy. I saddled the stallion and rode as fast as I could toward the ancient city of Granada.

The sun was low on the horizon and long shadows carpeted the ground as I approached the great fortress city of Santa Fé, headquarters of the garrison surrounding Granada. Isabella the Catholic and her husband Ferdinand sometimes called the great fortress city their home. There seemed too few guards around the fortress for the queen and king to be in residence. Still, I rode up cautiously. "Hola," I called when I was within shouting distance of the fortress wall.

"Hola," came the response. "Who goes there?"

"A lone caballero come to join the holy cause of the Reconquest," I called.

"Wait there," called the gate man. "The archers have you in their sights. If you move, you will die."

"I will not move," I acknowledged, then patted my horse's black neck, calming him.

Soon, a gate man rode down the trail from the fortress. "It is not wise to approach Santa Fé at night, Señor. Where do you come from?"

"From Córdoba," I answered.

"You should have waited until morning to volunteer," he said. "Come, follow me." The gate man spurred his horse on, up the trail. I followed close behind. He led me through the gates of Santa Fé. There, he had me dismount at a horse block. A stable hand took charge of my horse while a man in light armor came out to the courtyard and spoke to the mounted gate man. The lightly armored man nodded to me and indicated that I should follow him. We went inside one of the buildings, where I was led down a dark, dank stairway. The guard opened the door of an underground room, went in and lit three candles on a simple wooden table. He motioned that I should sit in the room's solitary chair. "The Grand Inquisitor will be along to see you shortly," explained the guard.

The words filled me with dread, though I'm not really sure why. As a devout Catholic, I had nothing to fear from the Inquisition. The guard turned and left the room, leaving the door slightly ajar. I wasn't a prisoner, but I didn't feel welcome to leave the room either. From the chair, I peered into the shadowed corners of the room, trying to discern what was there. I grew cold in the dark little room and the hairs on my arms stood on edge.

Hours seemed to crawl by before the door swung fully open to reveal a tall, gaunt priest in austere black robes. The priest's white hair stood out from his head, as though he were a wild man. I stood, showing my respect, but the priest waved me back into the chair. "I am Father Miguel García, Grand Inquisitor of Granada and Santa Fé. Why have you come at this late hour?"

"I am sorry, Father," I said with sincere humility. "I am Rudolfo de Córdoba, son of Don Ricardo de Córdoba, a militia captain."

"Ah … The captain killed yesterday morning by Abu Abdallah's heretical adviser," said Father Miguel, nodding. "Though your father was not a friend – most Córdobans are not – he was a good commander. He will be sorely missed."

"I wish to challenge this Ibrahim Yousef to a duel for the cowardly murder of my father," I said forcefully.

"That may prove difficult," said Father Miguel. "Yousef is safe inside Granada."

"I would, at least, like to join the caballeros blockading the city. In some small way, it would allow me to honor my father's memory." I said.

"Yes…" Father Miguel peered over his beak-like nose with dark eyes, like a raptor, ready to strike. "Your story is certainly convincing. You even look like Don Ricardo. But, how do I know your story is true?" Father Miguel folded his arms and began pacing. His words took on a hard edge. "I could just as easily believe that Yousef shot Don Ricardo as a ruse. Under cover of darkness he sends one of his people out of Granada, lets him ride off a few miles, then come back, claiming to be the son of the man killed the day before. That man would then be a spy in our midst. It's a plan worthy of Yousef."

"I assure you, I'm not a spy!" At that moment, I regretted not heeding Don Diego's advice to remain in Córdoba.

"Draco?" called Father Miguel, peering over my head.

"He is telling the truth." A deep, oddly accented voice echoed from one end of the room. I whirled around and peered into the gloom behind me. I could just make out the outline of a man, his eyes reflecting the room's wan candlelight. I could have sworn the man had not been there before, nor had he entered with Father Miguel. "This man is indeed the son of Don Ricardo and has ridden out to help with the crusade against the Moors." It took me a moment, but I finally recognized the man's English accent.

"Indeed!" Father Miguel's dangerous brooding metamorphosed into an even more dangerous glee. The priest looked from me to the shadowy figure in the back of the room. "Could the Caballeros Escarlata use a man who desires the death of Ibrahim Yousef?"

"I planned to assign the matter to Roquelaure," said the shadowy Englishman, firmly.

"But you said yourself that Roquelaure is not always reliable in these matters, that he might be better suited to another task."

"That is true."

"Would this man serve you better than Roquelaure?" asked Father Miguel.

The Englishman slowly emerged from the shadows. I lost my breath. His skin was extraordinarily pale, almost translucent. He was dressed completely in black. A cloak covered a black jerkin and leggings. These were not a priest's vestments. Rather they were the raiment of a noble. The Englishman's hair was short and combed back, giving him a regal appearance, not like the wild-haired Grand Inquisitor. "Rudolfo here is a man of great passion," said the English nobleman, looking me over. "I sense that he is alone in the world. He may well do." As the nobleman spoke, I noticed fangs much like a dog's in his mouth.

I shrank down. "Am I to understand that the Grand Inquisitor consorts with demons?"

Father Miguel chuckled. "Not demonio. Vampiro," he said, as though that would make everything clear.

"I am Desmond, Lord Draco – Knight Commander of the Scarlet Order." The demonic nobleman introduced himself. "My brethren are known by varying names throughout the world. Here in Spain and in Rome we are called vampiro or vampire. Perhaps you've heard of the apes of distant India. They are similar, but different, from man. So are we."

"Apes?" I asked, growing more confused. I had never heard of creatures that were similar, yet different from men. Though I knew of India and the Far East, I was ignorant of the beasts that lived in those places. I looked at Draco's translucent skin and his animalistic eyes. "I was not aware that creatures such as you inhabited the islands of Britain."

Father Miguel shook his head. "It is premature to presume that Lord Draco is a natural creature. What's important is that the pope has never ruled that vampires are demons."

"We are not demons," said Draco, his jaw set. He turned and looked at me. "We are transcendent creatures possessing great power." Silently, Draco moved across the floor toward me, looking into my eyes the whole time and speaking softly. "Do you know how old I am?"

"I would say you are a man of nearly forty years, if I do not miss my guess." Draco seemed only a little older than me.

"Ah, but you do miss your guess. I am nearly a thousand years old." Draco smiled at my shock, as he put one of his hands on my shoulder and gave a gentle squeeze. My shoulder joint felt as though it would snap in his grasp. "Not only are we virtually immortal, we are very strong."

"Vampires make excellent warriors," added Father Miguel.

"I have the power to make you a vampire," explained Draco.

"You could join the Scarlet Order and I could grant you the opportunity for the very revenge you seek."

I stood quickly, upsetting my chair, and backed toward the wall. "I do not want to become a monster – demon or not. Revenge is not worth that price."

I found myself falling under the spell of Draco's eyes again. "You would never be plagued by death," he said.

"What is the price of such a miracle?" I asked.

"You will need to feast on human blood in order to survive," said Father Miguel bluntly as he stepped to the center of the room and righted the chair. "You will never again be able to walk in sunlight."

"And what becomes of my immortal soul?"

"That's up to God and the pope." Father Miguel shrugged.

Draco looked away, releasing me from the power of his gaze. "This offer is neither given lightly nor should you accept it lightly. You will be able to avenge your father's death, but after that, what will you do with immortality? Most choose to hide and become true creatures of darkness. A few of us, though, have chosen to serve human causes. Of course, service is fraught with its own difficulties. Though the powers of good and evil do not change, the clothes they wear often do." Draco inclined his head toward Father Miguel. "One's loyalties must remain flexible."

"Are you saying you're a mercenary?" I asked, finding my tongue.

Draco's nod was barely perceptible. "Though I must live exclusively at night, I do not wish to remain in the shadows. That choice requires gold. Otherwise, I must live in a cave or worse."

Slowly, I crept toward Father Miguel. Though he was an Inquisitor, I somehow felt safer by his side than by Draco's. "This is not an easy decision," I said. "I would like time to consider."

"You will have until tomorrow night. If you are safely ensconced in your chambers after sunset tomorrow, we will respect your wish to remain human. If, instead, you are out on the city's western ramparts, we will know you wish to join our order," said Draco. "If you do not join us, Father Miguel will take you to the Córdoban militia unit your father commanded. You may join them, if they will have you."

I swallowed hard and looked to Father Miguel. "How do I choose?"

"Pray," he said simply.

"And, if God doesn't answer?"

Father Miguel was as silent as I feared God himself would be.

Chapter Four

Rudolfo de Córdoba tells Jane Heckman how he became a vampire. The Year 1491.

In the early morning hours, a guard led me to comfortable sleeping quarters where, having spent a long night with the Grand Inquisitor and the mysterious Lord Draco, I slept much of the next day. When I did wake, I shaved, bathed and then went outside to bask in the sunlight as much as possible.

I walked through the fortress-city's streets and thought about the times I wrestled with my brother and son. I wept as I thought of my poor baby daughter, who had learned to crawl across the hacienda's floor a week before the Black Death struck her down. I remembered my wife, beautiful on the day of our wedding, in the great cathedral of Córdoba. The image of my father, proudly riding his beautiful Arabian horses across the plains, came to me last of all. Death had been stalking me. As the last member of my family, I felt as much of a victim as those who had actually died. Draco offered me a form of revenge against the grim reaper. I didn't need prayer to know what I wanted. In fact, I was afraid that were I to pray, God would advise me to go hide in my room.

As the sun descended in the western sky, I climbed the ladder to the top of the western wall. Longingly, I watched the sun sink below the gently rolling horizon from the fortress city's ramparts. Shortly after, I looked overhead and watched the first stars of the night appear.

"The time for the ceremony is nigh," said a silken voice near my shoulder.

I had not heard anyone approach and I gasped at the sound of the voice. Standing only a few inches away was a figure in a scarlet, hooded robe. At first glance, it looked as though Death himself had come to greet me. The grim reaper threw back his hood and revealed a stunningly handsome face framed by blond hair. He had vivid blue eyes and wore a thin mustache. "I am called Roquelaure," he said. "Lord Draco awaits."

Silently, Roquelaure turned and glided through a portico, entering a tall, nondescript building, not far from the one where I spent the previous night. He led me through numerous twisting, turning corridors that were strangely quiet and empty. At last, Roquelaure entered a great chamber where candelabras lined the walls. The flickering candles cast an eerie, ever-changing light across the room. In the center of the room stood eleven red-hooded figures. It was difficult to tell with the thick, heavy garments, but it seemed to me that a few of the figures might actually be women. Roquelaure took his place in the circle. With no further instructions, I stood awkwardly outside the circle of hooded figures, waiting to see what would happen.

A heavy wooden door at the far end of the room creaked open. Lord Draco appeared, carrying a basin of water. He wore robes of bright red silk, embroidered with an elaborate dragon. A towel was draped over his shoulder. He moved to the center of the circle of hooded figures and bade me to do likewise. I moved cautiously, aware that I was the focal point of hidden, predatory eyes. At the center of the circle was a wooden chair. With a wave of his hand, Draco indicated that I should sit. Kneeling in front of me, he pulled off my boots and eased my feet into the basin of delightfully warm and soothing water. With strong, yet gentle fingers, he massaged my feet in the water and the scent of frankincense rose from the basin to greet me.

"Know this," said Draco as he caressed my feet. "We vampires are not animals, nor are we walking corpses, as is rumored in some lands. We are transcendent beings of mysterious origin. As transcendent beings, it is our duty to care for one another. We are blessed with virtual immortality, but we are not unkillable. We are cursed to drink human blood to survive, but we have power to limit this need. Know that I am the master here and all who have accepted my invitation to join the Scarlet Order have sworn an oath of fealty to me. Know too that I am the Scarlet Order's guardian. As master, I am the absolute authority. Yet, I will never be afraid to kneel before my companions and wash their feet." He paused and looked into my eyes. "I invite you to join the Scarlet Order."

I took a deep breath, then let it out slowly. Something in the back of my mind told me to run – leave this place. Part of me wanted to return to the safety of the hacienda and find someone to help me tend the land. Perhaps even Sister Inez might be compelled to renounce her vows and marry me. Then I thought of my enemy, Death, stalking me all these years. I swallowed deeply. "I accept your invitation."

Draco eased my feet out of the water and dried them with his towel. He stood and helped me to my feet then embraced me as a father might embrace his long, lost son. Just as I returned the embrace, Draco nuzzled, then bit into my neck. The pain was blinding and I cried out, my hands trembling. Growing weaker with every heartbeat, I tried to claw, push and pull – anything to get this monster off of me. The weaker I became, the more timid my blows. Seeming to have taken his fill, Draco lowered me into the chair and stood back, opening his robe. My vision had blurred, but I could just make out his exposed chest. With a sharp fingernail, Draco opened a wound over his heart.

"Do you swear fealty to me?" he asked.

"I swear it," I mumbled.

He reached out and helped me to my feet, saying, "Take, drink. My blood will become your blood. You will transcend, never again needing bread or the fruit of the vine." With that, he cradled the back of my head and pulled my mouth to the wound on his chest. Tasting the blood, I swooned. Long suppressed instinct told me that I must drink to live and so I suckled at the master's breast and felt myself grow stronger. After a long moment, he gently pulled me away. I embraced Draco and lay my head on his shoulder. My breathing became more and more shallow and he eased me toward the floor. Shortly after, I lay limp, as though dead.

☦☦☦

I awoke later, in a dark, damp room that smelled of death. Seeing shackles on the wall, I realized I was in a dungeon, somewhere within the great city fortress. In spite of the foul smells of human waste, mold, and decaying flesh, I grew ravenous. Though the room was dark, I could make out many minute details. Somehow, my vision had improved. Behind me was Lord Draco, still in his scarlet robes. With him was Father Miguel. Looking forward again, I saw a lump of a man huddled in the corner.

"His name is Fuad Shawki," said Lord Draco in a calm voice.

"He is a Moor who refuses baptism," explained Father Miguel, coldly. "The Inquisition has sentenced him to death for heresy. You are to carry out the sentence."

I required no further prompting. Like a great cat, I pounced on the huddled man. Instinctively, I bit into the pulsing jugular vein and his blood washed over my tongue, filling me. Joyously, I drew his blood into me and felt the edge taken from my hunger. I continued to suck at the wound long after the heretic was dead. Draco gently pried the body from my arms.

"Still hungry?" asked Father Miguel, a gleam in his eye.

To my shame, I nodded.

"There are plenty more heretics where this one came from."

"The initial hunger is the worst," whispered Draco. "After this, it is easier to control."

☦☦☦

I soon learned that vampires normally do not require much blood to survive – a pint or two per day will keep us healthy and well. Under normal conditions, if we drain more than one body dry, we will feel bloated and sick. In fact, during that first night in the dungeons of Santa Fé, Father Miguel egged me on, encouraging me to continue draining the blood of heretics. My hunger had been so great, that I was willing to oblige. After the fifth unfortunate victim, I became sick and found myself doubled over. Draco's arms were around my shoulders as I vomited blood. For the next week, I lay in a darkened room, wishing I'd stayed in my chambers and not accepted Draco's gift of immortality.

Ultimately, I did recover and began to revel in my newfound strength and sensations. I discovered that I could hear distant conversations. From the ramparts of Santa Fé, I could peer into Granada's windows. Passing buildings, I could hear snippets of unspoken thought. "You begin to understand why kings, knights and the church value us so," said Draco, finding me one night, wandering the streets of the fortress city. "Your gifts will strengthen as you age. Soon, you will discover the animal spirit within. With practice, you may even be able to transform into that beast."

My eyes went wide. "Can you transform into a beast?"

Draco inclined his head.

"Can you show me?"

Draco pursed his lips. "I do not perform tricks for anyone's amusement."

"I am sorry," I said, humbly. "I did not mean to offend you."

The English nobleman waved my apology aside, quickly forgetting my faux pas. He then told me the time appointed for our strike against Granada approached.

The vampires of the Scarlet Order met the next night in the chamber where I'd been welcomed into their fold. Dread weighed heavily upon me that night. I was afraid our mission would be to rampage through Granada, killing as many of the citizens as possible. Instead, Draco spoke of killing only three Granadans: The first was a Sa'id visiting the city and rumored to be a friend of Emir Abu Abdallah's father. The second was an arms smith, said to be one of the best in the land. The third was one of the Emir's advisers – Vizier Ibrahim Yousef. One vampire would be assigned to assassinate each of these people. Without their support,

Abu Abdallah's hold over Granada would weaken substantially, hastening the city's fall. The remainder of the vampires were to seek certain texts and scrolls within the city. These texts contained knowledge that could also prolong the campaign.

"Do you still seek vengeance for your father?" asked Draco.

I nodded.

"Then your job will be to find and kill Ibrahim Yousef," ordered Lord Draco.

"Where will I find him?"

"Within the Al-hambra," said the handsome Roquelaure. "He often wanders the Courtyard of the Lions alone in the early evening."

The next night, the vampires of the Scarlet Order crossed the distance between Santa Fé and Granada in silence. I was amazed how fast I could run over land. It seemed I was even more fleet of foot than my father's prized Arabian horses. Roquelaure led me through the city to the great palace of Al-hambra. From the outside, the palace looked even more stark and featureless than the buildings inside hastily built Santa Fé. Effortlessly, Roquelaure climbed the palace walls. My improved vision and strength allowed me to find and grip foot and toe holds I would never have managed as a human. Though slower than Roquelaure, I found I could follow him up the wall. At the top, he gave me directions to the Lion Court. He went the opposite way, seeking several of the scrolls Draco wanted.

I crept along tiled roofs, stepping carefully so as not to shatter the tiles and alert guards to my presence. I found the Lion Court easily enough. It was a splendid, grassy courtyard. Four walkways cut through the grass and met in the center at a fountain guarded by a number of stone lions. Surrounding the courtyard were covered walkways. Narrow columns that blossomed into delicately carved arches supported the roofs of the walkways. The courtyard itself was empty and I had little to do but wait for Ibrahim Yousef – presuming he would arrive as Roquelaure indicated he would.

As I loitered among the columns admiring the fine work of the artisans who had built the Al-hambra, a lone figure emerged on the far side of the courtyard. He stepped into the open and stood near the lion-guarded fountain. Around the man's neck was a chain that held a metal disk with several metal circles mounted to its face. The man removed the chain from his neck, adjusted the circles on the disk's face, then held it up, as though sighting stars along its side. I presumed this man was Ibrahim Yousef, but I needed to be certain. Though I could detect some thoughts, my gifts were not sufficiently developed to probe this man's mind.

Casually, I emerged from the shadows and asked what he was doing.

"This is an astrolabe," he said, his eyes still skyward. "I'm trying to get a good measurement of the alignment of two stars – the swooping eagle and the hen's tail. It will help us maximize our resources by telling us when we can fertilize our trees and gardens, and harvest the fruits and vegetables from around the city. By getting as much as we can from our limited resources, perhaps we can survive this blockade of infidels."

"That looks like it takes a great deal of concentration," I said, idly wondering whether it might be better to take Yousef back to Draco – press his skills into the service of Isabella and Ferdinand rather than simply kill him.

"It does, and it would be easier outside the confines of the city. However, the last time I tried, I was attacked by one of the infidels. It's not safe to go outside the city at night." He paused in his stargazing and looked me in the eye, his wispy salt-and-pepper beard wafting in the breeze. "I don't know you. You are not one of the palace regulars."

"I'm not," I said. "My father was Don Ricardo de Córdoba, the man who attacked you outside the city."

He pursed his lips. "You've made it deep into the palace grounds without being detected. I presume you must be one of the red-hooded servants of Shaitan who are employed by the Castillian Inquisition."

"I serve Lord Draco."

"Shaitan, Draco," he said, rolling his eyes. "It makes no difference. They're both the same – creatures of darkness."

"Why did you kill my father?" I asked.

Yousef shrugged. "He interfered with my work and he was an infidel. That seems more than enough reason to me." I caught just a flicker of warning as Yousef dropped the astrolabe to the ground with one hand and drew a flintlock pistol from his robes with the other. He cocked the pistol's hammer as he leveled it at me.

A robed figure emerged from the shadows of the walkway behind Yousef and struck him. The pistol discharged and the ball hit me in the shoulder, whipping me around. I dropped to the ground, my shoulder seemingly afire. With a force of will, I turned my head and saw Roquelaure bent over Yousef, fangs in his neck, drinking the vizier's blood.

After a few moments, Roquelaure looked up at me and grinned. "Be wary of the time you spend among humans and what they say to you," said Roquelaure, still holding the limp form of Ibrahim Yousef. "They are dangerous, murderous creatures."

"Couldn't we have used his knowledge?" I asked, surprised that I spoke of my father's murderer.

"His knowledge lives on in the books that Draco ordered us to bring back to Santa Fé. Books are beautiful and permanent, much like us vampires."

"Books decay," I said, glumly. "What of vampires?"

"Books can be copied by patient hands. There are few hands more patient than those of immortal vampires," retorted Roquelaure. He snapped Yousef's neck to assure he was dead, then dropped the body in a heap near the lion fountain.

Gingerly, I reached up and touched the bullet wound in my shoulder. I was surprised to find it mostly healed. Roquelaure held his hand out to me, helping me stand. "Come, we need to go so we can get that tended to," he said, gently. "It is healing, but you need blood."

I sighed and looked at the crumpled form of Ibrahim Yousef. "Somehow, I thought his death would bring me peace. Instead, it just leaves me uneasy."

"That's because loss is cumulative – killing a person to avenge another only leaves two dead bodies. It does not reconcile anything," said Roquelaure. "The older you get, the more you'll value life. I've been watching Yousef's movements for months. However, I could not bring myself to kill him until tonight – until I saw for myself that he did not respect any life but his own."

"That seems an odd attitude for a mercenary," I said.

"It's just as odd an attitude for a vampire," he said. "However, I must live with my own conscience for the rest of eternity. Likewise, you must live with yours." With that thought, Roquelaure took my good arm and helped me back to Santa Fé.

Chapter Five

From the journals of Dr. Jane Heckman.
Present Day.

I have been a vampire for just over a month now and I'm still sorting out what exactly it means to "be a vampire." I am not aware of any formal, scientific study of vampires. It would appear that we are rare creatures. Classical studies such as Montague Summers's *The Vampire, His Kith and Kin* and *The Vampire in Europe* do little more than survey vampire literature and relate second and third-hand accounts of vampire encounters. More recent studies do little more.

My own field is ballistic and explosive physics, not anthropology, biology or any other field of study that might be more relevant to the study of vampires, which are also known by such names as nosferatu, revenant, vrykolakas and so forth depending on the region of the vampire's origin. This journal will endeavor to be a first-hand account of my observations. However, since the study of creatures such as vampires is outside my discipline, these notes may lack completeness.

I was born a human but became a vampire through a process of being attacked by a vampire that drank my blood. I, in turn, drank the blood of the attacking vampire. My attacker claims to be a 550-year-old vampire who calls himself Rudolfo.

✟✟✟

"For the record, my name is Rudolfo Jésus Juan Ramírez de Córdoba." Rudolfo's voice caused me to jump involuntarily.

"How long have you been looking over my shoulder?" I asked as I lay my pen down.

"Only a few minutes. I saw the title and thought I'd do what I could to clear up any misconceptions you may give your poor readers about me or about vampires in general." Rudolfo shrugged, nonchalant.

I sighed. "I'd rather you not stare over my shoulder."

Rudolfo grinned. "What do I have better to do than watch a beautiful woman work? Besides, it's interesting."

I waved my hands at the older vampire. "You could go watch television or something. There're lots of women to watch there."

"I hate television." Rudolfo wrinkled his nose. "The stories jump all around and just as they get interesting, some shill comes on to sell me something I don't need. It's very annoying."

"All right, all right," I relented. "Get a chair or something. Just don't stand there. It makes me nervous." I paused for a moment then looked at Rudolfo again, my brow furrowed. "Are you really a vampire named Jésus?"

"A rose by any other name would smell as sweet." His eyes twinkled as he pulled up a chair.

✟✟✟

As a vampire, I find my outward appearance is very nearly the same as it was when I was human. At the time I became a vampire, I was a woman of 42. Admittedly, some of the changes I record are qualitative: My skin has become smoother and more taut, yet somewhat more pale, taking on something of an alabaster quality. My eye color seems more vivid. My lips seem fuller and a brighter shade of red.

My senses also seem to be improved. I can hear fainter

sounds and see more distant objects. Looking up at the night sky, I am able to distinguish the rings of Saturn, something well beyond normal human ability. I should emphasize that my vision does not seem to magnify objects. I simply seem to have improved resolution, as though there are more rods and cones in my eyes. Perhaps an eye test with a qualified ophthalmologist would be in order.

I appear to have acquired the ability to sense the thoughts of others and to project my own thoughts into their minds. Though various studies have been made, I know of no study that has definitively demonstrated the existence of telepathy in humans. I also know of no satisfactory hypothesis describing a mechanism for telepathy. Perhaps further study of this ability with vampires would yield better results than it has with humans.

I have become stronger. It is much easier for me to load my crossbow than before I became a vampire. I can now easily subdue and feed upon human males that I estimate to be two and a half times my weight. Because I was neither a violent person nor the subject of an attack prior to becoming a vampire, I do not know what I was capable of as a human. However, I strongly suspect I was not capable of such a feat of physical prowess.

More quantitatively: My canine teeth now extend approximately 0.125 inches below the neighboring teeth. In spite of what is shown in many vampire movies, my canine teeth do not retract, they are fixed much like those of a dog.

✝✝✝

"What an unflattering comparison," muttered Rudolfo.

Turning around, I scowled at him. "What do you mean? Dogs have long canine teeth. It's a reasonable comparison."

"So do cats," he said, grinning wistfully, displaying his own fangs. "And I would say you have feline grace and charm."

"If you don't stop interrupting, you'll see what a bitch I can be," I growled.

✝✝✝

My canine fangs have a slightly serrated edge, reminiscent of a Tyrannosaurus Rex's fossil teeth. The purpose of my fangs is to allow me to quickly bite through skin and muscle, allowing blood to flow into my mouth. I ingest blood through my digestive system, just as an ordinary human would ingest food or drink.

Regrettably, when I first became a vampire, I had no control over my feeding instinct and I killed my first victim. At that point, I discovered Rudolfo had both an uncanny knack for disposing of bodies and strong powers of psychic persuasion. The police now consider my first victim and myself to be "missing persons." State Police are currently looking for both of us, but as time wears on and the trail grows cold, hope fades that we shall be found. Upon searching my house, the police only found Rudolfo, who persuaded them to search elsewhere. The police have not returned.

Fortunately, I've found that the taking of lives is not required. A pint of blood per night seems satisfactory for good health. I'm still learning how to control and use my telepathic powers. However, they seem largely geared toward causing the victim to forget our encounter.

I find that I can digest all liquids, not just blood. However, I become weak if I don't drink any blood in a 24-hour period. Alcohol proves even more intoxicating to me now than before I became a vampire. It's as though all of the alcohol I ingest goes directly into my blood stream. I cannot digest solid food. If I attempt to, I vomit the entire volume of what I've consumed.

According to Rudolfo, vampires do not require human blood for survival. They can drink the blood of other animals. Experimenting, I have found I can indeed digest the blood of rats and dogs. However, the taste is repellent and I can only consume animal blood with difficulty. Morally difficult as it is at times, it's simply easier to drink the blood of humans and I suspect more nutritious.

All of this leads to the conclusion that my digestive system has been altered. An ordinary human takes in food. The food is, in turn, broken down and nutrients transferred through the small intestine into the blood stream where blood nourishes the cells.

As best as I can determine without dissecting a vampire, the blood I ingest is transferred directly into my blood stream. I would hypothesize that this happens in the small intestine. As the nutrients in the blood are used up, it is expelled along with other wastes through the urinary tract.

✞✞✞

"That's distasteful." Rudolfo's face contorted in a grimace. "Must a woman write about her toilet habits for all to read?"

"It's scientific observation." I shrugged. "I'm trying to describe this objectively. And really, I'm not being very graphic at all. You should hear some of my friends talk about their menstrual flows."

Rudolfo's natural pallor turned a slight shade of green.

I grinned and couldn't resist prodding him a little further. "I bet you fainted the first time you pissed blood, didn't you?"

"I am a caballero!" he said, sitting bolt upright. "I was accustomed to blood long before I became a vampire."

"You didn't answer the question."

Uncharacteristically, Rudolfo looked down at his feet. "It made me nervous, the first time."

"I think that's one area where it's easier for women to become vampires than men. We're used to seeing blood in the toilet."

If anything, Rudolfo turned greener. "I think you should concentrate on your scientific observations."

✞✞✞

Vampire folklorists, such as Montague Summers, suggest that vampires are humans who have lost their souls. Further, the folklorists state that the vampire is possessed by a demon.

I regard the soul as a matter for theological discussion and beyond the scope of these observations. Likewise, I will not speculate as to the existence of demons or their activities. Regarding my own experience in becoming a vampire, I still remember my life prior to the transformation. My tastes in personal things such as art, clothing, music, and books have not changed.

It is too early for me to write about my emotions definitively. Over the past month, I have had several instances of depression. These bouts stem from several sources: I am disheartened by the fact that I must now feed on human blood to survive and that I took the life of my first victim. I am saddened and haunted by the loss of two of my students to the vampire who attacked me. To understand my vampiric existence, I have chosen to live with that same vampire.

✝✝✝

Tears welled up to the surface and I could not continue writing. Rudolfo rose from his chair and reached out to pull me close, but I beat him off with my fists. He collapsed into the chair, hands folded, and waited until my sobs subsided. I looked up at him. "Why did you do this to me?"

He reached out and gently brushed a tear from my cheek with his strong finger. He answered my question with two of his own. "Has it really been so bad being with me? Do you really hate what you are?"

I took his hand in mine and brushed his knuckle with a kiss, then shook my head. "But I feel like I ought to be guilty and hate myself." I let Rudolfo pull me to him, let him hold me for a time, comforting me.

✝✝✝

Though the depression exists, it is not as severe as I would have expected. I seem to have developed predatory instincts. Though I have qualms about attacking humans, those qualms are surprisingly easy to override. I am loath to admit it, but there is a part of me that enjoys the hunt. It would be easy to say it's simply the hunger for human blood that drives me to it, but there is something more. This point alone tempts me to revisit the notion that vampires may, somehow be possessed by some kind of spirit that could be called a demon.

However, as a scientist who has lived and worked by the principal of Ocham's Razor, I look for the simplest explanation. If there is a demon within me, she operates with great subtlety and stealth. Instead of invoking souls and demons, I believe a simpler explanation is that a vampire is a human who has undergone a physical and biochemical transformation. Changes in my brain's biochemistry could account for more willingness to be violent while most other things about me have not been changed. My bouts of depression seem natural in light of the violence of my transformation into a vampire. I suspect they will vanish with time. Even though I'm skeptical of the existence of souls, I fear for my own when my self-loathing of hunting humans vanishes entirely.

For my hypothesis to be sound, I must explore the reasons why the transformation of human to vampire would occur. All of the changes that occur when a person becomes a vampire enhance their fighting abilities. Vampirism would appear to be a process by which a human is made into a more efficient warrior. I do not have sufficient data to suggest how such a transformation may have been started, nor who or what would have had the ability to create the first vampires. The notion that vampires are engineered warriors is borne out by Rudolfo de Córdoba's personal history. The events recorded here are from a first-hand interview with Rudolfo de Córdoba. I should note that they have not been corroborated through literature or other interviews.

Rudolfo de Córdoba claims to have been born in 1456 to Christians fighting to drive the last of the Moors from Spain. He lived on a hacienda in Southern Spain and learned to be a soldier from his father. When his father was killed while blockading the Moorish city of Granada in 1491, he says he was invited to join an elite group of knights called the Caballeros de Reino Escarlata, literally Knights of the Scarlet Realm. I am somewhat skeptical of this story since I cannot find any record of the Caballeros de Reino Escarlata on the internet. It is a source I do not entirely trust, but a source that tends to propagate too much rather than too little information. Rudolfo says he was turned into a vampire as part of the initiation into the order.

✝✝✝

"'He says,' 'he claims,' 'I am skeptical.'" Rudolfo frowned deeply. "Don't you believe anything I have told you?"

"I'm a scientist," I said firmly. "I cannot report something as fact unless I observe it directly or have corroborating evidence."

Rudolfo leaned menacingly close to me. "If I tell you something, you can be sure that it is the truth, as surely as if you saw it yourself."

I shook my head. "This isn't about your word or the truth of what you said. It's about being able to verify what I'm writing."

"But you are skeptical." He stood and began pacing, waving his hands in agitation. "The Caballeros were a force to be feared. We were responsible for driving the Moors from Spain. We brought an end to the Ottoman Empire. If not for us, there would be no Europeans in America."

Standing, I put my hand against Rudolfo's chest, stopping him in his tracks. "All right, you told me about driving the Moors from Spain. What else did the Scarlet Order do? Maybe if you tell me more about your history, I can search and find more to corroborate your story."

"Have I told you how we dispatched Suleiman the Magnificent and what I saw in the aftermath of the Battle of Lepanto."

That gave me pause. Those would certainly be points of history I could investigate further. "Please tell me the stories."

He went to the kitchen, retrieved a bottle of wine and poured two glasses. He handed me one, then sat and began his tale.

Chapter Six

Suleiman the Magnificent's assassination as told by Rudolfo de Córdoba. The Year 1566.

"I loved it here in the Carpathians until the Ottoman Turks arrived." Desmond, Lord Draco stood on a rock pile, his cape pulled tight around him, and surveyed the remains of an ancient castle. Several forlorn walls leaned desperately into one another like drunks trying to stay upright after too much celebration. Any furniture that remained was out of sight. Cloth, whether from furniture, tapestries, or clothing had long ago decayed or been carried away.

"The Ottomans invaded about a century ago, wasn't it?" I asked, more captivated by the fog-shrouded mountain peaks surrounding us than by the skeletal remains of a castle I had never known. "Around the time I was born – as a human that is."

Draco faced me and his lips curled upward slightly. "Only a drop in the well of eternity," he mused. "In fact, this place has hardly changed since I first came here. It feels like I lived here a thousand years – though it really wasn't quite that long. The Turks destroyed my home in less than a week." The English Lord turned his back on the castle walls, closed his eyes for several moments, then opened them and took in the view of the valley below.

Green trees and grass carpeted wild, jagged slopes, barely visible in the deep gloom of the overcast night. The air was still – heavy-laden with fog that Draco seemed to breathe in like an elixir. The

Bistritza River flowed to the Northeast. Gypsies, who had arrived in the country little more than a century before, plied their trades along the waterway. Not far away was the town of Bistritz. All around were enough people to feed a vampire, yet standing on a rock mound, looking at a ruined castle nestled in a crag of rock, I felt isolated and alone. Though, I could see the appeal of such a place to an ancient vampire such as Draco, I had begun to miss cities like Córdoba and the company of humans.

"But why here?" I broke the eerie silence. "Why didn't you build your castle in England?"

Lord Draco snorted at the word, 'England.' "I left Britain when it was conquered by the invaders," he said, emphasizing the word 'Britain.' "What was left of my people were driven west into Wales or north into Scotland. I bear an English title only because I returned and did some favors for the invaders." Desmond looked to the ground for several minutes while pondering memories. When he looked up, his eyes were moist. "I came here because I had grown tired of empires ebbing and flowing across my homeland. In my youth, it was the Romans. While I was still human, I fought off Saxon invaders. After I became a vampire, the Saxons ultimately won. I came here to get away from it all. The Carpathian Mountains seemed like the ideal place to find peace."

"Then the Ottoman Turks arrived…"

"…and I fought to preserve my adopted homeland. Once again, the invaders won."

"Is that why you became a mercenary?"

Draco shook his head. "No … I was a mercenary here, too. Despite the combined experience of the Scarlet Order, my home was destroyed." Looking back at the castle, he sighed. "I settled here because I was foolish enough to think I could stop fighting and pursue intellectual challenges."

A patch of fog blew through and swallowed both scenery and sound. After it cleared, I became aware of a wolf prowling through a cluster of trees not far from where we stood. The creature seemed to evaluate the two of us, deciding if we were suitable prey. With an almost contemptuous snort, the wolf moved on.

"Since the castle is in ruins," I began, "where will we spend the day?"

"We'll spend it here," Draco said. "The crypt was spared and it's the best place to spend the day since sunlight doesn't penetrate its depths. The Turks didn't feel it was right to defile a burial site." Draco sighed and turned to face the castle again. "Besides, Roquelaure and the others expect to find us here."

"Why here?" I narrowed my gaze.

"You are full of questions, young one." Draco's lips curled upward slightly and I bristled. I might be younger than Lord Draco, but by this time I was over a century old. "This is a good place to gather before we travel to Hungary. My sources tell me that Suleiman is gathering his forces there."

"The Ottoman Sultan himself?"

"Indeed." Draco strode toward the castle, stepping gracefully and carefully over long-remembered stones.

I thought for a moment, then ran after the older vampire. "I thought we'd finished with the Ottomans when we dispatched the sultan's son, Mustafa, over ten years ago."

"That was part one of the plan. This is part two."

"It's taken a decade to move to part two?"

"Only a drop in the well of eternity, young one," said Draco with a nod.

✣✣✣

The vampire Rosen served as our spy in Suleiman the Magnificent's encampment. He kept his shock of red hair shorn and wore a turban so he blended in with the humans in the sultan's retinue.

Suleiman rode into the encampment on a lovely Arabian stallion. Even as an older man, he cut a striking figure with his thick, white mustache. Upon his head a great turban was adorned with feathers, and a brocaded silk caftan wrapped his body. These were not garments the sultan would wear into battle, but he wore them as he rode through the camp to inspire his troops. The fortress above was Szigetvár. The sultan and his forces were in Hungary, far from their home in Istanbul. The sultan's advisers were certain the Hungarian stronghold could not survive more than a month-long siege. Suleiman dismounted at the pavilion outside the tent set up for him, then surveyed the scene as servants led his horse away for grooming. Suleiman's grand vizier, Sokollu Mehmed Pasha emerged from the tent wringing his hands.

"You look troubled," observed Suleiman. "You should not be. This will be an easy victory for us."

The vizier sighed and asked to speak in private. Unhurriedly, the sultan turned and led the way inside. Servants, including Rosen, scurried about, fluffing pillows, laying out platters of dried fruit and spiced meat and pouring two goblets of şalgam. Seeing the sultan, they bowed low and backed out of the tent. Rosen blended into the shadows and doubled back to a place where he could watch the meeting.

"I have received word that your life is in danger from assassins," said Sokollu.

Suleiman threw his head back and laughed. "Assassins? What are they going to do, sneak past the janissaries and murder me in my sleep?" Surveying the platters, the sultan selected several pieces of dried fruit and grew serious as the vizier ignored the platters and continued wringing his hands. "Tell me more of these assassins."

"The information is limited, but the threat seems supernatural in nature."

"Some kind of wizardry?" The sultan sat in the midst of a stack of pillows and chewed the fruit, slowly.

The vizier shook his head and sat at the sultan's feet. "The peasants in the area talk of demonic creatures known as vampir. They are creatures of the night that lust after blood."

The sultan reached for a goblet of şalgam. "I have heard of such creatures, but I thought they were simply peasant rumors – stories to frighten young children."

"They may be," said the vizier. "However, the Christians take the vampir demons very seriously. I have agents who believe there is a vampir demon that will target you, personally."

The sultan heaved a deep sigh, took a drink, then reached for more fruit. "No doubt your agents are being fed lies designed to frighten us." The vizier opened his mouth to speak, but the sultan held up his hand. "Your sources haven't been wrong before, so no doubt there is a truth in what they say – though I refuse to speculate on exactly what the truth may be. Do they know of a way to prevent an attack by a vampir?"

"I have ordered my agents to send for assistance."

"What kind of assistance?" The sultan set the goblet down.

"It is said that parts of Greece are infested with these vampir. There are certain Greeks whose profession is hunting vampir demons."

"Christians?"

The vizier reached for a piece of meat. "It is said that they have the blessing of the Orthodox Church."

The sultan frowned. "I don't know if I like placing my life in the hands of Christians."

"A sultan does not always have the luxury of doing what he likes. Sometimes, he must do what is necessary for the survival of his realm." The vizier bit into the meat and chewed.

"Though I wish to survive, the realm does not depend on me, alone. If I were to die, there is Selim to succeed me."

The vizier coughed and looked to the ground to cover a disappointed frown. Rosen knew Sokollu dare not question Selim's competence. One day, the vizier may have to serve Suleiman's only remaining son.

"Is there anything else, old friend," asked Suleiman after a moment.

Sokollu looked up and thought for a moment. "No, your eminence."

"Then you are dismissed." Suleiman reached up and began removing the large turban. "Be sure to alert me when these vampir hunters arrive."

Sokollu bowed low and backed out of the tent.

Once assured the sultan had settled in for the night, Rosen left his hiding place, wrote a message and sent it via homing pigeon to Alexandra the Greek.

✝✝✝

I awoke from my death-like slumber early the following evening and blinked in near total darkness as I regained my bearings. Cautiously, I felt for the floor with my left foot, then sat up slowly while rubbing my lower back and cursing the stone slab I'd slept on. Much as I hated sleeping in the damp crypt, it was preferable to digging into the earth and waking to soil in my eyes and an earthworm crawling in my ear. I shut my eyes against the unpleasant memory and shivered, then shook my head and decided to find Draco.

Already outside, the British Lord watched the darkening sky. "There is an encampment of gypsies not far from here," he said, as I approached. "We should feed now so we can return before the others arrive. Have you been practicing your transformation?"

"I have, but must we transform?" I shook my head. "I always feel drained by the process and must take more blood than I would if I didn't transform into my animal self. Sometimes it is difficult to prevent myself from killing."

Lord Draco nodded. "I understand. But it is the fastest way for us to travel and assure we return before too late."

"Then lead the way."

Without further comment, Desmond, Lord Draco closed his eyes. His skin sprouted bristly fur and developed a life of its own, swarming and writhing. First, his body collapsed in on itself, then exploded into a swarm of flies. I must confess I almost grew ill at the sight. My own animal is a bat. Bats seem more noble creatures than swarms of insects. Fortunately for Draco, my bat self did not need to eat, otherwise the English lord would likely be in danger of being consumed. I spread my arms wide and ran along the grassy field, transforming into a bat. Together, Draco and I flew over the rocky terrain.

My sensitive ears picked up strains of song and the jangling of instruments before I could see the camp. Draco rarely discussed what it was like to be a swarm of flies and I often wondered exactly how the master vampire sensed the world while in his transformed state. Soon after I heard the music, Draco's flies coalesced into human form. I slowed and transformed into my human self. Unfortunately, my feet were a few inches above the ground and I tumbled into a nearby bush. Draco had the temerity to shush me, but I bit back a retort when I noticed him pointing.

A pair of young lovers sat on a log well away from the main camp. The two were engrossed with one another and did not see or hear us as we approached.

Draco attacked the young man while I took the woman. Neither of the gypsies had time to cry out. After drinking his fill of blood, Draco eased the young man into the grass and worked to make him as comfortable as possible. Once I finished drinking, I realized the woman's pulse had become weak and thready. I stroked her hair.

"Is she..." Draco's voice held a note of concern.

I shook my head. "Not yet, but I fear I may have taken too much blood."

Draco put his hand on my shoulder. "Unfortunately, tonight it cannot be helped. Move her next to her lover. His body heat will keep her warm until they are found. She may yet survive."

With care, I nestled the woman against her young lover, then stood and looked at the couple for a few moments, remembering my own family, killed by the black plague. "I became a vampire to defeat death. Now, it would appear that I am death's ally."

The vampire lord motioned for me to follow. We stepped quietly away from the gypsy camp so our voices would not carry. "Death is not an entity that you can be allied with or fight against. It is simply something that happens to all living beings." Without further comment, Draco fell silent and transformed into the swarm. With a sigh, I followed suit, becoming a bat again, and we flew back to the castle. Upon our return, we discovered nearly a dozen vampires milling around outside the castle walls. Some searched for us, some waited patiently, and others were visibly bored.

"The pope sends his regards," called Roquelaure.

Draco's swarm settled near the French vampire and coalesced into human form. "And how is Pope Julius?"

"Dead, as are Marcellus II, Paul IV, and Pius IV" said Roquelaure, dryly. "The current Pope has taken the name, Pius V."

Looking to the ground, Draco sighed. "Human life is so short – and each time there is a new pope, there is a danger the church will back out of its commitment to us."

Roquelaure frowned. "Indeed, Pius V is the fifth pope since the Council of Trent decreed that the Ottomans were a threat to the Holy Roman Empire."

Now transformed into my natural state, I shook my head. "There's something about that I don't completely understand. I didn't think the papacy allied itself with the Empire anymore. Why do they care whether the Holy Roman Empire falls to the Ottomans?"

A tall, young-looking female vampire stepped forward, her hips swaying. Thick, long hair flowed over her shoulders. She looked at me with large, dark eyes as she draped a delicate arm around Roquelaure's shoulder. "At least Charles V is Catholic," said Alexandra the Greek. "As such, I would think the Pope would consider him a better neighbor than Suleiman."

"And, Suleiman is a real threat, given the weakness of Charles' empire. As such, they call on us to keep the Ottomans contained," said Roquelaure, turning and putting his hand on Alexandra's slender waist. He kissed her on the nose, then spun out of her embrace.

Looking around at the ruins of his castle, Draco sighed. "At least this campaign should give me enough money to build a better library. The books I have in Wales are moldering. I need to get them back into a dry environment."

As Draco and Roquelaure conversed, two others appeared from the ruins with a long table and turned it upright. Other vampires brought wooden chairs and rocks on which they could sit.

Once they were seated around the table, I opened the meeting. "So, how do we proceed against Suleiman? He will be heavily guarded."

"Indeed," said Alexandra. "Rosen has sent us word he will be guarded by the Hunters of Santorini."

"The Hunters of Santorini?" My brow furrowed.

"The strongest league of professional vampire hunters we've ever met," explained a stoic African woman at the end of the table named Nabila. "You're lucky you've not encountered them yet. Of course, they've yet to meet the force of the entire Scarlet Order. Those of us unfortunate enough to know the Hunters have only dealt with them one-on-one."

"Years ago, there was a particularly imprudent master vampire on the island of Santorini in Greece," explained Alexandra. "He created many vampires on his home island and the surrounding islands. They were like a plague. Several humans using the resources of the Greek Orthodox Church made a study of our kind so that they could contain the plague." Alexandra closed her eyes and Roquelaure pulled her close, protective rather than playful.

"They are very effective at killing vampires," finished Nabila. "Alexandra is one of the few vampires I know who has survived an encounter."

Desmond, Lord Draco rubbed his chin and nodded. "Clearly we must do our best to account for the hunters in our plans." He signaled to Roquelaure who rolled out a map of Szigetvár and the surrounding countryside. I whispered to another vampire who retrieved candles and a candelabrum. We gathered around to study the map and make our plans for the attack on the Sultan of the Ottoman Empire.

✟✟✟

A month into the siege of Szigetvár, Suleiman had fallen into a routine. The siege itself went well and he grew complacent when no assassins appeared. Even so, the sultan allowed the recently arrived Christian bodyguards to watch over him. They unnerved him, but he made a show of accepting their presence as routine, even amid the objections of the janissaries.

After a particularly long day filled with the minutiae of

administration, the sultan entered his tent, did his best to ignore the Greek bodyguards and fell into a fitful sleep.

That's when we struck. Three of us attacked each of the Santorini vampire hunters. Suleiman awoke and reached for his oil lamp, but I knocked his hand away. He called out for his guards.

One of the Santorini hunters broke free of his attackers and shouted orders to another in Greek. I leapt on him, wrestled him to the ground and wrenched his head so hard it nearly came off in my hands.

One man cried out and another screamed. The sultan stood and ran for the door, a look of sheer terror on his face. Alexandra dispatched one of the hunters and threw the body in the sultan's path. Nabila leapt out of the shadows and grabbed the sultan. He gazed into her eyes and seemed to take comfort from her embrace. Then she opened her mouth, revealing fangs. He struggled to free himself, but I stepped over and calmed his mind. Nabila sank her teeth into his neck. I could sense the sultan's thoughts. He began to wonder why he had been so frightened. His eyelids grew heavy and he fell asleep in Nabila's tender embrace.

The mission complete, Draco ordered retreat. I remained behind with Rosen to see the aftermath of our attack and assure there were no loose ends. Rosen showed me his hiding place and I discovered that we could indeed see most of what transpired without being observed ourselves. A short, stout man entered. Rosen spoke to me in my mind. I understood the man was the leader of the vampire hunters and his name was Nikolas. He gasped at the site of his fallen comrades. His gaze moved from one to the other, as though trying to decide who to run to first. At last, he seemed to remember his duty and ran to the sultan. He checked the man's pulse.

A moment later a man in bright robes with a full beard entered. Rosen let me know this was the sultan's grand vizier, Sokollu Mehmed Pasha. "What happened? When did this happen?"

Nikolas's breaths came in deep gulps and his eyes glazed over. "Only a few minutes ago," he said, between breaths. A drooping mustache framed a frown of disappointment. "I have never in my life encountered so many vampires attacking at once in such a coordinated fashion."

"You knew these vampir demons threatened the sultan with assassination!" shouted Sokollu.

"We expected one or two vampires," said Nikolas, his voice and jowls trembling. "There were a dozen or more. I suspect this must have been the infamous Scarlet Order – once employed by the Spanish Inquisition. We didn't expect…"

As Nikolas spoke and pulled himself together, Sokollu made his way to the sultan's side. "How is he?"

"He has lost much blood," reported Nikolas. "I'm afraid there is nothing more we can do. I doubt he will see morning. If he's very strong, he may live the day through."

Sokollu's face flushed crimson. "I was told you vampir hunters could prevent this attack. Now, my sultan lies there dying!"

Nikolas blew out a breath. "Though we have known of the Scarlet Order, this is the first time our ranks have faced them. We were not aware they would pose such a challenge. We'll be ready for them next time." The vampire hunter retrieved a handkerchief and wiped his brow.

"There will be no next time," shouted Sokollu. Stepping carefully over the bodies of the sultan's personal guard and the vampire hunters, he stormed through the door and summoned as many soldiers as he could. He ordered them to surround the tent, then picked out two senior officers. All together they entered the sultan's tent and Sokollu swallowed hard.

Nikolas left and the bodies of those who had fallen were taken away. Only the sultan and the grand vizier remained. The sultan moaned in his sleep.

The senior janissary entered the tent and bowed low. "Why have you summoned us, Grand Vizier? Where are the sultan's guards?"

Closing his eyes for a moment, Sokollu composed himself. "The sultan is dying," he said at last. "He has fallen ill. I do not wish him disturbed in his last hours. If any men try to approach, have them brought to me. I'd like to interrogate them before they are executed. That includes his guards who appear to have abandoned their posts."

"Yes, sir," responded the soldier.

"And the siege on Szigetvár?" asked the other soldier.

Sokollu looked at the sultan as though willing him back to health. "The siege will continue. The sultan wishes it."

The janissary acknowledged the vizier, who dismissed him with a wave of his hand. Once the soldier departed, Sokollu dropped into a pile of cushions. I transformed into a bat while Rosen transformed into a fox. The two of us slipped out into the night, unheeded by the janissaries.

Chapter Seven

A voyage to the Gulf of Patras as told by Rudolfo de Córdoba.
The Year 1571.

Five years after the vampires of the Scarlet Order assassinated Suleiman, leaving the Ottoman Empire in the hands of his son, Selim II, I found myself spending the waning days of summer in Venice. Though the nights were short, I found the city quite pleasant. There were cafés where I could strike up conversations with learned men, art galleries where I could admire the works of the new Renaissance painters, and theaters where I could watch plays. The city was sufficiently large with enough peasants that it was easy for me to hunt with discretion and take a little blood here and there. As the summer gradually gave way to fall, the nights became cooler, longer, and altogether more pleasant. I came to realize I was a long way from my father's simple hacienda in Southern Spain, nearly a century before.

Over the course of the summer, I exchanged occasional correspondence with Draco, who had been expanding his library in Wales. Alexandra and Roquelaure were enjoying the Renaissance in Paris along with a few other members of the Scarlet Order including Nabila and Rosen. Pleasant as the Venetian nights were, I began to feel a longing. When I spoke to scientists and traders, I learned about places across the Atlantic and east of the Ottoman Empire. I longed to explore the world. Gradually, I started spending less time in the cafés and more time in the libraries, pondering maps of a place called America. So many of my fellow Spaniards had already gone and I began to think how my experiences as a caballero and a member of the Scarlet Order might serve me well in America. Likewise, being a vampire might also help me survive in the New World. There were even rumors of a lost city of gold. Though the gold held little appeal, a vast alien city to explore did.

While I pondered the maps, I found myself hunting more and more among the brothels and inns near the wharves to gaze out at the Mediterranean. Transient sailors made for easy prey.

One night, in late September 1571, I stalked a drunken sailor and the prostitute leading him to a private place when the sound of someone clearing their throat startled me. I looked up and blinked at the sight that met me. Desmond, Lord Draco stood in an alley, his hands behind his back with a red-lined cape trailing behind him.

"Somehow it surprises me to find you hunting in this district," said Draco with an amused lilt. "However, it is fortunate. It saves me the trouble of trying to find you in the next few days."

I frowned. "What are you doing here?"

"Is that the way you greet your master and friend?"

I bowed low. "I'm pleased to see you again, My Lord Draco." Though tempted, I kept sarcasm from my voice.

Draco closed his eyes and turned his head, but I still saw the smile that played across his features. "There's no need for that, either." The vampire lord reached out, took me by the arm and began walking. "Just about two weeks ago, I received word that the Ottoman fleet had taken Cyprus from the Venetians and were on their way to Greece."

"Yes, it was quite a blow. The people here were not happy." I sighed. "Personally, it made me wonder if we'd done anything at all to damage the Ottoman Empire."

Pursing his lips, Draco nodded slowly. "I can see where you might wonder about that. However, I don't think the Venetians and the rest of Western Europe are likely to let this defeat go unchallenged."

I realized that Draco led me down a dock toward a ship. The

tips of oars peeked out from ports that ran the length of the vessel. "Where are we going?"

"To see an old friend."

As we approached the galley, I noticed the ship wasn't like any of the ones I'd seen before. Not being a seaman, I couldn't tell what exactly was different. There was something about the shape that seemed more box-like and less elegant than other galleys. I thought perhaps the ship sat higher in the water, and it was painted less colorfully, designed more for functionality than to impress other sailors.

"Ahoy on the deck!" called Draco. "Is Captain O'Malley aboard?"

The hour was late and most humans were sound asleep. For several minutes, it seemed as though Draco would receive no reply. However, a response finally came.

"Aye, Captain O'Malley's here on the ship," said a gruff, feminine voice. A window opened underneath the afterdeck and a gaunt face appeared. "She'll take your head off for asking such questions at this hour!"

"She'll try and she'll have as much luck as her father did and her father's father and her father's father's mother."

"You leave my great grandmother out of this you God-forsaken son of an Englishman," shouted the feminine voice in a growing rage and thickening Irish brogue.

"Who are you calling the son of an Englishman?" called Draco. He moved toward a rope ladder hanging from the side of the ship and ascended. "I'm as English as you are!"

"There's no reason to hurl insults!" Just as suddenly as it had opened, the window slammed shut. Draco indicated that I should follow him up the ladder.

Though I rarely feared humans, I felt nervous about climbing the ladder. When I reached the deck, Draco stood face to face with a tall, lanky person wearing close-cropped black hair and a nightgown that looked more like it belonged on a woman than on a sailor. Just then, I realized that the sailor was indeed a woman. She turned her gaze upon me and looked me up and down.

"It's bad enough that Draco's here. He had to bring a friend along, too," she groused.

"Is that any way to treat new members of your night watch, Captain O'Malley?" asked Draco. Rather than meeting the captain's eye, the vampire lord examined the rigging and the masts.

Confused, and not knowing what else to do, I bowed low. "I am Rudolfo de Córdoba. I am afraid I've not had the pleasure, my dear lady ... Captain ... uh ... sir."

The captain crossed her arms and tapped her foot. "So, where'd you find this one?" she asked. To me, she said, "You can call me Granuaile, everyone else does. I'm captain of this here ship and Chieftain of the O'Malley Clan."

I stood bolt upright. "You're Grace O'Malley, the Irish pirate?"

"No, I'm Gracie O'Malley the scullery maid!" She stabbed her finger at my chest. "O' course I'm Grace O'Malley the pirate! And any friend o' the dragon here is a friend o' mine. Unless o' course he's English and you sound more like a Goddamned Dago and that's good enough for me." Granuaile turned her back on me and shook lightly, as though laughing silently.

I turned to Draco, hoping for an explanation.

"The good captain has offered to take us down to the Gulf of Patras in exchange for some help manning the oars at night," explained Draco as though that would make everything clear.

"What's in the Gulf of Patras?" I moved so I could look down at the benches with the oars pulled up and locked into place and tried to imagine rowing the ship for hours on end.

"The Ottoman Navy," said Granuaile with a sneer.

"And soon, the Papal navy under the command of Don Juan de Austria," continued Draco.

"Either way, there's going to be a lot of salvage. Things I can use back home." Granuaile sounded hopeful.

"And what do we get out of this?" I looked up and down the length of the ship then back at the oars.

"I have craftsmen and artisans to pay," explained Draco, dryly. "The pope is late paying us for the work we did in Hungary five years ago. It seems, he thinks what we did was of no value – just as you worried."

I turned and faced Draco suddenly thinking about all of the money I had been spending in Venice. "And you hope to demonstrate that the Ottoman Empire is diminished?"

Draco closed his eyes and nodded. He turned to Granuaile. "Would you care to show us to our berths?"

She grimaced and nodded. "There are a few crewmen who've volunteered their blood in exchange for shortened watches. You vampires'll be on rations. No killing any of my crew. Do you understand?"

Draco inclined his head and I swallowed hard, then nodded rapidly. I had no desire to face the wrath of this Captain O'Malley or Granuaile or whatever else she called herself. As she turned her back, Draco leaned close to me and whispered. "She'll be in port another night or two, then we'll be underway. You can show me the hunting grounds of Venice, then we'll have to behave ourselves."

"I can believe it," I whispered in reply. "As long as our quarters are light-tight."

"Believe me, it's hard to get more light-tight than aboard a galley below the waterline. We'll be fine."

✝✝✝

A week later, my legs, arms and back were sore. Though I was a vampire with the strength of many humans, rowing a galley through the water was hard work. The winds had been light and, thus, the sails flapped impotently overhead. My stomach growled and I longed for more than the taste of blood offered by those sailors who had volunteered to donate. I was tempted just to kill one of the crewmen, but Draco had sternly warned me that Granuaile was a master of both the sword and the crossbow. "Remember, we are strong, but we are not unkillable."

Fortunately, when I had gone to bed as the sun rose that morning, we were nearing Greece and a strong wind began to blow. Seeing the coastline as I came on deck, I had reason to hope that if we weren't already in the Gulf of Patras, we were near. Wood groaned as oarsmen rowed through the water. I groaned at the thought of returning to work. Fortunately, I saw Draco leaning on the deck railing. Rather than go directly to my bench, I joined my master and looked out over the water then swallowed hard.

The water was littered with broken masts, pieces of ship hulls, and bodies. Enough blood had spilled into the gulf for the water to have a red cast. I closed my eyes and willed myself not to vomit. "I take it we've arrived at the Gulf of Patras."

"Up oars!" came a shout from a man in the afterdeck. "Lower the anchor! All hands to the gun ports!"

"I suppose that means us, as well." To be honest, I didn't feel like getting closer to the water.

"No," said Granuaile sharply. I turned, surprised that I had not heard her approach. "I don't want you two any closer to that bloody water than need be." The Irish captain looked as though she was fighting to keep her own dinner down.

"I would just as soon not go. The brine and the smell of the blood – it's like rotten meat." I wrinkled my nose.

"At any rate, I think you're a hazard to my crew," she said seriously.

"What happened?" I concentrated on looking into Granuaile's eyes. "What are we doing?"

"It looks like we've just missed a major battle," she said as she replaced me at the railing and evaluated the gulf. "It must have happened either today or yesterday. More likely yesterday since we didn't hear any gunfire as we came into the gulf. What we're doing is casting nets and lines in the hopes of finding salvage." She pulled out a telescope and scanned the area.

"Who won?" I asked.

Draco gazed off into the distance and pointed. "Look over there on the far bank – the ships anchored at Lepanto. Tell me what flags you see."

I returned to the railing and tried not to look into the water. "They look like Vatican flags. The papal fleet is docked over there, but that doesn't necessarily tell us who won. The Ottomans may have simply fled."

Granuaile collapsed the telescope and shook her head. "They didn't flee. They're right here."

"Where?" My brow creased.

"Under our feet," she said harshly. "The papal fleet sunk the lot of them. Maybe a few prize ships over there against the shore under new flags, but with all this wreckage in the water, I'd say very few of the Ottoman ships survived."

Draco smiled wolfishly. "This could never have happened under Suleiman."

"But surely the Ottomans can rebuild their fleet," said Rudolfo.

"Perhaps," said Draco. "However, it's humiliating to the Ottomans and it will give the pope and the Holy Roman Empire hope. A good leader such as Suleiman would never have put his fleet into such a position. It says that the Ottoman Empire is declining."

"How long will it be before the empire falls?" I asked. "A decade? A century?"

"It's hard to tell," admitted Draco. He turned to Granuaile. "If you recover a set of Ottoman colors, and could provide a sworn statement to the pope detailing what you've seen here, that would pay my friend and I back for our hard work."

"As agreed," nodded Granuaile. I tried to read the captain's look, but was unsuccessful.

Draco and I stood at the railing and watched the galley's crew tend to the grisly task of sorting through the wreckage drifting in the harbor. They worked for an hour, then weighed anchor, rowed forward about a mile, dropped anchor and resumed work. Though I was offered refreshment, I declined. Before the night was over, Draco had his colors, Granuaile salvaged spare parts for three galleys and her ship was rowing back out to the Mediterranean.

Pleased to be leaving the Gulf, I leaned over the ship's rail. I enjoyed the chill night wind as it blew through my hair, cleansing me. Draco stepped up next to me and leaned on the railing, watching as the waters of the Mediterranean opened before us. "We won my friend, but you do not look happy. Soon, money will be flowing again."

I looked down and shook my head. "This defeat of the Ottoman fleet seems shallow. Unless the empire actually falls, the Church will eventually stop paying."

"The Ottomans are dying and sometimes death takes a long time," mused Draco. "To humans, it may take several lifetimes. Yet, we are patient. Popes, emperors and sultans may come and go, but we'll still be here, influencing the destiny of the world."

"And what do we get for it all? Some more books? More Old World knowledge?" I looked into Draco's blue-green eyes.

"They say gold corrupts." Draco smiled warily.

"There are those who say we vampires have no souls to corrupt."

Draco folded his arms and examined me. "This isn't about gold, is it?"

"I'm thinking about going to America and Mexico."

Taking a deep breath, Draco closed his eyes. I wondered if he shared my dream. "You wish to explore…"

"Perhaps there is more to be learned by exploring new worlds than there is in plundering old ones." I turned and faced the Mediterranean again. "Queen Isabella granted you title to lands in the New World. Why don't you come with me and claim them?"

The vampire lord turned his back on the sea and slumped against the railing. "I don't think I'm ready yet."

I snorted. "For centuries, you sat locked up in a castle in the Carpathians. Only now do you search for meaning. What makes you think you'll find it here?"

"What makes you think you'll find meaning in the New World with a bunch of savages?"

"Perhaps it's not meaning I seek. Perhaps I am simply looking for life. Perhaps in a New World, I can be reborn."

"Perhaps…"

Orange streaks appeared on the horizon. Without further word, Draco snorted and clambered down the ladder into the hold. I watched the sky lighten for half an hour, longing to watch the sun rise, but ultimately went below decks before it actually crept above the horizon.

Chapter Eight

From the journals of Dr. Jane Heckman.
Present Day.

"Thank you for the stories, but they don't tell me much. You and Draco were just bystanders at the Battle of Lepanto. In fact, you weren't even at the battle, you arrived after it had already been fought."

"I have read a little about Grace O'Malley on the..." he searched for the right word "...on the internet. She became famous after the battle. She had an audience with Queen Elizabeth. I would imagine her papers have survived. Our voyage with her would provide you records..."

I held up my hand. "All right, lets say I can get Grace O'Malley's manifests and logs so I can check out your story, I still have a question. If these Caballeros de Reino Escarlata were such bad-ass fighters, where are they all today?"

Rudolfo's eyes bore into my own. "We were a secret society and mercenaries do not seek fame or glory. I left the order in 1597 to become a conquistador. Others followed our general, Señor Draco, to his manor house in Wales."

"That's awfully convenient."

"You didn't really believe that there were vampires until you became one," he snorted. With that, he turned around to leave.

"And just where do you think you're going?"

"Hunting," he said. "I'll leave you to your 'scientific' pursuits."

Sitting down, I took a deep breath and shook my head. I had no intention of questioning Rudolfo's word. Why he should be so upset was beyond me. While I had no intention of hurting his feelings, I couldn't get too upset about it either. After all, he was the one who attacked me and made me a vampire against my will. Though I'd say he's correct that I'm adjusting and, dare I say, enjoying elements of my vampiric existence, I don't think I'll ever be able to forgive him for his attack on me or on my students. The more I sort out what it is to be a vampire, the better equipped I'll be to know what I'll do about Rudolfo.

✝✝✝

Rudolfo de Córdoba came to the American Continent with the Juan de Oñate expedition in 1598. He marched with Oñate along the Rio Grande in New Mexico to Santa Fe, where he remained until 1615. That year, he was assigned to protect the Franciscan missionaries in Socorro. He has been in Socorro ever since. After the Pueblo Revolt of 1680 caused Socorro to be abandoned, Rudolfo took refuge in a cave under Socorro Peak. When food ran out, Rudolfo hibernated until he was awakened by a routine weapons test near the mountain.

Rudolfo stored many of his volumes of literature and writings in the Socorro Peak cave, a fact that lends credence to the claims of his history and pedigree. Rudolfo has shown me some of the texts he had stored away. Among them is a fascinating volume written by a league of professional vampire hunters from the Island of Santorini in Greece. So far, this volume is the closest thing I've seen to a scholarly study of real vampires. However, its focus is entirely on how vampires may be destroyed and does little to explain their actual nature.

Though the hunter's guidebook goes a long way toward explaining the origins of classical vampire lore, I find many of these topics leave me with more questions than answers. On the other hand, there are topics that the hunter's guidebook explains quite satisfactorily.

For example, the hunter's guidebook explains that garlic is unreliable as a means to drive off or delay a vampire. The reason garlic works at all is due to the fact that vampires cannot digest solid food. Since smell is one of the most evocative senses, aromatic foods such as garlic and onions can cause a vampire to long for their former, human existence. I could imagine that the smell of freshly baked bread or chocolate chip cookies might do just as well to distract me. The point the hunter's guidebook makes is that only a very unfocused vampire would even care about garlic or other food.

More fascinating to me, as a physicist, is what the hunter's guidebook says about crosses. According to the hunter's guidebook vampires fear the cross not for its Christian significance but, because the cross can, under certain circumstances, create a gateway between the "worlds."

"Through this gateway a vampire's soul may be restored," wrote the hunters of Santorini. They pointed out that the cross is a powerful weapon, capable of making a vampire mortal long enough to allow him to be killed.

With that notion in mind, I wonder if there isn't an implication for Christians. Before writing further, let me state that I don't believe that the historical Jesus was a vampire or anything like it. If he was, or is, immortal, then the cross may have been a necessary instrument for the Romans. They may have needed power of the cross's magnitude to kill a person of Jesus's strength. I'm digressing in my thoughts and straying from my topic. This is a subject best left to historians, theologians and the faithful.

At this time, I don't have enough data to speculate what "worlds" the vampire hunters are referring to. My guess is that the word is used metaphorically, that the cross is not a gateway to literal worlds. It would appear that the cross does have to be fairly large, at least as big as a Roman crucifix, to open the "gateway." A small cross may make a vampire uncomfortable, but it will hardly hurt him very much. I do not pretend to understand the mechanism by which a cross may be used to restore a vampire to their human form. It is another piece in the puzzle of understanding vampirism.

There are other tools that would appear to be effective when trying to fight vampires. For example, certain stones will fluoresce in the presence of a vampire. Understanding why that would happen could be another route to understanding the nature of vampires.

✟✟✟

"I hate to interrupt your writing again," said Rudolfo, looking down at me. "But there is something I thought you might like to see." I gasped, not realizing that Rudolfo had returned. He appeared to have forgotten all about his anger over my perceived slight to his honor. If anything, he was distressed.

I followed Rudolfo through the streets of Socorro. He led me to the campus of New Mexico Tech where we went into Workman Center, the tallest building on campus. We took the elevator to the "PH" floor where a seismology lab is housed and there's access to the roof. I guessed "PH" must be short for penthouse. Though the door was secured, Rudolfo quickly twisted the knob, breaking the lock. We stepped out onto the roof and walked across to a red railing where we had a view of the grassy mall tucked among several buildings. Sniffing around a bricked-in fountain at the center of the mall was a coyote.

"Rudolfo, I've seen coyotes before," I said, irritated.

He pointed again. "That's no ordinary coyote. Keep watching."

With a sigh, I looked down again and watched the coyote roam around, sniffing, apparently hunting for a small animal to have as its food. I became aware of an odd pattern to the coyote's search. It seemed to be sticking to the sidewalks. If it were looking for mice or rabbits, I'd think it would be searching and pawing in the grass.

"It's retracing our steps," I said, astonished as I realized what the coyote was doing. "Why would it do that, coyotes don't eat vampires, do they?" I looked at Rudolfo who shook his head. Looking down again, I saw that the coyote stopped at the entrance to the building we were in. It appeared to grin then took several steps backward, then looked up at the building.

"That's no ordinary coyote, is it?" I asked.

"Different cultures know them by different names: gods, angels, devils. The Piro Indians call them kachinas or elemental spirits. In any event, they are probably the most powerful creatures that walk the planet. There are legends that say that some of their kind are responsible for creating us vampires in the first place."

"You mean like the legends that say vampires were created by Satan or his minions." I licked my lips, anticipating the knowledge that could be gained from such a creature. "Can we go down and talk to it?"

"Absolutely not," said Rudolfo sternly. "The kachinas are dangerous creatures. Most do not like vampires."

"You know, I don't know of many people who do like vampires. I'm beginning to feel very unpopular." Looking back to the ground, I was surprised to find the coyote staring straight at me. "Can he see us?"

"His eyesight is at least as good as ours. I suggest we get inside and get under cover."

The coyote's eyes glowed red and it began to rise from the ground toward us. "What do we do now?"

"Run!" called Rudolfo.

We turned and ran back to the penthouse and the comparative safety of the elevator. I started to look back, but Rudolfo pushed me forward. I bolted into the penthouse room. Inside, I pushed the elevator call button and the doors slid open. Before I could enter, the door to the roof exploded inward. Darting inside the elevator, I turned around to grab for Rudolfo but saw him standing still, fixed in place by the coyote-kachina's gaze.

"Close the door, it shouldn't know about elevators," Rudolfo called.

Without thinking, I did as he commanded. The door closed

and, out of habit, I pushed the button for the ground floor. I cursed myself as I descended for not trying to save Rudolfo. When the door opened at the ground floor, I bolted for the stairwell and bounded up the four flights of stairs. Rudolfo and the coyote vanished in a flash of light as I burst onto the penthouse floor. I ran to the spot where they once stood. There was no sign of Rudolfo or the coyote-kachina. Carefully stepping over the broken remains of the roof door, I stepped back out onto the roof. I stood, looking over the railing, listening to the hollow sound of the wind blowing across the roof. I hugged myself and looked to the stars, wondering where Rudolfo had gone and what I was going to do, now that I was alone.

It has now been a week since the disappearance of Rudolfo de Córdoba. I have not been able to find any clues as to what happened to him or the elemental spirit creature that disappeared along with him.

I have since conducted research into Native American shamans and elemental spirits or kachinas, as they are sometimes known. The role of the shaman in Native American society was a powerful and respected one, and was sought after. Shamans learned their craft from an older family member. They underwent a lengthy apprenticeship before they acquired their master's skill, learning how to control "the spirit helpers." The success of a shaman depended on the powers of the spirit helpers. These spirit helpers could be any number of forms, including birds, insects, reptiles, constellations or other elemental forces. They can also take the form of coyotes.

I also found a fascinating and somewhat disturbing account of Navajo witches called skinwalkers. Skinwalkers reportedly roam the night looking for victims. Like vampires, they can take on animal forms. According to Navajo legend, the trickster, Coyote, created the first Skinwalker.

Rudolfo's commander was an ancient vampire named Lord Draco. As it turns out, I have discovered that there is a rather reclusive English lord by that name with lands in Northern New Mexico. It seems that the King of Spain granted the lands to Lord Draco's family during the early 16th century.

If I am to find Rudolfo, I will need help. Without any other clues, I see no harm in seeking out Lord Draco to find out if he is indeed Rudolfo's one-time commander. The next challenge will be enlisting his aid. If he refuses to help or isn't even there, at least the drive north will give me a chance to consider other options.

Part II

Lady of the Evening

"When one becomes a vampire, one expects to encounter some strange shit."

– Marcella DuBois

Chapter Nine

From the journal of Christopher Garrett.
Present Day.

I had a few days' vacation, so I decided to throw my tent in the old VW and drive south to Carlsbad Caverns. I maintain the chemistry stockroom at the New Mexico Military Institute in Roswell. It's not a bad job as long as you don't mind the military-types at the school and the UFO nuts who hang out downtown. Of course, there are times I think I got along better with the UFO nuts than the guys in uniform.

I got to the caverns late on a Wednesday night. Being mid-week, the only other tourists were out-of-staters camping with their families. I checked into the campground, pitched my tent under a light post and set my dinner cooking. While dinner cooked, I watched the bugs flit to-and-fro in the lights. Bats would zing out of the darkness and scoop bugs into their mouths. At last, my own dinner was done and the bats and I ate in the campground's growing silence.

Next day, I went down into the caverns. Most tourists rent self-guided tour radios. At different places in the caverns, the radios give explanations of the various rock formations, stalactites and stalagmites. These radios are great if it's your first or second time in the cave. Mostly, I visit to get out of the heat of the Southern New Mexico sun. I take my hand lens and flashlight and amble through the caverns exploring the formations in detail. I like to see the yellow veins that run through the center of the pale limestone stalactites and stare into the ponds that are formed throughout the caves. One time, I saw a place where a bat had fallen on a stalagmite and died. Water saturated with limestone dripped on the bat, making it a permanent part of the stalagmite. The park service says it should take about an hour or two to hike the caverns. It usually takes me most of a day, just because I enjoy looking at everything.

That evening, I went to the amphitheater at the cave entrance to watch the bat flight. It's a time when all the bats of Carlsbad Caverns fly out to begin their nocturnal hunting. Before the bats emerged, a ranger named Loretta took the microphone to tell the audience about the Mexican free-tail bats that live in the caverns. I listened spellbound. To be honest, I was more spellbound by Ranger Loretta than the talk itself. She had lovely dark hair and eyes along with a body kept trim by hiking cavern trails. Her bosom was nicely accented by the cut of her shirt. God, I love a woman in uniform.

Ranger Loretta's talk ended abruptly when the bats began to spiral out of the cave. They rose, almost like a smoke column, circling counterclockwise from the cavern mouth. Once the bats were high enough, they let the wind carry them to their nighttime hunting grounds. I sat and watched even as the other tourists grew bored with the show and left the amphitheater. It was almost full dark when I realized that I was the only one left besides Ranger Loretta. She sat down next to me. "They're great, aren't they?" she asked.

I nodded. "I could sit here all night."

"Well, I'm afraid the bats have all gone for the night and I have to close up."

I looked at her, trying to find the words to ask her to come down to my campsite for a beer or maybe go into town. The words just wouldn't come. Instead, I just nodded and mumbled, "Thanks for the talk."

A bat swooped down between us, its wings buzzing. Loretta looked after it, wide-eyed. "Wow, I hardly ever see them get that close. That one's pretty big too. Hard to tell in the dark, but I don't think it's a free-tail." She looked into my eyes just a moment too long then looked away, shrugging. "I really do have to close up."

I nodded again, thrust my hands into my pockets and shuffled up the steps. Outside the amphitheater, on the trail back to the parking lot, I walked along looking up at the stars. Again, a bat buzzed me. I followed its path with my gaze and wondered if it was the same one that had dive-bombed us back in the amphitheater. I soon lost sight of it among the other bats and continued walking. A moment later, someone shoved me into the mesquite bushes lining the trail. Something pinched, or more like, stabbed the side of my neck. Disoriented as I was, I thought I must have been knocked into a Spanish dagger bush. Someone lifted me into their arms. The stabbing sensation intensified and my head began to spin. My neck wouldn't move. I turned my eyes and caught sight of black, spiky hair framing a pale forehead.

With an effort, I turned my head enough to look into the unnaturally bright green eyes of a pale woman as she lifted her head from my neck. A thin line of blood trickled down her delicate chin. She gazed into my eyes and I began to feel numb. The woman opened her mouth to speak, revealing a hint of a fang, when something pulled her attention away from me. I managed to turn my head away from the green-eyed woman.

Two bald, human-like creatures with pale, almost gray skin made their way through the brush like crabs scuttling across the ocean floor. Their eyes were solid black and bulged slightly, glistening in the moonlight like rats' eyes. The woman vanished and all I could feel was a strange scrabbling sensation around my chest, as though some small animal crawled into my shirt pocket. I raised my arm to brush the animal away when one of the gray creatures leveled a weapon at me. An electric shock set my teeth rattling. My eyes rolled back and I fell asleep on the cold, hard ground.

✝✝✝

Something pinched my arm and my eyes flew open. I was on my

back, naked with my arms and legs bound to a cold, metal exam table. One of the gray creatures drew a blood sample from me. While the creature withdrew the needle, it occurred to me that it was frighteningly similar to the pictures of aliens at the museum in Roswell.

The room was dark, but I became aware of a second exam table. Strapped to it was the green-eyed woman who had attacked me earlier. Like me, she was nude. Unlike me, her body was not riddled with goose bumps. Her lips curled into a snarl as a second gray alien-like creature approached her with a needle. It seemed to take some effort for him to insert the needle. He withdrew it and tried again. He never succeeded in drawing any blood.

The second creature looked at the first, holding the useless sample tube in long, claw-like fingers. Without a word, the two creatures turned and left the room.

The woman closed her eyes then took a deep breath. Her right arm tensed as she pushed it against the metal band holding her wrist. With a pop, the band gave way. Reaching over, she grabbed the band holding her left wrist and pulled until it too broke. Ignoring me, she sat up and freed her ankles. Lithe as a cat, she sprang to the floor and examined the metal table. She found a drawer and retrieved a red leather bustier and black leather pants. As she dressed, I grew aroused. Turning around, she sat on the exam table to pull on a pair of boots. Then, as though really seeing me for the first time, she smiled wickedly. My cheeks grew hot under her scrutiny and I tried unsuccessfully to hide my erection by turning my hips as far as possible.

"Where am I? What's going on?" I stammered, my voice echoing in the room.

The woman held her finger to her lips and virtually glided across the floor toward my table. "Our abductors are nearby. Quiet!"

"Our abductors?" I asked, trying to keep my voice down.

"Actually, they only abducted you. I stowed away in your shirt pocket, in the form of a bat," explained the woman quietly. "But they seemed delighted to discover they had me as well."

I licked my lips. "Who are you? What are you?" My voice began to rise again.

"My name is Marcella. I'm a vampire."

I couldn't help myself. I began to giggle. "Vampires and aliens? I must have hit my head harder than I thought." Marcella stared at me with green eyes that seemed to glow. Images formed in my mind and I could feel the joy of rushing out of the cave and flying to the hunting grounds. I "saw" hints of a life in the Wild West and how the west changed into the modern world. Visions played through my mind and there was no doubt that she was, in fact, a vampire. I knew the fact as surely as I knew my own name was Christopher. "You're a telepath," I stated, almost reverently.

Marcella inclined her head. "Indeed. Most vampires are, at least to some degree." She broke the metal straps holding my wrists and ankles. "Your last name is Garrett. Are you kin to Pat Garrett?"

"Seems a lot of people ask that. He was my great grandfather's cousin, so the story goes." I sat up, doing my best to pull my legs into a position to hide my nudity. "Were you going to kill me?"

She shook her head. "No. First off, I would have only taken a pint or so of blood. I might have paid a visit to the park ranger as well. Between the two of you, I would have drunk my fill for the night. Secondly, I could never hurt anyone who was kin to Pat." She reached under the examining table and produced my clothes from a drawer. "If we hadn't been interrupted, I would have figured that out on my own earlier." Marcella folded her arms across her stomach and grinned. "Well? Aren't you going to get dressed?"

I shrugged. "I'd be more comfortable if you'd turn your back."

That made her grin widen. "It's not as though you have anything I haven't seen, even more pronounced than now." She shook her head, bemused then turned. "You know, you really do look a lot like Pat Garrett."

Afraid to inquire further about just how well this vampire knew my distant relative, I pulled on my underwear and pants, then winced as I pulled on my shirt. Gingerly, I touched the sore spot on my shoulder. Marcella turned and looked at me. "They implanted something there," she explained. "If you want, I can get it out. We can see what it is."

Nervously, I nodded.

Marcella leaned over. Her fang pierced the sore spot. Involuntarily, I yelped. She spit a small spherical nodule into her hand. "It looks like plastic or glass," she observed, handing it to me.

I took it and examined it. Indeed, it looked like a simple glass sphere – like a marble, only smaller. I began to toss the nodule over my shoulder when she grabbed my wrist. "Wait," she called.

I dropped the nodule into her hand. "There's something about this thing," she said, holding it up to a wan light in the ceiling, and squinting at the nodule. "There's something crawling around in there." She dropped the sphere back into my hand.

I held it up and squinted at it myself. "I don't see anything."

She grabbed the nodule from me, dropped it to the metal floor and crunched it under the heel of her boot. "Of course not – they're too small."

"What did you see?" I asked, backing toward the table.

Marcella shrugged. "At first guess, I'd say it's like one of those time-release capsules. After a while, it would break open and those things, whatever they are, would start crawling around under your skin."

Self-consciously, I hopped back onto the metal exam table and looked at the floor. I couldn't really see anything, but I imagined little bugs flitting to and fro across the floor. Looking back up into Marcella's eyes, I cleared my throat. "So, do you have any idea how we're going to get off this ship?"

Her eyes narrowed. "Ship? What makes you think we're on a ship?"

"You're the one who said we were abducted," I cried defensively. "What about the aliens?"

"Aliens?" she asked, then looked toward the door. "You mean those guys?" She laughed lightly. "I'm not exactly sure what they are, but they're from Earth."

"What about that ray gun they zapped me with?"

"That was a Taser. Half the police forces in the country are equipped with them." Marcella put her hands on her hips and shook her head. "When I said we were abducted, I meant like kidnapped."

"Why couldn't they get any blood from you?"

She opened her mouth and pointed to a pair of fangs. "Vampire." When I shook my head, she explained further.

"I can turn my heart on and off like you can choose not to blink or not to breathe for a time. No heartbeat, no blood pressure, no blood flow into their little vial."

"So, where are we?" I asked.

"I'm not exactly sure, but they brought us west. I'm guessing we're either at White Sands Missile Range or the Fort Bliss Military Reservation. In either event, we need to get out of here."

"And go where?" I asked, dropping back to the floor. "Look, I work for the Army. If they're really the ones that grabbed us, they're not going to make it easy for us to leave."

Marcella's expression changed. She looked at me as though I had finally said something startling. "I know. We need to get outside. Maybe with your Army experience and my stealth, we can figure something out."

At that point, I wanted to tell Marcella that I didn't really have any combat experience. I was just a lab tech, after all. Marcella's spiked hair and leather outfit didn't inspire a lot of confidence in me.

I chewed on my lower lip for a moment. On one hand, having worked for the Army, it didn't seem impossible that they would conduct secret experiments on human guinea pigs. On the other hand, I felt betrayed. After nearly a decade of service, I thought I'd be treated better than that. I swallowed hard. "Whether this is a military base or not, we'd better get out of here before those creatures get back."

Marcella nodded in agreement, then led me from the exam room through a sliding door into a silver corridor. There were only five doors aside from the one we came through; two on each side of the corridor and one at each end. Each of the doors had a little round view port. The first room we looked into was empty.

Across the way, was a laboratory. Three of the gray creatures stood around a lab bench, in conversation with a human in a white lab coat. The human held a test tube of blood – possibly my blood – and seesawed it gently in his fingers. He scowled as one of the tall gray creatures spoke to him. I noticed that the gray creature had a mouth full of sharp, pointed teeth. I looked at Marcella. She only had the two pointed canine teeth.

"Can you make out what they're saying?" I whispered.

Marcella peeked through the viewport. She took me by the hand, leading me back to the exam room.

"As best as I can tell, they're trying to figure out how to get a blood sample from me," said Marcella, closing the door behind her.

"From you?" I asked, raising my eyebrows.

"It seems I'm the one they were really after." She looked through the window in the door. "They only grabbed you after I disappeared."

"Why did they want you?"

"I don't know." She shrugged. Marcella looked at me, then looked away again.

"Anything else?"

Marcella looked down at the floor. "They've got some kind of experiment going, but they don't know if it's 100 percent reliable yet. They took you so you could be a test subject. They seemed to be debating what to do with you if the experiment didn't work."

"What experiment?" I looked at the glass splinters on the floor where Marcella had shattered the nodule. "Did it have to do with the thing you took out of my shoulder?"

"It would seem so," said Marcella.

I stepped out of the room and sneaked up to the laboratory door. The creatures and the scientist simply appeared to be standing around the bench. After a few moments, the human opened a centrifuge and retrieved the test tube containing the blood sample.

"How are they doing?" Marcella's voice startled me and I jumped with my hands on my pounding chest.

She replaced me at the door. Marcella watched the activity with fascination. I eased my way further up the corridor to look inside the remaining three rooms. The one next door to the laboratory was empty except for some filing cabinets. The room at the end of the hall contained a very prosaic wooden desk. A uniformed guard sat in a chair with his arms folded and head down on his chest, apparently dozing. Behind him was a pair of glass doors maybe leading outside.

"Come check this out," called Marcella in a whisper.

I returned to the laboratory door. The human scientist had opened a locker. Inside, there were literally hundreds of the nodules, like the one Marcella had removed from my arm.

"Just what the hell are those things?" I said, aghast.

"Who can tell?" Marcella shrugged. "I don't think we should hang around here too much longer. We're too much in the open."

I started walking up to the last door, leading to the room I hadn't looked into.

"Hey!" called Marcella in a harsh whisper. "Where the hell do you think you're going?"

"I'm curious," I said, looking in the window. What I saw brought a rush of saliva to my mouth and a thick lump to my throat. I dropped to the floor and tried not to vomit.

Marcella joined me and looked in the window. She opened the door and entered the room. Lying on a table, much like the one I had been strapped to were the remains of a man's body. His larynx had been ripped out and what was left of his intestines spilled out of a jagged, bloody hole in his abdomen. The man's hair was graying. I guessed he had been ten or fifteen years older than I had when he had been killed.

I looked at Marcella icily. "I've heard that vampires kill people too," I said, my breath coming too quickly and my voice too loud.

"Not if we can help it," said Marcella calmly. "It gets the locals riled up. They start going after us with stakes and sickles." The vampire shivered. "Makes my skin crawl just thinking about it." She looked at the body again. "I'm guessing this is what they would do to you if their implant failed." She looked down at the torn and bloody remains with a mixture of disgust and hunger.

"It riles the locals?" I asked in disbelief. "Is that all that's wrong about what those creatures are doing?"

She looked up at me, holding me in her gaze. "No, it isn't," she said sharply. "Believe it or not, I have some feelings for you as a fellow … human. I too was human, once. My plan for tonight was to drink my pint of blood from you and the ranger. You would have awakened with nasty looking hickeys. I would have bespelled each of you to think it had happened in a night of passion." She paused. Her grin wasn't wicked. Instead, it was almost that of an embarrassed schoolgirl. "I could tell you had feelings for each other. If it worked out, maybe you would have become a couple for real. You may have even thanked me if you could have remembered."

I blinked several times. "You would have played matchmaker to a couple of humans?"

"Something like that." She shrugged.

"Why? So you could continue to feed off of us?"

"No!" She took a deep breath, calming herself. "I take just enough blood for nourishment. These creatures are nothing more than wild animals."

I turned my back on the body, doing my best to pretend it wasn't there. I looked down at my feet and tried to think what to do.

"I think it's high time that we get out of this building," said Marcella, as though reading my mind. "We've taken too long as it is."

I swallowed hard and nodded. "Even if we do get out of here, what then? If we're on one of the bases, do you think they're going to just let us walk out the front gate?"

"We'll worry about that when we get there."

"There seems to be an outside door leading out of the next room. The only problem is the guard who looked like he was asleep."

"One guard?" asked Marcella, lifting her eyebrows. "I suppose with those creatures, they don't need any more."

"Or, there are more guards outside the door." Looking down, I saw a tray next to the body. On the tray was a set of pristine surgical instruments. I picked up a scalpel. "It's a better weapon than nothing."

"Leave the guards to me, unless there are more than I can handle alone." With that, Marcella cautiously peered out into the hall. Seeing no sign of the creatures or the scientist, she stepped around the corner into the atrium. I followed close behind.

Silently, Marcella crept toward the guard, stalking him almost like a cat might stalk its prey. I gently closed the door behind us. Turning around, I realized that I didn't recognize the guard's uniform. It reminded me of the Army uniforms worn at the Military Institute, but the insignia were all wrong. Marcella lifted the guard's hat and almost lovingly stroked his hair. His eyes flew open and went wide, but before he could cry out, Marcella lunged at his throat. The guard's cry became a muffled gurgle. His eyes rolled back in his head as Marcella fed. Finally, she lowered the soldier to the floor and looked up at me with a dazed look in her eyes. For a moment, I thought she might pounce on me. "Let's get out of here," she said.

An alarm sounded as we ran out through the double doors. I looked around, expecting to see armed soldiers descending on us. There weren't any surrounding buildings. We had left a large Quonset hut isolated in the middle of a moonlit desert – scrub brush dotted an otherwise barren landscape. A single paved road cut a straight line to somewhere. A truck and two unmarked jeeps were parked alongside the road.

"Stop them!" shouted a voice from behind us.

I turned around, the scientist and the three gray creatures flanked the Quonset hut's door. One of the creatures raised a gun and aimed it at Marcella. I expected the gun to fire an energy ray of some sort. Instead, it launched a probe attached to the gun by two wires. The probe bounced off of Marcella's bare shoulder. With a snarl, she rushed the creature that had fired the Taser. Faster than I could see, Marcella grabbed the creature's bald head and twisted. I expected to hear the crunch of broken bones. Instead, the creature knocked Marcella's arms away and sent her flying.

I ran forward with the scalpel and thrust it into the eye of the first creature I came to. The rat-like eye exploded into black tar-like pus. The creature's mouth opened in a silent scream as it fell back into the wall. The scientist and the third creature pulled me off and dragged me struggling into the building. They hauled me into the laboratory. The creature pushed me into a chair and held me while the scientist examined my arm.

"I see the vampire bitch removed the nanite nodule," he mused as he poked the tender spot on my shoulder none-too-gently. "I suppose she didn't want any competition. We'll soon fix that." The scientist moved toward the locker containing the glass nodules.

"I don't think so!" called Marcella. She stalked through the doorway carrying in her arms the body of the gray creature who had fired the Taser. She hefted the body over her head and hurled it at the scientist, knocking him into a chemical storage shelf.

The creature that held me let go and stomped toward Marcella. She threw herself at the creature, forced its head to the side and drove her fangs into its neck. The creature struggled; threatened to dislodge her. I jumped up from the chair and grabbed one of its arms. The creature kicked backwards, catching me in the shin. With a crunching of bone, I collapsed to the floor. Marcella continued to hold the gray creature and drain the life from it. Ultimately, it collapsed to the floor. She spat out a mouthful of blue-gray ichor. Her tongue, dyed blue, hung out. "I think I'm gonna be sick. That thing is definitely not human."

A scream interrupted Marcella's thought. The scientist stood up from where he'd been knocked into the shelf of chemicals. The skin of his face was like a bloody rag, barely concealing the skull beneath. Apparently, one of the bottles that spilled on him contained a corrosive acid. Falling backward, he knocked over several more bottles.

"Oh my God," I said, watching the vapor rise from the chemical soup.

Before we could react, the chemicals exploded in a blaze of glass and metal fragments. I screamed as Marcella threw herself on top of me, sheltering me from the blast, but wrenching my broken leg.

Marcella lifted me out of the clutter of body parts and rubble and started running. Once outside, she put me down on the far side of the truck and jeeps. Another explosion sounded within the building. The force sent me tumbling into a mesquite bush. Marcella helped me sit up. Fire blazed from the building crowned by a plume of smoke.

Marcella looked drawn and pale, even for her. Her spiked hair had wilted and she looked as though she would pass out. With my broken leg, there was no way I could drive. If we didn't get away, we'd soon be recaptured. Even if we were a long way from any other buildings, the alarms would surely have triggered remote alerts at another facility not far away.

Marcella looked at me with her eyes pleading. "May I have just a little of your blood? I won't kill you."

I reached up and lowered my collar.

I winced as she sank her fangs in. She clung to me and I became very aware of her bare skin and the smell of the leather she wore. I returned Marcella's embrace, and my breathing became raspy. My grip on Marcella weakened and just as I thought I would black out, she released me and eased me to the ground. She stood slowly, then picked me up and lifted me into the back of the truck.

"Did we do good?" I asked as she lowered the canvas at the back of the truck bed.

"We did," she reassured. "I'll get you to a hospital, then come back and see if there's anything I can learn about these people." That was the last thing I heard before I passed out.

✝✝✝

I awoke in a hospital in Roswell with an IV in my arm. There were a dozen blood-red roses at my bedside and a sheaf of papers. The card read, "Thanks for the best time ever. We'll meet again. M."

I lay the card down and looked at the papers. They were pages from a diary. It seemed Marcella had decided to share her story. I read her tale as new blood dripped into my arm.

Chapter Ten

From the diaries of Marcella DuBois.
1874 to 1881.

It was early evening. A chill mist clung to the Spanish moss that hung low from the trees. I trudged through the swamp, a rude sucking pop sounding each time I lifted my feet. My body, once that of a sturdy Acadian woman was now a pitiful sight. Translucent skin barely clung to my bones. The blood in my veins was a weak rivulet that struggled as I did just to survive. My life as a vampire was off to a really bad start. You might even say it sucked.

Sorry, I try not to descend into puns, but I deserve some slack. Those early days are painful to remember. The year was 1874 and I'd been in the swamp for about four months with no blood other than what I could get from the occasional snake or swamp rat. I was simply too weak to try to drink the blood of one of the many alligators that were all around me. Looking back, it's hard to believe that the August before that dreadful night I was a respectable schoolteacher in Bayou Sorrel, Louisiana. Late one afternoon, I'd gone to the schoolhouse to read up on things and straighten up my classroom before the students arrived for the fall. Time got away from me and it was dark by the time I got hungry and decided to head for home. As I locked the schoolhouse, I noticed a tall, thin man in a red smoking jacket leaned up against the building. A pencil-thin mustache framed his easy smile. If Sir

Lancelot from the King Arthur stories really existed, I imagine he must have looked just like this man.

"Mademoiselle, I am called Roquelaure. I am a traveler passing through and I was wondering if you know of a restaurant in this fair town."

"I'm afraid the closest restaurant is in the city, Baton Rouge," I said with a shrug.

"Ah, what a shame," he said in a silken continental accent, truly French as opposed to Cajun. "I like to have company when I dine."

I looked at my feet and wrung my hands like the schoolgirls I taught. I foolishly invited the stranger to my house to dine with me. I gave him directions and he arrived about an hour later. He brought a bottle of red wine and surprised me by driving me out of the kitchen where he cooked dinner. The Frenchman watched admiringly as I ate a delicious meal that seemed miraculous in that it was produced from the stock of my meager pantry. Oddly, he refused to join me. Being a simple Cajun woman, I was afraid to ask about his lack of appetite, thinking this might be some continental custom and that this handsome man would perceive me as an ignorant American.

After a couple of hours the wine went to my head. I laughed too loudly and I vaguely remember unfastening the top buttons of my blouse as a prelude to an invitation to my bedroom. All the time, the Frenchman's eyes never left me. At one point, he stood and I feared he had grown bored and was going to leave. Instead, he swept me into his arms right at the table and sank his teeth into my neck. As my blood flowed into him, I began to ride a wave of orgasmic euphoria that refused to stop even after he withdrew his teeth. My own mouth explored his body starting at his neck then moving down across his chest and abdomen, taking nibbles as I went. The taste of his sweat and blood was more exhilarating even than the wine he'd brought. I don't know how long I feasted on his beautiful body before I blacked out.

I awoke the next night with a blinding headache and a mouth that tasted of raw meat and cotton. My tongue probed my sore mouth, stopping short when I discovered two sharp fangs where my canines should have been. Putting my head in my hands I began to cry, wondering what kind of monster I'd become. Self-loathing and pity were soon replaced by hunger. I went to my pantry and looked at the vegetables with disgust. Going to the icebox, I found a sausage that seemed more palatable. I ate it greedily, but soon found myself running outside to vomit in the grass. Newly found vampiric instinct dawned and I realized that it was blood I needed.

"Are you all right?" came a concerned voice. Kneeling on the ground by my front porch, I looked up and felt some of the remains of the un-digested sausage slip down my chin. Standing by my front gate was the fat, bald form of the parish priest. He tried to mask his disgust with concern. "No one's seen you all day. I came by to see if you were feeling well."

I heard the priest's heart pounding in his chest and could sense his blood coursing through his veins. Without a word, I leapt on the priest and clumsily sank my teeth into his pulsing jugular. I smiled to myself when the sanctimonious son-of-a-bitch grabbed my breast and began thrusting his broad hips into my leg. I drained the priest dry, standing there in front of my house. Unfortunately, Roquelaure hadn't taught me about stealth. My neighbors came out of their houses, undoubtedly attracted by the gasps, grunts and moans of the dying priest. I found myself the focal point of a sea of astonished faces. The parish sheriff emerged from the crowd and knelt down by the dead priest. His exact words didn't register, but I knew I'd better get out of there. Surrounded now, but feeling invulnerable, I tried to run through the crowd of on-lookers.

That night I learned that a lone vampire cannot outrun or defeat a mob of enraged humans. Fortunately, the mob I faced knew little of vampires. My fellow residents of Bayou Sorrel were very Americanized, living far from their European roots and knowledge of vampire lore. I was lucky these people knew nothing of stakes through the heart. Instead, they treated a devil-woman who killed the parish priest the same way they would treat a black man who raped a white woman. They dumped me in the swamp as food for the alligators.

So, there I was. Frightened and alone, confused by my craving for blood and my fangs, I was not certain if I could ever live among humans again. I wondered what became of Roquelaure. Did he come looking for me? I learned that I could live on the blood of the myriad small creatures that lived in the swamp, though it barely sustained me. Fortunately, the thick growth and water of the swamp shielded me from sunlight during the day. Too many months passed by before instinct kicked in and taught me that the only way I'd regain my strength would be to drink human blood. Depleted as I was by this time, I didn't dare return to town. I would be overwhelmed and dumped right back in the swamp. I had to wait for someone to come to me.

Then, I saw them: two Acadian men hunting in the swamp. I broke into the clearing where the men stood. One screamed, dropped his rifle, and ran a distance before stopping and calling back to his friend, transfixed by the horror of my hag-like body. My teeth tore into his neck and I fed on that luscious human life. My breasts swelled ever so slightly as my thighs and calves firmed, giving me the strength to run after his friend. Before giving chase, I cradled the body of my victim and longed for my own lost humanity.

✝✝✝

After escaping the swamp, I decided to move west. First and foremost, the mob that had thrown me into the swamp convinced me of the truth of the old saw, "you can never go home again." While I was in the swamp, I began to feel that Texas, New Mexico, and Arizona, known as the Wild West, had a certain appeal. Guns blazed and blood flowed very easily there. It seemed a natural enough place for a vampire to live. Looking back on it, I'm actually a little surprised that I didn't meet many vampires in the West in those days. Of course, vampires thrive on human blood and there simply weren't that many people living in the desert Southwest.

Another lesson I learned from the mob at Bayou Sorrel was that small towns are hazardous to a vampire's health and well being. I searched for an area with sufficient population so I could preserve some anonymity. I spent most of a year in Dallas, Texas, but found that the city was trying too hard to become "civilized" and "acceptable" to people from back East for my taste. It was too hard to hide my activities from the law. However, quite a few people passed through Dallas and I was able to make inquiries about places farther west. Ultimately, I decided to move to the village of Las Cruces, an old Spanish town located on the banks of the Rio Grande. At the time, I didn't know that vampires were supposed to fear holy relics. If I had, I might have thought twice about moving to a city named, "The Crosses."

I moved to Las Cruces in early 1876. I found a small adobe house and convinced the local undertaker to sell me a coffin without asking too many questions. While living in Dallas, I'd learned that coffins are one of the best ways to seal out sunlight while sleeping the day away.

Living among humans meant needs besides blood such as clothes, a hot bath now and then, along with other trappings. Fulfilling those needs meant taking a job. There was no demand for a school marm who worked only at night. In 1876, that left few options for making money. I went to work at the Long Dobé: an adobe house on Mesquite Street that extended for a city block where the farmers, ranchers, and outlaws came to seek female companionship.

I gained a reputation at that "cat house" and came to be known as the French Gringa. Few people in Las Cruces in those days could tell the difference between Cajun and French accents. Grimy from dust and dirt and smelling of cow manure, men would come and rub their coarse hands over my smooth alabaster skin. Our bodies would intermingle, but their passion never lasted long enough to satisfy me. Riding me like one of their foul horses, they would gaze into my eyes and fall under my spell. At the height of passion, my teeth would enter them, much as they had entered me. Just a little blood – not enough to kill. Leaving soon after, they would tell their friends to visit the French Gringa for the bite. I made good money and took enough blood to satisfy my hunger, but I felt as though Roquelaure, my beautiful French vampire, had taken a part of my soul with him and was carrying it further and further away with each passing night.

It was not uncommon for teen-aged boys to visit the Long Dobé to prove to themselves that they were men. There was one day that will be hard for me to forget: November 23, 1876. To be honest, I would have forgotten the exact date except that it was almost exactly two years after I'd escaped the swamp and the boy who came in that day was in the process of descending into history. He called himself Henry William McCarty and I was given to understand that was his real name. Later, I would learn that Henry's aliases were even better known: William H. Bonney or Billy the Kid.

Henry came into the Dobé with a friend named Jim McDaniels. McDaniels was somewhat older than Henry and one of my "regulars." He pointed me out and Henry came over, tightly clutching a sombrero. His words stumbling over his buckteeth, he introduced himself.

"You're a little young to be in a place like this," I said.

"I ... I can pay." He held out a bag of coins.

I sighed, took the coins, and led Henry down the long hallway to my room. Once inside, I shut the door. He stood, dumbstruck, as I undressed in front of him. As a prostitute, I didn't wear as many clothes as other women of the late nineteenth century – it simply wasn't practical. Naked, I turned around and faced him. He stood there, in the middle of my room, slack-jawed. He'd only managed to take off his gun belt. I helped him remove his shirt, then gently guided him to my bed where I helped him take off his pants and drawers.

Henry had long, delicate hands that he seemed hesitant to use for fear they might break. I sat down next to him and guided one hand to my cool, but soft breast. His hand rested there, unmoving for a moment, but finally began to explore the alien territory of my body. I moved back on the bed and guided Henry's body over mine. With care, I guided him into position. Before entering me, his face grew pained. "Will this hurt you?" he asked.

"It'll feel delightful," I lied. After all, I was paid to lie. Actually I'd grown quite numb to sex, working as a prostitute. It didn't help that my vampire strength came with the price of a certain lack of sensitivity.

He climaxed shortly after entering me. I longed painfully for the only release I could have under the circumstances. I didn't dare bite such a young man as Henry McCarty, but I allowed my fangs to scrape along his neck, teasingly.

With just that small tease, Henry leapt back off the bed, wide-eyed and flailed at the floor for his gun belt. Jerkily, he pulled the gun and pointed it at me. "What the hell kind of monster are you?" For the first time, I think he looked right into my eyes.

I flashed to that night in Bayou Sorrel when a mob grabbed me, kicking and screaming, then threw me into the swamp to die. I narrowed my eyes and evaluated Henry carefully. "You were so busy eyeing my body that you never even looked at my face – never noticed my unusual dentition, eh?" I stood slowly. The gun wavered for just a second. Striking, I snatched the gun from his hand and pinched the barrel shut.

Henry McCarty then did something that amazed me. He collapsed to the floor, put his face in his hands and began to cry.

"What am I?" I asked, moving back to the bed. "I'm a predator, Henry, just like you. When you threaten another predator, you'd better be prepared to kill." I picked his drawers up from the bed and flung them at him. "If you ever come at me with a weapon again, you'd better be prepared to kill me. Comprende?"

He looked up. "But you're a woman. How can I kill a woman?"

"What does being a woman have to do with anything? A predator just kills. But a predator never kills without a reason." I dropped my voice slightly. "Do you have a reason to kill me, Henry?"

He wiped the tears from his eyes and snuffled. "No," he said, quietly.

"Then get out of my sight, and hope I never find a reason to kill you." Sheepishly, Henry McCarty, Billy the Kid, got dressed and left my room. That night, I was certain that he would walk out into the night and disappear into obscurity. Just goes to show what a really bad judge of character I can be.

✝✝✝

Two years later, I still worked at the Long Dobé, much to my shame, when a group of cowboys came in. Among them was a tall, handsome man who reminded me of the creature who had turned me into a vampire back in Louisiana. Instead of immediately coming to ogle the ladies, the handsome cowboy with the droopy mustache went to the bar and bought a drink. He stood there, sipping contentedly, and chatted with the bartender. The cowboy's voice caught me off guard. Instead of the West Texas drawl I'd grown used to, I recognized an accent straight out of Louisiana's Cajun Country. I went up and said, "Hello."

"Pleased to meet you, ma'am," he said. "Name's Pat Garrett." He lifted his glass in salute. "May I have the pleasure of your name?"

I caught my breath at the question and tears welled up in my eyes. How long had it been since someone had asked my name without wanting something from me? I closed my eyes and answered softly, "Marcella DuBois."

"Marcella DuBois," he repeated gently, apparently recognizing my accent as I'd recognized his, "a lovely lady from Louisiana. What brings you to this house of ill repute?"

I almost laughed outright. "You know, sir, I could ask you the very same question."

"My friends brought me." He lifted the glass and looked into it. "They told me I could get a decent mint julep here."

I laughed. "That's not why most people come here."

Pat took a sip of his julep. "I'm not most people."

"Now that, I believe."

Pat placed a coin on the bar, buying me a drink. Juan, the old bartender, poured a small glass of watered-down whiskey. There was no need to waste the good stuff on me. I wouldn't drink it anyway. Alcohol went straight to my head and I was useless for work the rest of the night.

"You still haven't answered my question," said Garrett as he leaned back against the bar.

I picked up my glass and looked into it. "I killed a man," I said softly. "I had to leave Louisiana. I've been moving west ever since."

Pat gazed into my eyes with an intensity that made my icy, vampiric heart melt. "Did he deserve it?"

I took a deep breath and thought about the parish priest. There had been rumors that he molested young boys. Henry McCarty's young face haunted me just then. Was I much better than the priest? "Yes," I said softly, fighting back tears. "He deserved it."

"Good," said Pat, surprising me. He put down his cold glass and took my free hand. I was so lonely. That tender, icy touch was enough to make me wish there was someone, anyone, to share my dark existence. I was tempted to make Pat a vampire that very night. "I don't like the idea of killing, but it seems sometimes there's no choice." He squeezed my hand, then picked up his drink. "Me, I came west for some adventure. Haven't killed anyone yet, but I'm sure I'll have to one of these days."

I sighed. Pat Garrett just seemed so nice, so trusting. How long had it been since I'd just talked to someone like this? Much as I'd have liked to make Pat a vampire, I realized that he wouldn't last long as one. "Killing's a terrible thing." I lifted my glass. "Here's to Pat Garrett. May you never know the pain of taking a human life."

He nodded and lifted his own glass. "Here's to Miss Marcella DuBois. May you find your way out of this house of ill repute." He drank while I pretended to sip my drink.

"Why do you care about me?" I asked.

"There's a strength about you, Miss DuBois," he said. "You're wasting away here. I think you'll find there's something better for you out in the world."

I snorted. "I'm a woman. What is there for me unless I marry someone?"

"What does being a woman have to do with anything?" I'd heard that question before from my own lips. However, I think I listened to it for the first time when Pat Garrett asked it of me.

"Mr. Garrett, you've given me something to think about."

"I'm glad to hear it." With that, he knocked back the rest of his drink, tipped his hat and exited into the night, leaving his friends to their choice of amusements.

✝✝✝

During the course of my life, it has fascinated me how some people achieve notoriety. Certain people seem to blaze into history like a shooting star and shortly after, are gone. Soon after my night with Henry McCarty, I saw a familiar-looking woodcut in the local newspaper. That's when I first learned that insecure Henry was blazing into history as Billy the Kid. According to the newspaper, Henry was working as a hired gun for a rancher named John Chisum up in Lincoln County, New Mexico. By Henry's 18th birthday, he was already suspected of murdering several people.

I heard nothing further about Pat until the fall of 1880. Even then, I nearly missed the small notice in the newspaper. According to the article, Pat Garrett had been elected Sheriff of Lincoln County. None other than Billy the Kid had killed Lincoln County's previous sheriff, William Brady, and there were high hopes that Pat would bring "the Kid" to justice. As I continued to read the article, I sighed, sadly. The article mentioned that Pat had married a Fort Sumner woman named Apolinaria Gutierrez. I've always been a romantic and somehow knowing that Pat had found lasting love with another was sufficient to end any lingering thoughts I'd had of making Pat a vampire. Be that as it may, the tiny article about Pat Garrett becoming sheriff had another effect on me. If Pat could make something of himself, then so could I. I'd saved up quite a bit of money in four years of working at the Long Dobé, never needing to buy food helps, and quit my "job" as a prostitute. Most of the girls at the Long Dobé didn't work much more than three to four years anyway. The owner, while disappointed to see his French Gringa go, was not surprised.

During the fall and early winter of 1880, I rested. I fed lightly off the wanderers and vagabonds that came into Las Cruces and neighboring Mesilla and spent most of my nights exploring the beautiful countryside around my adopted home. This is something I hadn't really had time to do before. One remarkable thing happened to me during that time. I'd gone down to the little town of Anthony on the border of Texas and New Mexico. While exploring the small town, I was startled by the sudden appearance of a frail, wisp of a vampire dressed all in black. A broad-brimmed hat covered her face. Her chin and hands seemed remarkably smooth, as though she'd been quite young when she became a vampire. However, I sensed she was a creature of great age.

"You tread lightly on my hunting grounds, Chica," said the vampire.

I wanted to ask a thousand questions. The question I asked was, "Who are you?"

"Mercy," she said. "It is Mercy that lets you live this night and Mercy that lets you go with a warning. Las Cruces is your territory. Anthony and south to El Paso are mine. Do not come this way again."

I watched wide-eyed as the slender vampire turned and vanished into the night. If I were to judge her by size alone, I'd say I could easily overpower her. However, something in my sense of her age and in the tone of her voice warned me not to try. I accepted her warning and kept to the North.

In the meantime, things began to move quickly for Pat Garrett and "the Kid." Pat tracked the Kid through Northern and Eastern New Mexico and finally caught him just before Christmas of 1880. Pat took Henry to Santa Fe and turned him over to Marshall Neis, who was anything but "nice." I could tell you some stories about his nights in the Dobé. Anyway, the "nice" Marshall brought Henry to Mesilla for trial. Two trials were held in March 1881. I would have gone to them, but even today, judges and lawyers like to spend time with their families and rarely hold trials at night. I had to content myself with reading about the proceedings in the newspaper.

The Kid was convicted of the murder of Sheriff William Brady on April 1, 1881. Sentenced to hang, the Kid was given back to Pat Garrett to carry out the execution. Before the end of the month, the Kid would be a fugitive from justice, yet again.

On April 28, 1881, Henry McCarty tricked one of his guards, stealing his gun. The Kid killed that first guard, then broke into Pat's office and stole a shotgun. Henry surprised and killed the second guard. Taking the horse that was in the corral behind the jailhouse, the Kid rode to freedom. Henry McCarty had learned to be a good predator. I worried about Pat and wondered if he was a good enough predator to deal with the situation. In fact, my worry was well founded. While Pat would go on to write a popular novel and even come to the attention of President Theodore Roosevelt, his predator instincts never fully developed. He was ultimately shot in the back while relieving himself.

I decided to go north. I found that Pat and his deputies had ridden out to old Pete Maxwell's shack. Maxwell, a known friend of Billy the Kid's, was a rancher, working land just outside Fort Sumner.

I found Pat and his deputies outside Pete Maxwell's shack shortly after sunset. I didn't approach them, figuring it was dangerous to go up to a group of nervous, armed men at night. Instead I found a hiding place and watched things for a bit. I wasn't sure why Pat hadn't just gone in and asked Maxwell his questions. Being a vampire, I had very good hearing. From their conversation, I learned there was a man staying with Maxwell. The deputies and Pat were arguing among themselves about who that man was. I decided to take matters into my own hands and find out.

I made my way through the rocks around Maxwell's shack, staying out of sight of Pat Garrett and his deputies. Behind the shack, I went up to one of the windows and looked inside. Sure enough, sitting on the bed was Henry McCarty. He was whittling a piece of wood and talking to a man in another bed, apparently trying to go to sleep. I presumed the other man was Pete Maxwell.

I rapped lightly on the window glass.

Henry looked up from his whittling. I smiled and licked one of my fangs. He gasped, but quickly recovered. "I'm gonna go and get me some meat," said Henry, hungrily.

"Fine, whatever…" said Maxwell, sounding glad to be rid of Henry.

A few minutes later, Henry came around the corner of the house and stopped cold. "It is you, isn't it, from the Dobé in Cruces? What are you doing here?"

I smiled and swayed over to him. I wore a riding outfit of leather pants and jacket. I knew I looked good – sometimes I wish I still had that outfit. "I heard you'd broken out of jail, and I wanted to say, 'hi.'"

He eyed me suspiciously and pointed his knife at me. "Stay back."

"Now, Henry," I sighed. "What did I tell you about pulling weapons on me?" I leapt forward and took Billy the Kid into my arms. He fought to get the knife into a position where he could stab me while I once again teased his neck with my fangs. Before he could strike with his knife, I bit into his neck. My lips caressed Henry's neck and I luxuriated in the taste of his blood. I heard Pat's voice from inside the shack and I briefly allowed myself to be pulled into a fantasy where it was Pat I drank from and not obnoxious little Henry McCarty.

I stopped short of killing Henry – stopped short of even causing him to lose consciousness. I put my revolver in Henry's hand, and sent him dazedly stumbling in the direction of the shack's door. I heard Henry shout, almost drunkenly, as he entered the shack, "Quién es? Who's there?"

Pat's revolver rang out and Billy the Kid died. I leaned against the back wall of Pete Maxwell's shack and hugged myself, wondering whether I should let Pat know I was around. Taking a deep breath, I drank in the fragrance of mesquite and pine. I decided I liked the freedom of the mountains and the freedom of anonymity. I'd leave history to Pat. With that, I made my way back to my horse and rode off to shelter before the sun rose.

Chapter Eleven

From the diaries of Marcella DuBois.
Present Day.

When one becomes a vampire, one expects to encounter some strange shit. That said, one of the last things I ever expected to happen during the course of my vampiric existence was to be abducted by the military and taken to a Quonset hut out in the middle of nowhere for a series of experiments. What's more, the military was in league with some kind of monsters, not unlike vampires in their own right.

For the past several years, I'd made my home in the caverns of Southeastern New Mexico, the Carlsbad Caverns in particular. There's no sunlight down in the depths and plenty of tourists camping nearby to feed upon at night. One such tourist was a man named Christopher Garrett, who bore more than a passing resemblance to a distant relative that I still dream of over a century after I last saw him.

I'm getting ahead of myself, and I'm afraid I'm giving the impression that feeding, sleeping and unattainable romantic fantasies are the only things that occupy a vampire's mind. When I get an urge to feel like a sentient being rather than some kind of predatory animal, there are a handful of small towns nearby. I can go to bars or cafes and interact with the local ranchers. I don't tend to see people down in the caverns since they're closed from sunset to sunrise, when I happen to be awake. When I'm asleep, I'm back in one of the side caves not open to the public.

Recently, I've taken to spiking my hair and wearing more leather than lace. Doing so, I've turned the heads of more than a few cowboys. That's fine with me, being sentient doesn't necessarily mean being nice. That said, I'm the first to admit that the way I dress blurs the line between "sentient being" and "predatory animal."

Living in Southeastern New Mexico, I've become familiar with both the government and the military and the ways that both alter the political and physical landscape to suit their needs. Shortly after World War II, the Air Force built an air base outside Roswell. They say a spacecraft crashed on a nearby ranch and the remains of the UFO were secreted away. As a vampire, I've spent more than my share of time outside at night and I've yet to see anything that resembles a spacecraft from another world.

More recently, Congress authorized the Waste Isolation Pilot Plant outside Carlsbad. It's a facility not far from the caverns where they're supposed to store radioactive waste from nuclear reactors. It's definitely a frightening place, almost enough to make me want to find new hunting grounds, or even move back to the city.

In the end, I wasn't really all that surprised to discover that there was a secret base out in the middle of the desert. What really bothered me were the monsters. Over the past century or so, I'd met a few fellow vampires and the occasional lycanthrope. I've never met anything like the creatures that had abducted Christopher Garrett and me. Like I said, the creatures reminded me of vampires; they had sharp teeth and were nearly as strong as me. However, they seemed more single-minded and savage. What did the creatures want with me? What did they want with Christopher? Were there more of the creatures? Somehow, I felt there were.

Escaping that stupid Quonset hut was the closest I'd ever come to losing my life after I'd become a vampire. Sensing how much blood Christopher had lost, I realized I needed to get him to a hospital quickly, or he would die. I'd hefted him into one of the trucks parked near the destroyed lab and followed the one road, not certain where it would lead. The road was unguarded and eventually I came to a hastily constructed gravel turnout that took me onto a highway. Making an educated guess and judging direction from the stars, I started driving north. Before long, I came to a sign that told me I was on Highway 285 that ran between Roswell and Carlsbad.

Within half an hour, I was driving down the main street of Roswell. Stopping at the first gas station I came to, I asked directions to the hospital. I did my best to ignore the strange look the attendant gave me. I suppose it's not every day you see a woman with spiked hair and a leather bustier driving an unmarked military truck.

Once I reached the hospital I unloaded Christopher and carefully put him over my shoulders and hauled him inside. Morning twilight was already brightening the sky and I didn't want to take longer getting him inside than absolutely necessary. I carried him into the Emergency Room, settled him into a chair and was on my way out just as the admitting nurse started calling after me. I shook my head, Christopher's injuries were self-evident and I didn't know, or frankly care, about his insurance.

With little more than 45 minutes until sunrise, I found a motel and checked in. The room was nice as motel rooms go, but suffered from having curtains that didn't completely come together. Thinking fast, I draped the bedspread over the window to keep the room as dark as possible. Just in case I'd missed a crack where sunlight could get in, I snatched a pillow and squeezed under the bed. I sneezed a couple of times at the dust I'd stirred up. As a human, I'd have never been able to sleep in such a cramped, dirty space. As a vampire, sleep came to me during the day whether I wanted it or not.

I had a few minutes to reflect on my abductors before "the little death" took me. I shivered at the thought that I could be captured and overpowered so easily. For a moment, I wondered where those creatures came from. Were they the same kind of monsters as I am? Could they have been a new species of vampire, or something similar? Perhaps they weren't even from Earth. That thought really gave me shivers. If not from Earth, where did they come from? Was it Mars or a distant star or even a whole different galaxy?

Though it had been vitally important to get Christopher to the hospital, I realized that I'd missed an opportunity to learn more about our abductors. Just as the thought came to me, I fell into my dreamless deathlike sleep.

✝✝✝

Early the next evening, just after dusk, I checked out of the motel. In spite of growing hunger pangs, I was filled with both curiosity about our abductors and stricken with whimsy. I stopped by the hospital to drop off some roses for Christopher and left him a note along with some pages I'd scribbled about my history some time back. I thought he should know about my connection with his famous relative. You may wonder where I store my stuff if I live in the caverns. Well, you can keep wondering. I won't write down all my secrets.

Whimsy satisfied, I thought about returning to the site of the destroyed Quonset hut. Realizing it would be unwise to drive back in the stolen truck, I ditched the vehicle in the parking lot of a convenience store then transformed into a bat and flew back to the lab. I reveled in the feel of the wind as it blew through my short fir and remained attentive to distant sounds.

I love my bat form. It's exhilarating to fly quickly from point to point and, for the most part, not be noticed. When I transform, I don't exactly become a bat. It's more like stepping into a virtual reality game. I still feel my own body, but I control all of the actions of the bat and sense everything it feels, like a spectator wearing an apparatus. That doesn't diminish the fun any. It's just a curiosity.

As I approached the ruins of the facility, I detected the movement of many people and saw numerous bright lights mounted on stands. Straining my ears, I could make out snatches of conversation.

"Unit A, why don't you have that Northern Perimeter Secure?"

"We're getting troops in place now, Lieutenant. We'll have it locked down within the hour."

"Sergeant, I'm detecting traces of hazardous chemicals at 2-0-7."

"Take precautions, Private."

Apparently, the military had moved in and secured the site. Fortunately for me, bats don't tend to attract soldiers' guns. If they did, there would be far more targets out here than just little old me. In my bat form, I'm an anomaly, a fairly large vampire bat that's bigger than the Mexican free-tail bats that populate much of the Southwest. Even so, the average soldier can't tell the difference. The real danger comes from scientists who see me as a curiosity requiring further study. They usually spend a few days trying to hunt me down to capture me.

At any rate, I joined my Mexican free-tail brothers and sisters and circled the charred remains of the building. There was more left than I thought there would be. Beams, metal plates, and glass were strewn across a charred stretch of desert. The free-tail bats swooped in and out of the Army's light beams hunting the swarming insects. Instead of insects, I hunted clues. Admittedly, I wasn't sure what I was looking for as I circled the area. Even if I did find something of interest, I wasn't sure what I could do about it as a small bat.

At the perimeter, a soldier began adjusting one of the lights. As he did, the beam glinted off a jagged piece of metal that stood out from the rubble. Swooping lower, I saw that the object was the battered and ripped-open remains of a filing cabinet. The light beam flitted across the cabinet a couple of times, then settled on the ground a few feet away. A mostly-complete wall stood between the light and the cabinet, casting long shadows. Descending into those shadows I felt the bat form dissolve, as though I was taking off a suit of clothing.

Quietly, I approached the cabinet. Papers and bits of drywall crunched under my feet and I cringed in spite of the fact that the soldiers were making much more noise than I was. The top drawer of the filing cabinet was somewhat askew and jammed in the railings. Tugging forcefully, I could not get the drawer to open.

I was able to open the second drawer down. Rifling through

the plastic, multicolored file tabs, I tried to discern if there was anything useful. Mostly, there were names of chemical compounds and files labeled "DNA Sequence" followed by a series of numbers and letters. In the third drawer down, I found a thick file labeled "vampires." Pulling the file, I saw a mishmash of oddly sized papers and immediately wished I'd brought a knapsack or a box to carry what I found.

Another light beam sliced the darkness as it scanned across the rubble. I backed away from the filing cabinet, doing my best to melt into the shadows. I remained still for several minutes, barely breathing while listening for anyone who might have seen me move. The voices I heard all sounded like routine status reports and check-ins.

While trying to figure out how I was going to get away from the site with the file folder, my mind touched something. It was like a thousand tiny voices crying out in the night. Listening carefully, I realized that these new voices weren't traveling through the air. They were like the whispers of thoughts we vampires routinely sense. At first, I thought I was just picking up the thoughts of the soldiers but I soon realized the source was too close to me.

Peering cautiously over the crumbling wall at my back, I saw several nodules, like the one the scientist had tried to implant in Christopher's arm. Clutching the file folder tightly, and avoiding the beams of light, I crept around the wall. So many of the nodules littered the ground that I had to step gingerly to avoid crunching them under my boots.

I reached down and picked up one of the nodules. Like before, it seemed to me that there was something alive inside. I now realized that these "living" things weren't simple creatures like bugs, but possessed something approaching higher thought.

The hairs on the back of my neck stood up. I sensed more than saw a new presence. Not far from a cluster of soldiers, a figure began to rise from the rubble. I couldn't quite make it out, but I watched as the thing pushed itself up on eight legs. The nearby soldiers seemed oblivious to the figure. Looking down, I saw that the nodule in my hand began to glow. Swearing at the fact that I hadn't brought a bag, I realized that several nodules around my feet also started glowing. Carefully I tucked one of the nodules down the front of my bustier, between my breasts. I grabbed a second nodule for good measure, then quickly moved away from the faint glow. I knew if the soldiers saw me, they wouldn't hesitate to shoot. While I can survive bullets, they sting like Hell.

Remembering the snippets of conversation I'd heard earlier, I made my way toward the northern perimeter, where things hadn't been secured. As I approached, I discovered that the soldiers had been more efficient about securing the perimeter than they'd reported. Though it hadn't taken an hour to search the files and locate the nodules, there were guards spaced within eyesight of each other. There was simply no way I could lift the nodules or the thick file folder out as a bat. Some things would transform with me, like clothes, but some things didn't. The nodules might have transformed, but the folder wouldn't. I had to find a way past one of the guards. Looking around, I picked a guard that looked tired and dashed toward him.

Why did I assume the guard was male? It was nothing more than a combination of statistics and wishful thinking. There are advantages to sneaking out of heavily armed military blockades when you are a beautiful woman scantily dressed in leather. Almost all of those advantages vanish when you find out that the guard you want to bypass is, in fact, a woman. I had to make a decision at that point. I could gamble that the woman was lesbian and my original plan of seducing her would work. Alternately, I could just attack her and take my chances. Given my speed and reflexes and the unlikelihood that the woman was gay, I liked the latter option best.

I approached the guard and I realized luck was on my side in ways I'd not anticipated. Though the guards were in position, the lights were still being set up. I could approach in shadow. Though the guards could see each other, they could only do so in silhouette. I gripped the file folder tightly with one hand and moved along awkwardly on my free hand and knees. I hoped that if I was spotted, the guards would simply think I was a lame coyote making my way toward safety. At the shadow's perimeter, I reared back on my haunches, checked my grip on the folder, gauged my distance and leapt at the guard praying that papers wouldn't fly everywhere. Grabbing the guard around the neck with my free hand, I held her in close to my body. Silhouetted as we were, the other guards weren't able to distinguish two separate figures.

Stroking the guard's hair, I looked into her eyes, willing images of her mother to the forefront of her mind. Panic, fear and anger slowly subsided in the wake of calm. Gently, lovingly, I bent my head to her neck and pierced her jugular with my fangs. Wonderful, wet, life-giving blood gushed into my mouth. Her pulse sped up from the attack and almost caused the blood to flow faster than I could swallow. I had no desire to kill the guard but, hungry as I was, I had a difficult time stopping. Ultimately, she passed out and I lowered her to the ground. Realizing I had mere minutes before the other guards noticed their comrade's disappearance, I looked about. Luck was still with me. There was a generator close by. Sparing a moment, I looked back at the rubble. The strange, spectral figure I'd seen earlier seemed to have vanished.

Clutching the folder, I sprang to the generator then jumped into the shadows. Revitalized by the guard's blood, I started running at full speed toward the highway. I guessed I was about a mile away when my ears picked up faint sounds from a radio: "Corporal, report! Corporal!" A few minutes later guards were conferring with one another. I would be at the highway again by the time they would strike out after the corporal's attacker

I ran toward the highway and a dry, cool breeze blew across my skin. It evaporated sweat and gave clarity to my thoughts. I considered the nodules and the file then considered who would appreciate what I'd found and be able to help me unlock their secrets. One name kept coming to me again and again. The only vampire I knew experienced enough to help was Desmond Drake. If I was lucky, he would be at his American home, a ranch in Northern New Mexico, neighboring land owned by Ted Turner. Unlike the television magnate, Desmond Drake, Lord Draco of England has held title to his land since New Mexico was a province of New Spain.

Near the highway, I paused and caught my breath then reached out with my mind, feeling for Drake's presence. Drake was so strong that it was not impossible to sense his mind from hundreds of miles away. I caught a light prickling, like the after effect of a monsoon's lightning strike. There was a good chance I'd gotten lucky and Drake was in New Mexico.

The challenge I now faced was how to get the clues I'd found from where I was in Southeastern New Mexico to Drake's ranch up north. If I didn't have to carry so much, I'd just turn into a bat and fly. What I needed were wheels. Though I could retrieve the Army truck, it didn't seem like a safe vehicle to be in. That's when I remembered that Christopher must have driven down to Carlsbad Caverns from his home in Roswell. It was time to pay a visit to Christopher in the hospital. Resuming my run and turning northward when I reached the highway, I came to a place where someone had erected a white cross and lain a wreath where someone had once rolled a truck. I marked off five paces from the cross and buried the file folder and the nodules. Taking a deep breath, I transformed into a bat and flew back to Roswell.

Late at night, the hospital in Roswell was nearly silent. I simply walked past the reception nurse. His feet were on the desk and his head slumped on his chest; snoring quietly. I found my way back to Christopher's room. Thankfully he had a double room without a second occupant. He opened his eyes and tried to sit up when I entered the room.

"How are you doing?" I asked. The question sounded far too casual.

"Better," he said weakly. "I got the flowers you sent and the story."

I smiled in spite of myself. "Really? Did you like them?"

He recoiled slightly as I smiled and I realized he was reacting to the sight of my fangs. I reverted to a gentle close-mouthed grin.

"I liked them," he said nervously. "I've been wondering if everything that happened was a dream or some kind of hallucination. Your story made me think it must have all been real."

I nodded. "I was just out at the building. Last night's events did happen."

"You went back?" His brow furrowed. "Why?"

"Perhaps, like you, I needed to convince myself that the whole thing really happened."

"Fact of the matter is," said Christopher, shifting uncomfortably. "I think I'd rather forget the whole thing happened at all and just get on with my life."

I frowned, somewhat puzzled, then told myself that this was Christopher, not Pat Garrett I was dealing with. I didn't want to tell him that I thought he might be in danger if the Army found out he knew about their experiments and the creatures. "Say, is your car still down in Carlsbad?" I decided it was safest both to change the subject and get to the point of why I was there.

"Yeah…" he said, as though reluctant to admit the fact.

"I was thinking, if you don't mind me borrowing the car for a couple of days, I'd bring it back up to Roswell for you. I'd make sure to gas it up and take good care of it."

He sighed and shook his head. "I'm not sure if that would be a good idea. It might be better if I went down with a friend after I recover."

"Hmmm…" I reached down and slowly unlaced the leather bustier I wore. Having worked at the Long Dobé, I knew how to get material things from men. Though he wasn't Pat, he looked the part enough that it was easy for me to give into a long-unrequited fantasy. I allowed Christopher a brief view of my breasts before I turned around, pulled off my boots and lowered my pants to the floor. Lithe as a cat, I sidled over and closed the door. In one fluid motion, I climbed onto the narrow hospital bed and straddled Christopher's body with my legs. I brushed his neck with my fangs and said, "I wanted to thank you properly for letting me have some of your blood last night. It almost certainly saved my life." I dropped my voice a few registers and breathed, "Can't I borrow the car for just a couple of days?"

Christopher's heart rate increased and he grew aroused. I tensed the muscles of my inner thigh ever so slightly and felt him twitch. At that moment, I knew that Christopher was not the predator I was. He was poised to strike, yet did not. I held power over him.

"I'd be very grateful," I purred, flexing my thigh muscle again and feeling him twinge in response.

"The keys are in my pants pocket," he rasped. "In the closet."

I slid down onto Christopher letting him fill me. The sensation was not at all like the bite of a vampire, I was still the predator and he was still the prey. My vagina was the mouth that swallowed him whole. A couple of minutes later, non-life-sustaining fluid tepidly surged into my body. I think I grinned a little as I thought about the fact that, like all vampires, I'm sterile. He smiled back at me and his eyes fluttered. He was still weak after the fight and, no doubt, I'd just weakened him further.

I kissed Christopher gently on the mouth and thanked him for the keys then dressed quickly. Looking in the closet, I found his trousers and retrieved the car keys then put them into my own pocket. Before leaving, I filled his glass with water and told him again that I'd be back. He was sound asleep with a smile on his face.

✝✝✝

The next night I took the bus to Carlsbad and found Christopher's abandoned VW Bug in the campground. A note on the window warned that if the car was not moved within the day, it would be towed at the owner's expense. I knew I'd found the right car. He should have thanked me for rescuing his vehicle. I packed up his camping gear and made my way north on highway 285, stopping briefly at the memorial where I'd hidden the file and the nodules. The papers in the file were slightly damp from a night in the ground, but they were still readable. Though I had no reason to suspect that anyone would have taken the things, I breathed a sigh of relief when I found them right where I'd left them.

Continuing north, I was nearly to the junction of Highway 285 and I-40 when I had to stomp on the breaks suddenly. Standing in the middle of the road was a creature that I can best describe as an eight-foot-tall spider. Two multi-facetted red eyes glowed eerily. Below them were a nub-like nose and mandibles that opened and closed in front of a frightening maw. I realized that this was the same creature that I'd seen at the site of the ruined Quonset hut. I also realized that this must be one of the creatures that some Native American shamans called a kachina. The tribes back east would call it a manitou. Over the years, I'd heard that the kachinas were real, but I'd never actually seen one.

The kachina did not seem interested in me. Instead, it raised one of its forelegs and I saw the trunk space in the front of the car shudder. The kachina was after either the file or the nodules. Adrenaline surged and suddenly it seemed as if alarm bells went off in my head. With a great force of will, I cranked the engine over, put the car in gear and slammed on the accelerator.

I don't know whether the spider kachina tumbled over the top of the car or whether I simply drove through him as though he were a ghost. When I looked in the rear-view mirror, I saw the spider receding in the distance.

Turning my eyes forward, I pushed the accelerator to the floor and continued toward Santa Fe, praying that Desmond Drake would be home and that I wouldn't meet another kachina.

Part III

The Astronomer and La Llorona

"How many boys can say that La Llorona is watching out for them?"

– Mercedes Rodriguez

Chapter Twelve

From the notes of Daniel McKee.
Present Day.

Twilight darkened the sky and I was groggy, barely awake. I sipped a cup of coffee, trying to stimulate the old blood in my veins. I needed new blood, but it'd be a while before I could partake of my "night lunch." Instead, I dutifully stepped into the console room of the 2.1-meter telescope at Kitt Peak National Observatory in Arizona and sat behind a computer console. I began my ritual of preparing the telescope for observations. At the other end of the room sat a visiting astronomer. He controlled the camera and I controlled the telescope.

Using the computer, I opened the observatory dome and pointed the telescope to the first star of the night. It all appeared on my screen like a video game. Even now, I long for the past when I used ropes and pulleys to open the dome, then sat on the cold, lonely observing floor pushing the telescope by hand. Now, astronomers sit in a room apart from the telescope. Body heat disturbs the frail air around the instrument. Little does anyone know that the only heat I generate comes from the coffee I sip and the new blood I drink. Both sources of heat dissipate rapidly. No wonder I had been one of Percival Lowell's best observers at the beginning of the 20th century.

The visiting astronomer that night at Kitt Peak was a painfully cheerful sort. He tried to engage me in conversation but I just glared at him. He was the type of person who found natural bodily noises and lewd jokes wildly entertaining. If he hadn't been so disgusting, I'd have happily put an end to his life. The only reason I didn't, was that I'd have to deal with too many questions about the fate of the astronomer in my charge. They said he was a genius. I suppose he could have been, but it didn't mean I liked him any better. I smiled warily, then sat back sipping my coffee. Scanning the computer monitors, I confirmed the telescope was behaving as it should. The astronomer requested that I point the telescope to a new target and I complied with my usual cool efficiency.

For the most part, I actually liked working at the observatory. It gave my life of darkness a sense of normalcy. After all, I was no thief. Working as an astronomer paid the bills and kept me clothed and housed. It was a life to which I had become accustomed. I was an astronomer before I became a vampire. As I alluded, I worked for the great Percival Lowell at his observatory on Mars Hill in Northern Arizona. He'd built the observatory to look for canals on the planet Mars.

One cold night in 1899 I walked from the dome of the 24-inch telescope to my sleeping quarters when a low growl drew my attention. Wary, I thought I'd stumbled upon a mountain lion. Seemingly, my fears were confirmed when something pounced on me in the darkness. Teeth tore into my jugular and my own blood left my body for the last time. The body on me was not covered in fur as I expected and it was not a mountain lion. It was more like a man. I grew euphoric as the creature's blood passed to my body. I became a vampire there in the snow, on a clear winter's night on a hill outside Flagstaff.

The vampire that attacked me taught me how to feed and how to sleep during the day so that others would not find me. Coffins come in handy, but I really do prefer a soft bed. He taught me the basics and little more. I've met only a few other vampires. We have conversed some, but for the most part we leave each other alone. We seem to be creatures of solitude. Maybe it's just me but there are times I long for a new master.

The astronomer at the other end of the room broke wind and

giggled. I looked at the clock on the wall. Thankfully the time had passed quickly and midnight approached – time for lunch. I excused myself.

Most of the astronomers who operate telescopes walk to Kitt Peak's cafeteria and eat a stale, prepared meal. Fresher fare was on my menu. I left the building and looked around to see that I was alone; then looking up at the clear, crisp Arizona night, I stretched out my arms. Bone and skin lightened and became more leathery. My hearing improved and my sight went gray. I transformed into a bat, able to glide on the air. The strange part about transforming is that, although I could feel the transformation, somehow, I still felt like my human persona. It's like I become two separate entities.

There is a small Native American settlement near the base of Kitt Peak. The mountain is on the land of the Tohono O'odham, a proud people whom I had come to respect. However, they were human and served as my prey. I flew quickly down the mountain and assumed my natural form. I crept into the village and spied a Native American woman walking alone. There is little to fear out here in the desert but she turned and saw me. Before she could scream, I pounced on her.

My teeth tore into her jugular and as the blood began to flow, I became acutely aware of my arm against the woman's soft breasts. Her broad hips struggled against me and she moaned softly as the blood left her. The reactions to my attacks vary. For some the attack is sexual, for others, it's almost comforting. Still, for others it is simply terrifying. My master explained that it's all related to the victim's state of mind. After a time, I was satiated and the woman fell unconscious, dreaming of her demon lover. I left her where the others of her tribe could find her. I turned my attention briefly to the village. I would not be able to take too many more from there. They would seek the demon who attacked their people to protect either their spirits or their honor. Bullets couldn't harm me, but an arrow through the heart would be just as effective as a stake. With a sigh, I allowed the updrafts to carry me back to the observatory.

Back in the control room, the visiting astronomer belched as he devoured his own lunch. After feeding, I like to be alone in silence.

The visiting astronomer played his music too loud. I sighed, longing for the dawn, when I would be truly dead to the world.

I turned my attention to the computer. The World Wide Web offered a way to pass the time. It absorbed my attention so I did not have to interact with the beast at the other end of the room. As I scanned the web, I saw a job posting and wondered if it could be a dream come true. New Mexico State University sought an astronomer to operate its facility on Tortugas Peak. The job required many solitary hours operating a telescope, observing the planets. The university was in a city called Las Cruces. I giggled in spite of myself. It would be an ironic choice for a vampire. Las Cruces was Spanish for "the crosses." Before retiring for the day, I decided to email my résumé.

✟✟✟

Professor Vera Bode, the planetary astronomer in charge of the Tortugas Observatory, found it only slightly odd that I should request a night interview. Even so, she granted the request and I spent an enchanting evening in her company. I found her a vast improvement over the buffoon who I had been forced to work with that terrible night at Kitt Peak. Most of the visiting astronomers were not like that fellow. Working with astronomers night after night was an imposition. Like the Native Americans of the village, it was only a matter of time before one of the visitors would become suspicious of my long midnight absences from the telescope. I needed to work in a more solitary location.

Professor Bode was nearing retirement. She needed someone who could work long nights independently. She preferred someone who could spend weeks on site. The living quarters had fallen somewhat into disrepair, but that was a problem easily fixed. Bad as they were, I had lived in worse. The site was only a couple of miles from Las Cruces itself. She explained that I could make trips to town for food and supplies. I nodded understanding and stated my willingness to stay at the primitive site.

The Tortugas observatory's primary mission was to provide

ground-based support for spacecraft visiting Jupiter and Saturn. Clyde Tombaugh, who discovered Pluto when he was employed at the Lowell Observatory, founded the Tortugas Observatory. The telescope that Tombaugh used to discover Pluto had not been built when I left in 1905. I explained that I used to observe Mars when I worked at Lowell. I was vague about exactly when I worked at Lowell though. My descriptions of the instruments and knowledge of astronomy were sufficient to offset any feelings of uncertainty she had about hiring me.

After a few nights of instruction, Professor Bode left me to run the Tortugas Observatory as I saw fit. She sent observing instructions to me via email and I sent my data back to her over the same pipeline. I was alone at last, with time to explore my surroundings.

I found Las Cruces to be a charming town with one exception. There were, in fact, far too many crosses in the city. In the northeast, there is a neighborhood called "three crosses." Three metal crosses overlooked the main street. In the center of the city, in front of the downtown plaza, lay three concrete cross-shaped flowerbeds. Most of the time, they were bare and only the heads of sprinklers were visible.

There were crosses on the police cars. There were crosses in every city correspondence. Those damned crosses were everywhere.

The fact of the matter was, I'd never understood exactly why vampires hated crosses. Bram Stoker would have you believe that it has to do with the creator and the fact that crosses are a holy symbol. However, Stars of David have never made my skin crawl like crosses. Were Christian symbols the cause of my distress? Hardly! As an experiment, I tried eating sacramental bread back in the 1950s. It gave me a stomachache because I hadn't eaten solid food in almost fifty years, but nothing more. Images of the Virgin Mary are rather pleasant to look upon. Yet, I'd always felt uneasy around crosses.

Fortunately, I was not required to spend much time in the city. When I did go down to hunt at night, I simply avoided the big crosses. Even when I did go near, they did no more than make me uneasy, as long as I didn't get too close.

Hunting in Las Cruces was a pleasure. The warm climate attracted the homeless. Likewise, Cruces was near enough the border with Mexico that there were plenty of gangs. I suppose that partly explains the appeal that some vampires seem to find in urban areas. If you kill accidentally, as does happen, especially when hunting among society's least healthy segments, the homeless and the gang members won't be missed. I'm a creature of a century past, from a time when there were far fewer people than alive today. I find myself discomfited by large, modern cities but Las Cruces was perfect. It was large enough to provide anonymity but small enough that I didn't suffocate. If the police knew why the gang and homeless populations were being attacked and weakened, I think they would have thanked me.

In spite of the crosses, I was quite content with my new situation. I enjoyed the job at the observatory. Professor Bode did come up from time to time but, for the most part, she left me in peace. Though the telescope did have a computer interface, it could be run by hand. I spent many quiet nights moving the telescope to targets and taking pictures. I looked out upon the clear New Mexico sky. My vampire eyes let me see details in the sky that no mortal could imagine. I could see the rings of Saturn without a telescope. Would Galileo have been branded a heretic if all humans could see the moons of Jupiter as clearly as I could?

Given the choice, I would never have traded my vampire senses for those of a mortal. I may have been lonely at times but I would never return to my mortal frailty. Though I spent too many nights feeling cold in those domes, I ultimately became a creature of the cold. I was thankful for that, even if I was damned.

My routine was simple. I woke during the twilight hours then took my first data of the evening and sent it to Professor Bode. I flew down to Las Cruces for my night lunch avoiding the crosses, of course. I returned to the observatory and finished any work that needed to be done. I enjoyed the night sky and communed with my fellow night-creatures such as bats and owls that hunted on the mountain. I would return to the dormitory to sleep during the day.

✟✟✟

Some nights were cloudy and I didn't need to observe at all. I spent those nights in Las Cruces finding new hunting grounds. Las Cruces might have been the second largest city in New Mexico, but it was small compared to Tucson. Hunting for too long in one neighborhood could have jeopardized my idyllic existence. The police and citizens might have approved of my helping with the homeless situation and the gangs, but if they disappeared too fast, suspicions would be raised.

On one particularly cloudy night, I found myself in one of Cruces's poorer neighborhoods, not too far from downtown. Those hideous cross-shaped flowerbeds were not in sight. Unfortunately, there were almost no humans in sight, either. I grew bored and contemplated moving on to more fertile hunting grounds.

Just then, I spotted a chola walking alone. In fact, her walk was more of a swagger. She was tough and she knew it. She wore a halter-top and tight jeans. Her long hair was black and lustrous in the streetlights. Given the gangs and drugs in that part of town, you didn't tend to see even the cholos walking alone much less the cholas. Intrigued, I wanted to know where she was going and what she was doing.

In an almost hypnotic trance, I began to follow her. I didn't know whether she saw me and, in a way, I didn't care. My eyes were drawn to her muscular arms, her straight back, and yes, even to her swaying hips and taut buttocks.

I remembered my first kill back in 1899. The act of killing a human frightened me. Even more frightening was the fact that I had become aroused during the killing. The vampire who made me explained that it was natural and that I shouldn't be embarrassed. I still find the attack arousing, but taking blood is primarily for food. The pleasure I get is the pleasure of a full belly.

There was something about this chola though. My groin led me more than my empty belly. A woman had not made me feel that sensation in decades. I could tell she was more than prey.

I grew queasy and looked down, finding myself surrounded by concrete crosses. Looking up, the woman had vanished. My heart pounded of its own accord. I sensed I was trapped and I started to turn.

A dull thud resounded in my ears and I dropped to the ground, looking up at my beloved stars. They didn't seem as brilliant as I remembered. A sprinkler head poked me in the back. I was on the cross being held down.

"Don't even try to move." It was the voice of the chola. I smelled blood on her breath.

"You're a vampire," I said.

"Smart boy," she replied.

Weakened, I pushed against her hand, which lay hard against my chest. I struggled to free myself, but she didn't move. I noticed she avoided touching the cross, even with her shins.

"What are you doing?" I shouted.

"I've got you on the cross." She smiled, revealing her fangs.

I grew aroused much as I did during that first killing. Other than my master, I'd never had another vampire hold power over me. "Why?" My head began to throb. I hadn't had a headache in nearly a century.

"Don't you know about the cross?" she asked, her head cocked.

I shook my head in response.

"The ultimate symbol of human mortality. They killed the Son of God on one of these."

"But the Son of God rose from the dead," I protested.

"And so shall you. The question is, will you be mortal or will you be vampire?"

I started to pant, and worried that I was going to hyperventilate. I fought to regain control. "I don't want to be mortal."

"Tsk, tsk." She wagged a finger at me. "Mercy could give you a quick death or Mercy could make you a vampire again."

"I don't want death. I want to be a vampire."

She laughed. The sound echoed from the buildings.

I managed to knock her hand away and kicked her in the stomach. Stunned, she fell hard to the ground. I ran for the center of the downtown plaza.

Near the round tile semi-circles that formed the "Entrada" memorial commemorating Juan de Oñate's entrance into New Mexico, the chola caught up to me and shoved her cold hand into my upper spine. My head snapped backward and I dropped onto the bricks. Blood gushed from my nose. The chola pulled me up by my collar. "I'm in control here. Beg for Mercy!"

I spat blood and a tooth at her. I didn't notice whether the tooth was a fang.

Again she laughed. Her tongue played over her teeth. Slowly her head descended to my neck and she sank her fangs into my jugular. I moaned, feeling a painful longing. "I want to be a vampire again," I whispered hoarsely. "I want to be a vampire."

She fell with me to the ground, not stopping me as I gently kneaded her cool breast, grasping it like a comforting pillow.

Chapter Thirteen

From the notes of Daniel McKee.
Present Day.

Swimming in a light-headed delirium, I sat cross-legged on cold, hard concrete and watched the chola vampire. She was a tough street girl who had just drained most of my blood. Now she perched on the edge of a marble and tile memorial. The structure commemorated the 400th anniversary of Spain claiming New Mexico. The words of Captain General Juan de Oñate, painted on the tile, swam above the chola vampire's head like unspoken words: "Finding myself on the banks of the Rio del Norte, I take possession of this land..."

The chola vampire's jeans were old and faded with holes worn through at the knees and inner thighs. In a leisurely, serpentine motion, her right hand moved to her thigh and talon-like fingernails gashed soft flesh. Briefly her hand hovered over the oozing blood, as if in longing, then reached out, settling on my neck. She pulled my head to her thigh where my lips closed around the bleeding wound and I drank my own blood that had passed through her body.

The memorial we occupied stands on the site of what was once Las Cruces, New Mexico's oldest church. It was torn down to make way for the downtown mall. At one end of the memorial, a steel-frame sculpture stood in a fountain depicting the old church's portico. In a sense, the chola vampire and I desecrated a holy site.

We were not the first. Surrounding us were banks and lawyers' offices.

Growing stronger, I drank more forcefully. The chola vampire threw her head back and shut her eyes fast. After a moment, she pushed me back gently with some apparent regret. "Stop for Mercy's sake – More later…" she sighed.

Falling back on my haunches, I panted and my heart pounded furiously, threatening to burst through my chest. The water flowing in the nearby fountain roared in my ears. The world spun and I fell over sideways, hitting the ground with a soft thud. Looking up, I read the last of Oñate's words, "…this 30th day of April, the Feast of the Ascension of Our Lord." My heart stopped pounding as though someone had simply thrown a switch and apparently, I died for the second time in my long existence.

✟✟✟

My eyes fluttered open and I swallowed air in great gulping gasps. I had no idea how much time had passed. Shortly, my breathing softened and my heart settled into a more normal rhythm. Cautiously, I probed my teeth with my tongue and I was delighted to feel fangs. There was a gap where one of my molars was missing, but experience told me it would grow back. To this day, I do not know if the chola vampire really unmade me, or just played some trick on my mind.

I sat up, looked around and realized that I was still on Las Cruces's downtown mall, in the memorial. It was my night off and I had been stalking prey when the chola vampire attacked me, held me down on one of the great crosses and said she'd made me mortal again. I begged and pleaded for the restoration of my immortality and, apparently, she had given it back to me. Or, had she? Looking around, I saw no sign of the chola vampire. Then, hunger hit me like a blow to the stomach, insatiable hunger.

Whether real or illusion, I was reborn a vampire. Feeling the welts on my neck, I knew what was coming. What was then a mild burning in my neck would erupt into blinding pain. My back felt like it had been broken in a number of places and my head throbbed. It would get worse before it got better.

Right that instant, the need for blood overrode all other discomfort. A blinding light seized me and a wailing assailed my ears. A police car approached from the small street that dead-ends on the memorial. Two police officers, a man and a woman, stepped out of the car. Thinking I was a homeless man, they came to enforce the city's anti-vagrancy law. Headache and other pains notwithstanding, I leapt forward faster than they could see and knocked the man to the ground. The woman drew her gun, but before she could aim it at me, I was on her. Grabbing her wrist and pulling her toward me, I looked into her eyes. Her gun clattered to the ground as she came under my spell. I embraced her and found the natural suppleness of her body ruined by the leather, metal and plastic of the uniform. Closing my eyes, I bit into her jugular. Warm blood entered me and flowed into my stomach, lessening the hunger. Even my headache abated some. After a few minutes, she grew heavy in my arms. Gently, almost lovingly, I lowered her to the ground.

Looking up, I saw that the chola vampire had returned and drank the male police officer's blood. Releasing her hold on him, he collapsed to the ground in a heap. "Thanks for saving me some," she said with a wry grin.

My knees turned watery and buckled. Before I collapsed, the chola vampire came to my side, steadying me.

"Can you walk?" she asked with genuine concern.

I took several deep breaths. "With some help."

"You've had a hard night," she said, nodding. "I have some friends who live in that building," She pointed to an abandoned brick and adobe structure. The lower level was boarded up with plywood. Broken windows with tattered curtains adorned the second floor. "You can rest there and they can help me clean up this mess."

We walked over to the building. Big, red letters on a white sign proclaimed that it was the Rio Grande Theater owned by the local arts council. "Under Renovation, Get Involved," invited the sign in smaller letters. The chola vampire knocked on the plywood boarding up the entrance. Graffiti of a smiling face adorned the plywood. Someone had altered the face so that it had vampire fangs. Looking closely, I realized that one of the sections of plywood was hinged to allow workers access to the building. Bailing wire held it closed. Nimble fingers appeared, reaching through a gap between two of the plywood sheets and undid the wire.

A vampire with long hair and a wiry, unkempt beard opened the makeshift, plywood door. "Hey, Mercy," he called. For a moment, I wondered if 'hey, mercy' was simply an expression, but then it dawned on me that Mercy was the chola vampire's name. "Who's your friend?" he asked when he saw me.

"We have a situation, Hunter," explained Mercy. "Our friend here has just had a run-in with a cross. He's also had a run-in with the law." She looked over her shoulder at the police officers lying in the middle of the memorial.

"Your friend took out a couple of pigs?" asked Hunter, gleefully. "Right on!"

"He had some help. Let's get him inside. Is Alice here?"

Hunter nodded his shaggy head.

"She can watch over our friend while you and I get rid of the bodies and ditch the car."

"They still alive?"

"They're alive," said Mercy.

"Cool." Hunter continued to nod, like a bobble-head doll. "We can play with their memories, give 'em a new story to tell. That'll keep the pigs out of our hair for a while." Watching Hunter's shaggy mane flop about as his head bobbed, I grinned at his choice of words.

We entered the darkened theater. Hunter closed the door behind us and the light all but disappeared. Something flickered around the corner, but I couldn't discern any details. We must have been in the theater's lobby, making our way toward the auditorium. The pungent aroma of incense assailed my nostrils. Feeling our way along the wall, we eventually turned a corner and saw the soft glow of a ring of candles.

A tall, willowy woman with long blond hair tamed by a red bandana sat cross-legged on the floor surrounded by candles. She stood as we came near. She wore bell-bottom jeans and a white peasant blouse, both thin with age. Her face brightened into a smile as we approached. "Welcome traveler, I am Alice." Her voice was a little distant, but sincere.

"Daniel McKee." I introduced myself and wondered if I'd fallen down the rabbit hole. The abandoned theater seemed more like a movie set than a real place. All of the seats had been removed from the auditorium – undoubtedly as part of the renovation. At one end of the room, I made out a wooden stage and an orchestra pit. Dust and cobwebs were everywhere. I gathered it had been a while since anyone had actually done any work.

Hunter smiled, then reached out and shook my hand. "I'm Hunter. It's been a long time since I've met a vampire that uses his old man's last name." Mercy cleared her throat. "Present company excluded, of course. It's just that a lot of vampires don't think it's cool."

"And you?" I asked, genuinely curious. Of the vampires I've known, some used their surnames, others didn't. I was never really sure why the discrepancy existed.

"It's an establishment thing," explained Hunter. "I didn't much like using my last name before I became a vampire. Know what I'm sayin'?"

"Only some of the time," said Mercy with an amused grin. A sharp pain shot through my back and I sank to my knees, gasping involuntarily. Mercy caught me and led me to a large futon on the floor just beyond the ring of candles. "I still use my late husband's last name out of memory and respect," she explained. I stared at Mercy as she helped me get comfortable on the futon. She didn't look older than 19 or 20. I wondered how she could have been old enough to have had a husband before she became a vampire.

"If it's not impertinent of me to ask, how old are you?" I threw the question out to everyone.

"There are no rules here, especially about questions," said Alice. "Hunter and I have been vampires for over 30 years. We're over 50 years old now." Her eyes took on a faraway look. "It doesn't seem all that long ago that we were talking about not trusting people over thirty. Now we find it hard to trust humans at all." With a sigh, Alice sat on the futon next to me, leaned over and examined the wound on my neck.

"Well, I've been a vampire over four centuries, dear Alice. You guys are still just kids to me." Mercy studied me for a moment. "I'm guessing Daniel here is at least a century old. Still young in my book, but he is one of your elders so be nice to him."

Alice nodded to herself, stood, then glided into the darkness where she shuffled and rummaged through boxes and bags.

Mercy turned to Hunter. "We'd better go take care of those cops. I hope we're not too late."

"I'm with you, Mercy." Hunter looked at me. "Take it easy, man. Alice will take real good care of you." He flashed two fingers; a peace sign, something I hadn't seen in years. He turned and caught up with Mercy, who was almost to the lobby.

Alice returned from the dark, dragging a duffel bag. From it, she pulled some small pouches, satchels and bottles. Looking into the pouches, she plucked out leaves and placed them on the bite wounds on my neck. "These will help you heal."

"Leaves?"

"It's an herbal remedy. Just because we're supernatural creatures doesn't mean we should avoid the natural."

I lay back. A warm heat rapidly overtook the pain in my neck. A large balcony loomed in the shadows above. Crumbling adobe walls surrounded us. In some places the adobe had been repaired. It was quality work with painstaking care to assure that the structure's form had been preserved. I guessed that the adobe brick theater must have been over a century old, just as I was.

Alice turned on a hot plate plugged into an orange extension cord left behind by the workers. "Only a few of the outlets along the north wall work and none of the lights," explained Alice. "We don't want to flip any breakers that aren't already on. Using too much power will attract someone's attention." Gingerly, she placed a teapot on the burner.

"Aren't you afraid of being discovered by the workers renovating the theater?"

"No. The workers aren't here right now. There were money problems and they had to stop." Alice continued puttering, pulling some dried herbs from a jar and stuffing them into a tea ball with her thumb.

I nodded to myself, remembering the sign outside. The renovations were being funded by an arts organization. "So, how long have you known Mercy?"

The teapot whistled and Alice poured out a cup of hot water then set the tea ball in to steep. "Hunter and I met Mercy before we became vampires."

"Was she your sire?"

"No," said Alice, shaking her head. "I'm from San Antonio, Texas. I camped out one night here in Cruces while on my way to college in Berkeley. That's when I met Hunter and Mercy. She was really cool. Hunter was a straight-A student at UTEP. Mercy knew a lot about the natural places of the area and some of the old legends. Hunter knew a lot from books, but didn't know the world that well. Mercy suggested I take him along to Berkeley with me. A few months ago, Hunter and I wondered if Mercy was still here." Alice removed the tea ball from the cup and handed it to me. "Here, drink this."

I sat up on the futon, took the cup and sniffed at its contents, making a face. "What is it?"

"My sire back in Berkeley taught me how to make this tea. It'll help ease the hunger and the pain." Alice sat on the futon's edge, looking at me with bright, blue eyes that seemed strangely innocent for a vampire.

I pondered Alice's words and sipped the tea. A warm glow absorbed the pain. "Did Mercy really turn me human again? I didn't think it was possible."

"My sire told me that there are ways to weaken a vampire, so they're virtually human, but I've never seen it happen."

"The cross is a powerful talisman," said Hunter, entering the auditorium with Mercy on his heels. "Don't underestimate its power, man."

"And, don't underestimate your own strength," said Mercy. "Most vampires who are weakened by the cross, die soon after."

"Does that mean you were trying to kill me?" I put the teacup down and scanned the big auditorium, looking for escape routes.

"Not at all." Mercy sighed and threw herself down on the futon, next to me. Bending forward, she put her face in her hands and rubbed her eyes. "It's hard to know where to begin."

Hunter settled to the floor in front of Alice and rubbed her bare feet. "Start at the beginning where Alice and I came back to Cruces looking for a family."

Mercy shook her head. "That's not really the beginning." She sighed and looked into my eyes for a moment, then looked down again. The flickering candlelight formed deep shadows on her face. "I've been looking for a family for centuries; ever since I killed my own family. I used to baby-sit just so I could have children of my own. Hunter was one of my 'kids.'" She turned to Hunter. "Why don't you tell Daniel the story of how we met."

Hunter closed his eyes and thought, then he took a deep breath and began his tale.

Chapter Fourteen

Hunter Morgan tells how he met Mercy Rodriguez.
The year 1960.

"Get away from that fence!" called my new friend, Jesse Baca.

I looked at the picket fence. White paint peeled from splintered wood. The house and fence looked like something straight off TV, but in worse shape. "It's just a stupid fence." I shrugged.

Jesse pointed to the dilapidated gray house beyond. The remains of lace curtains hung in the windows. The grass surrounding the house was the uncut, verdant brown of the African Veldt. "The woman who lives in that house, she's a bruja, man."

"A brew-ha?" I asked. I knew Jesse was using a Spanish word, but I didn't know what it meant. "What's a brew-ha?"

"Don't you California boys know nothing?" He leaned close and whispered in my ear. "A bruja is a witch."

"A witch? You mean like in a fairy tale?" I laughed. My friend's face was serious. "Okay, if you're so smart, what makes you think she's a witch?"

Jesse leaned close and whispered in my ear. "My dad knows her. He says she hasn't aged a day since he was a teenager. She only comes out after dark. You never see her out working in the yard. She's never at the store, except at night and she never buys food."

I shook my head at this last bit of information. My mom

had just taken a new job in this small town of Anthony, New Mexico, right on the Texas border. We moved from Santa Monica, California. I missed skating by the ocean and all of the stores. I certainly was not used to people knowing or even caring about the shopping and lawn care habits of their neighbors. "That sounds more like a vampire than a witch."

"I never heard of a small-town vampire," said Jesse, nervously edging away from the house. Whether the home of a vampire or witch, my friend didn't like being too close. "I thought vampires liked cities. There's more people."

"We're not that far from El Paso." I took one more look at the house then started moving up the street. Jesse had edged almost a full house-length away. He waited for me to catch up, then fell in step beside me, letting out a breath.

"What's her name?" I asked.

"Mercedes Rodriguez," he whispered so lightly that I could barely hear.

"Sounds like a Mexican luxury car." I laughed. He glared at me with no humor at all in his sullen brown eyes. "Hey," I said trying to lighten his mood – this time by changing the subject. "Wasn't I going to teach you to roller skate?"

Jesse licked his lips and looked up the street, toward the future. As he did, his face brightened, as though he'd just awakened from a dream and remembered that the boogey man was just a story used to frighten bad children. "Last one to your house is a rotten egg." With that, he ran up the street.

"Hey, wait!" I called and ran after my friend.

After an hour of trying out my skates, Jesse was covered with bruises and a number of scrapes, but he started to get pretty good. Finally, we parted to return to our homes for dinner. I wasn't too thrilled with the idea of dinner. I guess I was a strange kid as far as my tastes went. I actually liked things like salads and home-cooked casseroles. Maybe it was because my mom was always so busy and never had time to cook. On her way home from work, she would stop off at a burger joint by the highway. For a real gourmet night, she would stop off at the little grocery store in town and pick up fresh bread and ham or sausages. Those things are all great when they're treats, but every night just got boring. I only ever had a good tuna casserole when I went to visit grandma, and that wasn't very often since she still lived in California.

As I walked through the door, mom greeted me with a smile. "Hi, Pumpkin. How're you doing?" She wore her "special" dress that she used to wear only for dad.

I sighed, hating her nickname for me. "Fine," I shrugged.

"There's hamburgers for dinner," called mom, retreating toward her bedroom. "French Fries,too ... in the bag on the counter."

I dropped the skates by the door and shuffled into the kitchen. Peering into one of the grease-spotted brown paper bags, I cautiously pulled out a cold French Fry. Ambling back to mom's room, I looked around the door and saw her staring into the mirror, putting on makeup. She seemed to catch sight of my reflection, because she turned around, with a wistful look on her face. "Pumpkin, I have a ... meeting in Cruces tonight. The sitter will be here within the hour."

I caught my breath and I think my lower lip may have stuck out. "A sitter?" I asked. *A meeting?* I thought. I saw the dress she used to wear only for dad, the extra special attention she gave to makeup that she never did for work. She had to be going on a date. How could she be going on a date? It's only been a year since dad died. "I'm eleven years old. I don't need a babysitter," I squawked aloud. My mind whirled. Maybe mom really is just going to a meeting ... but the special dress and makeup? Mom was a schoolteacher, not a businesswoman with nighttime meetings she needed to dress up for.

"Pumpkin," she sighed. "I'm going to be gone late..."

"But this is a small town, not Santa Monica. What's going to happen to me here?"

"She's nice," mom said, seemingly oblivious to my question. She turned back to the mirror to finish applying eye shadow. "Her name is Mercy and even though she's young, she's very polite and full of interesting stories about Anthony and the towns in the area."

"Mercy? What kind of name is Mercy?" I asked, my eyebrows raised.

"She says it's short for Mercedes," explained mom, with a toss of her hand.

"Mercedes … Rodriguez?" I asked, my heart skipping a beat.

Mom's eye shadow applicator paused mid-stroke. "You know her?" Slight puzzlement in her voice.

I licked my lips. "I think Jesse's dad knows her."

"It's a small town. Everybody knows everybody else." Mom finished her makeup, then inspected herself in the mirror. She nodded, seeming satisfied with the job she had done. "So, did Mr. Baca say nice things about Mercy?" asked mom, turning to face me.

"Mr. Baca didn't say anything," I said slowly, trying to think how to tell mom that my babysitter was rumored to be a bruja, a witch. "Jesse just said that his dad knew Mercedes Rodriguez a long time ago."

Mom smiled again. "He must know an aunt or someone with the same name. Mercy can't be more than nineteen years old." She reached out, putting her hand on my shoulder. "You'd better eat that hamburger before it gets cold."

I nodded, trying to find comfort in my mom's words, but somehow I knew that the Mercy Rodriguez coming to watch me that night was the very same Mercedes Rodriguez that Mr. Baca knew. After a moment, I trudged back to the kitchen. Dumping the contents of the bag onto a plate, I ate about half the fries then nibbled on the hamburger. One of the problems with a teenage babysitter is that she'd actually like this stuff. Why couldn't mom find a nice older woman who could cook?

More bored with the meal than full, I chucked what was left in the trash just as the doorbell rang. The sound of mom's high heels echoed down the hardwood hallway to the door. Cautiously, I went to the kitchen door and peered down the hall.

I always pictured witches as skinny, old women with long, hooked noses and a green tint to their skin. My new babysitter didn't look anything like those witches. Like mom said, she looked about eighteen or nineteen years old. She was short, with a flat stomach, but bigger hips and boobs than I'd seen on most of the teenage girls hanging around town. She had skin that looked as though it had been dark once, but was now strangely pale, like coffee with too much cream. Her long, black hair hung down her back. She stood with her hands on her hips, projecting more attitude than mom ever let me get away with. I wondered why mom considered Mercy an acceptable babysitter for me since she was, after all, a girl who looked like she was from the wrong side of the tracks, as Jesse might say. They shook hands and turned toward the kitchen. I ducked back into the kitchen before they saw me staring.

I couldn't think of a good place to hide, so I sat down at the table to await my fate. Mom and Mercy entered, speaking to each other. Without looking at me, they sat down. My heart beat so fast, I only caught snippets of the instructions my mom gave the sitter – "Make sure he does his homework" – "Here's a list of phone numbers if there's an emergency" – "Make sure he gets a shower. You know how boys are, they can really stink…"

I don't remember Mercy saying much of anything. She just nodded a lot as mom spoke. There was a strange, almost knowing, look in Mercy's eyes as mom spoke. After a few minutes, I felt mom's moist lips touch my cheek and she said, "Be good. I'll see you tomorrow."

Mom turned, looked at us briefly from the kitchen door, then disappeared. Her footsteps echoed in the hall and were punctuated by the sounds of the door closing and the car starting. I turned and saw Mercy looking at me, her eyes narrowed. It was then I figured out what was strange about the way Mercy looked at mom. Mercy hadn't looked at mom the way a teenager would. It was more like the way my grandmother would look at her. Eyes that had seen the world for a very long time had evaluated mom carefully. "You remind me of my boy," said Mercy, evenly.

"Your boy?" I couldn't keep the shock out of my voice. I knew that teenage girls could have babies, but something in the tone of her voice sounded like she was talking about something she remembered from long ago.

"He died ... some time ago..." Sadness weighed down her voice. A tear emerged from the corner of her eye.

I gasped in spite of myself. "Just how old are you?" I blurted out.

Hurriedly, Mercy wiped away the tear and straightened as if summoning some inner resolve. "Your mother says to do your homework, then get ready for bed. Don't forget a shower." It seemed as though years had fallen away from her voice. She sounded like a teenager again.

"Do you think I smell bad?" My voice was faint. Even I barely heard the question.

"You know," she began. Her eyes projected less age and wisdom and more attitude, "Girls don't appreciate sweat enough. They want everything to smell like flowers. Well, you know what? Flowers make me sneeze. Men are supposed to smell like sweat. You don't need to take the shower unless you want to. You do need to do the homework though."

My heart began to pound again as I considered Mercy's words and the way she looked at me. I began to think that she might well be the bruja that Mr. Baca knew from his childhood. Maybe she could cast a spell on herself to look young. I began to be afraid that when I started my homework, Mercy would cast some kind of spell on me. Then my thoughts turned to mom and I began to wonder about her "meeting."

"You're nervous." Mercy's eyes narrowed again. "There's nothing to worry about. It's not like I'm a witch who's going to throw you in the oven and cook you." She leaned forward, almost conspiratorially. "Your mother will be gone late, but don't worry. She'll get bored with the man she's gone to see before long."

I couldn't help but gasp. It was as though she had read my mind.

Mercy sat back and folded her arms across her stomach. "I may look young, but I've been babysitting as long as I can remember. You're worried about your mother and you're just a little nervous about your strange babysitter." She pursed her lips and nodded. "Are you too old for bedtime stories?"

I hadn't heard a bedtime story in years. In fact, I never really thought about whether I was too old or not. I shook my head, no.

"Good," she said. "Do your homework and I'll tell you a story. I know quite a few stories about the way things used to be around here."

Too stunned by the sudden offer to say anything, I rose from the table and went to my room to do math homework. When I was done I pulled off my clothes, leaving them on the floor, and pulled on my pajamas. Suddenly and silently, Mercy was in my room, picking up the discarded clothes and folding them. While she folded the clothes, she told me of a family who had moved to New Mexico almost four hundred years before. "It was Nuevo México before México had declared its independence from Spain. The province was named for Ciudad México. The family came to farm the land near the Río Grande, to work for the Franciscan Monks who had come to 'convert the savages.'" She told me about those days and how the river was full of life, unlike today. "In the 1800s the Texans came and straightened the river. When they did, it was like putting a man on the rack. It took all the life out of it."

I listened to Mercy's story but my eyelids grew heavy. I was fascinated by this tale of long ago, but her sing-song voice lulled me into a sound sleep.

✝✝✝

I woke from a nightmare, sweating. Mercy came in and pulled me close to her. She placed my head gently on her breast, which was like a refreshingly cool pillow on a hot night. The cloth of her blouse smelled faintly musty, like a house recently opened after being closed for a long time. She sang softly in Spanish. I drifted in and out of sleep. Groggily, I looked up at her face. She smiled at me as though she were smiling down at her own boy. I wasn't even afraid when I saw that two fangs broke the line of her smile. She lowered me gently to the bed and knelt beside me.

When I was just a little younger, my mom had told me about

sex and how it worked. I remembered wondering why people would want to do that to each other. When Mercy's fangs pierced my neck, I wondered if that was what a girl felt the first time she was with a boy. There was a fierce sting followed by a wash of blood, then contentment just to feel the fangs within my neck and the gentle pressure of Mercy's soft lips. My baby-sitter held me as she suckled my neck. I should have been scared to discover that my baby-sitter was a vampire, but I didn't want her to stop. Yes, there was a certain horror, but the closeness she gave me was more than I'd ever felt from my mom. Before dad died, he allowed me to cuddle up to him, but something masculine prevented him from returning affection to me. After a time, Mercy withdrew her fangs. Drained, but feeling loved, I drifted off to sleep.

✟✟✟

When I awoke the next day, I was embarrassed by the two red marks in my neck and ashamed of the feelings that Mercy aroused within me. Most of the shirts I had were T-shirts. I sorted through my closet until I finally found a button-down shirt with a collar. In the car on the way to school, mom looked at me. "My, that's pretty dressed up for you," she said.

I shrugged. "I couldn't find any clean T-shirts."

She looked at me, her lips pursed. "I just did the laundry two nights ago."

"How was your meeting?" I asked, quickly changing the subject.

Mom's face took on a faraway look revealing emotions not unlike those I had felt the night before when I was under Mercy's spell. "It was good," she said simply. "Hey, I hear the truck stop has pizza now. Wanna give it a try tonight?" It was mom's turn to change the subject.

"I'm going to eat with Jesse's family tonight," I said. I was a little scared of the green chile enchiladas that Jesse said his mom made, but at least it would be a home-cooked meal.

"Good," said mom. "I hope you eat well … You're looking a little pale."

I pulled the collar up a little higher.

The green chile enchiladas that night turned out to be great. The chile was a little like Mercy's bite: both painful and satisfying. Afterward, I found myself craving the chile. I wondered how I could want more of something that hurt so much. I wondered when Mercy Rodriguez would babysit again. Secretly I hoped it would be soon.

After dinner, Jesse and I ran for the door, planning to go down to the river and look for frogs and tadpoles.

"Boys," called Mrs. Baca. "Don't stay out too late. Remember La Llorona!"

We ran outside, the screen door banging shut behind us. "What's a Law Yorona?" I asked.

"La Llorona is the weeping woman," explained Jesse. "She threw her children into the Río Grande and cries for them now that they're gone. They say she walks up and down the riverbanks weeping for her children at night. Some of the stories say she'll throw you into the river if she catches you. Others say she's looking for kids to take her children's place."

I stopped in my tracks, again thinking of Mercy and her boy who died "long ago."

"Don't worry," said Jesse, his brow creased. "La Llorona can't get you unless you're outside at night."

"What would happen if you invited her inside your house?" I asked, not able to keep a tremor from my voice.

Jesse laughed. "No one would be stupid enough to invite La Llorona inside." With that, Jesse ran off toward the river.

✝✝✝

A week later, Mom had another one of her meetings and Mercy Rodriguez was invited back to babysit. Like before, she made sure I did my homework, and offered to tell me a bedtime story if I finished it.

Once I was finished with my homework and was in my pajamas, Mercy silently appeared in my room. Before she could begin her story, though, I took a deep breath then looked her in the eye. "Are you La Llorona?"

For a moment, I expected Mercy to laugh at me. Her face contorted, flashing several different emotions before a single tear fell. "I miss my boy so much." She shook her head and wiped the tear angrily away. "There are days I feel like La Llorona, but I'm not her."

Looking back on it, I probably should have been afraid of my vampire babysitter. Instead, I was afraid that she would never hold me again. "What really happened to your son?" I asked in a daze.

"About four hundred years ago I worked the land with my husband, a good but hard man. I suppose you could say he was a product of the land he was raised on. I met a dashing caballero from Spain named Rudolfo. He told me I was beautiful and he could make me live forever. I imagined him sweeping our family away from the hard life and taking us back to Europe. He smelled like flowers. I let him turn me into a vampire, which was a mistake.

"A new vampire must feed right away. Without thinking I took the life of my sweet young boy, then my baby girl. Once I had done that, I was satisfied, but realized the horror of what I had done. They say La Llorona was mad and drowned her children. I didn't drown my children. I tossed their bodies into the river to hide them. They say La Llorona killed herself. I was killed by a vampire named Rudolfo de Córdoba. I wasn't swept away to a better life. I was cursed for all eternity."

"But you're so young," I said softly. I wondered how a teenager could have been a wife and mother.

"Things were different then. I was 15 when I married Juan, only four years older than you. Your mother thinks I look 19, but I was only 17 when Rudolfo turned me into a vampire. When I look in the mirror, that 17-year-old still looks back at me. Before I was a vampire, I was a respected woman. Now people look at me and see a young girl. Part of me feels so very old and part of me feels like I've grown younger with the centuries."

"I've heard La Llorona is looking for new children to replace the ones she killed. Would you make me a vampire so I could stay with you, forever?"

Mercy sighed. "I work as a baby-sitter because they don't give teen girls any other kind of night time job. At least not one that I'll do." She shook her head. "You still have so much life ahead of you, Hunter, don't give it up for darkness. Walk in the light."

"If you don't want me with you, why did you drink my blood?" I asked. Emotions of fear, love, lust, and anger all made war in my body.

"I drank your blood because I needed it to survive and it wouldn't kill you."

"I'm so confused. I love you and I'm scared of you all at the same time. I want to feel the way I do when you drink my blood. Help me to understand," I pleaded.

Mercy put her face in her hands. "Maybe I've shown you the true nature of love before you're ready." Her voice cracked. "I never wanted to hurt you that way."

"Hurt me?" I almost yelled the question at her. "It might have been scary, but it was wonderful too." I looked at my feet and thought about my mom, away from me at a "meeting." I thought about my dad, no longer around to cuddle against. "I'd rather die in your arms than grow up an orphan," I said as tears welled up in my eyes.

She reached out and folded me into her arms. I sighed contentedly and listened as her heart pumped my blood through her body. Gently, she wiped the tears from my cheeks. "Take some time to grow up, then we'll talk about it. In the meantime, I promise I won't harm you or let anyone else harm you. How many boys can say that La Llorona is watching out for them?"

Chapter Fifteen

From the notes of Daniel McKee.
Present Day.

"Have you ever turned a child into a vampire?" I asked. My mind whirled through the possibilities, wondering what a child vampire would be like. All of the scenarios I imagined frightened me.

"No." Mercy's voice shuddered. She lowered her face farther and the shadows deepened. "I've come close, dangerously close, especially with Hunter. When he and Alice returned as vampires, the chance to make my dream come true was irresistible."

"We left the Bay Area because the vampires there started getting weird, dark and frightening." Alice frowned then looked hopefully at Hunter. "We just want to be good to each other, love each other and be part of a family. We used to share equally with each other."

"We vampires were doing our part to tear down the establishment." Hunter looked sadly into Alice's eyes. He shimmied next to Alice and began to rub her lower back. "Now, it seems like the San Francisco vampires are just part of the establishment."

Understanding dawned on me. "You want me to be part of your family. Why? And, why did you attack me?"

"Why does anyone become a part of a family?" asked Mercy.

When I didn't answer, Hunter answered for me. "Human families come together to raise children and to protect each other."

"But, vampires don't have children," I protested.

"Vampires can be killed, though." Alice shuddered. "We need to protect each other. Like all living creatures, we need love and affection."

"You seem strong and I thought you were one of the most beautiful vampires I'd ever seen." Mercy looked up into my eyes. "If I'd just asked you to come in and hang out, would you have stayed?"

"I like living alone," I admitted. "I might have been willing to meet you all, but I don't know if I would have stayed."

"Now, though, you know just how vulnerable vampires are." A tear escaped Mercy's eye. "If you decide you have to leave, we won't stop you. Though I hope you spare us a few days and see if you like it here."

There was an undeniable appeal to this invitation. There have been times in my vampiric life when I'd almost been discovered. The astronomers I worked around were liable to figure out my secret some day. "What if you decide you don't want me to be part of your family?"

"I don't think that will be a problem," said Mercy. "I've watched you come and go from the observatory. You're comfortable in your vampirism. You're not an overblown, brooding creature of the night like some vampires I've met. I'd be surprised if you weren't right for us."

I sensed honesty from both Hunter and Alice. I still wasn't sure whether or not to trust Mercy, but I decided that the idea of being part of a family was tempting enough to try for a few days. "I'll go to the observatory tomorrow and email my boss to tell her a family situation has come up and I need to be away for a few days. She'll understand."

Both Hunter and Alice lifted their hands into the air and shouted, "Hooray!" Mercy reached out and gave my shoulder a squeeze. Alice leaned over and kissed Hunter deeply. The kiss went on long enough to make me blush. After a few more moments, Hunter broke the kiss and stood. He helped Alice to her feet and, as if the two were on their own private wavelength, they moved a short ways off into the shadows.

Still sitting beside me, Mercy removed her black tennis shoes followed by a pair of white socks then wriggled her toes in the air. She shimmied closer to me and put her head on my shoulder. "I said you were a beautiful vampire and I meant it. Do you find me beautiful?"

She pressed her supple body into mine and I instinctively wrapped my arm around her shoulder. I allowed myself to look at her. She had long, lustrous black hair. Her eyes were dark brown, almost black. Her breasts were lovely and round and for just a few moments, I fantasized about my fangs teasing her nipples. "You are beautiful," I said. My voice caught in my throat and I feared that I didn't sound as suave as I'd have liked. From the corner of my eye, I saw Hunter and Alice with arms wrapped around each other. I thought Alice's blouse lay in a crumpled heap on the floor and I wondered what I'd gotten myself into.

"They say vampires love more passionately than humans." Mercy's voice grew husky. "You and I have already shared blood. How many humans have ever been that intimate?"

Instead of answering her question, my mouth closed on hers. Her tongue darted into my mouth and I teased it with a fang. After a few breathless moments, we parted. I sat back and looked at Mercy again and this time I saw the teenage girl that she had been when she became a vampire. "You seem so young," I whispered.

Mercy stood abruptly and put her hands on her hips. "The time has come to get one thing perfectly clear. I am not your teen fantasy girl." With careful precision, she placed her hand on my sternum and shoved me back onto the futon. "Though I may look like a young girl, never forget that I am the master here." She knelt down and removed my shoes and socks then slid onto the futon and embraced me, nuzzling my neck where she had bitten me.

Mercy's hand traveled to my belt and unbuckled it. After unfastening my trousers, she sat up. One hand caressed my chest while the other worked my pants down and off. She took a moment to run her finger around the tent-like form of my plain white underwear before standing and removing her own jeans. It both amused and comforted me to see that she, too, wore plain white briefs.

Distracted as I was, I did not notice Hunter and Alice approach. They were nude and slick with sweat. Mercy was beside me again. "There is little more intimate or exquisite than a blood circle."

Without further explanation, Mercy bit into my thigh, near the groin and I moaned. The pain of the bite and the urgency of my arousal were almost more than I could bear. Hunter settled onto the futon, and bit into Mercy's femoral artery on the leg opposite the one I'd bitten earlier.

"The blood flows from you to Mercy to Hunter to me and back again," said Alice, as she settled into position between Hunter and I. She bit his thigh and it was clear that Hunter was as aroused by the act as I. I allowed myself a moment to tease the soft flesh of Alice's thigh, not far from her golden pubic triangle before biting in.

I felt all of our blood coursing together – as though we were all one body. My body responded to the experience with a fierce orgasm. The thoughts and emotions of my fellow vampires invaded my mind. I felt the intensity of Hunter's first acid trip. My belly glowed like Alice's did the first time she was kissed by a boy. Mercy's loneliness and sense of isolation came pouring into me. Part of her feared being alone and longed for companionship while another part of her feared being trapped and wanted to push everyone away.

They felt my experiences as well and Hunter delighted in my memories of looking at the stars for the first time. Alice knew my pride at being able to repair a telescope, saving a precious night of observation. Mercy enjoyed my memories of communing with the night creatures on a lonely mountaintop during a break from observations. The sensations continued. I knew the feeling of a penis thrusting into my body, both lovingly and forcefully. There was a flash of terror as I 'remembered' exams at Berkeley. I lay in bed, exhausted after laboring in the field. I don't know how long we were like that, but Mercy eventually removed her fangs from my thigh and, regretfully, I extracted my fangs from Alice.

A mass of tired, sweaty bodies, we lay in a heap on the futon and one by one, we fell into the death-like slumber that only a vampire knows.

✝✝✝

Early in my days as a vampire, I slept, or perhaps I was literally dead, the whole day through. Even as I've aged, I still tended to sleep from sunrise to sunset. Only certain things can wake me. Usually, it has to do with a sense of danger.

When I woke in the Rio Grande Theater, I was surprised to find that it was just after three in the afternoon. I only remembered waking that early once or twice before. The auditorium was pitch dark. I could not see anything except for the light from my digital watch. Feeling around, I found Hunter and Alice, but no Mercy. I sat up and stared into the darkness for a time. A distant glow came from the lobby so I tossed on my jeans and shirt, then crept forward to investigate.

Approaching the lobby, I made out two figures in silhouette standing by an electrical box. Just as I was about to leave the auditorium, Mercy jerked me to the side. "We have intruders," she breathed. Like me, she'd tossed on some clothes.

"Who are they?" I asked. "Workmen?"

"Don't know yet. Since they're at the electrical box, I'd guess they're trying to get the lights turned on."

"Hunter and Alice are still on the futon, in plain sight. Is there somewhere we can hide them until they wake up?"

"There's a storage closet under the stage, behind the orchestra pit. If you can help me, we can get them there."

We made our way through the darkness, feeling our way to the futon. Silently, we agreed to take Hunter to the closet first, to get the heavier load out of the way. If necessary, we could move faster with Alice. We lifted Hunter and began trudging toward the orchestra pit.

"What do we do with the futon and candles?" I asked in a hoarse whisper.

"We don't do a damn thing," growled Mercy in a harsh whisper. "They'll just think some homeless hippies took up residence in here for a while."

"They wouldn't be too far from the truth."

"Now, shut up and keep moving," ordered Mercy.

We carefully made our way down the steps into the orchestra pit. There, we lay Hunter down and Mercy fumbled for a time with the storage closet's knob. It rattled loudly and I feared the workmen would hear us and come to seek us out with flashlights. She leaned into the moisture-swollen door and forced it open with a thud.

"There's no way those workers didn't hear that," I whispered.

Without saying a word or asking for help, Mercy drug Hunter into the storage room and closed the door. Just as she pulled the door to, light flooded the auditorium.

I was blinded at first. In reality, only about three of the big bulbs on the ceiling were on. It was enough to see clearly in the big auditorium. Mercy and I peered over the edge of the orchestra pit. A man in coveralls made his way to where Alice lay naked and vulnerable on the futon. The man in coveralls carried a spray tank and a wand.

"Exterminators?" I asked, my eyebrows knitting.

"It would seem so," said Mercy. "Weren't there two of them?"

"Shouldn't we go and get Alice?" I was more worried about the exterminator we saw than the one working elsewhere. The exterminator we saw didn't look very threatening. He was of moderate height, clean-shaven with big ears and short, curly hair.

"What's he going to do?" asked Mercy. "Spray her with bug poison?"

Something seemed wrong about an exterminator striding through the middle of a room. It struck me that an exterminator should work the room's periphery, where the bugs are, not stalking cat-like through the center of the room. Of course, he may have simply been going to check out the form on the futon.

"We're safer where we are for the moment," Mercy said, seeming to agree with my assessment. "He'll see the 'dead' body, get scared and run out to call the cops. That'll give us time to hide Alice."

Instead of showing signs of wariness toward the body on the futon, the exterminator stopped. He put his tank on the floor and with a brief look around, aimed the wand directly at Alice's vulnerable form.

"Maybe he's going to spray her with bug poison after all." Mercy raised her eyebrows at the odd scene.

The few times in my life I've had to deal with bug poison, I'd been struck by how much the stuff looked like water or mist. Only its strong scent told me it was anything other than water. The mist coming out of the exterminator's nozzle was definitely not water or any ordinary bug poison. It looked like a fog or even a dust cloud. I would have thought this was simply a new kind of poison, except that the exterminator wore no mask, gloves or other protective gear. Almost like a living creature, the mist enveloped Alice. Alice continued to sleep in her death-like state, unaware that anything had happened.

The mist dissipated. As it did, I sensed Alice less and less. We vampires have almost no brain activity when we sleep. Even though Alice's danger sense was not as well developed as mine, the mist shut down what senses she had developed. I began to wonder if she would even be able to wake with the sunset. My eyes grew wide and I turned to look at Mercy. She was just as shocked as I was. "What the hell."

"Larry!" Both Mercy and I whirled around and saw a woman standing on the stage over our heads. She wore a plain blue dress. Her hair was brown, collar-length, and wavy, distinctive in its indistinctness. "Get over here! We got two more vamps down in the pit and they're awake." Around her neck was a gaudy necklace that looked like something from the Wizard of Oz with big green stones strung together that glowed softly. I realized it was the source of the glow I'd seen earlier.

Larry the exterminator whirled around, picked up the tank and began a shuffling run toward us.

Mercy looked at me again. "Can you transform?"

I nodded stupidly at her.

"Time to show your stuff." With that, she made for the stairs of the orchestra pit at a run, collapsing in on herself. In two bounds, she was on all fours as a jaguar. I looked up and saw that Larry the exterminator was almost to the pit. I started running toward the stairs at the opposite side of the orchestra pit holding my arms out to the side. I hated to transform into a bat inside a building. I preferred to be in the open air where the wind would give me some lift. Larry set down his tank and aimed the wand at me. Becoming a bat just in time, I fluttered away from the approaching cloud. The mist continued on its way and collided with the wall, dissipating as it did so. I spiraled up toward the ceiling.

Mercy, in jaguar form, bounded onto the stage and lunged for the woman with the necklace as I continued my upward spiral. Even though I could only see in black and white as a bat, I noticed that the woman's necklace flared to blinding brilliance as Mercy pounced. I expected that the woman would be dead soon, but she turned and side-flipped out of Mercy's way, coming up in a fighting stance. The necklace diminished in intensity. Mercy landed and skidded on the slick wooden floor of the stage.

Larry the exterminator aimed his wand again, this time at Mercy. I darted down from the rafters and swooped in a hyperbolic arc around Larry's head. He spun, trying to follow me with the wand.

"Larry, quit fucking around with that bat and get this jaguar before she manages to nail me," ordered the woman. Risking a look over my wing, I saw that the woman was actually holding her own. Dodging another of Mercy's lunges, she ran for the other end of the stage where a broom leaned against the wall. As the woman ran, the necklace faded in brilliance. She broke the broomstick across her knee and stood ready to drive a stake through Mercy's heart on the next pass.

The exterminator grimaced and, seemingly out of frustration, discharged the spray wand in my general direction, before turning back to Mercy. I easily evaded the mist and darted back down again.

Mercy and the woman glared at each other, each poised to strike, both hesitant to make the first move. I realized that the woman was just buying the exterminator time to strike.

As I neared the auditorium floor, I transformed back into human-shape. Mistiming my transformation, I was still a little high and moving too fast. I careened into Larry with a full body tackle that sent us both tumbling to the floor. My vampire reflexes and physique allowed me to recover just a little faster than Larry. I rose and ran for the tank. Grabbing it and the wand, I ran for the back of the auditorium. Halfway to the lobby, I heard a shout of "Larry!" from the stage.

"What is it now, Georgia?" asked the exterminator, speaking for the first time.

Mercy looked around and saw what I'd done. Seeing her distracted, Georgia leaped at her with the broken broomstick. Just before she struck, Mercy leaped across the orchestra pit and charged after me. Georgia's necklace faded to a soft green glow as Mercy left the stage.

Mercy passed me with a growl and I gathered that she meant for me to follow her. She led me out of the auditorium and into the lobby. Bordering the lobby were two glassed-in rooms. Sunlight trickled in under the plywood front of the building giving us some light to see by. The glassed-in rooms appeared to be old storefronts. It seemed to me that some interior walls had been knocked down at some point in the theater's past. Mercy made a sharp right and led me into one of the rooms. In the back, we found a storage room and pulled the door shut. I tried a wall switch and the lights came on. The room was furnished with a desk, chair and cabinets. Surprising for such an old building, the room had a drop ceiling. I climbed on the desk and moved a ceiling panel aside.

Mercy transformed into human form and helped me lift the tank and wand up into the ceiling. I did my best to straighten out the panels once we finished "Looks like the work crews converted this into an office before they were ordered to stop work," I commented, noting the newness of the room's furnishings.

"Yeah, this old office was one of the first places they renovated." She looked around nervously. "We can't hide here for long. Did you notice that necklace the woman has?"

I nodded. "It glows more brightly when a vampire is nearby."

"Kind of a vampire range finder. They'll use it to locate us," she said.

"What concerns me more is what's in that spray bottle. What the hell was that stuff? Did they kill Alice?"

Mercy pursed her lips. "I don't think she's dead."

"How can you tell?" I asked.

Mercy shook her head. "This isn't the time to discuss the possibilities. If we can get out of here alive, I know someone who can help us understand what the spray is."

We took a few minutes to catch our breath. "Okay," I said, "What's the next step?"

Mercy closed her eyes and considered for a few moments. "I say we go on the offensive. We have their spray canister. If we're going up against two vampire hunters stake to fang, we'll have the advantage out in the open. As we are now, they have the advantage. They have a device to track and corner us."

"I agree," I said. "We're in greater danger the longer we stay here and they might very well have more of the spray."

Mercy leaned over and pulled my head to her. She kissed me deeply, probed my mouth with her tongue, then released me. "Just in case we're wrong about this being a good idea, I wanted one more chance to taste you."

We stood, turned out the light, then very cautiously made our way out of the back office. Emerging from the side room, we stopped when we heard Larry and Georgia speaking. Scraping, scuffling sounds indicated they dragged something heavy in our direction. We stayed in the shadows.

"I say we make a stand and get all the vamps at once," said Georgia.

"Look, we've already got two and that's a pretty tidy bounty right there. I've got more of the spray. We can come back early tomorrow morning and see if the other two are still here. If they are, we can deal with them. Otherwise, our job's done. We get paid for these two and move on." Larry's voice was reasoned and persuasive. They entered the lobby, dragging a heavy body bag. As best as I could tell, either Hunter or Alice was in the bag or perhaps both. Georgia's necklace glowed brightly from the vampires' proximity.

"But those vamps made off with a sample of the spray. What if they figure out what it is?" Georgia's normally commanding voice approached a whine.

"So what if they figure it out? What are they gonna do? It's not like there are chemist vampires who can trace the spray back to its makers." Larry pushed the plywood door open and I instinctively fell deeper into the shadows as sunlight spilled into the lobby. "Besides, vamps just aren't that loyal. The other two will just run away from here rather than fight us for their friends."

"I'd like to show you just how disloyal vamps are, pal," murmured Mercy. Wanting to hear as much of the conversation as possible, I hushed her. She slapped at my hand. "Let's rush 'em while we can."

"They're in sunlight, it'd be suicide," I whispered harshly. "Now shut up and let me listen."

"Do you really trust that the spray works?" pressed Georgia. "What if they wake up en route?" The vampire hunters dragged the bag out into the sunlight. I prayed that the bag was thick enough that the vampires within would not be harmed.

"Yeah," said Larry. "Well, there's always the old reliable stake through the heart…" Larry's voice trailed off as he closed the door behind him.

A padlock rattled as it was secured outside. We were locked in. That's not to say that the plywood would stop us. I suspected that locking the door was just habit for Larry and he counted on us not being at the theater in the morning.

Mercy stood up, putting her hands on her hips. "What the hell kind of friend are you, letting them take Hunter and Alice away?"

I took a step past Mercy toward the back room. "It didn't sound like the spray kills. It just knocks the vampires out. Even you didn't think Alice was dead."

"But those guys are taking Hunter and Alice somewhere," said Mercy. "What if the people paying the bounty kill Hunter and Alice?"

"If we'd rushed out there, we'd only have gotten ourselves killed. The people paying a bounty for vampires apparently want them alive. That gives us time. There's nothing we can do to stop them now." I put my hands on Mercy's shoulders. "You said you have a friend who can help us understand the mist?"

Mercy nodded. "His name's Desmond Drake. He's not exactly a friend, but he can help."

"Desmond Drake?" I asked, my eyebrows rising. "You mean the English billionaire? You know him?"

"Of course I know him," said Mercy with a sigh. "I thought all vampires in New Mexico did." She moved back into the office then pulled the chair out from behind the desk and dropped into it.

I sat down on the floor next to Mercy and laid my head in her lap. "Well, the exterminators expect us to be gone in the morning. I suspect we shouldn't disappoint them. We'll take the tank and see what Mr. Drake can make of the contents. I have a car parked at the university. We'll be able to use that to get across the state."

Mercy smiled wistfully and stroked my hair. "I hope you're right. I hope we'll be able to find Hunter and Alice."

"We will," I said, nuzzling Mercy's thigh, trying to be as comforting with my words as she comforted me by stroking my hair. I wondered just how much I could trust Mercy. Though she frightened me, I'd have been more afraid to be alone at that moment. I wasn't sure that I wanted to be part of this strange family. By the same token, I would have hated to see Hunter and Alice gone forever.

Slowly, I stood and offered my hand to Mercy. Taking my hand, she stood and we embraced, holding each other for a time. At last, she pulled back and looked up into my face with fire in her eyes. "Let's go get our friends back."

Chapter Sixteen

Mercedes Rodriguez and Daniel McKee travel to Northern New Mexico. Present Day.

A creature hovered over a bed of pine needles against a backdrop of heavily scented forest. The confluence of the Rio Grande and the Rio Chama was nearby. Night fell. The creature resembled an eight-foot tall beaver that stood upright, wearing brown monk's robes. Its paws were peaked, as if in prayer. Native Americans knew the creature as one of the great spirits and called him Beaver Man. Throughout the world, Beaver Man and the other great spirits were known by various names: angels, demons, gods, manitou and kachinas. Beaver Man liked the word manitou. Their origin was so steeped in history that the manitou had their own myths to explain their existence – some similar to the mythology of humans, others, quite different. Beaver Man and the other manitou were elemental creatures – more creatures of the cosmos than of the Earth itself.

Beaver Man opened a portal and transported himself from the forest to the World Apart. Many humans sensed the World Apart in their dreams. Native American medicine people sometimes referred to the World Apart as the Place of Power: the place where spirit quests began. The World Apart was, in fact, a universe parallel to the one inhabited by humans. Physical laws behaved differently in the World Apart, allowing Beaver Man to perform, for lack of a better term, magic. Beaver Man could come and go as he pleased and the World Apart served as a conduit to the World of Origins. To Beaver Man, it was as natural to move between the worlds as it was for a human to cross from one room to another.

Beaver Man sensed a dreaming human. He knew of few creatures as wonderful as humans. The dream stopped as suddenly as a candle flame being snuffed out. A creature that controlled a limited amount of elemental magic was responsible. The creature had attacked the human, ending the dream prematurely. Beaver Man had encountered creatures like this before. Humans called the creatures vampires. They were left over from an experiment that had gone wrong. Anra Mainyu and Iktome were responsible for unleashing the vampires on humanity.

The vampire was in the human city called Santa Fe, not too far from the mountains Beaver Man enjoyed on Earth. He stretched out his thoughts and could sense that the vampire was traveling Northward. He would go back to Earth and wait for the creature. A shaman from the East had petitioned Beaver Man for help finding vampires. Though the shaman had no love of vampire-kind, he did not want these vampires killed.

"An evil is brewing," the shaman had explained. "An evil far greater than vampires, and I fear we need them to purge this evil from the world." Reluctantly, Beaver Man agreed to help.

✟✟✟

Mercedes Rodriguez awoke in darkness to a pungent, soapy smell and the feel of stiff sheets that reminded her instantly that she was in a motel room. Her mouth was dry and she longed for the warm rush of blood that would fill her and give her energy. The rest of her languorous body longed for a male vampire's touch and caress. Only a fellow vampire could endure her desire long enough that she might be fulfilled. She reached out to the other side of the double bed. "Damn," she whispered. Daniel had already slipped away.

The door opened and the fading day's muted light filled the room. Daniel entered, holding a steaming cup of coffee. Mercy pulled the stiff sheets around her body and sighed. He had long hair worn in dreadlocks and an anachronistic, handlebar mustache. Daniel's shoulders stooped a bit from long work hunched over scientific equipment. He had a penchant for button-down shirts and loose-fitting, comfortable pants. He seemed a man out of time and something about his quest for knowledge, his love of the stars, and the fact that he embraced the night even before he had become a vampire attracted her.

"How can you stand to drink that awful stuff?" grumbled Mercy, eyeing the Styrofoam cup in Daniel's hand.

Daniel grinned wistfully and sipped the coffee. "How can you live without it?"

She lowered the sheet and held out her hand. Daniel took another drink, then sat on the bed. "Blood is life. It's the only life we need." Her arm encircled Daniel and she pulled herself close, nuzzling his neck.

Daniel set the coffee on the nightstand. "Is that really true?"

"Perhaps. Learn by example, young one." In one lithe, continuous motion, she shoved the one-time astronomer onto his back and pulled his pants down around his ankles, effectively binding his legs. Her claw-like fingernails traced lines along the insides of his thighs, drawing blood. Leisurely, she licked the blood and grinned slyly when he reacted as she expected.

Mercedes straddled Daniel, embracing him fully. She sighed as he thrust into her. "Mercy!" It was unclear whether he cried her name or asked for quarter. She kissed him deeply, then lay down beside him. After a few moments she sighed. "I'm getting hungry."

"Me too." He stroked her long, black hair for several minutes, then sat up and noisily sipped his coffee.

Mercy looked at him quizzically then shook her head. "I'm going to take a shower, then we'd better hunt and get on the road. Drake's ranch is near Chama. It's only about three hours away, but we don't want to get there too close to morning. I hate these short summer nights."

Daniel looked at the clock on the nightstand and nodded.

After a quick shower, Mercy pulled on underwear and Daniel

stepped into the bathroom to shave. "You know, it's like some evil trickster made the vampires," he moaned. "We're impervious to harm and virtually immortal, yet we still grow whiskers that need shaving."

"Speak for yourself," called Mercy as she pulled jeans over legs that only had a few fine, silky hairs that did not require depilation.

Settling in front of the mirror, Mercy carefully redrew "tattoos" on her smooth skin. Starting in the mid-twentieth century, she maintained the image of a chola – a tough girl. Fashions change, she thought as she carefully inked a pattern on her forearm. On a vampire, tattoos are very permanent. The tattoos a chola would have in 1990 would be very conspicuous by the time 2090 rolled around.

Mercedes Rodriguez had been seventeen when the Spanish conquistador, Rudolfo de Córdoba, had come to her in the night and made her a vampire. Guilt hammered when she remembered her human family, the sturdy Juan and their beautiful children. They had been her first victims during the initial ravenous, uncontrollable hunger that followed her birth to darkness. The guilt had muted with time, but still persisted.

Four centuries later, Mercy had planned to restart a family, but this time a family of vampires. Two of the vampires in Mercy's family of four were missing. She paused in drawing her tattoos and watched Daniel hastily packing bags, impatient to get on the road.

Daniel and Mercy made an odd couple. People stared at the apparently middle-aged man traveling with the teenaged chola. At four in the morning, they had checked into the motel on the outskirts of Santa Fe, New Mexico. Daniel recoiled under the critical gaze of the sleepy desk clerk. Mercy grinned wickedly. Let the old guy stare, she thought at the time, amused that she looked younger than her charge but was, in fact, over three centuries older than him.

Dressed and tattooed at last, Mercy stood up from the motel room's vanity and eyed Daniel, her hand on her hip. "Time for dinner," she said.

"Finally! I was wondering how long it was going to take you to finish."

Mercy threw back her head and laughed. "Men always seem to say that."

Daniel sighed and shook his head. He crumpled the Styrofoam coffee cup and tossed it into the trashcan. He grabbed his own suitcase, leaving Mercy's behind. She fought to suppress continued laughter as she grabbed her suitcase and followed.

The two vampires placed their suitcases into the trunk of Daniel's red and white 1975 Buick Century. Mercy started giggling again as she thought about how well the car fit the astronomer-vampire's persona.

Checking out of the motel, the young desk clerk scrutinized Mercy and Daniel. The blond woman was pretty in a country-girl kind of way. Her name tag read, "Billie Jean." Mercy guessed that Billy Jean was in her mid-twenties. Her too-dark scrutiny ended Mercy's mirth. Reaching out with her mind, Mercy found herself looking into Billie Jean's memories and saw the leering gaze of an older man. She felt his rough touch and wanted to scream. Billie Jean had been abused as a child. Though Mercy had married young by contemporary standards, she had been considered an adult when Juan had come to her in 1596. Mercy frowned and excused herself, leaving Daniel to pay the bill.

Mercy hugged herself and waited by the car. Finally, Daniel arrived. "Bill's paid," he said too cheerfully for her mood.

Silently, Mercy led Daniel down Cerrillos Road to a neighboring motel. The building was a tacky faux adobe box with turquoise doors. It would be an unusual building in the heart of Santa Fe, but it resembled many of its neighbors on the outskirts. They walked up concrete and metal steps to the second floor. Mercy searched the rooms with her mind. Daniel relied more on senses of smell and hearing. After a short search, the two vampires found themselves in front of a turquoise door. Mercy handed Daniel a hairpin. Using strong, but sensitive fingers, he skillfully picked the lock.

Inside the motel room were a woman and a man, both asleep. The vampires surveyed the room. Hastily tossed-aside clothing littered the floor and tousled blankets barely covered the bed's occupants. The air in the room was heavy with the sweet-sour smell of sweat. The vampires surmised that the couple in the bed had made passionate love to each other then fell into a deep sleep.

With a quick look over his shoulder, Daniel eased the door shut. The woman's eyes darted from side to side behind her eyelids. She was in REM sleep, dreaming. The man breathed softly – not so deeply asleep as the woman. With a sharp motion, Mercy pointed to the man.

"I don't like men," Daniel complained in a harsh whisper.

"You'll do as I say," hissed Mercy.

The man stirred and his eyes popped open, as he searched the dark room.

"Take him now," ordered Mercy. Without further comment, she leapt to the side of the bed and cradled the woman's head. The woman's eyes still searched behind closed lids. Mercedes whispered gently to her, keeping her in the dream. The man was transfixed by Mercy's gentle whispers. He didn't seem to grasp the reality of what was happening to his lover. Sure that the woman was too lost in her dream world to waken, Mercy lovingly sank her fangs into the woman's neck and began drinking the life-giving blood.

Daniel remained transfixed by the scene of Mercy drinking the woman's blood. He waited too long and the man screamed, as he realized what Mercy did to his lover. Shaken from his reverie, Daniel pounced. Without careful forethought, Daniel's first strike at the man's jugular missed. The man screamed even louder, thrashing at his attacker. Mercy almost wished Daniel would break the man's neck and be done with it, but drinking blood from a corpse was like sucking thick pudding through a straw. It could be done, but without the victim's heart pumping, it took a real effort to suck out the congealing blood. Daniel pinned the man's arms and struck again. At last, he succeeded and settled in to drink. The man's screaming ceased at last.

Mercy finished and rested her elbows on the woman's hips, watching Daniel. At last, he looked up. "You certainly took your sweet time about that," she said dangerously. "Suppose the cops are outside waiting for us? I'd rather not drive full speed to Drake's ranch."

Daniel sighed. "It's early. I doubt anyone even heard. Besides, motel walls are deliberately built thick. These two were counting on it." Daniel pointed to the severely rumpled blankets as evidence that the lovers' rendezvous had been an athletic one. "What can I say? Men's aftershave and blood don't mix well."

Mercy rolled her eyes and stood, putting her hands on her hips. "You know what your problem is? You're not tough enough. I don't care whether you like boys or girls, you gotta learn to strike fast when the time comes."

Daniel stood and put his hand on her shoulder, but she batted it away. "What's the matter?" he asked, frowning.

Images of Billie Jean the desk clerk and the gray-haired "uncle" kept flashing in Mercy's mind. She kept hearing the girl's screams of "No" and seeing the old man's leering grin. Mercy found it too easy to cast herself in the role of the leering old man. "I don't really want to talk about it."

Daniel sighed and opened the door a crack. As he'd surmised, no one waited to arrest them. Breathing in the scents that wafted in on the breeze, Mercy wanted to transform into her jaguar body and run as far and as fast as she could. No matter how far or how fast she ran, she couldn't escape her dark mood and they had farther to travel than she could run as a jaguar or Daniel could fly as a bat. She sighed and led the way back to the car.

✠✠✠

Mercy remained silent as Daniel drove down the highway. Several times, Daniel thought about turning on the radio, but he was too transfixed by the road and what he saw to take action. Driving in Northern New Mexico at night, there was so little traffic on the road that he could allow his attention to wander. The white lines of the highway were like lasers shooting into the car. The headlights faintly illuminated the scrub brush on the road's side. Scent of mesquite hovered lightly on the air. Occasionally, his eyes would glimpse a coyote or even an antelope just outside the headlights' range. Interesting as the wildlife was, what really kept Daniel's attention was the sky. His vampire vision could just make out the rainbow colors of Lyra's Ring Nebula – the leftovers of a star that had died of old age and shed its outer atmosphere. His thoughts turned melancholy as he wondered what it would be like to die a natural death.

Daniel caught a glimpse of something by the side of the road. His first impression was that he had seen an eight-foot tall beaver wearing a monk's robe. "What the hell was that?"

"What the hell was what?" grumbled Mercy. She sat slumped in the seat, her arms folded across her stomach, brooding.

"That beaver thing by the side of the road."

Mercy sat bolt upright. "Beaver thing?"

"Yeah, behind us." Daniel looked into the rear-view mirror. "I hate to say this, but I think it's following."

Mercy turned and looked out the rear window. Facing forward again she slumped low in the seat. "Shit! Step on it. Get out of here!"

Daniel turned his head and saw the beaver-like creature floating beside the road, easily pacing the car. With quick glances forward to make sure he wasn't about to run off the road, he examined the creature that pursued them. It really was just like his first impression of an eight-foot beaver in a hooded robe. Daniel eased the accelerator to the floorboard. "I've never seen anything like that. What is it?"

"You don't wanna know. The only way we're gonna live is if we get away from it."

Daniel played his tongue over a fang, curiosity getting the better of him. He slammed on the brakes and the car spun. Mercy's body, in turn, slammed into Daniel's. The Buick came to a stop facing the wrong way down the road.

The beaver-like creature hovered a few inches from the asphalt. The car's headlights made the creature stand out in stark relief against the black night. Its red eyes glowed, focused more above and beyond the car than on the passengers. Its buckteeth shone brightly. Whiskers and pelt glistened. The brown robe lay in rolls of carefully woven fibers framed by shadowed folds. Its paws were peaked, as if in prayer.

"What's this beaver want from us?" Daniel narrowed his gaze.

"Start the car and drive away from here." Mercy's voice quavered slightly.

He turned and blinked at her. "I've never seen a creature like this and you just want me to up and drive away?"

"Yes. You don't know how powerful it is. Neither do I ... not really, anyway."

"So ... why's it just standing there?"

"I don't know and I don't wanna know. Just start the car and let's get out of here."

Daniel pursed his lips and his hand hovered over the car keys for a moment. Instead of turning the keys, he reached out, pushed the door open and stepped from the car. Mercy slapped her forehead. The beaver creature continued to stare straight over the car. One of its paws crumpled from the prayerful peak and swept grandly to the side in a swoosh of fabric.

Chapter Seventeen

Mercedes Rodriguez and Daniel McKee journey into the World Apart. Present Day.

Daniel blinked as sunlight illuminated the landscape all around him at once. Still standing, now on pink sand instead of pavement, he dropped and rolled instinctively into a fetal position, protecting himself from the onslaught of the light.

After a minute, he realized that his skin was not scorching. Slowly, he eased himself into a sitting position. He looked around to see Mercy sitting in the sand, hugging her knees to herself. "Now you've done it." She shook her head then dropped backwards onto the sand.

Daniel stood and looked around, evaluating the landscape. Sand dunes extended as far as he could see in one direction, he wasn't sure whether it was east or west. Was it even morning or afternoon? He could not tell. A low mesa stood nearby in the opposite direction. The beaver-like creature was just visible, hovering over rocks near the mesa. High in the sky hung a bloated, blood-red sun. The astronomer gasped, realizing it could only mean he was no longer on Earth.

Though not dissimilar to the landscape through which they had been driving, there were differences. No vegetation dotted the landscape at all. The sand was strangely uniform in color. No scent of mesquite tickled the air. In fact, the only scents that Daniel could detect were some vaguely animal smells: beaver, and hints of bat and cat. The source of beaver was apparent. The bat and cat smells could be from the vampires themselves. If anything, the most unusual thing was the lack of any other identifiable scent at all. Mercy's eyes were closed and her nose twitched.

"Where are we?" asked Daniel. "This desert seems more dreamlike than real."

"That's 'cause you've probably dreamed of this place at some time or another," said Mercy, sitting up, sand clinging to her bare shoulders. "There're all kinds of names for this place. Shamans call it 'the Place of Power.' I've heard Drake refer to a place called 'the World Outside' or 'the World Apart.'"

Daniel sat down in the sand and shot a glance over his shoulder at the beaver-like creature. "Are we dreaming, then?"

Mercy took a deep breath, then let it out slowly. "No. This is a physical place. What do they call it in those science fiction movies? A parallel dimension?"

Daniel rubbed his chin, then looked at the red sun and considered the lack of smells. A century of precise, practiced scientific language came to his mind. "Dimension isn't exactly right. It would be more like a different universe, perhaps a bubble in our own universe. How did we get here?"

"That's easy." Mercy looked over her shoulder at the beaver creature. "He brought us here."

Daniel followed her gaze. "I mean, precisely. How did he do it?"

"Magic. He's an elemental, after all."

The astronomer massaged the bridge of his nose. "Why did he bring us here?"

"You probably threatened it by getting out of the car." She closed her eyes and thought how best to explain. "You see, vampires and elementals aren't all that different. Each of us has some elemental magic within us. That's why you can turn into a bat and I can turn into a jaguar. The thing is, elementals like Beaver Man back there are much more powerful."

"So, we're related to that beaver thing somehow?"

Before Mercy could answer, a wind-like howling cut through

the near-perfect silence. The hairs on Daniel's neck stood up when he realized that the air was absolutely still. Mercy knelt forward, her head inclined cat-like, listening. Her nose searched for scents as she continued her explanation. "Drake told me a few of the legends shortly after we met. In ancient times, the elemental creatures got along with each other and with people. They became teachers and protectors."

"Kind of like gods?"

"You got it. Some of the elementals became very protective of their people and adopted certain territories."

Daniel looked back toward the mesa. "It's protecting its land from us."

"More like its people," corrected Mercy. "A lot of Indian tribes have elemental protectors."

Daniel nodded, understanding dawning. He'd spent much of his professional life working on or near Native American reservations. "They would call it a kachina or a manitou depending on the tribe. I take it we were brought here to die."

Mercy pursed her lips and nodded.

"Well, I'm not just going to sit around and wait to see what happens. We need to find a way home." Daniel stood and brushed off his pants. He spread his arms and started running further into the dune field. After running nearly fifty yards, he realized he was still running along the ground and not flying. He stopped and turned back to Mercy. "Something's wrong."

Mercy stood, closed her eyes, and concentrated. "It's gone," she said. "My jaguar won't come even when I try to summon it."

"The beaver thing is keeping us from changing."

"Maybe…"

The wind-like howling sounded again, dropping in pitch to a moan. As Daniel walked back toward Mercy, the sand undulated slightly, as though a wave had passed through it. He struggled to balance himself and goose flesh appeared on his arms.

"Something's coming," said Daniel. "We've gotta get out of here."

The moaning sounded again, louder. Mercy looked toward the

mesa. A fog bank swirled into existence near the summit. An arc of blue lightning flashed and Beaver Man turned, drifting toward the mesa. "What's happening?" asked Mercy, pointing.

"I'm not really sure, but I think it's worth a look. It's better than standing around here."

"What about the beaver?"

"We'll deal with him if we need to but something tells me we'd be safer on the rocks than out here in the dunes." Daniel turned his head, trying to determine where the moaning originated. As best as he could tell, it came from the mesa itself. The ground rolled again and Daniel toppled off his feet. The sand surged like water around the astronomer's body, then began to spiral. Fighting the sand-currents, he reached Mercy just as the sand collapsed into a whirlpool right where he'd been.

The moaning rose in pitch, climbing to a wail. "Come on, let's get to the rocks," said Daniel, taking Mercy's hand. He tried to take a step, but found that sand had drifted over his feet and he couldn't move them. Mercy tried to lift her feet with no more success. Sweat beaded on Daniel's forehead and he looked helplessly at Mercy. "What do we do now?"

Mercy shook her head then gritted her teeth. "The Beaver Man is controlling this place with his mind. We're going to have to use our minds to get out of here."

"But how?" The astronomer looked at the sand-whirlpool growing in their direction, not wanting to accept that it was real. "There's got to be a solution to this puzzle."

"You're over-thinking. This is elemental magic. Concentrate on elemental solutions. Think about escape, release and that sort of thing. When we make love, do you analyze me like a gynecologist or do you just follow your desire?"

Daniel blinked several times, then laughed in spite of himself. "Since when do four hundred-year old vampires visit gynecologists?"

"Just answer the fucking question, you moron! I know you're capable of real passion. Use it now!"

The whirlpool slowed then spiraled into a wave that crashed into the vampires, burying them up to their knees.

Daniel stopped laughing, and fought to clear his mind. Fingers of sand emerged and began snaking their way up the vampires' thighs.

"Shit," growled Mercy, as she struggled to free herself. Within seconds, the fingers of sand snaked their way inside her halter-top like an unwelcome lover. The fingers of sand were only as far as Daniel's hips. Mercy's eyes widened. "We need to be a little of each other. I need to be as calm as you are while thinking about escape and release. You're mostly calm, but need to feel more." Mercy took several deep breaths and appeared to relax.

Daniel reached out with his mind. He could tell Mercy sought the jaguar. It was not within her, but neither was it far away. She called to the cat with her mind. *Come, my dear, for Mercy's sake. You are the embodiment of the predator. You are my other half.*

A sleek, spotted, cat topped a distant sand dune. It glanced around, searching. Finally, the cat saw the vampires and ran down the dune toward them.

Mercy was buried in sand to her stomach and the fingers had crawled over her breasts, toward her neck. Though Daniel's analytical mind kept the sand from working as quickly as it did on Mercy, it still embraced him like an abrasive, deadly lover.

The jaguar sidled up to Mercy and rubbed its head against hers. She reached out, rubbing its soft pelt. She grew stronger with each stroke. The jaguar purred in response. Mercy stopped sinking. She reached out and hugged the cat around its middle. Gathering resolve, the jaguar moved forward, pulling Mercy from the sand's grasp. She reached out to Daniel, who took her hand. The jaguar and Mercy worked as a team and pulled Daniel free.

"Together, my jaguar and I are a whole. We're stronger than the magic of this place," explained Mercy.

"How is that possible?"

Mercy brushed sand from her jeans. "When you become a bat, you reach inside yourself, don't you? The bat is part of you."

"You're talking metaphysics."

"Okay, here's some practicality. How do you suppose a big

man like you turns into a little bat? Isn't there something called conservation of mass?"

"We need to get away from this sand," said Daniel, changing the subject, "before it gathers strength for another attack."

Mercy nodded. She looked at the jaguar, which in turn looked at the mesa. The fog descended, shrouding the mesa. The jaguar took a few tentative steps toward the rocks, then picked up the pace when it saw that the vampires followed.

"So, how do you turn into a bat?" Mercy prompted as they walked.

"I hadn't really thought about it. I just do it."

"Has it ever occurred to you that you and your bat are really not one and the same, but two separate creatures much like a witch and her familiar?"

"Then where do I go when I become a bat? And, where's the bat when I'm in human form?"

"You're the puzzle boy. You figure it out."

Daniel studied the surrounding landscape: the sand, the mesa, the fog alive with electricity, and the red sun. "I suppose if this place exists, our animal familiars," he made a face at the word, "could exist in a universe parallel to ours until needed, then somehow, we swap places."

"Sounds like a hypothesis to me."

"Perhaps, or just a wild-ass guess. How did you know to look for the jaguar in the first place? How did you know she would be here?"

"It occurred to me that Indians go on spirit quests in this place. We needed to find our spirit animals." She let the astronomer chew on that for a moment. "Spirit animals are guides, like familiars. They help those who go on quests find that which they seek. It occurred to me that our familiars could help us navigate our way through this world."

"Does your jaguar know the way out?" asked Daniel, stopping in his tracks.

Mercy knelt beside the majestic cat and looked into its yellow eyes while stroking it behind the ears. She looked up. "I don't think she knows. We really need your bat. It can fly and survey the area. Is it here?"

"I don't know."

"Clear your mind, don't try to over-think. Do you feel it here?"

Daniel closed his eyes and forced himself to relax. "I think the bat is here," he said at last, then pointed toward the mesa. "In that direction. I wonder if that's why I felt the need to go there in the first place." Just then the wind-like moaning sounded again.

"I don't like that wailing." A tear escaped the corner of Mercy's eye then she sniffed and angrily slapped the tear away.

"We're dead if we stay here, and it seems that your jaguar wants to go that way too. Let's try it and see what happens."

Mercy nodded, making a sound that was halfway between a sob and a sigh. The jaguar led the way to the mesa. Once again, the sand tried to attack, taking the form of sandstone hands that emerged from the ground like vampires rising from a new grave. With the jaguar in the lead, the sand never quite got a grip on a foot or an ankle. The ground grew rockier and the wailing grew louder and more mournful.

Clambering through rocks at the base of the mesa, Daniel pointed to something in the sky. "It's me," he cried. "That's what I look like as a bat." Mercy and the jaguar strained to see where Daniel pointed. The jaguar nudged Mercy's arm and she turned to face the fluttering, spiraling little animal.

The bat spiraled downward, buzzing Daniel's ears. He watched it flutter away, then return. "I think he's telling us to follow."

"Think, or feel?" asked Mercy, sounding more confident in spite of the wailing.

"I feel like it's the right way to go."

Mercy nodded. "All right then. Let's go." With that, they continued picking their way through the rocks. The fog-like mist grew thicker as they climbed. The bat flew ahead and disappeared into the fog, but always circled back to show them the way. Daniel looked around, trying to see the beaver creature, but it stayed out of sight.

The rocks smoothed out and ultimately Mercy and Daniel found themselves atop a large, flat rock that faced a path that disappeared into the fog. A tall, thin man in a white suit with a broad-brimmed white hat planted on his head emerged like a specter from the fog ahead of them. A salt-and-pepper goatee framed his mouth. Lightning arced through the clouds just overhead, illuminating the man in shades of blue. Though he didn't appear to be armed, both of the vampires kept their distance.

"So, you've finally found me," said the man, stepping forward. Though the man held a cane, he didn't put any weight on it.

"Found you?" asked Daniel. "I didn't know we were looking for you."

Beaver Man drifted out of the fog and took a position at the man's side. The creature's red, unblinking eyes stared into the distance beyond Mercy and Daniel.

"We weren't looking for him," sneered Mercy. "We were herded, like sheep to the slaughter."

"I have no more power here than you do," said the man in white. "This is neutral ground for us, a place where we can speak without being a threat to one another."

"So, why did you bring us here? What is this place?" demanded Mercy, her hands on her hips.

"First off, I did not bring you here, he did." The old man pointed his cane at the Beaver Man. "Secondly, you were not brought here so that I could answer impertinent questions. You were brought here so that I could impart a warning."

"You could have written a letter," said Daniel. "There was no need to bring us to a place where we'd nearly die."

"This place is tied to your origin," said the old man. "It is a place of power and many of your abilities as vampires are rooted here. There are humans who would duplicate the powers of the vampire. You had to know that there are deeper and more potent magics at stake than your strength and your enhanced senses. Your ability to transform into beasts, hear thoughts and still other powers, are rooted in this place. An evil that controlled the full power of the World Apart could rule the Earth. Even a good human given full control over this place would have a difficult time remaining good."

Daniel's eyes went wide. "I don't believe in magic."

"Be that as it may," said the old man, pointing his cane at Daniel. "You believe in technology, no doubt. Arthur C. Clarke probably said it best when he declared that any sufficiently advanced technology is indistinguishable from magic."

"All right, suppose we buy this." Mercy stepped toward the old man. "Are you trying to tell us there are humans tampering with this place, trying to gain the same powers as vampires."

The old man nodded.

"Who are they?"

"Humans who already have a great deal of power," said the old man, cryptically. "You are on the right path, seeking Drake. He is one of the only vampires with sufficient power to combat this threat. Tell him the answers may be found where the journey of death begins."

"Why don't you tell him yourself? It sounds like you know him," challenged Mercy.

"Because it would be dangerous, should we meet. The Holy Order of Santorini has been working to contain Drake and his Scarlet Knights for centuries, ever since we discovered he was meddling in human affairs. You see, I am a vampire hunter." The old man reached into his jacket and retrieved a business card. With a flip of the wrist, he flung it to Daniel and Mercy. Daniel picked it up and put it in his shirt pocket. The old man turned, as though to leave.

"If you're a vampire hunter," called Daniel. "Did your people capture our friends, Hunter and Alice?"

The old man stopped, but did not turn around. "Your friends are in great danger. The exterminator and his wife work for the enemy, not for my order. That same exterminator stole a valuable artifact from us."

"Stones that glow when a vampire is near?" asked Mercy.

"The same. Should they be returned to our order, we would be most grateful." The old man continued down the path. Before the fog swallowed him, a cross-like portal materialized in his path and he stepped through. Once through, the portal vanished in a flash of blue light.

The Beaver Man's paws swept out in an arc and a second portal appeared on the path, directly in front of Daniel and Mercy. Daniel gulped and shrank back from the cross-like form. The jaguar nudged Mercy's hand. "Are you crazy?" she asked her cat-self. "You want me to get closer?"

Daniel watched as his bat-self drifted lazily around the top of the cross, not seeming to fear it at all. Scared to move, but prompted by the fearlessness of his bat, Daniel eased toward the glowing cross. Electricity arced along its beams. Mercy reached for Daniel's trembling hand and the two stood transfixed by the sight. Mercy's jaguar-self nudged her free hand. The bat circled lower, even closer to the spectral cross.

"I've felt what crosses can do to vampires," said Daniel softly.

Mercy nodded. "I know, but the animals seem to want us to go through."

Mercy and Daniel squeezed each other's hands and took several purposeful steps toward the glowing cross. A rift appeared. Through it, Mercy and Daniel could see the desert with the Buick parked where they had left it. Daniel took a breath and looked into Mercy's deep brown-black eyes. She nodded and squeezed his hand once more. Together they stepped through the rift followed by the jaguar and the bat.

✝✝✝

Back in the New Mexico desert, the sky was brightening ever so slightly, turning from full dark to the slate gray of early twilight. Daniel still grasped Mercy's chilled hand. He reached out and touched the Buick's reassuringly solid metal. He looked around for the jaguar and the bat, but they had vanished. He realized they must have returned to the place where they normally live. "So much for getting to Drake's ranch tonight. We'll be lucky if we make it to Española before daybreak," he said, trying to sound confident.

Mercy pointed. Beaver Man hovered by the car. Its paws were by its sides. Slowly, the beaver-like elemental folded its paws and nodded. It turned away and drifted over the highway back toward Santa Fe.

Mercy released Daniel's hand and opened the car door. She sat down on the chill leather seat and shivered. Daniel opened the driver's side door and started the car. He turned it around and drove along the highway.

"What does it mean? Powerful people are trying to harness the magic of the vampire," said Daniel after about thirty minutes. The sky brightened more with just a hint of pink on the horizon. Fortunately, the lights of Española, New Mexico twinkled like fairy dust strewn carelessly on the ground before them.

"I don't want to think about it right now. We'll take the message to Drake and figure it out together tomorrow." She looked out the window at the passing scenery. "In a way, I'm glad I'm a vampire, I don't think I could sleep, otherwise, after what happened today."

Daniel nodded then drove in silence for a little while longer. "Something was bothering you earlier tonight. What was it?"

Mercy swallowed. "It was something I saw in the mind of Billie Jean, the desk clerk." She shook her head. "It all seems so distant." She chewed her lower lip. "It's one thing to be a predator that takes life. It's another to be a predator that feeds on the spirit."

"Do kachinas feed on spirit?" he asked, not certain how the memory of Billie Jean related to her thoughts about predators. He slowed the car as they passed the Española city-limits sign and began scanning for a motel.

"Not exactly," she mumbled. She looked at Daniel, her eyes haunted. "The vampire hunter was right about one thing, though. We're in great danger. The kachinas wouldn't be involved if this was something small."

Daniel turned the car into a motel parking lot. Shutting off the engine, he looked at her with worry transparent on his face. "You look pale tonight, even for a vampire."

"I'm scared," she said, all the mock bravado gone. For the first time, Daniel saw her as the seventeen-year-old girl she had been when she became a vampire. "Hold me this morning. Die, with me in your arms. I'll be strong for you tomorrow."

Part IV

New Scarlet Order

"We vampires are not animals, nor are we walking corpses, as is rumored in some lands. We are transcendent beings of mysterious origin."

— Desmond, Lord Draco

Chapter Eighteen

From the notes of Daniel McKee.
Present Day.

We awoke in a motel in the small town of Española, just north of Santa Fe. The night before, Mercy and I quickly checked into the first place we came to since the sun was nearly up. As it turned out, the motel was an uncivilized little hovel. The room's carpet was worn and tattered and the cockroaches were so numerous that they didn't fear the room lights. Even worse, when I went to the lobby, they told me they turned off the coffeepot before noon. They directed me to a nearby Conoco station for coffee. That was fine with me since the car needed gas.

After my disappointing sojourn to the motel lobby, I returned to the room and found Mercy awake, but in a somber mood. "No coffee?" she asked. "Are you feeling okay?"

"I've felt better." I sighed, sitting down on the edge of the bed.

Mercy rubbed her eyes then snuggled up to me. "I almost wish I'd stayed home in Anthony. Here I go trying to move into the city to start a family and look what happens. In just under a week, Hunter and Alice disappear. Then, the two of us are nearly destroyed by a kachina and a vampire hunter. Some master vampire I turned out to be, eh?"

I ran my fingers through Mercy's long, lustrous hair. "We'll get Hunter and Alice back. Remember I was the one stupid enough to get out of the car. You're the one who told me to leave Beaver Man alone. If I'd listened, we'd never even have met the vampire hunter."

Mercy chewed on her lower lip for a moment, then looked into my eyes. "I'm not sure I'm looking forward to tonight." She sighed. "I have a bad headache and I need to eat."

"Where should we start?" I asked. "I hate hunting in small towns. It's too easy to be spotted."

"I know what you mean. Everyone knows everyone else. Even the gang members are somebody's grandchild." Mercy looked at her hands.

"I would have thought you were used to hunting in small towns. You lived in Anthony for so long."

"Yeah, but even though Anthony is small, El Paso, Las Cruces, and Mesilla are fairly close by. When you can turn into a jaguar, it's not that much of a run to any of those cities."

"We could always go back to Santa Fe."

She shook her head. "We'd risk crossing Beaver Man's path again."

"Are you scared?" I asked gently.

"Aren't you? It's not like you get carried into the spirit world every day." Mercy shook her head and stood up from the bed. In spite of my hunger and anxiety, I found myself longing to caress Mercy's supple curves just concealed by a black halter-top.

"Let's get hunting," she said.

"How about a shower first?" I suggested playfully.

"What! You don't like the way I smell?" She threw her head defiantly to the side and folded her arms. Then she shot a glance over her shoulder. "Besides, have you seen that bathroom? We should stay out, for Mercy's sake."

Although disappointed, I agreed that we should get moving. As we checked out, I asked whether there was anything to see in town. The clerk shook his head and shrugged. "Not much to see here, unless you're into low-riders."

Mercy took the cue, perking up at the word. "Low-riders. Where are they?" She was tired and her accent sounded more Old World Castillian than New World chola. Either the desk clerk didn't notice or didn't care. He gave us directions to one of the local bars, where we'd find some of the "Chevys" gathering in the parking lot.

We paid our bill then went to the Conoco station for gas and a cup of coffee. From there, we made our way to the bar and parked about a block away.

Chevys, Fords, and even a Toyota, all painted in a fantastic spectrum ranging from bright reds and oranges to greens and purples were parked out front. A cholo in a metallic purple Chevy Mustang – I guessed it was a '69 – exhibited the car's hydraulics to a small crowd of onlookers.

Mercy nodded to me and crept behind the building where we discovered two young men in their twenties and a girl who couldn't have been out of high school. One of the guys offered the girl a half-full bag of marijuana. Before I could ask Mercy about a plan, she leapt from our hiding place and ran toward the threesome. With a shrug, I bounded after her. Mercy slammed one of the guys into the wall. His friend drew a switchblade, but she knocked it from his hand and grabbed him by the crotch.

The girl's face contorted and I realized she was about to scream. If that happened, the cholos and vatos in front of the bar would be on us in a second. Leaping forward, I practically tore the girl's throat out with my teeth. Business-like in the eerie silence that followed the attack, we drank their blood, made sure they were dead, then shoved the spent bodies into a dumpster.

"Did we really have to kill them? If we'd planned the attack, maybe…" My voice drifted off.

Mercy sighed. "I'm sorry, but stealth and care take time we don't have. We need to get back on the road."

I nodded agreement and we returned to the car. As we left town, I retrieved my Styrofoam cup of coffee from the holder, hoping to drive away the taste of the THC-laced blood.

"Damn!" I growled when I tasted the liquid in the cup.

"What?" Mercy's eyes widened with concern.

"The goddamn coffee's cold." I tossed the cup out of the window.

"Litterbug."

I sighed and eased the accelerator toward the floor.

✝✝✝

Leaving Española, we wound our way along Highway 84 toward Chama. Normally, I like to drive with the window down, feeling the wind in my hair and absorbing the delicious desert scents. After meeting Beaver Man though, I felt a need to keep the windows up, as though something out in the dim landscape would leap through the open window and grab me. It seemed ludicrous, a vampire afraid of the night, but I could tell that Mercy was afraid too. She turned on the car radio to break the silence.

In most parts of the country, driving late at night and listening to AM radio, you're almost guaranteed one of two types of programming: country music or talk radio. The fact that we could pick up neither was a sign that we were in Northern New Mexico. My car's old speakers distorted the haunting melodies of R. Carlos Nakai's flute into a shrill keening. The hairs on my arms stood on edge.

"So," said Mercy, interrupting the music. "What does it feel like when you drive?"

I lifted my eyebrows. "What? You mean you don't know?"

"I never learned to drive and never needed to."

"It feels almost the same as when I'm a bat only I can go faster in a car."

"But you're not as maneuverable."

Pursing my lips, I nodded and we fell silent again, letting the Native American flute music fill the empty space. Listening to the music, I realized that Native American myths and legends were full of spirits, ranging the gamut of forms from rabbit to frog to coyote. Considering other cultures, there was a veritable zoo of mythological animals from around the world. Did they all come from the same parallel universe as Beaver Man? What kinds of powers did they control? Were there other creatures like vampires? Perhaps werewolves or other species of vampire existed somewhere.

Mercy hoped Drake could give us answers. I wanted to be able to ask specific questions when we met him.

Just past the old site called Ghost Ranch we turned onto a gravel road. Somehow it seemed appropriate to find a ranch occupied by a centuries-old vampire near Ghost Ranch: a place in the Canyon of the Rio Chama long said to be occupied by spirits of the dead.

Along either side of the gravel road were tall pine trees, obscuring a view of the surrounding terrain. When we passed a break in the trees, I could see rolling hills and grass dotted with wildflowers. Even in the moon's cold, wan light, it was much more colorful and greener than the sere sand and grass of Southern New Mexico and Arizona. "So, what exactly is the deal with this Lord Draco?" I asked as we bumped our way along the gravel road. "Is Draco really his name? He almost sounds like a Hollywood vampire."

"When an Englishman is granted peerage, he gets to choose the name that goes with his title. Draco's full name and title these days is Desmond Drake, Lord Draco of Angelsey, Knight Commander of the Scarlet Order. He took the Draco part to amuse himself. When he was human, he was a British peer, a Dragon serving King Ambrosius."

"Who's King Ambrosius?"

"Ambrosius was King of the Britons before King Arthur. This was all around the year 480 A.D."

I whistled, hardly able to comprehend a being over 1500 years old. "I thought you were going to tell me that he was the real Dracula or something."

Mercy's answer surprised me. "He's about as close as you're going to come. The way he tells it, he was minding his own business on a piece of real estate in the Carpathians when the Ottoman Turks invaded. He fought with Vlad the Impaler to drive them out of Wallachia and Moldavia. After that, the Catholic Church hired him to drive the Moors from Spain."

"What is he, some kind of mercenary?"

"He was a mercenary. Now, he pretty much lives in seclusion. Last I knew, he spends about half the year in Wales and half the year here."

"So, how did he get his current peerage?" I turned the wheel, following a bend in the road. The Rio Chama was now to our right.

"I don't know much about that part of his story," said Mercy. "I gather he did some favors for the likes of King Henry VIII."

My mind whirled, thinking about the history that this Lord Draco would have witnessed. "Okay, so we have someone who knew King Arthur and Henry VIII. You say he also knew Vlad the Impaler and I gather from the time period, Queen Isabella of Spain. Don't people get suspicious of a 1500-year-old Englishman who was apparently pivotal to several points in history?"

"He says the English Monarchy knows exactly who and what he is. For other people, he's simply a lord in a very long line. The name Desmond Drake gets passed down from generation to generation."

The roof of a large house came into view over a neat tree line. Once clear of the trees, we drove past an adobe wall into a courtyard surrounded by buildings. Stables and a barn stood near an enormous two-story house. Only the soft glow of the setting moon illuminated the scene. I pulled up behind a Volkswagen Beetle, already parked near the house.

I snorted. "So, can't this Draco afford a better car than a bug?"

"Draco would be parked in the garage behind the house," she cautioned. "That isn't his car."

A small, whitewashed house sat next to the stables. "Servant's quarters?" I asked. "Surely Draco doesn't take care of this place by himself. Maybe the Beetle belongs to the housekeeper."

Mercy pursed her lips. "I don't know." Slowly, she opened the passenger side door and stepped from the car.

I followed suit, habitually locking the door. Even in the city my car was not likely to be stolen, but old habits die hard. Mercy stood next to the car listening. All I could hear was the crunch of my own footsteps on the gravel as I circled around, surveying the area. Mercy held up her hand and I stopped. The Rio Chama flowed nearby, crickets chirped and mosquitoes buzzed. The grass whispered whenever the soft breeze blew through. All seemed peaceful.

Moving almost silently, Mercy approached the ranch house's

front door. She tried the handle, but the door wouldn't budge.

I caught a hint of movement in my peripheral vision. Dismissing it as a squirrel or chipmunk, I turned to Mercy. "Would he really leave the door unlocked?"

"What's he got to fear? Besides, I don't really think he's here. There would be lights on – at least a few."

"Let's check out the grounds and maybe the servant's quarters."

Mercy nodded. We made our way toward the smaller, whitewashed house. When we walked past the stables, I looked in. A well maintained old carriage occupied one stall. A horse knickered in another stall further on. "Someone must be coming by to feed the horses."

Again, I thought I saw movement from the corner of my eye. Just as I was about to comment, the air was knocked from me and I dropped face down in the gravel. Sputtering and coughing, I pushed myself up. Mercy traded blows with a tall, gaunt woman who seemed like she belonged in a gang. She wore leather pants and a red bustier. Her hair bristled, spiked with gel that glistened in the moonlight. I rushed forward just as the woman lifted Mercy by the throat and growled, "What have you done with…"

She didn't complete her sentence. I tackled the woman, sending all three of us sprawling to the ground. The woman kicked and elbowed me, forcing me to let go of her waist. Kicking gravel into my face she turned and lunged for Mercy who was just sitting up. Rising up on my elbow, I saw the woman punch Mercy. She turned and pounced on me, her hand around my neck, her knee in my crotch.

"Where's Drake?" she hissed. Feeling her strength and looking up into her eyes, I realized the woman was a vampire.

"We don't know. We're looking for him ourselves," I managed to sputter.

Mercy appeared behind the woman and reached down to pull her off me. The woman reached back to elbow Mercy and I started to throw a punch.

"Ahem."

All three of us stopped mid-strike and, as one, we turned toward the sound. Standing just a few feet away, a third woman aimed a crossbow at us. Slowly we stood and raised our hands.

Chapter Nineteen

From the notes of Daniel McKee.
Present Day.

This new woman wore a simple white blouse and tan slacks. Her light brown hair was pulled back in a ponytail. Keeping the crossbow pointed at us, the new woman looked at me. "You Drake?"

I shook my head.

"Where is he?"

"That would seem to be the question of the hour," said the spiky-haired woman smugly. "Coming in a close second would be, 'who the hell are all of you?'" The tall, thin vampire took a step toward the woman with the crossbow.

"My name is Jane Heckman," said the woman with the crossbow as she aimed it at the spiky-haired woman, who stopped in her tracks. When she spoke, I noticed Jane Heckman had fangs. We were just one happy gathering of vampires. "I've come looking for Desmond Drake."

"Why?" asked the spiky-haired woman.

"We're looking for Drake too," I offered. "We were hoping he'd be able to help us find some friends."

Jane Heckman's crossbow dipped just a little and her eyes narrowed. "You lost track of some friends? Vampires?"

I nodded.

"Okay," said the spiky-haired woman, putting hands on her

hips. "It sounds like we all have a mystery. I've lost track of a vampire too. Just so happens, his name's Drake."

"You could tell us who you are." Mercy folded her arms across her stomach. "You look like someone I've met before."

"You first, sweetheart," snarled the spiky-haired woman.

"Never mock the virtue of Mercy," said Mercy with a sneer and a wag of the head. "I just so happen to be Mercedes Rodriguez."

The spiky-haired woman took a closer look, then threw her head back and laughed. "I should have known that Southern New Mexico's one and only bloofer lady would come looking for her grandsire some day. Still playing La Llorona down by old El Paso?"

Mercy's eyes narrowed, evaluating the spiky-haired woman carefully. "The hair gel's a new look for you, isn't it? We should be honored to be in the presence of the one and only French Gringa. Still whoring for a living?"

Gritting my teeth, I stepped between Mercy and the spiky-haired 'French Gringa.' "I'm Daniel," I said, keenly aware of the two women glaring through me at each other.

"Pleased to meet you, Daniel," said the tall, spiky-haired woman icily. "I'm Marcella DuBois – an old friend of Desmond's. I'll thank you never to call me the 'French Gringa.'"

"You used to live in Las Cruces, didn't you?" I asked, remembering a display of sepia colored photographs from the University Library that showed the history of downtown Las Cruces's old Mesquite Street district.

"A lifetime ago," Marcella said softly.

Jane allowed her grip on the crossbow to relax. "Okay, so we're all here to find this Drake. Where do we start?"

Mercy sauntered over to Marcella and cocked her head. "First, I want to know why you attacked us."

Marcella sighed. "I got here yesterday and searched both of the houses and the grounds. I can sense Drake's presence, but I can't find him." Marcella turned and walked toward the line of cars. A third car, presumably Jane's, had pulled in behind my car and the Volkswagen. "When you guys showed up, I thought you might have been responsible for his disappearance." Marcella inclined her head toward Mercy and me. "I could smell Beaver on the two of you."

Jane threw her free hand into the air. "Just because we're vampires doesn't mean we have to be crude."

I laughed lightly, feeling some tension fall away. "She means beaver, the animal. Not beaver, the..." My cheeks burned. "...womanly musk."

It was Jane's turn to blush.

"There's a good reason for the smell," I explained. "We had a run in with a beaver creature last night."

Marcella pursed her lips. "You met up with Old Man Beaver, then." She stopped in front of the Volkswagen and surveyed the landscape. "I've seen him hanging around here. I thought he might be responsible for Drake's disappearance. When I smelled the Beaver on you, I thought you might have some answers."

"We have no more answers than you do, dear Gringa," said Mercy. "The only thing we know is that the beaver had a friend with a message for Drake. Apparently, they couldn't find him either so they gave the message to us."

"What message?" asked Marcella.

"The message is for Drake, not for you."

Marcella turned away, but her neck muscles tensed. She fumbled in her pants pocket, then pulled out a set of keys and opened the VW's front compartment and retrieved an old-fashioned sateen bag. Reaching in, she pulled out a small sphere, like a marble. "Drake missing is one mystery. This nodule is another."

The nodule began to glow as though lit from inside.

"A nanite nodule" whispered Jane, letting her fingers drift toward the marble-like orb. "Where did you get this?" Marcella tensed, resisting the temptation to draw the nodule back toward herself. Jane's fingers brushed the orb. "Oh my," whispered Jane.

Like Jane, I found myself drawn to the nodule. The best way I can describe it, is like a familiar, seductive voice much like when you're a child and your mother calls you with a promise of freshly baked cookies. It wasn't a voice like you could hear, it was more a sensation that ran through every cell in my body. "I've heard a little about nanites," I whispered. "I didn't know anyone actually made them."

"If you knew they existed, it would mean there had been a security breakdown somewhere," said Jane. "Even so, these are like nothing I've worked with. I think we need to study this more."

Mercy gently pulled me back into her arms. "Is there somewhere we can sit down? The sun will rise in just a few hours. We'll need to figure out where to sleep for the night."

Marcella looked over her shoulder at the house. "We can spend the night in there. I know a way inside." Putting the nodule back in its black bag, Marcella pulled the string, and drew the top closed. From the way she held the bag, there seemed to be another nodule inside. She started to place the bag back in the VW's front compartment, then decided to hand it over to Jane. Stepping a little away from us, Marcella folded in on herself and darkened. Parts of her body shrunk more than others. Folds of skin appeared under her arms and she began to flutter. Marcella could transform into a bat like me. She flew upward, towards a gable over the second floor where I could make out an attic ventilator covered with mesh. Taking care not to cut herself, she slipped through a hole in the mesh.

I looked at Mercy. "So, you and Marcella seem to know each other."

"Best little whore in the territory," sniped Mercy. "Or, so they said. There's a rumor she even slept with Billy the Kid."

"Billy the Kid?" asked Jane, wide eyed. "Wasn't there an old movie called *Billy the Kid versus Dracula*."

"There was," said Mercy with a wink. "I guess you could say it was Marcella's life story."

"So, what exactly is a 'bloofer lady?'" I asked.

"Oh, it's a reference to Bram Stoker's novel, *Dracula*," said Jane. "After the Count killed Lucy she became the 'bloofer lady' and starts abducting children."

Mercy shot both of us a dark look. "Some parts of the past are best left alone."

Just then, the door's latch clacked. The door opened and we faced the front hall of Desmond Drake's ranch house. "I couldn't agree more," said Marcella, turning on the light. "Let's leave the past behind. Our job is to figure out these nodules and find our friends." Marcella turned her back and strode into the house. Mercy, Jane, and I followed.

Desmond Drake's ranch house was a veritable mansion. The entry hall alone was enormous. Marcella led us through the house to a small room with a massive wooden table in the center and tapestries covering the walls. Silently, I wondered if any of the tapestries were antiques, or if they were all modern replicas. Searching the room, Marcella located a shallow crystal bowl and set it on the table. She opened the black drawstring bag and placed the two nodules inside to keep them from rolling off the table.

"So, where did you find these?" asked Jane, carefully leaning her crossbow against the wall.

Marcella told us a tale of being captured by vampire-like monsters and then taken to a secret military installation near Roswell. "They implanted one of these nodules into a human."

I looked at Jane. "You seemed to recognize the nodule. You called it a nanite nodule or something like that."

Jane nodded and pursed her lips. "They're top secret. I'm not supposed to tell anyone about them who doesn't need to know and who doesn't have the necessary security clearance."

Mercy snorted. "You're a vampire. What're they gonna do, arrest you and give you the chair?"

Jane smiled a little at that. "I hadn't thought about it that way, but I guess you're right." She closed her eyes for a moment then looked up. "Nanites are basically microminiature robots. The ones I worked with were very simple. When the nodule dissolves, the nanites seek out suitable material and begin replicating themselves until they reach critical mass."

"What happens when they reach 'critical mass?'" I asked.

"There's an explosion," said Jane. "The main application for my nanites is as a weapon against armored vehicles. They weaken the armor then blow a hole in it." Jane reached over and picked up one of the nodules. "These seem much more sophisticated, though, decades or maybe even a century beyond what I thought was possible."

"Why would anyone go to all the work of doing surgery on someone just to blow them up?" Marcella's eyebrows knitted.

"Theoretically, there are many more applications for nanites," explained Jane. "They could be used medically to hunt down and kill diseases. There's even talk of using them to alter cell structures, maybe even cure cancer."

"That makes sense." Marcella nodded. "When I found the nodules, I also found a file folder. I'm afraid I didn't understand much of what was written in it, but there were a lot of reports on 'nano technology,' 'DNA,' and 'cell structures.'"

"Could I see the file?" asked Jane. "Perhaps I could make some sense of the experiments."

"Certainly." Marcella stood and left the table.

"So, if these are just little robots, why do I hear them like they're talking to me?" I asked.

Jane shook her head. "Perhaps they're tuned to humans somehow."

"Maybe it's escaped your notice Miss Jane Scientist, but we're not humans anymore." Mercy leaned forward, injecting herself into the conversation.

"But, we're so similar to humans it hardly seems to make a difference," retorted Jane.

"Tell that to the corpses we've left behind." Mercy folded her arms in defiance.

I tried hard not to think about the girl and young men we left behind in a dumpster earlier that evening. Jane closed her eyes, as though trying to block out her own personal pain. After a moment, she opened her eyes and looked at me. "So, Daniel, what is your chosen line of work? You sound like you have an academic background."

"He's an astronomer," huffed Mercy, answering for me.

I rolled my eyes just as Marcella returned carrying an overflowing file folder and handed it across the table to Jane. She took about half the stack and handed the remaining papers to me. She started going through her own stack.

Biology and robotics are hardly my specialties, but I did my best to understand the papers in front of me. For the most part, the papers reported research into the possibilities of increasing human strength and agility. The papers concluded that it might be possible to alter human cells to bring about those traits. Another paper I looked at talked about improving the senses, particularly hearing and vision. Another was entitled "Shape Changing" and reviewed reports of vampires and their "reported ability to transform into different species of animal." That paper's conclusion was that the ability could not be reproduced and was probably nothing more than folk legend.

Jane shook her head in disbelief as she rifled through the papers. "'Blood as a Fuel Source for Nanites,' 'Increased Life spans of Nanite-Infected Humans,' 'Accelerated Healing in Vampires' – What in the hell were these jokers trying to do?"

"It sounds to me like they were trying to build vampires," I said.

Jane nodded. "I hate to admit it, but I think you're right."

"Why would anyone want to create their own vampires?" Marcella shook her head.

I shrugged. "There's a lot to be said about being a vampire, like the increased strength and vision."

"But there's a lot going against it," said Jane. "Not the least of which is the fact that we are murderers even when we try to avoid it. I suspect each of us has killed, at least once." Silence fell over the table with that observation. Remembering my own vulnerability when Mercy held me on the cross, I was inclined to think that vampires may have a number of unanticipated weaknesses.

"Well, the kachinas seem interested in stopping whoever is behind this," said Mercy, breaking the silence. "Otherwise why would Beaver Man have grabbed Daniel and I?"

Marcella leaned forward. "Not just Beaver Man, at least one other spirit is after these nodules; a giant spider. I'm afraid it could be Iktome, the Spider Man."

"The Spider Man?" asked Mercy, leaning forward on her elbows. "Wasn't he the 'evil trickster' of the elementals?"

"Wait a minute." Jane held her finger up. "Are we talking

Native American legend? If so, I thought the trickster in most tribes' legends was Coyote … and I think I had a run-in with him."

Mercy nodded slowly and chewed on her lip, then answered. "Coyote is a trickster, but he's not generally considered evil, like Iktome. Spider Man is one bad dude."

"Well," said Jane. "There's nothing in these files about who wants to make these artificial vampires. Without that, it's difficult to guess the reason for the kachinas' interest."

"I'd guess the government's behind the experiments," said Marcella. "The base I was taken to certainly looked like a government installation."

"But what branch of the government?" Jane sighed. "And, for what purpose?"

Marcella shook her head. "I have no clue, but the idea of the government creating their own vampires is depressing."

"You know, Chica, they have a pill to cure depression." Mercy sneered.

Marcella stood and put her hands on her hips. "You know, this world isn't going to get any better until the doctors realize that the biggest mental health issue is not that people are depressed. It's that some people are assholes and depress the rest of us!"

I stood up and held out my hands trying to calm the situation. "Jane is right, we need to focus on who is creating these artificial vampires." I looked down into Mercy's eyes. "If we learn that, we might just find out who's behind Hunter and Alice's disappearance. Sniping at each other doesn't help."

Mercy looked down at her hands on the table. Marcella sighed and sat down.

"The kachinas were trying to warn us about the people creating these vampires." I looked at Jane. "Did the coyote you encountered say anything to you?"

Jane shook her head slowly. "No, he didn't say anything at all. He just abducted a fellow vampire. I gather my 'friend' knew Draco, that's why I came here." Jane wrinkled her nose in distaste at the word 'friend' and I wondered about the vampire she sought.

"Perhaps the coyote creature took your friend to warn him," I said.

"Perhaps." Jane seemed to consider that.

"So," said Mercy, "how do we find out who's behind this vampire project?"

"Some of my funding and data comes from colleagues at Los Alamos National Labs. They're privy to more secrets than I am. There might be some clues down there," said Jane. "A couple of us could drive down and poke through the offices tomorrow night. It could take a while to follow up on the leads, though."

"We're vampires." Mercy's tone turned philosophical. "If anyone has time to kill, it's us."

Marcella looked at the clock. "Speaking of which, dawn will be approaching soon. All of the bedrooms here in the house have blackout blinds, so we can sleep safely. I suggest we get some rest then maybe we can take turns learning more about the nodules. I'd sure like to know what became of Drake"

"He's been in a cave, carefully avoiding the kachina spirits," came a booming voice from one end of the room. We all turned to see an imposing figure in the doorway of the dining room. "I see you have all made yourself comfortable in my home." The figure emerged from the shadows. His black hair was slicked back and he had a hawk-like face. "It is good to see you again, Mercedes and Marcella."

"Lord Draco, I presume." I stood and gave a respectful nod.

"You presume correctly," he said with a brief nod in reply. "In the meantime, the sun is, indeed, rising. Allow me to show you to rooms. We will speak again when the sun descends."

Chapter Twenty

S ensing it was early evening, I awoke but found it difficult to crawl out from under the blankets into the dark room. I longed to wake to the first rays of the morning sun but knew that was never again likely to happen. With a sigh, I threw back the luxurious blankets that covered me. I found my way over to the windows and unlatched the blackout shutters. The broad sky was painted in shades of deep orange and lavender. Standing there watching the sky darken, I grew hungry. Even more than the sun, I longed for the simple medley of tastes offered by something as ordinary as a hamburger with onions, tomatoes, lettuce and mustard. Blood may sustain me, but I couldn't tell any difference in flavor from one Rh factor to another. With a sigh, I closed the shutters then moved to the far side of the room and turned on the lights.

An elegant bathroom adjoined the bedroom that Drake let me use. The tub looked large enough to float in and I was tempted to try it out. Ultimately though, I decided to forgo the bath and settled for a shower. Feeling gritty after my long drive the night before, I allowed myself to luxuriate under the warm spray of water longer than I normally would.

I had mixed feelings about Rudolfo, but I felt I needed to find out what had happened to him. I had to admit this business of searching for him grew stranger with each passing day. An "elemental creature" had apparently abducted Rudolfo himself. Only last night, I met a vampire named Marcella who claimed she had been abducted by the government. I laughed to myself as I washed my hair. Rudolfo almost had me believing that vampires were somehow more civilized creatures, more evolved than humans. Then I met Marcella, Mercy, and Daniel.

It wasn't so much that the three vampires were uncivilized. If anything, the astronomer Daniel seemed quite civil. They just didn't seem at all different from ordinary humans. Were vampires really nothing more than humans who'd acquired a taste for blood, developed super strength and long life spans, if not immortality? Somehow, that seemed disappointing.

Despite that thought, I realized the situation could be far worse. In most vampire movies I'd seen, the vampires were awfully animalistic, always wanting to kill people indiscriminately. Would it have really been a better life if I'd been turned into a true monster? As it was, I didn't even need to kill to survive. I could drink enough to feel content without taking a life. Perhaps stumbling on elemental creatures wasn't so bad. Perhaps the quest for their understanding would help me better understand vampires.

The water turned cold. It seemed that even ancient, aristocratic vampires had limits to the capacity of their water heaters. With a sigh I turned the knob and stepped from the shower. I dried off with a large, warm, fuzzy towel. Stepping back into the bedroom, I dressed in clean clothes, then went downstairs to find out how ancient aristocratic vampires fed themselves on isolated property out in the middle of nowhere. Halfway down the stairs an image of a freezer full of corpses – lost travelers on New Mexico's highways – suddenly came to mind. It was far harder than it should have been to drive the image away. The aroma of fresh-brewed coffee wafted up the stairs and, in spite of my trepidation, I was seduced into descending the remaining stairs.

I heard the sound of voices already deep in conversation, at the bottom of the stairs. Marcella, Daniel, Mercy and Drake sat around an ornate wrought-iron table out on a terrace, overlooking a breathtaking view of the Rio Chama and the surrounding forest. Stunning as the scene was in shades of gray, I knew it would be even more amazing bathed in warm sunlight.

Drake stood and smiled charmingly, offering me his seat. "Please join us. Mercedes and Daniel just finished telling me of an extraordinary encounter with Old Man Beaver. I'm sorry you missed the twilight, Professor. The view from here is absolutely gorgeous."

"I saw some of it from my room." Looking around the table, I saw that Daniel clutched a steaming mug of coffee.

Drake nodded in response. "Actually, your timing is good. I was just about to offer nourishment."

The nobleman's phrasing caught me by surprise. He offered neither refreshment nor dinner, simply nourishment. "I do feel rather hungry," I said. "But a cup of coffee sounds even more welcome at the moment."

"Our astronomer friend found some coffee beans in the kitchen. I'll bring a cup along with something more substantial." Drake turned to leave.

Marcella stepped up to him and touched his arm. "Lord Draco, could you use some assistance?"

"I would be a fool to turn down company as charming as yours, my dear Miss DuBois," said Drake with a guarded smile. The nobleman offered Marcella his arm and the two left together. Once again, the image of a freezer full of bodies came to mind and I could almost picture the two dragging corpses up the stairs. I was repulsed that the idea actually tantalized me a little.

Mercy brushed Daniel's cheek with a kiss, then looked at me. "Did you sleep well?" she asked.

"Very," I said, perhaps a little too sharply. She looked at me with pursed lips, evaluating me. "So, has Drake told you where he's been hiding?" I forced my tone to be cheery, hoping to lighten the mood I'd inadvertently set.

"No. He just told us that he went into hiding when Old Man Beaver started hunting for him." Daniel sipped his coffee.

"Drake's just as scared of the thing as we are," interjected Mercy.

"So, what is the deal with these elemental creatures? Why are ancient vampires like Rudolfo and Drake frightened of them?"

"I don't know about Rudolfo and Drake, but I'm scared of them because they can kill me just as easily as I can kill a human," said Mercy. Daniel nodded agreeing with Mercy's evaluation.

Before we could continue the conversation, Marcella and Drake returned. She carried three pints of blood packaged in plasma bags. Drake carried one more along with a cup of coffee, both of which he placed in front of me with a curt nod. Mouth watering at the aroma of freshly brewed coffee, I was tempted to swallow it down right away, but thought my stomach would do better with something on it. I grabbed the plasma bag instead and was surprised to find it warm to the touch. I tore the seal at the bottom and after experimenting with a couple different ways of drinking the blood, I finally settled on sucking it out, as though through a straw. "This is very good," I said at last. Judging from the looks of contentment on the faces of Mercy and Daniel, I could tell they agreed with me.

"Emergency rations, I'm afraid," Drake apologized. "I keep a supply of blood in a refrigerator in the kitchen. I have a hospital warmer that brings it all up to body temperature to make it tolerable. It's a poor substitute for blood directly from a human, but one does have to make due out in the wilderness."

"Where does the blood come from?" I couldn't contain my curiosity.

"Let's just say that my suppliers are highly motivated to see that I have sufficient blood on hand so I don't feel compelled to go hunting," explained Drake.

I nodded. Though curious about Drake, I felt it would be more appropriate to pursue my questions later. After finishing the blood, I took a sip of the coffee. The sensation of a new flavor was almost overwhelming.

"So, Daniel, what do you make of the vampire hunter's dire warning?" asked Drake.

"'The answers may be found where the journey of death, begins,'" quoted Daniel.

"The journey of death," I interjected. "Jornada del Muerto? That's a lot of desert."

"Perhaps, but it is also desert with many places for keeping secrets like White Sands Missile Range, New Mexico Tech, New Mexico State's Physical Science Laboratory…" Drake finished his pint of blood then looked from Marcella to Daniel. "On our way to the kitchen, Marcella told me that she also stumbled on a mystery."

Daniel described what he had seen in the folders and I followed suit.

"It seems to me that whoever is behind the manufacture of these creatures is quite imaginative and ambitious." Drake sniffed.

"Imagination and ambition are well and good," said Daniel. "But I think we need to find a few concrete answers."

"Like, what happened to Alice and Hunter?" Mercy leaned forward.

"Just who are those bastards that abducted me? Can we stop them?" Marcella gritted her teeth.

"What is the World Apart? Is it a parallel universe?" asked Daniel.

Desmond Drake fell back into a chair, as though knocked over by the sheer weight of the questions. I began to wonder whether we'd all overestimated Lord Draco's ability to help us in our quests. In spite of that, I set my coffee cup down and posed my own question. "What are the elementals and what do they want with Rudolfo?"

"Rudolfo?" asked Drake, turning to face me. "Not Rudolfo de Córdoba?"

"The same," I said. "He's the one who made me a vampire."

"Then either your sire is a ghost or you are a much older vampire than you appear," said Drake, as though noticing me for the first time. "Rudolfo vanished over four hundred years ago, during the Pueblo Revolt here in New Mexico. We assumed he had been killed."

"Rudolfo went into hiding in a cave. I inadvertently woke him. I presume this means that Rudolfo's stories of the Scarlet Order are true." I picked up the coffee cup and studied Drake's reaction.

Desmond Drake nodded slowly. His eyes focused beyond the

treetops, as though he looked back through time. "Oh yes, the Scarlet Order was real. We were the greatest warriors the Earth has ever seen." Drake lay two long and delicate fingers alongside his nose. A tear escaped the corner of his eye only to be flung aside by those fingers. "Rudolfo was my second-in-command for a time. He decided to seek adventure and fortune in the Americas. Once the pope decided that vampires were demon-possessed corpses several others including me followed. That marked the end of the Order." Drake looked down at his feet.

Daniel frowned deeply. "It seems to me the Catholic Church has made many decisions throughout the centuries based on fear. Look at the story of Galileo."

Drake sighed and nodded. "Thank you, Daniel," he said with a wan smile.

"What about the elementals?" I pressed.

"They are powerful beings and I wish I knew more. How I would like to see Rudolfo again..." Drake looked away. "No, I'm afraid all I know is really mythology and folklore. Don't give up hope though, there might be other lines of inquiry."

"Indeed." I drank the last of the coffee in one swallow. "I was hoping to drive down to Los Alamos tonight. I wanted to see what I could learn about the agency that abducted Marcella and if I could learn more about those creatures. Perhaps Marcella could come along and help me, since she was at their facility near Roswell."

Drake stood and put his arm around Marcella's bare shoulder. "A worthy suggestion, Dr. Heckman. However, I am not without resources of my own."

Marcella narrowed her gaze. "So, tell me my dragon, what resources do you have to help us in our quests?"

"Every dragon has his treasure," said Drake with a twinkle in his eye. "Follow me and I'll lead you to mine." Lord Draco turned with a flourish. We all followed as he led us through the house to a room with two large gold-inlaid doors. He threw them open and I gaped at the sight before me: a circular room over four stories high with every inch of wall space covered with bookshelves. It was literally the largest single-room library I'd ever seen. The shelves were filled with books, both new and ancient. Some had paper covers, others leather. Some shelves even had scrolls. My skin grew clammy as we entered the room and my nose detected a faint tang to the air. I wondered if the atmosphere in the library contained more nitrogen than normal. Then I realized a human might not even be able to survive in this room. There might not be enough oxygen. However, the atmosphere was perfect for preserving an antique book collection.

Less reserved than I, Daniel practically leapt at one of the shelves. He turned around clutching a book to his breast. "Is this really a first edition of Kepler's *The Harmony of the Worlds*?" he asked, eyes wide.

"It was Kepler's own copy," explained Drake. "You'll find notes in the margin written in his hand."

"You knew Kepler?" asked the astronomer, jaw slack.

"Who cares about dead astronomers?" snarled Mercy, her hands on her hips. "I care about Hunter and Alice. I want to know if they're still alive. We're not going to do that in a room full of books."

"This has to be one of the greatest collections of antique manuscripts ever collected," I said, unfazed by Mercy's outburst.

"Quite right, Dr. Heckman," said Drake. "But Mercedes is also right. Some answers are here, and others will be found in less ancient collections. We need a starting place. Running out aimlessly in search of Rudolfo and the others will only get us lost. Let's see if there's something here to get us started." Drake stood back and examined the rows of bookshelves. After a moment, he nodded to himself then ascended three flights of stairs to a shelf near the top of the room. He returned, clutching a book. Setting the book on a table, he opened it to a grainy black and white photograph.

Marcella gasped, putting her hand to her mouth. After a beat, she examined the photograph more critically. "That creature is very close to what I saw," she said.

Daniel leaned in and looked at the photo. The astronomer still clutched the Kepler volume lovingly, as though afraid to let it go. "That's from an old German film, isn't it? Max Schreck as Graf Orlock in *Nosferatu*."

I leaned over from the far side of the table. Like Daniel, I recognized the still, but would not have known the name of the actor. The bald head, black, piercing eyes, claw-like hands and bat-like ears were all unmistakable to anyone who'd ever seen the film.

"This is undoubtedly a human in makeup," said Marcella, still evaluating the photograph. "The creatures that abducted me had darker, bigger eyes, more rat-like. This fellow's ears are too big but they're about the right shape." Marcella chewed on her lower lip for a few moments more. "I'm not familiar with German film," she said, her Cajun drawl suddenly more pronounced. "When was this movie made?"

"1925 or so, if I don't miss my guess," said Daniel.

"1922," said Drake, assuredly.

"The creatures that abducted me couldn't have been around that long," said Marcella, perplexed. "What kind of creature is this?"

"Nosferatu is a vampire movie." Mercy's voice dripped with contempt. "That's what the Germans think we vampires look like."

"I guess there's a good reason I don't care much for German films," snorted Marcella.

Drake shook his head. "Actually, it's what a lot of cultures think vampires are like. The Greek vrykolakas, the French revenant, the German nosferatu, all seem much closer to this 'handsome' fellow than to us. I long assumed these creatures were just exaggerations of stories of real vampires. Fear often causes the human mind to see things that aren't there. Hideous gray creatures began to vanish from the public consciousness as the twentieth century progressed, at least until the 1950s."

"What happened in the 1950s?" Mercy's tone seemed less aggressive and more curious than before.

"The UFO craze," I answered slowly. "The crash at Roswell in 1947, sightings of UFOs all over the country shortly afterwards, Project Blue Book…"

Drake nodded, then ascended another flight of stairs. This time he stopped at the middle level. The book he retrieved this time had a foldout illustrated page that resembled a police line-up. "I managed to acquire this from a base up in Nevada," said the ancient vampire, off-handedly. "These are renditions based on all of the 'reliable' eyewitness accounts of UFOs."

On the page was an assortment of creatures. One was short and gray with very large eyes. Another was similarly short, resembling a goblin with sharp teeth and toad-like skin. Some of the creatures were tall and menacing, others were almost comical.

Marcella nodded. "You know … if you took a bit from one and a part from another, you could make up a creature that looked a lot like the ones I saw."

"So, are you trying to tell us space creatures abducted our Chica?" Mercy narrowed her gaze, evaluating the page.

Drake shook his head. "Aliens and vampires inspire a certain … related terror. We come in the night when people are helpless. If someone wanted to build a creature for the purposes of inspiring terror, what models might they use?" The English Lord looked into my eyes sending a chill down my spine. "I begin to wonder if the 'journey of death' that our friend the vampire hunter warned us about so ominously wasn't Jornada del Muerto, after all, but rather the place where humans began the journey of death with atomic weapons. Dr. Heckman, if you and Miss DuBois are going to make it to Los Alamos and back tonight, I suggest you start soon."

Marcella looked down at her leather outfit, then shrugged apologetically. "I wonder if it would be better for me to stay here and send Daniel down instead." Mercy shot Marcella a dark look. "Hey, I don't exactly fit in at a top-secret lab."

I smiled, looking at her spiky hair. "I see your point, but you might be surprised. Besides, if we get caught, we're in trouble no matter what we look like. You're the one who's seen these creatures. I need you to tell me if I've found anything real."

Marcella frowned, then nodded. "All right, let's get going. Your car or mine?"

"I've got a parking permit." I shrugged. "Probably better to use my car. That way we won't get towed away while we're breaking and entering." She grinned at that and the two of us left the library.

Chapter Twenty-One

From the journals of Dr. Jane Heckman.
Present Day.

The heightened senses and reflexes I obtained from becoming a vampire made me both a faster and safer driver. Though it would normally take me almost four hours to drive the twisting, turning mountain roads between Ghost Ranch and Los Alamos, I was able to cover the distance in about half that time. Fortunately, my heightened senses could also pick up the subtle pinging of police radar. I could slow down in plenty of time to avoid speed traps, not that many police officers patrolled the twisting roads. Most of the cops must have been home watching television as we sped toward our destination.

During the drive Marcella spoke very little, as though lost in her own thoughts. I asked her a few questions about her life and learned that she'd spent much of the past fifty years following the migration patterns of a Mexican free-tail bat colony. Though her tone was somewhat romantic and it sounded as though she described a peaceful, almost monastic lifestyle, her existence sounded lonely to me. I probed further into her life before becoming a vampire and I realized she'd been very much alone as a human too.

"So, how did you become a vampire?" I asked at last. My gaze darted briefly her direction and she turned quickly away, as though afraid I'd see her expression.

"He was beautiful," said Marcella, almost too quietly even for my vampire hearing to detect. "The most beautiful vampire I'd ever met … His name was Roquelaure."

In spite of myself, I turned to look at her. When I remembered I was driving, I quickly turned my attention back to the road. "Rudolfo mentioned Roquelaure once. He was one of Draco's Scarlet Order."

From the corner of my eye, I could make out a barely perceptible nod. "Draco told me."

"Didn't Roquelaure…"

"After he made me into a vampire, Roquelaure vanished. I never saw him again. I wasn't even allowed the opportunity to decide if I could forgive him or not."

"If you ever did see him, what would you do?"

Marcella didn't answer. I fell into my own silence and thought about Rudolfo. Though I was angry at him, he had stayed with me after becoming a vampire. What happened to Marcella seemed more like rape. She still seemed drawn to the creature that made her. Marcella's shoulders trembled slightly, and though she faced away from me, I could tell she wept quietly. All through my drive from Socorro, I'd asked myself why I should even bother trying to rescue him. I kept justifying my feelings as self-preservation and curiosity about the creature that grabbed him.

"Do you want to see Roquelaure again?" I asked aloud.

Even before Marcella answered, I knew what she'd say. "More than anything … but don't ask me why."

There had been a niggling voice in the back of my head that kept denying that my feelings were simple academic curiosity. The niggling voice returned and told me that, like Marcella, I wanted more than anything to be with Rudolfo. There was no way I could tell anyone why. I didn't want to think about it right then and needed to talk about other things to take my mind off the situation. Somehow the words never came and we remained silent until we arrived at the labs.

I turned into the parking lot permitted by the sticker in my window, switched off the ignition, and turned to Marcella. "Well, I guess this is it."

With a gulp, Marcella reached up and touched her hair. "Are you really sure this is a good idea?"

I pursed my lips and thought for a moment before I answered. "Well, it's true that you're likely to turn some heads and bring some unwanted attention to our search, but you really don't look that different than some of the grad students I've seen around here. Just look like you belong."

"Somehow that doesn't exactly reassure me about the state of National Security, but if you say so…" Marcella took a deep breath and closed her eyes for a moment. When she opened them, she nodded sharply. "Ready."

I got out of the car and habitually strapped on my fanny pack then led the way to an old adobe-colored building toward the right-hand side of the parking lot. One of my close colleagues had an office in the building. "We need to get to a computer inside the lab's firewall. Once there, I can learn enough to proceed." Marcella simply nodded. At the door, I retrieved my ID from the fanny pack and waved it in front of the electronic scanner.

"Somehow, I would have thought there would be armed guards here," said Marcella, her brow furrowed.

"There are in parts," I explained. "My colleague works in a less secure facility."

I led the way through the halls. It had been almost a year since I'd visited Ralph Crest's office and it seemed like all the buildings at Los Alamos were somewhat maze-like. I'd always wondered if that was done deliberately. After only two wrong turns, we found ourselves in front of his door. I started to move my ID toward the scanner beside the door, then paused and checked my watch. It was just about an hour before midnight. Most likely Ralph had gone home hours before, but there were some nights that he worked late. If he was here, how would I explain my presence? Realizing I was just losing time I held the card to the scanner and let out a sigh of relief when the door opened into a darkened room.

Stepping in, I turned on the lights then sat down behind the desk and wiggled the mouse next to Ralph's computer terminal. It came to life and prompted me for a login. A moment later I scanned the internal Los Alamos web. At loose ends, Marcella looked around at the books lining the walls. She picked up a few papers and glanced through them, then studied a couple of Ralph's spaceship models. Finally, she made her way behind me and peered over my shoulder.

"Learning anything?" she asked.

I pointed to several listings for something called "Project Tepes" being headed up by the Biological and Quantum Physics Group. All of the links indicated that one needed proper clearance to access the data.

"Do you have the clearance to find out more?" asked Marcella.

I shook my head. "No, but the project leader would." I scrolled down and pointed to the screen. "Looks like we need to pay a visit to the Project Leader's office, Dr. Immanuel Love."

"You've got to be kidding," said Marcella incredulously. I just shook my head. "So, where is Dr. Love's office?"

"Over in P-21. Just a couple of buildings away." I looked back at the screen. "If these records are any indication, I suspect we'll meet a couple of armed guards on the way. We need to be careful so we don't set off any alarms."

Marcella nodded. I logged out of Ralph's computer and we left the office, being careful to lock the door on our way out.

"So, what does the Biological and Quantum Physics group do?" asked Marcella.

"If you wanted to turn someone into vampires, they're just the group you'd ask," I said. "They do robotics and adaptive systems, computational neuroscience, nanites in biological applications…"

A few minutes later, we arrived at the building that housed the P-21 group. Surprisingly no guards stood outside. I'd never been in the building and wasn't really sure whether or not my ID would work there. I tried it anyway and smiled when the door opened.

As we stepped inside, a guard stood up from behind a desk and crossed his arms in front of his chest. "May I help you ladies?" asked the guard.

Marcella looked around as though searching for an escape route. I knew the only escape route was behind our back and the only way to go forward was to talk to the guard. I only hoped he hadn't perceived Marcella's actions as too suspicious. "I'm Dr. Jane Heckman," I said, quickly flashing my ID at him. "I was working with Dr. Love today and I think I left one of my folders in his office. I was wondering if I could go look and see if it's there."

The guard held out his hand, silently asking to see the ID. I knew it wouldn't give me permission to access anything in this part of the facility but I didn't have any choice, or else I would seem too suspicious, so I handed him the badge.

He started to insert it into a scanner, and Marcella stepped forward and leaned over the desk. She gave the guard a good look down her bustier. I gritted my teeth, knowing that a well-trained guard wasn't going to fall for such an obvious ploy. It seemed I was right when the guard quickly averted his gaze from her full, white breasts to her green eyes with a suspicious scowl. She reached out with her right hand, and I was afraid she was going to rip out his throat, leaving a bloody mess for the shift change to find, perhaps in only a few minutes. Instead, she gently caressed his cheek.

"You don't need to see Dr. Heckman's ID," she purred. "You know her quite well, mon ami. She's left her keys back at her office and I'm afraid we need you to let us into Dr. Love's office so she can look for the folder."

My heart pounded so furiously, I feared it would burst. For a moment I thought the guard would reach for his sidearm. Instead, he pushed himself out of his chair and made his way down one of the corridors with his arm around Marcella's shoulder. Blinking a few times, I broke free from my own reverie and hurried to catch up with them. The guard took out his keys and opened the door to Dr. Love's office. Marcella eased her way out from under the guard's arm, then looked into his eyes again. "Now, mon ami, you need to go back to work before anyone finds out you're not at your post. If anyone asks about us, you've not seen anything. Understand, cher?"

The guard nodded and, as though in a trance, then turned away from us and walked down the corridor. I reached out and turned on the light. "I knew vampires could manipulate thoughts, but I haven't mastered it to that degree."

"You don't need to be a vampire to manipulate men's thoughts, Jane," said Marcella with a wink.

I shook my head and wondered whether she was just teasing me. I filed the question away as something to pursue later. Now I needed to attend to business. Looking at my watch, I saw it was just about midnight. If we wanted to get back to Drake's ranch before dawn, we didn't have much time. I went to the desk and directed Marcella to a set of binders in a neat row on the bookshelf.

Opening drawers, I rifled through papers. Most of the papers were mundane budgets and purchase requests for things like liquid nitrogen, cell growth media, markers, and microscope slides. Nothing there pointed toward the mysterious "Project Tepes" nor seemed at all surprising for an empirical biophysics group to order. I looked up at Marcella, who shook her head, not seeming to have discovered anything.

I stood and stretched my legs while looking at my watch. Only a half hour had gone by, but still I wondered if we'd run into a dead end. I looked at the file cabinet. Nothing stood out at first. The top drawer was labeled A-C. The next one down was D, the third was E-N and the last was O-Z. I tried the bottom drawer looking for anything labeled "Tepes" or "Project Tepes" but had no luck.

Marcella came up behind me and studied the file cabinet. "D," she said. "That's the way Dracula signs his name in Stoker's novel."

I nodded. "I'll bet that's it." I tried the drawer, but found it was locked. I went back to the desk to see if Dr. Love had left any keys behind. In the meantime, Marcella approached the cabinet, grabbed the handle and pushed the silver lock button with her thumb until the catch broke. She slid the drawer open. I gritted my teeth and sat silent for a moment listening, trying to determine is she'd set off any alarms. "That was just the kind of thing I warned you about," I hissed.

"It's getting late," said Marcella without apology as she rifled through the drawer. "We've got to hurry if we're going to find anything."

"We can't afford to be careless either." I moved to her side.

She had a file out and glanced through the papers. "I think this is it." She handed a stapled sheaf of papers to me.

I leafed through the papers and quickly saw they were a proposal from the Department of Energy to the National Security Council. The proposal's abstract discussed attempts by the FBI and CIA to recruit vampires for counter terrorism activities and "decapitation" of certain regimes known to be unfriendly to the United States. Even from my limited experience with vampires, I would have guessed that they found our kind to be uncooperative in the long term. Dr. Love and the research scientists of P-21 thought they could use nanites to convert ordinary soldiers into vampire-like super soldiers, both loyal and effective.

"There are a few supporting papers and some progress reports here," said Marcella.

I looked at my watch. Our time limit approached. "I think we need to get going. Hand them here, and we can take a closer look when we get back to Drake's."

Marcella nodded agreement and handed me the papers. I folded them as neatly as I could and stuffed them into my fanny pack. Marcella returned the folder and closed the drawer, making it look as undisturbed as possible.

"You know, even if you didn't set off an alarm, they'll move those files as soon as they discover the broken lock."

"It was a cheap lock," said Marcella. "I'm guessing they'll think it was broken just by wear and tear. I may live in a cave, but even I know about the security problems they've had here at the labs. They'll keep it pretty quiet."

I shook my head. "I hope you're right."

We left the office and found ourselves caught in the beams of two flashlights. "Hold it right there ladies," said one security guard. I couldn't tell if either of these was the same fellow that Marcella had seduced earlier, but I suspected he'd gone off duty over an hour before. "Please come with us."

"I don't think so," called Marcella. Before I could react, she pushed past me and knocked the left-most guard into the wall.

The other guard dropped his flashlight and drew a gun. With a growl of frustration at Marcella and the guard, I jumped forward and knocked the gun out of his hand, then elbowed him in the sternum. There was a crack and he collapsed to the ground. I gasped in surprise at Marcella who was hunched over the first guard, drinking blood.

She looked up at me. "I'm not going to kill him, but if we take some blood, it'll be longer before they can call for help."

I hated to admit it, but Marcella was probably right. The guard I hit didn't seem like he would get up any time soon. I allowed myself to take some of his blood. Standing up, I tried Dr. Love's office door, but found it had closed and locked behind us. "We've got to find some place to hide them, or the next watch will find them and be after us," I said.

Marcella reached out as though she was going to break the office door's handle. I put my hand on her forearm and shook my head. "The file cabinet alarm was minor. If you break a door handle, you'll trigger a major alarm and the whole force will be after us," I said.

"Well, we can't just walk out of here with them over our shoulders," she said.

"We can't leave them here." I looked down the hall feeling at an impasse. Then I spotted the manhole cover in the floor. "The old steam tunnels. We can take them down there."

Marcella saw the cover too and nodded. She hefted one of the guards over her shoulders and I followed suit. Even with our strength, it was tricky maneuvering the guards through the manhole cover and getting them past the pipes and conduits that ran beneath the floor. We had them situated in a place where, even when they did wake up, they would take a while finding their way out.

"How much time have we lost?" asked Marcella, looking up at the open manhole cover.

"More than I'd like." I looked around in the darkness, trying to get my bearings. "I think we should go down the tunnel a ways and come up at a different point. If someone follows quickly it should throw them off our trail."

Marcella looked up then down the length of the corridor. Without a word, she climbed the short ladder and replaced the manhole cover, then climbed back down and joined me. I expected a new access port just a few yards away. Instead, it seemed as though we walked at least fifty yards without finding another cover. I began to think we weren't even under the same building.

Behind us, something rattled, then thumped. My heart skipped a beat. My first thought was that the guards we'd attacked and stranded had just awakened and were following us. Marcella pointed at something ahead of us. At first, I didn't see what she indicated, then I noticed a narrow shaft of light. We were coming toward the end of the tunnel. I looked behind us again. "Damn!"

Two creatures shambled through the tunnel toward us. They were about six and a half feet tall with large black eyes, beak-like noses and large, pointed ears. Instead of the silver suits Marcella had described, these creatures wore black jumpsuits. "Run," shouted Marcella and she crouched low, as though ready to pounce. One of the creatures reached for her and she tried to spring between them while I looked for something to use as a weapon. The second "vampire" struck her on the back of the neck. Marcella fell to the ground in a heap, immobilized. "You are coming with us," stated one of the creatures in a low, guttural voice.

The creatures shuffled toward me. I thought about trying to fight, but realized that even though Marcella had more experience with hand-to-hand combat, she had fallen. I needed help. I turned and bolted down the tunnel toward the shaft of light we'd seen, hoping I had enough night left to make it to my car and find a better hiding place.

Chapter Twenty-Two

At Drake's Ranch House.
Present Day.

A fter Marcella and Jane left, Daniel turned to Drake. "So, where exactly do vampires come from?"

"I'm afraid the answer to that question is shrouded in history. Perhaps even prehistory." Drake shrugged.

Daniel held his hands out, indicating the sheer number of books surrounding them. "Surely one or more of these books has the answer."

"Perhaps," said Drake, "but there are more books here than even an ancient vampire can study."

"Do you mind if I browse for a while?" Daniel asked.

"That's why I brought you here."

Mercy stepped up to Daniel, hands clenching and unclenching at her sides. "You know, I don't really have a problem with you trying to figure out the origins of vampires. However, it doesn't get us any closer to finding our friends."

"Is it simple coincidence that creatures who abducted Marcella bear more than a passing resemblance to vampires?" Daniel retorted. "Why was a kachina interested enough in vampires to abduct Rudolfo? What are these elementals? Like vampires, they seem to be ancient too. Could there be a connection? I think it's worth checking out."

"What about that canister of gas we have out in the car,

do you think maybe we should try to figure out what that is?" retorted Mercy. "It contains something strong enough to knock out vampires and could be used as a weapon against us."

"There's a lot to investigate." Drake rubbed his chin. "We should approach this in an organized fashion. Like Jane, Daniel has a strong scientific background, it seems that he's the best candidate to try to figure out this 'gas.' I have a small lab that you can use."

Daniel looked longingly at the books, a retort barely held in check. After a moment, he stepped heavily toward the bookshelf and returned the copy of Kepler's *Harmony of the Worlds*.

"Mercy, given your recent encounter with vampire hunters, you should look through their texts for clues about the weapons they've used over the centuries. Though this 'gas' you mention seems new, you might find references to something similar. I also have a subscription to several newspapers. You may also want to look through those and see if you find reference to any incidents similar to those Marcella describes. I'm most familiar with the library and have some acquaintance with the history of vampires, so I'll see what more I can learn about our origins that might be of use to our current problems."

With that, Drake led Daniel out of the library to show him to the lab, leaving Mercy to stare open-mouthed at the vast library before her.

Daniel looked at the paintings as they made their way down the wide hallway. A worry tugged at him. "Mr. Drake ... Lord Draco..." sputtered Daniel, searching for the proper form of address.

Draco's lips turned upward slightly as he waved off-handedly. "Draco is fine, or even Desmond if you prefer. I'm far too old to care about titles and royal pomp."

The ancient vampire looked very nearly the same age as Daniel. The astronomer smiled self-consciously. "Draco, then," Daniel settled on a choice as Draco opened a door. Daniel followed him inside. "The fact of the matter is, I'm an astronomer, not a chemist. It's a little daunting to know just where I should start."

After the library, the "laboratory" seemed a bit disappointing. It looked more like a kitchenette equipped with a few racks of test tubes and flasks with only one Bunsen burner and a shelf of books. Draco stepped over to the bookshelf, as though answering Daniel's question. "Through the Renaissance, a scientist was a scientist. Galileo didn't over-worry about the distinctions between anatomist, engineer, astronomer, and natural philosopher. All of the disciplines start with curiosity and a hypothesis." Draco paused and studied Daniel for a moment. "I presume you have a hypothesis about the nature of the gas…"

Daniel shook his head. "I'm afraid I really don't have enough knowledge to know where to begin."

The English lord closed his eyes and stood silent, gathering his thoughts like a patient schoolteacher. "Surely there have been times you have awakened early from your daily slumber?"

Daniel remembered the morning the exterminator and his wife had arrived at the theater and he nodded. Draco turned and retrieved a book from the shelf. "I suspect the compound you have is related to fluoxetine hydrochloride." The master vampire thumbed through the book until he found what he sought, then set it down on the table. "The hunters of Santorini have been experimenting and I believe they've had promising results. Some of the tests are described here."

Daniel stepped over and studied the book for several minutes, then rubbed the bridge of his nose. "Okay. I think I can perform the tests, but what the hell is fluoxetine hydrochloride?"

The ancient vampire shrugged. "The active chemical in Prozac."

"You mean if vampires aren't depressed, they don't wake up early?" asked the astronomer incredulously.

"It's almost certainly not that simple. Since vampires seem to have different brain chemistry than … ordinary humans … it stands to reason that chemicals that affect the brain would behave in related, but slightly different ways, don't you think?" Draco stepped over to a makeshift chemical hood and turned on a blower fan, then he moved to a cupboard and retrieved goggles, gloves, and a breathing mask. "Make sure to take precautions. I don't want to find that you've passed out in here." Without further instruction, Draco turned and left.

Daniel let out a breath and shook his head. Finally, throwing his hands up, he decided to go to the car and retrieve the gas canister and see what he could learn.

✟✟✟

Mercy stared open-mouthed at a shelf of books. An engraved plaque read, "The Lost Vampire Texts." She pursed her lips and silently wondered how they could be "lost" when they were sitting there under her nose. She shook her head to clear it of irrelevant thoughts, but found her mind wandering to Hunter and Alice. She'd known other people and vampires over the years, but no others had quite brought the promise of unconditional love they had. A part of her consciousness prickled, wondering if they really could deliver what they promised; if anyone could really deliver unconditional love.

As her mind wandered, Mercy's eyes fell onto a volume in Spanish. She lifted it from the shelf and opened it to the first page. The book claimed to be a Spanish translation of the vampire hunter's guide from the Island of Santorini. The book was actually hand-written in a special translation commissioned by the Church in Spain. She shrugged, thinking it was as good a place to start as any.

Sitting down with the book, she began to struggle through. The handwriting was gothic calligraphy much like the Germans seemed to favor. Moreover, the text had a strongly Castillian flavor. She kept seeing the word, infección – infection. It seemed that vampirism was attributed to one of two things: demonic possession or an infection, like the black plague. Though Mercy had been called a bruja or a witch woman many times over her life, she seriously doubted that she had a demon inside her. She'd heard about blood-borne infections and began to wonder whether vampirism could simply be an infection. It would partly explain why one needed to ingest a vampire's blood to become a vampire. The only problem was that the blood borne infections she knew required the blood itself to mix.

Mercy stood and stretched then ambled over to the section of shelves labeled, "Biological Reference." In this case, she wasn't so much interested in ancient texts as newer works that would tell her about the different ways an infection could be transferred. However, she found those books even harder to read than old Spanish tomes written in gothic calligraphy. A couple of hours later, Mercy found herself turning pages in a general reference book about molecular biochemistry. She found a passage that stated it was theoretically possible to ingest a molecular agent through the mouth that could affect the body at a cellular level. She had yet to find any evidence of agents that produced anything like vampiric transformation. Rubbing her eyes, she sighed, wondering if she would even recognize the right clues if she saw them.

Drake sat down next to her. "How is the search proceeding?"

"Too damned slow!" snapped Mercy. She looked down and put her face in her hands. When she looked back up, Drake wore a concerned frown. "I'm sorry, I want to help, but I'm just not any good here. Get me in a fight and I'll kick ass. But this isn't really my element." She sighed, looked down and, without thinking, opened the vampire hunter's book again. It fell open to a page that detailed the effects of crosses on vampires.

Drake's eyes drifted to the page. He pulled the book toward him and read. "Though you are not a scholar, you seem to have found something interesting. According to this, after several minutes' exposure to a cross, a blue halo or glow will surround a vampire. They will vanish entirely if exposed to the cross long enough."

Mercy looked at Drake wide-eyed. "I held Daniel on a cross down in Las Cruces, but he didn't disappear…"

"How long were you able to hold him?"

"Only a minute or two," she said, shrugging. "I'd get sick too if I held him down much longer."

"You didn't see a blue glow?" asked Drake.

Mercy shook her head.

"It's hardly definitive," said Drake. "Still, things begin to fit in place. The cross may be a means of transference from one plane to another."

"Like a portal?"

"It seems we still have more questions than answers. I have some ideas but no proof. Unfortunately," said Drake closing the book, "that's the way research works sometimes."

Just then, the library doors opened and Daniel appeared. "I think you're right," he said. "It seems that the gas in the canister we brought is related to fluoxetine hydrochloride."

Drake let out a long breath then sat back with his hands behind his head. "Then it would seem that your exterminator friend was working with the vampire hunters of Santorini."

Daniel shrugged. "Not necessarily. The exterminator could have discovered that fluoxetine knocks out vampires all by himself."

"In any event, we have learned the vampire hunters only rendered Hunter and Alice unconscious. If we can find your friends, they should be all right." Drake placed a consoling hand on Mercy's shoulder.

"That's if he didn't take them from the theater so he could drive stakes through their hearts." She looked away from his eyes.

"He could have done that at the theater," said Daniel.

"Not with me watching!" Mercy jumped to her feet.

Drake raised his hand. "No, Daniel has a point. I suspect that the exterminator and his wife took your friends for some reason. Whoever was paying them wanted the vampires alive. Though fluoxetine will knock out our danger sense, it won't kill us. The real question is, who wanted your friends and why?"

"What about the people who kidnapped Marcella?" asked Daniel.

"A reasonable hypothesis," said Drake.

"Okay then," said Mercy, who began to pace, "how does all of this tie together? Our French Gringa was kidnapped and she found these little robot thingies…"

"Nanites," interjected Daniel.

"Robot thingies," said Mercy stubbornly. "We think the robot thingies make people into vampires. We think maybe Alice and Hunter were kidnapped by the same people that caught our French Gringa, but the exterminator dweeb doesn't look a thing like that

German vampire guy in the movie book. And you know what, I still haven't figured out how the UFO aliens fit into all this." Mercy stopped, put her hands on her hips and looked at Daniel and Drake, expecting an explanation.

"Well," said Daniel, refusing to meet Mercy's gaze. "We do seem to have quite a few loose ends…"

"Did you learn anything else from the vampire hunters' guidebook?" The master vampire looked pointedly at Mercy.

"Just that vampires are either demon-possessed puppets or humans carrying a disease of some kind," snorted Mercy.

"Well, you know," mused Daniel, "if nanites are really being developed and from what Jane says, that seems to be the case, they could be used to infect a person like a disease. In principal, they could radically alter DNA allowing for a transformation of one creature into another."

Mercy's eyes glazed over slightly, but they rapidly cleared. "So, then how do the kachina spirits fit into all this?"

Drake answered her question with another one. "What if the first vampires were created for some purpose by an advanced power?" He looked at Daniel.

"That power might have used something like our nanotechnology to infect humans and give us our abilities…" Daniel trailed off, lost in thought.

Mercy shook her head and made a sound in the back of her throat like a disgusted growl. "I've had enough of this speculation. Once you two get around to figuring out where I can go to kick some butt, let me know and I'll follow. In the meantime, I'm going to read the paper." She stormed off gathering a small stack of newspapers.

"I have to admit, she has a point," said Daniel, looking at Drake. "I'm not really sure that we've gotten anywhere. We have a few facts and a hypothesis that ties them together. Are we right about any of it? If so, what do we do about it?"

Drake opened his mouth to say something when Mercy cried out.

"Shit!" she exclaimed. She looked down at the newspaper atop the stack in front of her. Daniel and Drake stepped over expecting to see an article related to their quest. Instead, they saw that the newspaper was opened to an advertisement for a figurine of a Teddy Bear dressed in military fatigues, carrying an AK-47. Inscribed over the image was the banner, "Securing the Blessings of Liberty."

"Doesn't look much like a vampire to me," quipped Daniel.

Mercy sighed. "What is the artist trying to say with this? Is the artist trying to say that soldiers are really cute and cuddly and we should love them in spite of their guns? Or are they saying something about soldiers? Maybe they're not really human, so don't mourn for them when they pass."

"Only a people denying what they've become create such images," said Drake. "Over the last century, I have watched the United States denigrate and sabotage its warrior class. Today a handful of children are sent around the world to fight battles so that their cowardly elders may sit at home growing fat from the spoils of war. When the children come home, their elders don't even see fit to honor them with a living wage, much less the riches they are due."

Daniel's eyebrows came together. "I take it the United States is not the highest bidder for mercenaries, such as yourself."

Drake looked down at his feet for a long time without answering. "Being a mercenary isn't necessarily about money. It's about being the best warrior you can be and only accepting contracts from those willing to pay fairly for service." He frowned. "Still, I think Mercy has helped us stumble on another clue. Those in power don't want to fight their own battles and they want to spend as little as possible for those who do fight. What if these vampires are meant to be warriors?"

Mercy grabbed the newspaper and crumpled it up. "It's a sick image, whatever it means. On one hand it corrupts a child's plaything. On the other hand, it dishonors soldiers."

"I can't help but agree with you," mused Drake.

Mercy frowned. "So, what do we do with these bits of intelligence?"

"I'm afraid we'll need to hit the books again tomorrow night,"

Daniel sighed. "Unless Marcella and Jane come back with good news from the labs."

"Shouldn't they be back by now?" asked Mercy, glancing up at a nearby grandfather clock.

"I suspect they have found something and been delayed. In the meantime, we should not despair. We've made good progress," said Drake. "We can resume our inquiries tomorrow."

Mercy shook her head. "I hope tomorrow won't be too late."

Daniel looked at her and silently agreed.

☩☩☩

After Mercy and Daniel left for bed, Desmond Drake sat alone in the great library with his hands steepled under his nose. He felt the weight of nearly 1500 years of life and sensed that something major was happening. It was not coincidence that the kachina spirits were interested in the vampires' activities. It also had not been coincidence that Merlin and the druids followed the Pen-Dragon's activities with interest in old Britain. It was not coincidence that Rudolfo had returned, as though from the grave, only to be abducted by one of the kachinas. It had not been coincidence that Arthur, rather than Desmond, had been chosen to lead the Britons in their conquest of the Saxons. Desmond Drake considered the people who occupied his house and wondered whether the Knights of the Scarlet Order were about to be reborn. Perhaps governments with technology hadn't any need for vampires. Drake sensed that someone, somewhere needed the Order.

☩☩☩

Daniel led Mercy into their room. He closed the door gently and turned to find her sitting on the bed. He sat down next to her then took her in his arms and kissed away tears that had blossomed on her cheeks. She nuzzled his neck. Slowly and deliberately, they undressed each other. Mercy lay back on the bed and lazily explored Daniel's body with her hands. She felt neither predatory nor lustful, but didn't want to let Daniel out of her grasp. She wanted to hold onto him with her whole being, afraid he might vanish just like Hunter and Alice. Mercy lured Daniel on top of her then pulled him into her and held him there for a time, savoring his presence. She rocked him like a child in her arms and delighted in the feeling of his mustache on her cheek. Climax washed over her like a sigh. Outside, the sun neared the horizon. Regretfully, Mercy released Daniel. The two slipped under the blankets and closed their eyes with hands touching ever so slightly.

✝✝✝

Rudolfo de Córdoba found himself sitting on solid ground. The sky above grew rapidly brighter and he sensed sunrise was imminent. Looking around, he saw Lord Draco's manor house. He'd been told that was his destination. Two cars were parked in front. With the sun rising, Rudolfo knew he didn't have time to walk in unannounced and explain his sudden appearance. Next to him were long-abandoned servant's quarters. Striding over, he tried the door, but found it locked. With a quick twist of his wrist the knob gave way and Rudolfo pushed the door open. He made his way into an interior room without windows. He found a corner where sunlight would not touch him then curled up to sleep. While his eyes fluttered closed, the words of Coyote echoed in his thoughts, "Whether we want it or not, war is upon us."

Chapter Twenty-Three

From the notes of Daniel McKee.
Present Day.

I awoke the next evening with a head full of questions and a rather insistent erection. It was as though curiosity and sexuality were linked, which I suppose they are in many ways. Mercy rolled over and threw her arm across my chest and her leg around my waist. "You are fortunate that Mercy is generous."

"Mercy is a kind mistress," I said, gently teasing. She looked up at me and sneered, very much the four-century old master vampire. The real years seemed at odds with the smooth, supple skin I caressed. "Will Mercy linger a while before a shower? I burn with inquiry and wish to be satisfied."

"Only if you say, 'please,'" she said as her hands roved downward from my chest.

Instead of saying "please," I covered her mouth with my own. Later, she arose and strode leisurely to the bathroom where she took her time with a shower. When she emerged, the ink-tattoos were scrubbed clean and her hair was pulled back into a conservative bun. She looked older than before.

A stiffness in my joints made standing an effort, so I went to take my own shower. I sensed the hour was early and guessed the sun sat right on the horizon. The water washed over me, waking and refreshing me. After drying and dressing, I looked at Mercy. "Shall we find the others?"

She nodded and the two of us went downstairs where we met Drake on his way up the staircase. He nodded politely and wore a pleasant expression, but his brow was knitted as though concerned about something. "Have either of you seen any sign that Marcella or Jane have returned, perhaps last night, while we were still in the library?"

"No," I said. "We hoped they would make it back, but there certainly weren't any guarantees."

"True." Drake glanced downstairs at the front door. "There's been a prickling at my consciousness, as though a vampire is on the grounds. The only other vampires I'd expect would be you two or Jane and Marcella."

Right on cue, there was a banging at the front door. We exchanged perplexed glances. "Do you suppose that's them now?" asked Mercy.

Drake turned on his heel and led the way downstairs. We stood behind Drake at the door. The nobleman threw the door open and stood ready to attack or welcome whatever stood on the other side. Drake, Mercy and I gasped at the man standing on the porch. He stood straight, with a nobleman's bearing. His lip, framed by a neatly trimmed goatee was curled, as though somewhat amused by the expressions on our faces. He wore a simple button-down white shirt and black trousers that would have looked elegant had they not been rumpled and dust-covered. It appeared as though he'd been wearing them for several days and possibly even sleeping in them.

Drake eased closer to the visitor. "I thought you were dead." His voice held a curious mixture of humor and awe.

"We vampires are immortal, don't you know that, old friend?" asked the new vampire with a devilish gleam in his eye.

"But they aren't unkillable," said Drake. The British lord reached out and the two men embraced. Drake led the stranger inside.

"It's been a long time, Rudolfo." Mercy stepped up to the stranger with fire in her words and ice in her gaze.

At last, I understood who the stranger was. It was Jane's

infamous Rudolfo de Córdoba. He looked at Mercy for several seconds, blinked, then flashed an arrogant smile. "Mercedes? Is it you?"

She returned a curt nod, her body ramrod straight.

Rudolfo reached out, took her hand in his and kissed it tenderly. "It has been so long."

"I don't know if it's been long enough," she said with a tremor in her voice. She allowed her hand to linger in Rudolfo's for a moment, then pulled it back and took a step backwards toward me. My stomach hardened and I put my arm around Mercy's shoulder, wanting to protect her.

"Come," said Drake with open arms. "Let us have nourishment and you can tell us where you have been and the tale of your return." Drake led us to the dining room and seated us, then departed to the adjoining kitchen to retrieve plasma bags. Mercy followed Drake to help him.

Rudolfo seemed at ease sitting at Drake's table. He gazed at me and I shifted uncomfortably. "I am glad to see that Mercedes is still alive after all these centuries." Though he maintained a civil, conversational tone, I detected a slight edge to his words. "I'm glad she's found someone. She deserved better than me ... better than the person I'd been, at any rate."

I didn't know quite how to answer, but was spared the need when Drake and Mercy returned and handed out the warm blood-filled plasma bags. Drake put extras in the center of the table. Though this method of drinking blood did seem more civilized than attacking a human, it struck me that the sight of four vampires sitting around a dining room table sucking blood out of plasma bags was gruesome in its own right.

"May I have another," asked Rudolfo. "It's been several days. The elementals made certain I was nourished, but not with blood." Drake nodded and Rudolfo took another bag, and tore it open.

"So, you've been in the company of a kachina spirit?" I appreciated Mercy interrupting the slurping sounds we made. Not only was it gruesome, but the sound itself was just plain rude.

Rudolfo nodded then looked at Drake. "We have wondered

about the nature of the elementals for a long time, my friend, and they have proven to be even stranger creatures than we guessed."

"Try us." Mercy seemed irritated that Rudolfo's gaze had moved from her to the nobleman.

"I was born into a fractured world. Some people were Jews, some followed Christ, and some followed Mohammed. One thing united us all: the belief in one True God. Those of us in Spain in the latter half of the fifteenth century were absolutely certain that all of the other gods were myths from a deluded past. That wasn't true of your time, was it, Lord Draco?"

Drake's eyes narrowed as he recalled his past. "No, my people were druids. We believed in the Celtic pantheon: Lug, Lir, Angus Og and the like. When I became a vampire there were few Christians in the Islands of Britain. Even the Christians clung to pantheistic beliefs, treating the Virgin Mary as a goddess in her own right. That seemed natural to us. Our gods were not so removed from human beings as the Christian God."

"Four hundred years ago, I found this New World much as the early Christians must have found Britain," explained Rudolfo. "The people here told stories of powerful beings from ancient times, much like your pantheon. The Native Americans called these beings elemental spirits, kachina, or manitou. Like the gods of Europe, the elemental spirits were a lot like people with many of the same pitfalls and foibles." Rudolfo looked down at the table for a moment, as though considering what to say next. "The kachinas are neither spirits nor gods. Rather, they are a people like us."

"What do you mean, 'people like us'?" Mercy cast Rudolfo a suspicious glare. "We vampires are hardly ordinary people and the elementals are a thousand times more powerful than us."

"I think Rudolfo means that the kachinas are intelligent beings," I speculated, brushing a stray mustache hair from my mouth.

"Are they transcendent beings like vampires?" Drake steepled his fingers.

Rudolfo shook his head. "They do not come from Earth, but they visit often. The kachinas are far older than vampires or humans. We think our technology is powerful because we could go to the moon in three days if we wanted. The kachinas have been able to travel between galaxies since before man's creation. Their technology is so advanced you can't even see the machines they use. Being in their world of crystal palaces is like being in a world of sorcerers."

"It's Clarke's Law again." I leaned forward. "A society so advanced, it's like magic."

Rudolfo's brow furrowed. "I don't know what Clarke's Law is, but the world was as you describe."

I grinned, admittedly satisfied with myself, then sat back. "Is the world of the kachinas the same as 'the World Apart?'"

Mercy looked at me with a cross between a grin and a sneer. "I didn't see no 'crystal palaces' when we were there. Just a lot of fucking sand."

"There is more than one World Apart. They are conduits from our world to theirs. The kachinas explained it to me using concepts I didn't fully understand. They said the Worlds Apart are 'bubbles' in the fabric of space and that these bubbles move faster than light itself." Rudolfo shrugged. "The kachinas seemed to think I should know that light was some kind of substance that moved. I just thought light was there or it wasn't."

Rudolfo's brown eyes turned downward and I sensed that missing centuries of life on Earth saddened him. Mercy stirred beside me. Though at times Mercy wanted to kill Rudolfo for making her a vampire and causing her to destroy her own children, this was not one of them. She stood and moved behind Rudolfo, to rub his shoulders.

Rudolfo sighed. "As it turns out, the bubbles are part of the reason we find ourselves here today. The bubbles allow the kachinas to travel to a thousand worlds, Earth among them. They liked the creatures they found here, particularly humans and tried to help. We vampires are a result of their attempts to help us ... evolve. The kachinas fear humans now work to repeat the mistakes of the past."

Mercy threw her hands into the air. "Now wait just a goddamned minute. What do you mean that we vampires came about because the kachinas were trying to help? That doesn't make any sense. We have a tendency to kill humans, if you haven't noticed. If anything, we're a threat to humans, not a help."

Drake waved Mercy's outburst aside and leaned forward. "Something went wrong, didn't it?"

Rudolfo nodded, then followed Mercy with his eyes as she returned to her seat next to me. The pieces of the puzzle started to come together.

"An ancient race of beings with powerful, invisible technology much like nanotechnology, came to Earth and started tampering with humans. They unleashed the infection that led to vampirism," I said after a few minutes, nodding to myself. "But why did they do it?"

"Like I said, the kachinas traveled through the universe. They found Earth fascinating." The edge of uncertainty returned to Rudolfo's voice. "What they said was, again, strange. They said they'd seen many different forms of life evolve then die off when some cosmic debris would strike the Earth. It seems the kachinas were fond of creatures called dinosaurs." Rudolfo paused and shook his head. "I always believed that humans were formed on the sixth day of creation in the center of the universe…"

I took a deep breath and shrugged. "It's hubris to assume that God works in any particular way. Science has discovered that the universe is a much bigger place than people thought in your day. I'm guessing you knew of Galileo and Copernicus."

"Even Copernicus believed that the sun was the center of the universe. The shock is in learning that even his revolutionary ideas were simpleminded." Rudolfo gripped the arm of his chair tightly, but continued his narrative. "When humans finally came about on the Earth, the kachinas did not want to see them go the way of the dinosaurs. Some of the kachinas, Spider-Man and Coyote among them, thought they might be able to give humans an edge. This edge was something that would allow them a better chance of survival in the event another comet or asteroid struck the Earth."

Drake laughed incredulously. "The evil Spider-Man and his trickster friend were the ones who created vampires?"

"The problem is that they didn't figure out all of the variables before they started tampering," I snorted. It disgusted me that beings so advanced would make such an elementary error. "They didn't account for the fact that we'd only be able to survive on the blood of human beings. Likewise, they didn't account for our being unable to walk in the sunlight."

"I've walked in the sunlight of their world," breathed Rudolfo. "Their sun is redder than ours. We can tolerate that light."

I caught Mercy's eye and could tell she remembered our experience in the World Apart, one of many bubble universes.

"So, are the Spider-Man and Coyote the same species?" I could believe in space travelers coming to Earth in ancient times and unleashing an infection, intentional or not, that created vampires. I couldn't figure out how giant spiders and coyotes could evolve on one planet, in one ecosystem.

Rudolfo shook his head. "Who knows? I don't even know if they know. You see, Spider-Man, Coyote, Beaver Man and all of the kachinas can change into any form they want. It's allowed by their magic-like technology and the ability to manipulate the bubbles within the universe."

"You mean like Daniel here can change into a bat and I can change into a jaguar?" asked Mercy.

"Exactly," said Rudolfo. "When the plague, as Daniel called it, was unleashed on us, it imparted certain abilities to us that were the same as the kachinas. The ability to change form, although we don't do it as well as the kachina spirits, is one of the things we have in common. They also gave us great strength and the ability to read and manipulate the thoughts of others."

"So, what exactly is it that these kachinas want us to do for them?" asked Drake.

"We were designed to withstand great catastrophe. It's why we make such good warriors..." Rudolfo was interrupted by the sudden appearance of a dirty and bedraggled figure in the dining room doorway. He turned and gasped. "Jane?"

"Rudolfo?" She squinted as though trying to be sure she really saw whom she thought. Where Rudolfo had merely looked rumpled, Jane looked downright miserable. Her blouse and slacks were ripped in several places. Dirt smudged her face and a palpable odor of offal wafted toward us.

In spite of the smell, Rudolfo stood and pulled Jane toward him. Given the reactions I'd seen from Jane when we'd discussed Rudolfo in the past, I was surprised to see how enthusiastically she returned the embrace. "Thank God you're alive," she said. "I thought you'd been killed."

Drake stood and pulled out a chair for Jane. Rudolfo helped her sit. "It takes more than a coyote from the far side of the universe to kill the last conquistador," said Rudolfo. He kissed Jane's forehead lightly and she closed her eyes. She let Rudolfo help her sit while Draco passed one of the plasma bags from the center of the table. Given Jane's previous tentative sips from such bags, it surprised me how quickly and gracelessly she drained this one.

She finally looked up and acknowledged the rest of us. "They got Marcella," she said at last. She opened her fanny-pack and pulled out several papers, smudging them with dirty fingers. "We were able to get some information about what's going on, but as we left the labs, two of the gray creatures appeared. They got her, but I managed to escape. I had enough dark to drive away from the labs and spend the night in the sewers underneath White Rock."

I swore to myself and Mercy gasped. Given the way she felt about Marcella, I almost would have thought she wouldn't have objected to "the French Gringa's" disappearance. Impassive, Drake reached out and took the papers from in front of Jane and scanned them quickly, then handed them over to Rudolfo.

Rudolfo nodded. "This is what Coyote wanted to warn us about. There are scientists who have learned some of the secrets of the vampires and they are arrogant enough to think they can use their technology to make pliable vampires of their own."

"It would seem the suspicions I voiced last night are correct." Drake looked down and took a deep breath. "More than once, people in Washington have called, asking me to recall the Scarlet Order to help with some war or another in the Middle East. Instead of offering a fair and honorable price they threaten and cajole. The most recent bureaucrat pulled the old line about vampires being demons and threatened to turn me over to the Church. I told the bastard what to do with his threats." The British Lord rubbed his eyes, as though weary. "Perhaps I should have accepted his offer."

Rudolfo put his hand on Drake's shoulder, consoling an old friend. "You would have been a pawn. It was right to refuse. Coyote told me that humans have been flirting with these magics ... these technologies ... for long enough that it was only a matter of time before they tried to create super soldiers."

"The desire has been there for a long time," conceded Drake. "Hitler wanted supermen, but he didn't have the technology. After him, it was Stalin. Both of them wanted to control the Scarlet Order, but I turned them down as well."

Jane looked up and tears streaked through the dirt on her cheeks. Whether the tears were a reaction to Drake's words or simply fatigue, I never knew. "Are you really trying to equate the United States of today with Hitler and Stalin?"

Drake sighed deeply. "Perhaps it's an ... unfortunate comparison. People who are frightened often take desperate and dangerous actions. Unfortunately, the United States has been frightened ever since September 11, 2001, when a force that had nothing but determination and organization proved it could hurt the country."

"Okay," interjected Mercy. "So the government is making these cheap knock-off vampires. What happened to Marcella?"

Rudolfo shook his head. "I don't know. The kachinas have been looking for Marcella for several days. Spider-Man himself almost managed to catch up with her the other night, but she got away from him. You see, the kachinas are afraid of tampering again, afraid they'll make the problem worse. They want our help because we are creatures of both worlds. You asked if I was the only vampire in the world of the kachinas, the answer is no." The one-time conquistador looked at his former commander. "I saw our old friends, Roquelaure and Alexandra the Greek along with one other."

"Did you see two vampires called Hunter and Alice?" Mercy leaned forward.

"I'm afraid not." Rudolfo shook his head. "They only took three besides myself," he said. "The kachinas aren't the only ones capturing vampires. The scientists who are trying to recreate us have also been abducting vampires to figure out those things they can't get to work, like our ability to transform and manipulate thoughts."

"They didn't grab Marcella for a specific reason then," said Jane. "Any old vampire would have done for their purposes."

"As many as they can get," affirmed Rudolfo.

"But why were the kachinas after Marcella?" I asked.

"The kachinas hoped they could convince either Marcella or Lord Draco to lead the vampire forces."

Drake played his tongue over his fang. "Though I like the company of Miss DuBois and find her quite intelligent, she hardly seems a general…"

"The kachinas are well aware of your talents. Though you are an experienced commander of vampires, Marcella has proven herself in battle with this new enemy. The kachinas wanted you two in joint command of the forces. Are you game for this challenge, old friend?" asked Rudolfo.

"To brave and know the unknown is the high world's motive and mark, though the way with snares be strewn," answered Drake, quoting the poem "Unknown" by John Davidson. "I would like to meet with Spider-Man or Coyote and understand the challenges better. Can you summon them?" Drake looked at Rudolfo. "I think the time has come to discuss plans."

Rudolfo nodded. "We can summon the Spider-Man. It may take a while for him to arrive, but he will come." Rudolfo said we should gather in a circle outside.

Drake led the way outdoors and mused aloud: "The chance to understand the mysteries of vampires, to understand the kachinas, is almost payment enough for this old mercenary."

Outside, the chill night air raised goose bumps all along my skin. Rudolfo began a low chant as we formed into a circle. Within a few minutes, something tugged at the circle of hands. Raising my eyes, I gasped, once again seeing a six-foot tall creature with the head of a beaver and the body of a human. Mercy looked as though she wanted to run, but Rudolfo and I held her hands. Rudolfo turned to face the Beaver Man. "Bring Spider-Man. We are ready," he said.

The Beaver Man nodded and vanished in a blue glow.

"So, now we wait," said Rudolfo.

Chapter Twenty-Four

From the journals of Dr. Jane Heckman.
Present Day.

We went back into the house after the encounter with Beaver Man. Not knowing what would happen next, I decided to go upstairs and take a shower. After a night crawling through steam tunnels and sleeping in the sewer, dirt, mud and worse things clung to my skin and clothes. Just as I finished my shower, someone knocked at the door to my room. I pushed the bathroom door slightly closed and called, "Who is it?"

"It's Mercy," came the reply. "Do you mind if we talk for a few minutes?"

"No, come on in." The door opened and Mercy flopped down on the bed. Nude, I stepped from the bathroom and noticed the door to the hall hanging open. "Do you mind closing the door while I get dressed."

Her thoughts seemed elsewhere but she stood and closed the door while I walked to the dresser and pulled out a blouse and slacks.

"I'm worried about Marcella," she said without prelude. "It feels like everyone I've ever known has been vanishing and reappearing. It's getting on my nerves and I'm worried about what it all means."

Now dressed, it seemed that I could think a bit more clearly. "You know, I didn't think you and Marcella were on the best of terms. From what I saw of your relationship, I'd almost think you'd be glad to be rid of her."

Mercy returned to the bed and perched on the edge next to me. "It's kinda complicated, but all of us vampires in this house are interconnected in some way. Drake made Rudolfo who, in turn, made both you and me. Marcella was sired by another of Drake's vampires – that Roquelaure who Rudolfo mentioned."

"Marcella told me a little about Roquelaure." I narrowed my eyes. "Are you saying we're all Desmond Drake's grandchildren?"

"In a way," she affirmed. "I don't think Drake actually sired Roquelaure, but there's a reason we were all drawn here. My problem with Marcella goes back a long way. You see, when I became a vampire, I was ashamed and I hid for years. Eventually, those years became decades and the decades became centuries. Marcella was a whole different kind of vampire. She was flamboyant, you know. She flouted her vampireness in front of the whole world. I hated her for that, but we're kinda like cousins and I can't let something bad happen to a cousin, you know?"

"Family's important to you, isn't it?" I asked.

She nodded. "That's part of the problem. You see, now that Rudolfo's back, I see that he's changed. He isn't quite the same man I knew all those years ago."

"Well ... it has been several hundred years," I said. "I suspect Marcella has changed quite a bit, too. I don't think all of it has to do with these elemental spirits."

"I know, and maybe that's the real problem. I'm afraid that it was wrong to be angry at Rudolfo and to hate Marcella all these years. They've grown and I'm afraid I've stagnated." I almost put my arm around Mercy, but something held me back. My family had been my students and my colleagues at the university. You don't exactly go around hugging students. At a loss for what to say, I looked at my watch. "Shall we go find out whether anything new has happened?"

We went back downstairs and found the others in the library talking about the history of the kachinas. "You know, I've been thinking about these elementals for the past hour and what I don't get is why they're all manifestations of Native American gods," I interjected a little too loudly, interrupting the conversation. "Why aren't gods like Zeus or Thor in on the action?"

"Ah..." said Drake holding one finger up. "In fact these archetypes aren't limited to Native American mythology. Take Spider-Man for instance. Couldn't he be related to the spider demon that Raiko battled in ancient Japan? There's also a Spider-Woman in pueblo lore. Perhaps Spider-Woman had a hand in the story of Athena and Arachne. For all I know, Athena could have been one of Spider-Woman's people, she was said to be quite a good weaver."

Daniel shook his head. "But what about coyote? Coyotes are unique to the American continent."

"So they are," said Drake. "But jackals and gray wolves are close relatives to coyotes. Perhaps Egyptians saw Coyote or one of his kin as Anubis. Look how often wolves show up as cunning tricksters in European folk stories."

"It sounds like you're saying that Erich von Däniken got it right in his book, Chariots of the Gods?" I said, incredulous.

Drake shrugged. "I think he was blowing smoke most of the time, but it seems he was on the right trail nonetheless. Ancient humans knew these powerful beings from other worlds and they tried to make some sense of them. Their images filtered down through the ages to become god-like archetypes."

"Maybe even angels?" suggested Mercy.

"Indeed," agreed Drake.

I looked at my watch. "So, how long do we have to wait for this Spider-Man?"

"It's hard to say," said Rudolfo. "It depends on the currents and conditions through which he must travel. It could be a few more minutes, it could be tomorrow."

"In other words, you wouldn't recommend waiting up on him." Drake's lips curled upward in a mischievous grin.

Rudolfo shook his head.

"Well, since it looks like there may be some time before our honored guest arrives," I looked at Rudolfo, "would you mind taking a walk with me? I'd like to talk."

Rudolfo stood and took my hand. Since it now appeared that Beaver Man really was not a threat, and even if he was, he was now away running an errand. I led Rudolfo outside so we could walk around the compound under the stars.

When I walked with Rudolfo, my stomach fluttered. I looked at his face, softly illuminated in the moonlight. He looked up toward the stars, thoughtful and perhaps a little worried. I closed my eyes appalled that I wanted to wrap my arms around the man who'd killed my students and forced this curse of vampirism on me. Spinning on my heel I started back toward the house, thinking myself a fool. Rudolfo's hand landed lightly on my shoulder and I stopped in my tracks. He used no force, his hand just rested there lightly. For some reason that was enough to keep me in place. He moved to my side. I stared at the ground, refusing to meet the eyes I knew looked down at me.

"You hate me." He spoke so softly, it almost broke my heart.

"I missed you," I corrected. "And I hate myself for missing you."

Rudolfo tucked his finger under my chin and turned my head so I couldn't help but look into his deep brown eyes. "Soon after Drake made me a vampire, the Spanish Inquisition used me to dispose of some of their enemies. All I'd seen at the time was food – a way to continue my survival. I did not think about the fact that those wretches in the dungeons outside Granada were prisoners, Muslim, or even human beings. Only later did their screams haunt my dreams and memories.

"When I went to sleep in the mountain, it took a force of will to stay asleep after the next sunset. Any time I awoke I forced myself back to sleep. This went on for many, many nights. After awhile I lost track. I was lonely, but I also wanted to die in that cave for the suffering I'd caused humankind. When I awoke after centuries in the cave, I was even more ravenous than I'd been when I first became a vampire. I was the animal again, unable to stop myself from killing. You've experienced that hunger and know how terrible it is. When it's quiet, their screams still resonate in my thoughts and again, I find myself unable to die."

"We could always ram a stake through your heart." I tried to be flippant, to lighten the mood, but I regretted the words as soon as I spoke them.

"I would fight it and you would almost certainly lose." Rudolfo's matter-of-fact response frightened me. "It would seem we vampires have an uncanny instinct to survive."

"What were you thinking when you made me?"

"I was thinking that perhaps I'd found the person who could make endless survival bearable."

I forced my eyes from Rudolfo's gaze. "Were you thinking the same thing when you made Mercedes Rodriguez a vampire?"

A long silence ensued. "When I saw Mercy, I thought I'd seen my dead wife resurrected. The problem was that Mercy was too much like the woman I'd married. She was too loving, too human."

Snorting, I turned around and pushed my finger into Rudolfo's chest. "So, what you really wanted was someone who already was an inhuman monster. You were fascinated by the woman scientist who had no emotions, no husband, and no children."

Rudolfo cupped his hands around my index finger. "I fell in love with the woman who could hunt me down to try to understand me, in spite of the pain she felt." Gently, Rudolfo uncurled my fingers, raised my hand to his lips and kissed it. "Even though you could imagine your students' screams, you were able to act."

"You acted by forcing yourself on me." I wrenched my hand from Rudolfo's tender grasp.

"The nature of love has changed over the centuries. I see that now." He looked at me with a mixture of sadness and longing. "However, I'm not sure you would have become a vampire had I not forced it upon you. You might have been content to watch from a distance and I couldn't stand that."

I turned away from Rudolfo and looked up at the stars and the moon. The craters on its gray surface stood out clearly. As a child, I'd imagined walking on the moon's surface. Growing older the dream vanished in the light of reality. A short time before, Rudolfo spoke of visiting worlds, light-centuries away. The thought both tantalized and frightened me. "So, why do you want to stop these new, artificial vampires? Are you hoping you might die in battle so as not to hear the screams of your victims anymore?" A chill breeze gusted by and I shivered.

Rudolfo's strong arms wrapped around my waist from behind. "I have someone to live for now. The kachinas' cause takes me back to the days when I fought alongside Drake. When it seemed as though there was a certain nobility to being a vampire."

The forest surrounded us. In the silence, I could hear myriad small creatures moving through the brush. "And what of Mercy?"

"Mercy has found Daniel."

I turned within Rudolfo's arms, looked up into his eyes of my own free will and put my arms around him. "I don't want to love you," I said.

"Don't want to love me, or are you afraid to love me?" Rudolfo's mouth found mine and we kissed. I shut my eyes against the waves of desire. I wanted to taste Rudolfo's body and his blood. Fantasies of entering him with my fangs as he entered me came unbidden. After a moment, I pulled away breathing deeply. Closing my eyes, I lay my head against Rudolfo's chest and listened to his heart beating.

With a sigh, I looked toward the mansion. "We'd better get back," I sighed.

Rudolfo held me a little tighter for a moment then released me. He held his hand out and I looked at it a moment before I finally took it. Together, we made our way back to the house.

Opening the door of the mansion upon our return, I gasped in spite of myself. I wasn't sure what I expected upon meeting a creature described as the Spider-Man, but I certainly was not expecting to see a literal spider, eight feet tall at the shoulder, practically filling the entrance hall. Drake, Mercy, and Daniel stood in the hallway beyond to make room for the Spider-Man. It's hard to describe what I heard when I entered the house. It was like I heard the spider's voice, which was surprisingly deep and reassuring. Later, it would occur to me that it was the perfect voice for an effective trickster. The voice seemed to resonate within my head rather than travel through the air of the room. It was almost like Spider-Man's voice directly stimulated the aural center of my brain. "I prefer to be called Iktome," said the voice in my mind. "Spider-Man makes me sound like Stan Lee's famous creation."

I laughed in spite of myself.

He resumed his discussion with the others. "Long ago, when we discovered the secrets of programming molecules such as DNA, enzymes, and proteins, we gave up tool building. The natural course of human technical evolution is following the same road. Possibly as a side effect of humanity's speedy evolution, the people of this planet are impatient..."

"They have a tendency to rush ahead and not think through the consequences of their experiments nor do all the appropriate tests." Daniel's voice held a note of bitterness.

"Indeed, we have made our own foolish mistakes." Iktome paused. I couldn't read any expression in his multifaceted eyes, but his mandibles opened and closed silently for a moment. "It would be wrong to prevent humans from making the same mistakes. Perhaps with your help, we can 'herd' this technology a little."

"What do you have in mind?" asked Drake, folding his arms.

"The vampire called Marcella already destroyed the secret facility near the area you call Jornada del Muerto where the nanite probes were being tested and the scientists were breeding their soldiers. However, there is a facility for the production of the nanites at the place you call Los Alamos. That facility must also be destroyed. I believe you have a stockpile of explosives here at the ranch capable of the task."

"Why would you think that?" asked Drake with an innocent expression.

"You are a mercenary who fights wars, are you not?" asked Iktome in flat tones. "This is the most secluded land you own, the least likely to be searched."

Drake grinned and gave a brief nod.

"You must also rescue the vampires held captive in Los Alamos. Marcella is among them, as are the vampires known as Hunter and Alice. The scientists who wish to unlock the secrets of the vampires hope to study the captives and learn more," explained Iktome.

Rudolfo's brow knitted. "I have yet to see the cell built by humans that could hold any vampire who wanted to escape."

"If the humans holding the vampires were foolish enough

to rely merely on concrete and steel, you would be correct. The people holding the vampires have the fluoxetine gas to keep them subdued. Vampire-like creatures also guard the vampires. Though these super soldiers are not completely the equal of vampires, they are a formidable challenge."

Daniel looked from Drake to Iktome. "So, is it really possible for the humans holding the vampires to discover their secrets."

Iktome's entire body tipped forward, in a gesture that was a cross between a bow and a nod. "Human scientists have become so specialized that the risk is, admittedly small. It's unlikely the people developing nanites and working in biotechnology will make the necessary connections to the scientists studying the universe's structure. These scientists are close to discovering the bubbles we use for so much. The discovery of the bubbles is close at hand and the risk is real."

"Supposing we are game to help out," I interjected. "Los Alamos is a big place. Marcella's already been captured and all we did was penetrate relatively low-security areas. We need information about the cells and a way in and out of the lab."

"Information is easy to provide," said Iktome. "We have members of Drake's old Scarlet Order and another skilled vampire who can help. We will send them to you tomorrow with maps."

"Maps alone won't be sufficient," I persisted.

In a move that seemed to stretch physical possibility, one of Iktome's legs reached from the floor and searched through the downy-like fur on his back. He held four colored nodules in a small claw at the end of his leg. The nodules were red, orange, green and blue. "Though our tool building is limited, these nodules will help you unlock one of your latent abilities, the ability to move outside the universe. You are beginners and cannot expect to travel large distances without help. If you are near your destinations, these nodules will help you pass unseen through walls. Breaking one on the ground will open a portal. The green and red nodules are a matched pair that will assist your entry into the manufacturing facility. The blue and orange will assist your entry into the holding facility. Green and blue send you in. Red and orange will take you back to your starting point."

"What if the people we're trying to get past capture one of these nodules?" asked Mercy with her hands on her hips.

"Only vampires or my kind can unlock the secrets within these nodules. The vampire-like soldiers and ordinary humans do not have the genetic programming necessary to make them work," explained Iktome.

Drake took a deep breath and examined Iktome carefully. "In the balance of things, it seems to me that you kachinas owe vampires, more than vampires owe the kachinas. You created us by accident. Why should we help you?" Though I'd known Drake had been a mercenary, I was surprised to see that aspect of his personality come out with such force.

Iktome pondered the issue for a moment before answering. "We have much to offer in exchange for your help. We can further teach you how to unlock abilities that we gave you. We can teach you better control of your powers of transformation. We can even show you how you can travel larger distances using your own programming. With time, perhaps you could even travel the stars. There is more; humans are at risk. If all humans die, vampires will also perish."

I gasped. "Is that really possible?"

"The risk is perhaps greater than that posed by atomic weapons," said Iktome solemnly. "Such concepts as the 'soul' are as mysterious to us as they are to you. Whatever constitutes the life force known as the soul is almost certainly destroyed when these vampire-like soldiers are created."

"How can you tell?" I took a half-step forward.

"It's apparent by their actions," responded Iktome.

"What about us?" My own voice was barely audible.

"It is less apparent." I wasn't quite sure what Iktome meant by that, but I was afraid to press the subject any further.

It was Drake's turn to consider what Iktome had said. He looked at each of us in turn to see if we raised any objections. When no further comments were made, Drake nodded to Iktome. "We accept your offer. What must we do now?"

"The rest of your force will be returned tomorrow evening." He turned to face Drake. "You know how to organize a strike force. You do not need further advice from me on that score." Without any further word, Iktome passed the nodules to Drake then turned toward Rudolfo and I who stood just inside the mansion's front door. We backed outside and I wondered how such a large creature as Iktome could get out of the room. Drake made his way around the Spider-Man and opened the second door. Iktome pulled his legs in toward himself, just like an Earthly spider. There was just enough room for his body to squeeze through the door. In the middle of the courtyard, Iktome vanished as Beaver Man had earlier in the evening.

Once he departed, we all gathered back in the entryway. I looked up into Rudolfo's eyes and saw resignation. He was prepared to follow Drake wherever his one-time general would lead. Like me, both Mercy and Daniel seemed shaken by the enormity of what had just transpired. Daniel put his arm around Mercy and squeezed her shoulder.

Desmond Drake looked around the room, as though evaluating his troops. "I suggest we all call it a night. I suspect the next two days are going to be the busiest of our lives," he said.

✞✞✞

The next day three vampires materialized, as promised. Two of the vampires, a man and a woman, were tall and elegant. They were the most "Goth" vampires I'd ever met. Rudolfo introduced them as Roquelaure and Alexandra the Greek. They were members of Drake's fabled "Scarlet Order" picked up when the kachinas had been searching for the British lord.

The third vampire, named Mendez, was short and stout. He appeared to be Native American. "My people call me a Skinwalker," he explained. "I have known Coyote and Iktome for years. They asked me to help with this endeavor."

Drake gathered us together for a meal of blood. He raised a toast to the reunited "Knights of the Scarlet Order." To me, it sounded more like what a street gang would call itself than an elite cadre of vampires. I looked around the table. Drake dressed a little too elegantly in black and red from head to toe. Mercy wore a T-shirt and jeans with tattoos redrawn on her arms. Mendez quietly watched everything happening around the table, like a predator. Both Roquelaure and Alexandra drank their blood with just a little too much enthusiasm and dark humor for my taste. Though absent, Marcella's leather outfit and spiked hair came to my mind. I had no doubt we would see her again. Even Daniel's button-down shirt and slacks said "homeboy" to me.

Perhaps we were just a street gang after all; a street gang going up against the military with the world's top scientists and their super soldiers.

After dinner, I went to my room to freshen up and make the bed. I really had no idea whether any of us would be coming back. It just seemed wrong to leave my room a mess.

The clocks in the house struck the midnight hour and Drake gathered us together to discuss strategy. He divided us into two teams of four. Drake, Mercy, Daniel, and I would attack the nanite production facility. Rudolfo, Roquelaure, Alexandra, and Mendez would free the captive vampires. I volunteered to stay with Rudolfo, but Drake argued that they would need my expertise at the nanite production facility. Even though I'd volunteered, Drake's firm decision was actually a relief. The vampire called Roquelaure also volunteered to go with Rudolfo. "I believe I owe it to Marcella," he said.

Drake's planning was sound and the cause we would fight for was just, but not for the first time. I wished I had never met Rudolfo and I was still a professor in a mundane little office in a mundane little town.

Chapter Twenty-Five

The Scarlet Order strikes Los Alamos National Laboratory.
Present Day.

The next evening, eight vampires assembled in Drake's front hall. With the British nobleman in the lead, they stepped out onto the manor's front steps. Drake fell behind and locked the big house's double doors. With one last look, he returned to the front of the group and led them to the courtyard where two vehicles were parked.

Even though she had been in on the planning session, Jane couldn't quite shake the image of eight vampires piling into Daniel's Buick and her Subaru and storming Los Alamos. Perhaps the ridiculousness of the scene kept the notion of what they were doing from being too real to her. Instead of a Buick, a Subaru, and a Volkswagen, two new vehicles stood ready and waiting.

Rudolfo, Roquelaure, Alexandra and Mendez made their way to a new, white fifteen-passenger van gleaming in the moonlight. The vampires to be freed would ride back in that. It appeared something of a clumsy vehicle for a quick getaway, but Jane had approved it. The white van was just the sort of government-issue vehicle that one would expect to see driving around the labs.

Meanwhile, Jane along with Drake, Daniel, and Mercy strode toward a less inconspicuous vehicle: a Hummer. It was not one of the flashy Hummers an overpaid suburbanite would drive to impress work colleagues and fellow dads at the soccer field. No, this was the real deal, newly built for operations in the Middle East. Quite a few well-placed dollars diverted it from the cargo hold of a C-130 at Kirtland Air Force Base to Drake's garage. Though more conspicuous than the van, no one would overly question its presence at the labs. Unlike the van, it could be used for assault or make a quick escape if things went wrong.

Silently, the vampires climbed into their respective vehicles, started the engines, and slowly pulled out of Drake's courtyard. In the Hummer, Desmond Drake was dressed in black like a commando. He faced forward with his eyes never leaving the horizon. At last he would lead an army on a noble quest, perhaps even nobler than the Pen-dragon's quest for the Holy Grail. Desmond Drake used his vampiric existence to gain knowledge that could not be obtained in a single lifetime. Knowledge alone had proven something of a disappointment, bringing little happiness into his world. Adventure was the process of gaining knowledge and it had been better. Now, he traveled across the desert on a mission like so many he'd led before. This time the knowledge he might gain as a reward seemed worth the risk. Desmond Drake was determined to see the mission through to its conclusion.

Like Drake, Jane Heckman was driven by curiosity about the universe. Sitting 'shotgun' riding in silence, she realized the reason she had hunted Rudolfo in the first place was to obtain what he had: eternal life unfettered by the rules that governed mortals. Though she sought knowledge and adventure like Drake, Jane Heckman was a loner who had no desire to be a leader. Growing more nervous and noticeably warmer with each passing mile, she rolled up her white blouse's sleeves and undid the top button. A few miles later, she rolled down the window and let the wind blow through her hair.

Daniel McKee had not chosen to be a vampire. More than any of the others, he seemed destined from birth to be a creature of the night. Riding in the seat behind Drake, he stared out at the comforting darkness. Like Drake, the hints Iktome had dropped about vampires traveling to the stars one day tantalized him. When he worked for Percival Lowell in Flagstaff, Arizona, Daniel heard the astronomer's claims of canals on Mars and imagined what it would be like to live on the red sands of that distant planet. After watching a century of slow scientific development, Daniel was dubious of the "magic" that purportedly had transported Rudolfo to a distant world. Even if the kachinas' purported magic was real, and after a visit to the World Apart Daniel had good reason to believe it was, he knew learning how to unlock those secrets would not be easy. It would take years, perhaps even centuries. Daniel McKee couldn't wait to begin.

Mercedes Rodriguez clutched Daniel's hand and longed for her reunion with Hunter and Alice. Part of her wanted to be in the van with Rudolfo and the others who were going to find and release the prisoners, but she liked being with Daniel. In many ways, he reminded her of her long-departed husband; knowledgeable in many ways, simple and unsophisticated in others. Her stomach knotted with guilt and she forced her thoughts to memories of coming to the American continent as a young girl. She'd imagined finding cities with streets paved of gold. Instead, she found a land poorer and harder to work than the land of her youth. It was hard for her not to feel cynical about promises of new and better worlds. To her, the kachinas might have higher levels of technology than what she knew, but did any technology really improve life? Was it just a way of distracting people from the basic human needs of survival and love?

Rudolfo de Córdoba felt lost in time as he rode in the van's front passenger seat. Not many days before, he awoke in a brave new world. Carriages, like the one he was in, traveled roads without horses. Boxes called televisions carried theatrical images into every dwelling. Perhaps he was the ideal vampire to have been taken to the world of the kachinas. Though strange, it was almost easier to accept the kachinas' world than the world of twenty-first century America. It was a world where people actually dreamed of becoming vampires and used their technology to impose the curse on themselves; a curse he long regretted accepting.

Rudolfo turned to stare at Roquelaure who, like a marble bust, appeared unchanged after centuries. "So, tell me," said Rudolfo breaking the silence, "how do you know this Marcella DuBois? You said something about owing her this rescue…"

Roquelaure smiled and continued to watch the road. For a time, Rudolfo thought his implacable friend would refuse an answer. After a moment he spoke softly. "Soon after the Scarlet Order vampires went their separate ways, I met the lovely Miss DuBois. Her gorgeous neck, her supple flesh and her fierce spirit tantalized me. I had to make her permanent."

Rudolfo thought of his own feelings upon seeing Jane the first time and eyed Roquelaure critically. "But you didn't stay…"

"I realized too late that the only thing that gives vampires a semblance of nobility is a mission. Missions like the ones Drake has called us to through the ages, missions like the one we're on now. When I realized that I'd turned Marcella into a vampire, I was afraid I'd simply unleashed more evil on the world. I had a difficult time living with that realization." Roquelaure clenched and unclenched his hands around the steering wheel, but kept staring straight ahead. "Later I grew lonely and I went back to Louisiana to look for Marcella. By then it was too late. She had gone." Roquelaure took a deep breath, then reached over and rolled down the window. His next words were barely audible over the howling wind. "The question is, when we meet again, will she forgive me or will she kill me?"

Rudolfo turned and sought the moon, hanging in the sky. "There's only one way to find out."

✝✝✝

Two hours later, Drake pulled the Hummer into the parking lot closest to the nanite production facility. Finding a parking space, he killed the engine and hopped from the vehicle. He retrieved a pair of binoculars with a built-in infrared digital camera and scanned the horizon. In the meantime, Roquelaure who had been following close behind in the van, pulled into the same parking lot and pulled into a space near, but not too close, to the Hummer.

Drake's team huddled and he showed them the photos he'd

snapped using the binoculars. Mercy pulled out the map provided by the kachinas. Drake stopped as he reviewed the pictures. "We're actually in line of sight with the building," he pointed to a structure in the picture, surrounded by a chain-link fence topped with concertina wire.

"That must be the outer security perimeter." Jane pointed to the fence. If the nodules provided by Iktome even get us past that, it'll be a help."

"We'll still have to get to the building's second floor," said Daniel.

"But it shouldn't be too strongly guarded on the inside," affirmed Mercy.

Drake retrieved four backpacks from the Hummer. Daniel was amazed that the explosives required for the job could fit in Drake's pack. Daniel's only experience with explosives had been the dynamite miners had used in his youth. Enough bulky dynamite to do the job would not have fit in Drake's pack.

"This all has to look like an accident," Drake reminded his team. "We need to alert as few guards as possible. Plan A is we make this look like an accident. Plan B is we make it look like a terrorist strike. I don't want the whole United States Army turning up at my ranch in a few days."

Rudolfo and his team stepped up to where Drake's team was huddled. Drake pulled up a few photos on the digital camera and showed them to his one-time lieutenant. Rudolfo nodded. "It looks like the security complex is next to the production facility."

"As we knew from the maps," said Jane. "It actually makes some sense that they'd keep as much of this project in the secure sections of the labs as possible."

"Enough chatting," hissed Drake, looking from Rudolfo to Jane. "The time has come for us to strike. We'll go in first." He looked back to Rudolfo. "Give us a few minutes, then follow. Good luck, my friend."

Rudolfo took a deep breath. "Good luck, Lord Draco."

Rudolfo and his team stood back, next to the Hummer and

watched as Drake hurled the green nodule to the ground. A green, glowing cross erupted into the night.

"I hope no one up there sees that or we're in a whole lotta trouble," whispered Mercy. Drake glared at her for a moment then strode toward the cross. The other vampires watched as it swallowed him up. The other three in Drake's team followed. As soon as they were through, the cross vanished.

A fluttery feeling settled into the pit of Alexandra's stomach. "I sure hope they ended up where they expected."

"I sure hope they ended up somewhere, at least," said Mendez nervously.

Rudolfo silenced his team with a look. Refusing to be silent, Roquelaure spoke up. "Mercy was right about one thing, I think we should be a little less in the open when we ignite the portal. One glowing cross may be a mere curiosity to the guards. Two will tell them something is wrong," he whispered.

The group looked around. Mendez spotted an alcove where a corridor joined two wings of a building. He pointed and Rudolfo nodded, acknowledging that the alcove was more hidden from view than the middle of the parking lot. They went back to the van and retrieved their own backpacks, then crossed the parking lot to the alcove.

Rudolfo stared at his watch and gave the first team five minutes. At the end of that time, he swallowed and drew the travel nodule from his pocket. With one last look around at his team, he hurled the nodule that would send them inside the prison complex to the ground. Much as Drake's nodule, this one erupted into a great blue cross. The vampires stood for a moment gripped by a mixture of awe and fear.

"I have spent my whole life fearing crosses," whispered Alexandra. "I can't help but wonder about the significance of the cross form."

Roquelaure shrugged. "Perhaps, it is symbolic of a cross-road," he suggested.

Mendez, looking less refined than the other vampires in his blue jeans and chambray shirt stood with his arms out to his sides and stared at the cross with his deep brown eyes. "You know, I think the cross has more to do with the Pueblo swastika than with the Christian Cross."

Alexandra considered that and nodded.

"I think we'd better get going before the portal closes," said Mendez.

The four vampires stepped into the shimmering cross.

✝✝✝

The trip through the portal seemed instantaneous. Looking behind as he stepped through, Drake could see they were just inside the fenced-in area. The concertina wire atop the fence glared menacingly in the soft moonlight. Mercy, Daniel, and Jane appeared out of thin air a few seconds later. Drake retrieved his map and the four crouched low to study it with him.

The nanite production facility was just ahead of them. The building was only five stories tall, but it was a veritable skyscraper by New Mexico standards. Looking at the buildings around them as well as the one ahead, they could tell they faced the rear of the building. "Excellent," commented Drake. "We don't have to get past the well lit front entrance. The basement loading dock should be just ahead."

"I think I would have preferred it if we'd ended up inside the building and could bypass the outside altogether," snarled Mercy. She looked around and saw they were adjacent to the building that held the security facility. She was tempted to turn around and head inside herself to rescue Hunter and Alice.

Jane indicated how dark the location was and the fact that only a few windows looked out toward them. "This is a good place to ignite the portals without being detected."

Their shadows softened as Jane spoke. Looking up, Daniel noticed clouds overhead, obscuring the moon. Jane sniffed the air and detected moisture and the sharp tang of toxins. Several pipes stood atop the building where the nanites were being produced. There were almost certainly chemistry and biology labs in the building, as well as the production facility.

The vampires stood and formed a circle. Slowly and quietly, they approached the target building. Jane put her hand on Drake's shoulder, stopping him. Without words, she pointed up to the corner of the building they passed. A security camera was mounted just ahead of them. Studying the camera for a moment, Jane saw the signal wires coming from the back. Going up to the building, she retrieved a pair of wire clippers from her backpack and held them in her mouth. Using immensely powerful fingers, she pulled herself up to the camera. With the wire clippers, she carefully cut part way through the wire, then dropped back to the ground. "Should look like a mouse chewed through the wires. With any luck, it'll be turned in as a routine maintenance report and no one will come around to follow up until long after we're gone."

Drake nodded in response, then motioned for the team to follow. Walking straight ahead for a short distance, they came to a guardrail and looked down to see a loading dock. A long ramp led from the level where they stood down to service doors at the bottom. The gate at the ramp's top was watched by another security camera. Drake pointed to it, but Jane shook her head. "If too many cameras start failing, they'll come out to see what's going on." Peering over the railing in front of them, Mercy estimated that the bottom of the building was about one floor below. Looking one floor up, Drake noted a darkened window.

He pulled out the map again and looked at it. "That window is in the room we want."

Scanning the building, Daniel saw that the only other window was several stories above them. Drake shook his head. "I wish we could get across there with the explosives. It might save us some fighting."

Looking down, then looking up to the windows, Mercy shrugged. "Wouldn't it be easier if Daniel just flew the explosives up?"

Drake handed the backpack with the explosives to Daniel. "Can you do it?"

Daniel hefted the weight and shook his head. "I know some stuff like my clothes will transform with me, but I think this is too much for me to carry in bat form." He handed the pack back to Drake.

"There's nothing to do, but go through the service door," said Drake. "With some luck, we'll be able to get upstairs without meeting any guards."

"What do we do? Jump?" asked Jane looking at the drop.

Drake had already climbed up on the railing. "It's not like our bones break easily." The nobleman patted his backpack and confirmed that the explosives were well padded and wouldn't jar too much as he dropped down. Satisfied, he let go of the railing. Like a cat, he landed on his feet and crouched low, to see if anyone had been alerted to his presence. Once convinced all was clear, Drake signaled that the other vampires should follow him down.

Once the others accompanied him, Drake looked both directions again, then strode across to the garage-like loading door. A simple locking T-handle near the ground secured it in place.

"What do you suppose we'll find on the other side?" asked Mercy.

"Only one way to find out," said Drake. He grabbed the handle and wrenched it clockwise, then lifted the door. Light washed over them. Two men in black coveralls, possibly janitors, smoked cigarettes and drank coffee from Styrofoam cups. "Damn," Drake swore under his breath. The last thing he wanted was to attack civilian workers. One of the janitors opened his mouth in surprise, causing his cigarette to drop to the concrete floor. The other seemed to have more of his wits about him. He leapt to his feet and made for a panel of some kind mounted on the wall. Drake leapt at the janitor going for the panel and knocked him back into the wall with enough force that he slumped to the floor, leaving a trail of blood on the wall. Startled from his reverie, the other janitor stood and his face screwed up as though he would either scream or cry. Mercy stepped forward, staring into the janitor's eyes, talking to him quietly. His face relaxed and his eyes fluttered closed. Gently, she eased him to the floor. Drake took a moment to orient himself, then ran to the other end of the loading dock, throwing open the door he found there.

Alarm klaxons sounded.

Drake snarled, but continued into a corridor that led roughly in the direction he wanted to go. Hastily, he motioned for the other vampires to follow. They caught up to him as a door opened at the far end of the corridor. Ten soldiers darted through and took up defensive positions, pointing assault weapons.

Chapter Twenty-Six

The Scarlet Order's assault on Los Alamos continues.
Present Day.

Marcella DuBois sat in a dismal, gray-painted cell. A single fluorescent lamp in the ceiling above glowed faintly, as though tired of being on all the time. The cell door was an imposing thing of steel and rivets. Ordinarily, she would have fought to break through, but ever since she'd been captured, she'd felt too weak to even defend herself. Her danger-sense didn't seem to be working. She couldn't tell if there was someone outside the cell or not. Perhaps she was sealed in the cell forever, as though in a tomb. The gray creatures had mentioned tests. Perhaps they were testing how long she could go without blood.

Marcella sat on the floor of the box-like cell and hugged her legs to herself. There wasn't any furniture, just an unwashed toilet in the corner. The vampire had too much dignity left to sit on the toilet even if sitting on the floor was giving her legs cramps and making her backside numb. Inside the windowless cell, she had no way of following the passage of time. She guessed that between one and two days had passed since she'd been captured in the steam tunnels. In addition to whatever disoriented her, she grew weak from the lack of blood. As a vampire who'd not eaten recently, she had no need of the miserable, metal toilet. She would be even more miserable if she'd been a human who had no choice but to use the cold metal thing that virtually taunted her.

Marcella ran her fingers through her hair and sighed. She normally kept her hair spiked, as if in defiance of human convention. Now it lay matted against her skull. She slept intermittently, but not well. Though her normal sleep was very death-like, it seemed her circadian rhythms were thrown off by not having natural day and night while sealed up in the cell.

Jane Heckman had told her about Rudolfo, the vampire who had slept for hundreds of years underneath a mountain in Socorro. She began to wonder if she could turn her own body off to the point that she could sleep until either someone came to rescue her or the scientists decided they were finished with her and turned her loose.

As Marcella sat in the box-like cell, she realized she might not live to be released. The scientists could be planning to weaken her enough to simply ram a stake through her heart, then dissect her for study.

Just as Marcella bowed her head and closed her eyes to try to get some sleep, the cell door creaked open. Two gray creatures entered.

"Just when I thought I was going to be left here forever," she grumbled cynically.

A scientist in a white lab coat stepped in behind the gray creatures. He wore a government nametag: Dr. Immanuel Love. "It's time to run some tests," he said in a chipper voice.

"Oh, really?" laughed Marcella bitterly. She had a difficult time rising to her feet. The vampire-like soldiers stood by and watched dispassionately. "Nice of you to feed your prisoner while she's locked away."

"What would you have us do? Throw in the occasional grad student?" Dr. Love laughed darkly at his own joke.

Marcella came to her feet and balanced precariously against the wall. Head swimming, she stepped over to the gray-skinned creatures who took her arms and led her out into the hall. They restrained her tightly, but weak as she was, she would have a difficult time resisting.

The gray creatures led her out into a corridor lined with metal doors, identical to the one she had been facing for the past day. Their destination was a door at the far end of the corridor. It shot open and a figure darted through, shoving Dr. Love's stoop-shouldered body into the wall. The figure stopped and faced Marcella. It was Roquelaure, the vampire who had sired her. "Now, I know I'm hallucinating," she said feebly.

The creature holding her left arm was quickly wrenched away from her side. Marcella began to slump to the floor as the second creature let go of her to draw a sidearm. Roquelaure caught and held her. To her side, a tall, stately woman crushed the skull of the creature as it pointed its weapon at Roquelaure.

"You're weak," said Roquelaure. "You must have some blood if we're to get out of here." The handsome vampire loosened his collar and offered his neck to Marcella.

Without thinking, Marcella lunged at the pulsing carotid artery and drank greedily. Roquelaure gently pushed her back. "That's enough for now, Mademoiselle," he said. "We can restore your health more fully once we get back to Drake's manor." Feeling better, Marcella looked down the corridor and noticed most of the cell doors had been opened. About a half dozen vampires milled around the corridor. Some of their faces seemed merely curious while others were more furtive. All looked as disoriented as Marcella.

"Just how do we get to Drake's manor?" asked a willowy, blond vampire standing away from the rest.

"We'll discuss that once we get back outside," said a tall, muscular vampire in a white shirt.

Marcella felt lost. Where had Roquelaure come from after all these years? Who were these other vampires? She blinked several times. After a moment, she could feel Roquelaure's blood making her stronger and she stood straighter. "I don't know who most of you are, but thanks for coming for me. Now, let's get the hell out of here."

Roquelaure took Marcella's hand and led her down the corridor toward the open door. The other vampires followed closely behind. The door slammed shut as they approached. The vampires whipped around and found themselves facing a contingent of armed, gray vampire-like warriors.

✞✞✞

The fighting was ferocious in the close quarters of the manufacturing facility's hallway. The soldiers crouched low and fired their weapons at the vampires who, in turn, fell back against the walls, presenting smaller profiles. Mercy and Daniel pulled Drake back behind them. "Sorry," said Daniel. "But we can't afford to have those soldiers detonate the explosives you're carrying."

Daniel, Mercy and Jane looked at one another, then launched themselves at the crouched, firing soldiers. The British nobleman fumed at having to stay out of the action, but he knew the logic in Daniel's words. If he fought and the explosives went off, all of the vampires would die. It was likely that the machines used to manufacture the nanites wouldn't be damaged at all.

Taken by the surprise and unused to fighting inside a building, most of the assault force ceased firing as soon as Daniel, Mercy and Jane struck. The vampires punched, kicked and clawed their way through the assembled soldiers. One weapon discharged seemingly by accident. Only vampires were left standing. The soldiers lay in a heap around them, not moving. In the end, Daniel, Mercy, and Jane were not covered in much blood. They had worked to pull their punches and avoided killing the soldiers, but they knew some would never move again. The alarm klaxon had gone silent during the fighting.

Drake gestured impatiently. The vampires carefully, almost reverently, stepped over the fallen soldiers and went forward. The strike force found a set of steps leading upward. At the top of two flights of stairs was a second featureless corridor. Choosing the direction that would take them toward the lab, Drake hurried along the hall. The other three followed close behind. Several feet along the corridor, the vampires came to a junction of two corridors. Drake relied on his sense of direction and picked one of the white corridors and continued his run. The vampires came to a closed door. "If I don't miss my guess, this is the right room," said Drake.

They faced a sliding door, activated by a badge scanner. Jane reached into her pack and retrieved her Los Alamos ID badge. Drake put his hand on her wrist and shook his head. "After your raid the other night, I suspect the locks will recognize your ID and set off another alarm."

"How do we open it then?" asked Daniel, as he examined the door.

Mercy rolled her eyes and cleared everyone to the side. Taking a few steps back, she ran into the door, hammering it with her shoulder. Though the door buckled, it did not give. "Give me a hand," she ordered. Daniel and Jane lined up with Mercy and the three vampires struck the door at once. The door gave suddenly and Daniel fell headlong into a table of glassware. Mercy came to his side and checked to make sure he wasn't seriously hurt then helped him stand.

Drake examined the machines in the room carefully as he removed his pack. Out of the pack's back pocket he retrieved a set of diagrams and handed it to Jane. She studied the drawing, then looked up. After a moment, she pointed to four machines that resembled washer-dryer combos set against the wall. She pointed to a large cabinet that looked like a refrigerator. "If you blow those up, I think you'll have it all."

"What about this thing called a 'molecular doping station,'" asked Drake pointing to the chart and then to a device that looked a little like a large freezer.

"Strictly speaking, it shouldn't be necessary, but it wouldn't hurt to get it," said Jane.

"Hell, is anything in here going to survive the blast?" asked Mercy.

"Probably not," said Drake as he removed explosives from his backpack. "But I'd rather turn as many of the critical components into scrap metal as I can." He quickly reviewed the instructions for the placement of the explosive devices with the team. They set to work and were done in five minutes.

Daniel spotted the window they'd seen from outside. Unlatching it, he swung it open. Alarm klaxons echoed again from within the building. "Now the real forces will come," said Drake. "Let's get out of here."

Daniel didn't need any further prompting. He pushed himself through the window and launched himself to the ground below. Mercy followed him. Tentatively, Jane climbed into the window and threw herself at the ground as Drake retrieved the detonator from his pack.

Five of the gray vampire-like creatures appeared in the doorway as Drake prepared to launch himself. He jumped and pushed the detonator button just as the gray creatures rushed at him. Fire, glass and concrete flew from the open window. The strike force ran toward the spot where they'd first appeared. Alarm klaxons sounded all around the facility by this time.

Drake retrieved the red transport nodule from his pocket. This time, Mercy put her hand on the British lord's wrist. "We can't leave without making sure the others are safe."

"Rudolfo can take care of himself!" shouted Draco.

"That may be, but you've got a do-hickey that can get us to safety the minute we get in too deep. Why not go check?" With that, Mercy ran off toward the detention facility. With a growl, Drake pocketed the transport nodule and ran after her. Jane and Daniel looked at each other, shrugged, then followed.

✟✟✟

The gray creatures cautiously closed the distance between themselves and the small group of vampires in the detention facility. Roquelaure and the large, muscular vampire looked for a way out of the situation. Marcella couldn't see what they could do. At least now, she would have company when she died. Just as she was about to resign herself to dying or being led back to the cell, she looked up and blinked in surprise. Mercedes Rodriguez appeared in the doorway behind the vampire-like creatures. Daniel, Jane and Drake followed on her heels. "Now I know I'm hallucinating," said Marcella.

The new arrivals fell upon the soldiers from behind. Caught by surprise, the vampire-like creatures were quickly overpowered. Mercy, covered in blue ichor, looked at Marcella and grinned mischievously. "You owe me big time, Gringa," she said.

"You might not have noticed," retorted Marcella, "but we ain't out of here yet."

Drake retrieved the red nodule from his pocket and threw it to the floor. A red cross erupted against the wall. "We're out of here now." Even with alarm klaxons echoing through the hallway, Drake bowed low and indicated that others should go first. Rudolfo led the vampires through the portal back to the waiting cars. It wouldn't be long before the whole facility would be closed down, but the guards and soldiers would waste time locking down the inner security area before they started searching parking lots. By then, Drake hoped to be long gone.

"Pretty good jail break, eh, Mademoiselle?" asked Roquelaure as he helped Marcella step over the bodies of gray vampire-like soldiers toward the portal. Stepping through the portal, she blinked in the comforting darkness as rain began to fall.

"I think I need an explanation," said Marcella.

"That's what you get for missing staff meetings," said Drake. He appeared from thin air behind her with a wry grin.

"Explanations will all come in good time," said Roquelaure. "We will get you rested and fed and then we'll tell you what's been happening."

As Marcella, Drake and Roquelaure spoke, Mercy and Daniel helped the freed prisoners into the van and out of the rain. Standing away from the rest were two vampires that seemed to revel in their newfound freedom and danced in the rain. They watched the nearby lightning strikes with fascination. Mercy nudged Daniel in the ribs and the astronomer smiled. Heedless of the wet pavement, Daniel and Mercy broke from the group and ran toward their friends. Mercy scooped the willowy Alice into her arms. "I was afraid I would never see you again."

Hunter beamed with his broad smile framed by his shaggy beard. Daniel offered his hand and Hunter pulled the astronomer close, surprising him with a strong hug. "When we woke up here without you, we thought you'd been killed back at the theater."

"It takes more than some would-be vampire exterminators to kill us," quipped Daniel.

"Let's get moving!" hollered Drake, as the rain came down even harder. Mercy, Daniel, Hunter and Alice ran for the Hummer. Moments later, the two vehicles rumbled back up the highway toward Drake's ranch.

Chapter Twenty-Seven

A tale concludes.
Another begins.

The Hummer and the van pulled into Drake's courtyard. The British lord hopped triumphantly from the front seat and a crossbow bolt narrowly missed him. Drake's eyes went wide as he crouched low, trying to determine what direction the bolt came from. Just as the van pulled to a stop next to the Hummer, Rudolfo and Roquelaure took in the scene. With a gesture and a few hastily spoken words, they sent everyone out of the van and toward the protection of the house.

Just as Rudolfo cleared the van, it exploded, struck by an anti-tank rocket. Most of the vampires were blown to the ground. Rudolfo scrambled to his knees and blinked several times, as though trying to clear the dust from his eyes. "Jane!" he called.

Drake coughed, then called out, "Quiet. We need to figure out what's going on." He joined Rudolfo as the dust started to settle. A short ways off, Roquelaure helped Jane sit up. Her face appeared dirty and scraped, but otherwise okay.

Mercy and Daniel, followed by Hunter and Alice, scrambled over to Drake and Rudolfo. "Who's shooting at us?" asked Mercy.

"Silence," said Drake in a commanding whisper. "We've got just a moment before the dust settles between us and the shooters." He looked at Rudolfo. "I need you to assemble a team and take out the one with the heavy artillery. I'll go after the crossbow."

Marcella joined the huddle as he spoke. "You're going after the crossbow alone?" she asked.

"I suspect the one with the crossbow is the more dangerous of the two," he said. "That one isn't relying on the big guns and doesn't feel the need for overkill."

"I'll come with you," said Mercy.

"No, we'll need to transform to get close enough. You make too big a target as a jaguar."

"Then let me come," said Marcella, leaning forward.

"Are you sure you're up to it?" Drake eyed her sleepy eyes and matted hair.

Marcella nodded, apparently determined.

Without any further instruction, Drake collapsed in on himself and became a swarm of flies. He took off through the drifting dust. Marcella ran away from the snipers, becoming a bat then swirled around, using her echolocation to find the fly swarm and follow.

Rudolfo turned to Hunter and Alice. "I want you two to get the others to safety as quick as possible. Go to the servants' quarters. There's a basement in there that should be safe. The snipers will almost certainly attack the big house first."

Hunter and Alice nodded quickly. Given their dispositions, Rudolfo was pleased to see how quickly and efficiently they followed his orders. They gathered Jane, Mendez and the other two vampires then made their way rapidly toward the servant's quarters.

Rudolfo summoned Mercy, Roquelaure and Alexandra to his side. "The rocket came from that ridge." He pointed. "Mercy, Drake was correct when he said you make a big target. You can help us knock over someone carrying around a shoulder-mounted anti-tank gun. I want you moving now. Go toward the woods behind the house to transform then circle around. We'll meet you up there."

Without a word, Mercy ran toward the house and appeared to stumble. A crossbow bolt narrowly missed her as she transformed into a jaguar and sprinted out of sight.

A second blast knocked the huddled vampires over. "Did the others make it to the house?" asked Alexandra, concern in her voice.

"No time to worry about that now," snarled Rudolfo. "We've got to get moving while we still have the cover of dust." The last conquistador stood and brushed the dust from his hair and trousers before running at the ridge and transforming into a bat. Daniel followed on his heels.

"Just like the old days," Roquelaure grinned at Alexandra. "Shall we give them a hand?"

"Indeed," said Alexandra, sweeping her long hair over her shoulder. "I think Rudolfo has forgotten our abilities. Your animal is a rat and I transform into smoke. Neither one will get up the ridge quickly."

"Indeed," sighed Roquelaure. "I suggest we run instead." The two stood and followed Rudolfo.

✞✞✞

Silently, Georgia Hawthorne cursed her husband's bungling. The rocket launcher should have been a weapon of last resort. She'd had several good targets picked out for the crossbow before he started blasting away, sending up clouds of dust. She lifted the crossbow again, trying to find a new target. A faint glow caught her attention. Her necklace indicated that one or more vampires approached. She looked around trying to find the vampire. Having no luck, she crouched low and set the crossbow at her feet. Standing slowly, she retrieved a wooden stake from her belt.

"I don't believe you will need that," said a velvety smooth voice from behind. She spun around quickly, aiming the stake at the chest of the elegant looking vampire.

The vampire caught her wrist and gently pushed her backward. Georgia sneered at the vampire dressed in black with his hair slicked back. Recovering her balance, she spared a moment to think, *Who does he think he is, Dracula or something?* The moment spared was a moment too long. A second vampire that looked a complete mess appeared at her side. Before Georgia could react, the female vampire made a sweeping toe kick, dropping her to her back and knocking the wind out of her. The elegantly dressed male gathered up the stake and the crossbow, while the female gathered up Georgia's crumpled form.

✝✝✝

As the dust cleared in the courtyard, Larry Hawthorne smiled at the damage he'd wrought. He'd destroyed the van and rolled the Hummer over on its side. Even more pleasing, no vampires remained in the courtyard. He must have blown them straight to Hell.

A cold chill of realization crept down Larry's spine. There were no bodies or body parts in the courtyard and even vampires left remains.

Something like a ton of bricks clobbered him from the side. He lay dazed for a moment and thought a jaguar looked down at him. The jaguar transformed into a female vampire. Gingerly, she reached down and turned him over. Blinking several times, he realized it was one of the vampires who had gotten away from him in Las Cruces. She helped him to his feet as two other vampires arrived, one of whom was the other vampire that had escaped from the theater.

The third vampire was tall, dressed in a white shirt turned gray with dust. He looked around as two vampires dressed in black approached. He remembered their names from files he'd seen: Roquelaure and Alexandra.

One of the vampires in black whistled, examining Larry's cache of rockets and explosives. "Looks like the kind of party favors Desmond likes," said Roquelaure.

The vampire in white, Rudolfo, grabbed Larry by the collar and lifted him to his feet. "Is there anyone besides you and your partner?"

"Why should I tell you?" growled Larry, attempting a menacing snarl.

"If you don't, we'll kill you," said Mercy.

Alexandra stepped up to him and looked into his eyes. "Tell me all about your plans."

The timbre of her voice and the soft touch of her hand sent waves of desire through the exterminator. He fought to keep images of Georgia in his mind. He did not want to give in to these creatures. His words came unbidden: "I kill you bastards for one simple reason," he said with tears rolling down his cheeks. "I kill you because what you do is worse than killing humans. You drain their blood and weaken them, but leave them alive to suffer the memory of the attack." He lowered his collar and revealed scars left by fangs.

He opened his eyes and let himself look into Alexandra's face. She had to look away. "He's alone, except for his wife. She's the shooter with the crossbow. Their job was to destroy us before we attacked the labs."

Daniel shook his head. "That means they knew about our plans."

"Obviously, they didn't expect us to strike quite so quickly," said Rudolfo.

"Well, that's a relief," said Mercy.

"Only a small one," said Roquelaure with doubt creeping into his voice.

Larry Hawthorne grinned feebly.

✟✟✟

Rudolfo, Roquelaure, Daniel, Mercy, and Alexandra returned to the courtyard, with Larry Hawthorne in tow. They found Drake and Marcella waiting with Larry's wife, Georgia.

"There's a nice supply of ammunition to add to your stockpile Lord Draco," said Rudolfo. "It's back there on the ridge where we found this fellow."

Draco looked at his toppled Hummer and sighed. "Small compensation for the damage they've done." He shook his head. "Who knows how long it'll be before Iktome delivers on his promise to pay us."

"So, what do we do with these two?" asked Alexandra.

"I'm not quite sure." Roquelaure faced the compound's

main gate. "The gentleman over there seems interested in them, though."

Drake looked over to see a man standing at the gate, like a vampire that couldn't enter without permission. He wore a white suit and a broad-brimmed white hat. A salt-and-pepper goatee framed his mouth and he held a cane in his right hand. Mercy gasped in spite of herself. "It's him," she said in a barely audible whisper.

Desmond Drake looked rattled. "Perhaps you and Daniel should speak to our visitor," said Drake, addressing Mercy.

Hesitantly, Daniel and Mercy approached the gate. The vampire hunter acknowledged them coldly and politely. "You and your friends have done well tonight."

"What are you doing here?" asked Mercy.

"I'm on a special errand," explained the hunter. "I'm here to collect the exterminator and his wife. Though they work for the enemy, they are of our kind – vampire hunters. We cannot leave them to the tender *mercies* of vampires. It is for us to administer justice."

Mercy ignored his quip. "How can we believe you? What's to keep you from taking them away then coming right back to kill us."

The vampire hunter removed his hat. "There are rules in any game. Honor in warfare is what makes the difference between civilized beings and savages. If I'd wanted you all dead, you would not be standing here talking to me."

Daniel and Mercy turned and looked back toward Drake who could hear the conversation even from the distance. He nodded, then whispered to Roquelaure and Marcella, who took the Hawthornes to the gate. With his hat planted firmly on his head, the vampire hunter stepped over to a limousine parked in the shadows and opened the door. He came back and retrieved Larry and Georgia from the vampires and led them toward the car.

As they climbed in, Georgia looked around with disgust. "Are you foolish enough to think the only cache of nanites was at Los

Alamos? You aren't the only vampires available to study," she spat. She grew silent at a whispered word from the vampire hunter and passively dropped into her seat.

Removing his hat one last time, the vampire hunter bowed then joined the Hawthornes in the back of the limousine and closed the door. The big vehicle turned and drove down the dirt road. Marcella, Roquelaure, Daniel and Mercy turned to join the other vampires gathered in the courtyard while Hunter, Alice and Jane led the rest from the servant's quarters.

Drake opened his mouth, as if to speak, but a noise from the manor house's front steps cut him off.

The vampires looked back to see a giant spider-like being emerge from Drake's front door. Hunter and Alice each let out an audible gasp at the sight of the creature that approached. It bowed low in greeting. Drake nodded at Iktome. The spider-like creature's body collapsed in on itself and reformed into a vaguely human-like shape. Iktome sprouted a round, dark-eyed and downy-covered head from a human-like torso, clothed in flowing black cloth. The creature still had four arms and four legs. With two of his arms, he gestured that the vampires should follow him back into the manor.

"So when do we get paid?" asked Drake as the group walked through the halls toward the library.

"What must we do now?" asked Daniel.

"By letting you use the travel nodules in the operation and by showing some of you the World Apart, we have already unlocked many of the secrets for you," said Iktome as he reached the door to Drake's library. He threw the doors wide open. "Knowing what you've learned, now you must return to the books. Many answers are already there."

"You call that payment for a job well done?" grumbled Lord Draco, the mercenary.

Iktome smiled. "I think you will find that you have been paid quite well." With that, the Spider-Man stepped away from the door and simply faded from sight. Mercy and Marcella were left with the feeling that the greatest trickster of all had just tricked them. Daniel and Jane considered the Spider-Man's words and were already deciding where to start looking for more clues.

Drake looked around at the group. "Perhaps the Spider-Man is a poor client, but I am still a good host. I believe we all need nourishment ... and rest." He led the group toward the dining room.

☩☩☩

The next night, Jane strolled hand-in-hand with Rudolfo through the woods around Drake's manor. The moon sat on the horizon and the air grew chill. "So, what was it like to walk in sunlight on the elementals' world?" asked Jane.

Rudolfo looked around at the trees. "It wasn't what I thought it would be. I still missed the clear blue skies of Nuevo Mexico and the smell of Spanish flowers. I prefer being here with you, even if we can't be under a blue sky." Rudolfo looked down to his feet, though his eyes seemed focused much farther away.

"There's something else wrong, isn't there?" Jane looked at him.

"I found that I missed the hunt." Rudolfo snorted and kept looking down, avoiding Jane's contemplative stare. "I missed the release that comes with the strike. I missed blood running over my tongue."

"So, how did you eat there?" Jane didn't want to think about hunting. She had been relieved that during the past several nights, she'd not had to attack anyone for their blood.

"Within the crystal palaces of the kachinas, there were wonderful rooms where you could enter and a glow enveloped you, like a mother's love. It was like entering a womb." Rudolfo chewed on his lower lip, as though searching for words to describe what he had experienced. "I suppose you're skeptical." He looked away.

"Not as much as you might think," said Jane, softly.

Rudolfo snorted. "The old blood in my veins was re-energized. Even though hunger pangs subsided, I had the sense that I couldn't go on forever like that. At some point, I would need more than the rooms could provide." He looked into Jane's eyes.

Jane caught her breath as she imagined the possibilities. Living on such a world she could have the best of being a vampire without the cost. Then she looked at Rudolfo and saw the sadness return to his eyes.

"Perhaps time has passed me by," he said at last. "In my day, humans were predators and so were vampires. Vampires were just a little higher up on the food chain. Now, vampires must learn to become peaceful creatures." Rudolfo stepped ahead, through a stand of trees.

Jane had to hurry to catch up. "Why do you want to hurt people?"

Rudolfo stopped and leaned against a tree. Jane had to stop suddenly to avoid bumping into his back. "It's not that I want to hurt people. You see, humans have no natural predators except for themselves and vampires. Long ago, I convinced myself that vampires were part of the natural order because we needed to feed on humans. We were the only thing keeping human population at bay."

Looking at the moon on the horizon, Jane considered this last statement. She began to think about the rising human population and wondered if there wasn't some truth there, even if she abhorred it.

Standing for several minutes in uncomfortable silence, Rudolfo finally looked at Jane. "Have you come to understand vampires more in the last weeks?"

Slowly, Jane nodded. "Quite a bit," she said.

"Are you still sorry you became a vampire?" Rudolfo watched her struggle with the answer to that for a long moment before he held up his hand. "Never mind. Let me ask a simpler question. Do you think we'll ever have the powers of the kachinas?"

Jane pursed her lips. "Maybe, someday. Mostly it's a matter of having the time to learn."

Rudolfo reached into his pocket and retrieved the orange travel nodule given to him by Iktome. "A gift," he said, putting it into her hand. "Study it. Perhaps it will unlock some of the secrets."

Jane couldn't help herself. She pulled Rudolfo close and kissed him. Arm in arm, the two returned to the manor.

✝✝✝

A phone rang, startling the vampires gathered in Drake's dining room. Daniel had begun to assume that Drake didn't even own a phone. The British lord retrieved the phone from his pocket and answered. He spoke to the person for a moment, then clicked off. "My sources tell me that it would be advisable to vacation in Europe for a year or two. This house will not be safe."

"More vampire hunters?" asked Marcella.

"Let's just say, the harder we are to find, the better off we'll be." Drake took a deep breath.

"How long will we need to hide?" asked Roquelaure.

"It will probably be safe to return once there's a new administration in Washington. Once the tide turns, as it does so often in the brief lives of humans."

"What will become of the manor house? The library?" Daniel's eyes grew wide and his breath came a little too quickly.

"As long as we're not here, it should be safe. They only care about us, not this collection of relics." Apparently not interested in further conversation, Drake hung his head and left the dining room.

"Well, where does that leave the rest of us?" asked Hunter with wide eyes.

"We could always go back to Las Cruces," suggested Mercy. She looked over to Marcella. "Would you and Monsieur Roquelaure care to join us in your old stomping grounds?"

Marcella smiled wickedly. A day of rest and a healthy serving of Draco's blood supply left her looking much better. Instead of spiking her hair, she'd washed and brushed it out. She wore a dress and resembled the schoolteacher she once had been. "Thanks, but I think we need some time to ourselves. We've been talking about going to Europe. He offered to show me some of the old haunts of the Scarlet Order." She reached out and took Roquelaure's hand. "I've always wanted to see Paris and Venice."

Jane and Rudolfo entered the dining room. "We just met Drake in the hallway." She chewed on her lower lip. "This is terrible. I was hoping we could stay here for a while and follow up on the secrets of the kachinas."

Daniel stood and stretched, then looked down at Mercy. "You know, I don't really think I want to go back to Las Cruces." He looked over at Jane. "How hard do you think it would be for a couple of scientists to set up a small laboratory in Colorado?"

Jane smiled so broadly, her fangs showed. "I don't think it would be that hard at all. Especially if Drake will let us take as much of his laboratory equipment and books as we can carry."

Looking into the corner of the room, as though she wasn't paying any attention, Alice said: "I've always wanted to go to Colorado."

Mercedes Rodriguez seemed crestfallen. "You mean you're going to leave me?" Horrified, she looked into each of their faces. Daniel was stunned by the suggestion. Hunter shook his shaggy head. Rudolfo seemed amused. Then realization dawned. "I don't know if I want to go to Colorado."

Hunter reached out and took Mercy's hands. "You said you wanted to get out of Southern New Mexico. This is your chance."

"We need you," said Jane, putting her arm around Mercy's shoulders.

A single tear ran down Mercy's cheek.

✟✟✟

Drake's manor buzzed with activity over the course of the following two nights. Vampires packed boxes and suitcases as fast as they could. On the first night after their return, Mendez borrowed one of Drake's cars and left with the vampires they'd freed from Los Alamos. He promised to return them safely to their homes and Drake promised to contact Mendez as soon as things settled down again.

Drake wired a tidy sum of money to Christopher Garrett in Roswell. Happily the stockroom supervisor sent the Volkswagen's title to the ranch by express mail as requested. Drake handed the title to Marcella, who in turn handed it over to Hunter. "A gift," she said. "You all need the car more than I do now."

Mercy hugged Marcella. "Thank you, Gringa," she said, then corrected herself. "Thank you, Marcella."

The next night, Daniel's Buick, Jane's Subaru, and Hunter's new Volkswagen were loaded so full of supplies and books that the suspensions seemed in danger of breaking. Marcella, Roquelaure, Alexandra and Draco stood on the manor's front steps and waved as the low-slung caravan drove through the gates. Rudolfo, Jane, Daniel, Mercy, Hunter and Alice were on their way to start a new life in Colorado. Drake's stomach felt hollow, much as it had one night in the Mediterranean when Rudolfo had announced that he would go to America.

"Do you really think they'll be able to unlock the secrets of the kachinas?" asked Marcella, sounding wistful, as though she wanted to accompany them.

Drake took a deep breath, savoring the mountain air. "If they don't, I'll be back to hunt for spiders. No one cheats me out of my payment." The British lord pulled out a pocket watch. "Time to go, or we'll miss our flight." With that, Desmond, Lord Draco reached back and locked the door, silently vowing that one day he would travel to the stars.

About the Author

David Lee Summers is an author, editor and astronomer living somewhere between the western and final frontiers in Southern New Mexico. His novels include *The Astronomer's Crypt, Owl Dance*, and *Dragon's Fall: Rise of the Scarlet Order Vampires*. His short stories and poems have appeared in numerous magazines including *Realms of Fantasy, Cemetery Dance, Star*Line* and *The Santa Clara Review*. When he's not writing, David operates telescopes at Kitt Peak National Observatory.

Learn more about David at http://davidleesummers.com